I0760681

Chronicles of Mirstone

EDITED BY RICHARD FIERCE

AND PDMAC

Interior design by Richard Fierce
Cover design by Keith Robinson
Cover art by Rosauro Ugang
Anthology Editer: Richard Fierce and pdmac

Dragonfire Press

Print ISBN: 978-1-958354-39-1

E-Book ISBN: 978-1-947329-07-2

First Edition: 2017

CONTENTS

INTRODUCTION

October 8th, 2016. That's the day the idea for this anthology was born. I was at a convention with my fellow author pdmac and we were talking about a number of things. I had the idea for a shared world where we could invite other authors to write short stories with a common theme. The idea was initially rough, but as it was fleshed out it became so much more than I could have imagined.

All of the authors in this anthology are masters of their craft and I am excited to share their stories with you. If you love what you read, you can find their other books on their biography pages. And as always, please leave a review. We authors live and die by them.

Happy reading!

Richard Fierce

The Dragon of Blackstone

Richard Fierce

Tringad journeyed to Blackstone seeking power.

At least, that was what he had told himself. Perhaps, in retrospect, he may have been seeking death. Yet it is an axiom of life that a dwarf never finds the one thing that he seeks—or perhaps never seeks the one thing he finds—and in those last hours he found neither power nor death on the blasted crags of Blackstone.

His tale did not begin with a beginning, but an ending. During the time of the Long Peace between dwarves and elves, the king of the dwarven clans decided to expand the boundaries of his kingdom. The problem, however, was that the forests of their elven neighbors surrounded the mountains of Rachdale. Tensions were high among their races, and after many heated arguments with both the elves and the clan's leaders, the King convinced the Stormguard clan to use their magic to extend their mountain home. With exception of a few, the Stormguard wizards used their power to rip mountains up from the grounds of the forest. And as some had predicted, the elves were furious.

The Long Peace had died amidst thunder, earthquakes, and darkness.

In the first days afterward, the elves demanded answers. *Who*, they cried. *Who had destroyed part of their homeland?* Through the dust, the King laughed at them. The answer was simple: greed. And from that moment, everything had changed.

Before the Plucking, as some called it, Tringad had left his mountain home behind. He had fallen in with powerful forces, choosing the life of a wanderer and hiring out his talents to the highest bidders. He frequently brought in enough gold that he constantly had purpose, food in his stomach, and believed himself safe and on the path to great things.

His employers had seemed so strong, so glorious, so indominable. But at the end, they had shattered like so much glass. Now he was on his own. The old ways of doing things, the old rules, were gone, burned to ashes with the bodies of his employers. There were new rules to be made, and Tringad knew that those who made them would come out on top. That was why he had journeyed to this place.

He was nearly upon it before he got his first view.

The scorched wind changed direction and tore a rift in the gritty clouds of dust. There it stood before him, rising five thousand feet into the sky, a great heap of jagged rocks the color of night.

Blackstone.

Tringad licked his blistered lips with his parched tongue. "Blast me to the Depths," he said, wondering if he hadn't already been, if he wasn't already there.

He craned his neck upward, and upward still, but the summit was lost in haze, and faded into a sky stained red with the soot of a thousand thousand fires. For a moment, he almost staggered. How could he possibly climb to the top of this … this thing? How could he even think to try?

But he had come too far. He could not turn away now. He let the wave of weakness pass over him, drew in a deep breath, and walked across the cracked uneven ground toward the tumbled base of the mountain.

He had first heard the story in a tavern, a filthy pub where swine rooted on the floor for scraps, and ate nearly as well as those who paid hard gold. A traveler from the east—a self-described merchant he called himself, a thief and a murderer Tringard guessed—told him, for the price of a cup of sour ale, of the great rock that had been thrust up from the bones of the earth by the tremors of the Plucking, and of the silhouette he had glimpsed by moonlight perched upon its summit: a winged, saurian shape that lifted its wedge-shaped head toward the sky.

Tringad had drank his ale, and wondered.

He heard the tale again in a village, told by a band of pilgrims who searched in vain for signs of the gods. Then once more, among a camp of outlaws, who pretended to take him in as a compatriot, and would have slit his throat in his sleep had he not cut theirs first. Again he heard it told, in a hovel, in a village, in a town. One telling he would have discounted, two doubted. But a dozen he believed, and so here he was.

The sun beat upon his armor. Sweat streamed down his brow, into his eyes, and stung them. A hundred times on his journey he had been tempted to cast off the steel that encased him, to toss it into some foul pit or to send it clattering down a cliff face, to be free of the heat and its stench. But his path had led through dangerous and broken lands. He had kept his armor, and kept his neck.

He was picking his way among the mountain's first jumbled boulders when he saw smoke.

A thin, dark line rose upward, from behind a large spur of stone. Tringad froze. He had assumed the beast would keep to the heights of the peak, but he had not been able to see the summit for the haze. Perhaps it had come down to prowl among the rubble for food. True, it might decide he was suitable prey before he opened his mouth and spoke a single word to it, as he intended. But at least it would save him the climb. Tringad scrambled over the rocks toward the pillar of smoke.

It was no dragon he saw in the gully below.

At first he thought to slink away through the rocks, to remain undetected, then he halted. Would it not be better to know who it was that climbed behind him? And there was still a part of him that remembered what he had been before, and the oaths of honor he had sworn. Hollow they seemed now, empty. But what didn't anymore? He hesitated, then stood and walked down the steep slope.

Dust-devils swirled around him. They must have blocked the elf's view, or else he was dozing in the heat, for he did not seem to notice Tringad until he was a dozen paces from him and his small campfire. All at once he jerked his head up, leapt to his feet, and drew his sword. He held the blade before him, turned to his left, his right, his left again, searching. Tringad frowned. He was plain before the elf. Did he not see him?

Only then did Tringad notice the dirty rag bound around his eyes, crusted with dark blood.

No, he did not.

Tringad approached, deliberately grinding his boot heel on the gravel. The elf spun to face him, sword before him. Beneath the patina of dust, he could see a rose embossed upon the elf's wind-scoured armor.

"Are you friend or enemy?" he called out.

"Neither," Tringad answered.

The elf frowned at this, and Tringad might have turned away then, might have left this ruined elf to himself, but for something he saw among the elf's few things: a large goatskin in a wicker frame. He worked his dry tongue in his mouth. It would be a long climb to the top, and he had precious little water.

The elf seemed to make a decision, then lowered his sword. "If you mean no evil, then I will count you a friend in this blasted place."

Tringad made no answer. It did not matter to him what the elf thought.

"I am Elaninir," he said, "Knight of Shanmour."

"My name is Tringad."

Elanirin made a stiff bow. "I cannot offer you a feast, Tringad, but I have some food and you may share it."

He gestured for Tringad to sit, and he did. He searched through his gear with blinds hands. Tringad watched him as he did. They could not have been more dissimilar, the two of them, and it was not only their race that made them so. Elaninir was fair, and tall, and lean, while Tringad was dark, and short, and powerfully built. Even wounded the elf was handsome and noble of face. Tringad had never in his life been accused of being comely. The pockmarks of childhood had taken care of that.

There was little more in the elf's pack than some hard tack and strips of dried meat, but Tringad did not turn up his nose at these. They ate, then when Tringad asked if he could fill his water bottle from Elaninir's goatskin, the elf said he would be honored if he did.

Honored. Tringad sometimes thought the word meant the same thing as dead. He almost laughed, but there was scant water in the elf's goatskin, and Tringad only filled his bottle halfway.

"You will go now, won't you, Tringad?"

"Yes."

The elf nodded. "I cannot fault you. That is why I came here myself. To stand before the monster of Blackstone, and to slay it."

"Why?" Tringad asked, although he had already guessed.

For a moment, beneath the bloody rag, his face shone. "After I perform such a glorious deed, how can the gods refuse to restore my sight?"

So, he was a fool then. A noble fool. But then, they were the most dangerous sort.

"Fighting a dragon is a deadly task even if one is blessed with eyes."

Elaninir shrugged. "If the will is strong, one can always find a way. I convinced a merchant to bring me here in his wagon. Now I have built this fire. Sooner or later the beast will see the smoke and will come to investigate." He gripped the hilt of his sword. "I was trained to fight in the dark. And now the dark is always around me—there is no difference. I will succeed no matter."

Tringad grunted at that. The elf had lost his eyes, but not his arrogance.

"You can keep on waiting for the dragon to come to you," Tringad said. "But I'm going to climb Blackstone and find the monster first."

"And will you attempt to slay it then?"

Why not tell him the truth? "No, I'm going to talk to it, forge an alliance with it."

The hauteur on his face turned to shock. "By the gods, why would you do this?"

One word Tringad said. "Power."

Elaninir shook his head. "No. The dragon is a thing of evil. I cannot let you sell yourself to it." The dwarf reached for him, but his boot struck a stone, and he stumbled. Tringad caught the elf before he fell. Elaninir gripped the dwarf's shoulder to steady himself, and his hand found hot steel. His mouth opened in surprise.

"But you are a knight as well! Why did you not say so, brother? From which order do you hail?"

Tringad said nothing. The elf's blind hands touched Tringad's armor, froze, then groped along the metal, tracing the hard outlines. Tringad grinned like the death's head on his breastplate. *Yes, let him touch me, let him know what I am.*

At last he pulled away.

"Now, I understand, dwarf. You have your path to follow, and I have mine."

His words were not angry, but rather filled with disgust and pity. This bothered Tringad more.

"Thank you for the water," he said.

The elf said nothing.

Then Tringad left him, and he did not look back.

He started up the sheer slope. He climbed with speed and with purpose, using his hands as much as his legs to scramble over the treacherous rocks. Hot air rose in dizzying waves from below and seared his lungs, but he ignored it. Elaninir had been right about one thing—they did each have a path to follow. Only the elf's path led to death, and his—if he was right, if he was lucky—would lead to mastery. Surely he could find a way to make himself useful to the dragon. If nothing else, he could catch far more meat for it than he would make as a meal. And with such a powerful ally beside him, there was no telling how far he would rise in the world.

He kept climbing.

Then it happened, so quickly he could do nothing but watch. With his hand he gripped the corner of a boulder to pull himself up. But it was loose, and precariously balanced. It shifted under his weight, tilted, then all at once came free. With a grating of rock on rock, the boulder slid down. There was no time to move. The ponderous block struck his left leg and pinned it against a spur of stone behind it. The steel greave he wore crumpled like paper. He heard more than felt the wet pop of his leg breaking.

A tingling clarity filled his mind. Injury, he realized, tended to do that. *You idiot! You allowed yourself to be distracted by the fool elf, and now you're going to pay for it!*

And he did, with the first bright shards of pain.

Tringad almost swooned, but he fought to hold onto his wits, and did so, though just barely. He drew his sword, slipped it under the boulder, and wedged it against the spur of rock that crushed his leg. Then he leaned on the hilt. A groan of rock. The boulder shifted, and he could feel the broken ends of his leg bone grind against each other. He paused to vomit, then leaned on the sword again. The boulder lifted a finger's breadth, then two, then three. He clenched his teeth against the pain and started to pull his dangling leg free.

That was when the blade of his sword snapped.

Tringad flew backward. The boulder lurched to the side, rolled over, and tumbled down the slope. His fingers clutched for a hold to stop his fall, but they found only loose stone. The boulder had set all the rocks around him into motion. He shouted a curse to all the gods of darkness. Then with a roar like thunder a large part of the mountain went sliding down the slope and carried his body with it. He might have screamed, but a stone struck his head, and all went black.

Tringad woke to the unfamiliar stars of the night sky.

For a moment he struggled in disorientation. A shadow hovered over him. The light of the moon glimmered off the steel outline of a rose. Then he blinked in understanding and let the strong hands ease him back to the ground.

"I knew the gods would bring you back," Elaninir said.

Tringad gave a bitter laugh at the conceit of his words. "Do your gods often break the legs of people just to get what they want? They sound more like common thugs to me."

Now anger twisted the elf's face. "And what of your dark gods? Do they not use others for their gain?"

"They do, only they are honest about it, and never disguise it as anything else. But none of that matters."

With a grimace, Tringad sat up and tried to piece together what had happened. Elaninir must have heard the boulders fall, must have followed the sounds of his moans, must have somehow dragged him back to his camp. Tringad searched with his hands. The elf had splinted his leg, and had tucked the hilt of his broken sword into its sheath. *Why hadn't he just killed me?* It didn't matter.

"I've got to go," Tringad said.

He struggled to his feet. The pain was manageable with the splint. Then he took a step. A moment later, he was on the ground again, clutching his leg, spitting and swearing.

Elaninir knelt beside him. "You can't walk well enough."

"Yes, I can." It was a lie. Tringad didn't care. At that moment, he hated the elf.

"No, it's a sign." Again, that utter confidence lit his sightless face. "You can see the way. And I'm strong. I can help you up the rocks. Alone we can do nothing, but together we can make it to the top."

Tringad fell still and gazed at the elf. "And what would we do once we got there? Or have you forgotten our differing intentions?"

Elaninir shook his head. "Perhaps it will be decided for us. Perhaps the dragon will be amenable to your talk of alliance. Or perhaps it won't, and then I will slay it. Let us see when we get there."

It was madness. Tringad knew it. The Shanmour Knight could only be trouble. He likely thought he could convert the dwarf along the way, to win Tringad over to his cause. Blast the righteous arrogance. It made him sick. Yet sometimes, in a mad world, madness was the only way.

"Yes," he said at last. "We shall see."

They began their ascent at dawn.

The sun heaved itself over the horizon, a baleful eye that glared at the land. In moments a hot wind sprang up out of nowhere and raced over them. Its gritty breath stung their hands and faces. Tringad looked up at Blackstone, but he could not make out the crown of the peak. Instead it was sheer slopes of ebony as far as his eyes could see.

"Are you ready?" Tringad asked.

Elaninir adjusted the rag that bound his eyes, then nodded. "I am."

"Then we'd better get moving. We'll want to make it to the summit before sunset if we can. Whether it's to talk to it or fight it, better to face a dragon in the light than in the dark."

Tringad pushed up from the ground with his arms, got his good leg beneath him, and stood, though in the process he drew in a hissing breath of pain.

Elaninir must have heard him. He reached out, found Tringad's arm, and placed it on the slender slope of his hips.

"I will help you."

Tringad hesitated. He did not like the idea of depending on another, not for anything. And Elaninir seemed too willing, almost too eager to help him, as if he enjoyed that the dwarf was weaker than him. But, whatever Tringad felt, the elf was right—there was no way he was going to climb the mountain alone. Tringad clenched his teeth, then looped his arm around Elaninir's waist and allowed the elf to take the weight off his splinted leg.

"Now you must show me the way," he said.

His face was so calm beneath the dirty bandage, so full of pride still. Was he not disgusted with his own deficiency? Was he not furious that he needed another to lead him like a child? But Tringad only grunted and limped toward the foot of the nearest slope, Elaninir beside him.

What an absurd sight they made, two broken knights, one dark and one light, one crippled and one blind, struggling together up the knife-edged side of a mountain. But there was no one to see them, only the hot, unblinking eye of the sun. Nothing grew or lived on the slopes of the blasted peak. Rock and sand and wind, that was all.

The slowness of their progress was agonizing. Every boulder, every ledge of stone was a battle. Tringad described what the way looked like to Elaninir, using words to guide his hands and feet to the scant holds, until he was able to leverage himself up. Then he would reach down to pull Tringad up after him while the dwarf pushed with his good leg. More than once Elaninir's blind hands missed their mark, and he skidded back down the slope, scraping his hands and face. And every time he heaved Tringad up, his broken leg was jarred and buffeted, sending sharp knives of pain up through his body.

Their armor was a hot and ponderous burden, yet they were loath to cast if off, knowing they might well need it at the top. And, too, it saved them from the worst of the scrapes and bruises. Still, by midday they were battered, bleeding, and exhausted. They sat on a broad ledge of rough stone. The land, flat and brown as the skin of a drum, stretched far below them and made Tringad dizzy to gaze down. He still could not glimpse the summit for the haze, but by his guess they had come at least halfway.

They ate some food, then Tringad pulled his bottle from Elaninir's pack. The water was scalding and tasted like the waste swill from a tanner's shop, but they drank it all the same, and it was an effort to keep from gulping. Tringad replaced the stopper. There was still a long way to go.

For a few minutes more they rested. Tringad gazed into the empty air before them, while Elaninir gazed into nothingness.

"Tell me, was it a vision that led you here?" the fair-haired elf asked suddenly.

Tringad gave the elf a sharp look, even though he knew Elaninir could not see it. "What do you know of visions, Knight of Shanmour?"

"Only that they are something each Knight of Stormguard has, something that guides them, that leads them onward to their dark purpose."

"No, not something that each has. I forsook my clan long ago, as well as the visions," Tringad's words were harsh, but he didn't care.

Tringad would never forget that day—the day he was brought before the leader of the Stormguard clan, the day the powerful dwarf lord had laid his hands upon him. Some said that his mother was a stone goddess, and Tringad believed it. The dwarven lord had given him a choice: go out to the streets and live with the thieves and murderers until he became one himself, and ended up swinging from a gibbet; or join his army, become one of his knights, and know honor and glory.

That ultimatum had made Tringad angry, he remembered. Who was he to offer Tringad such a choice? Who was he to tell him what his life would or would not be? But he could not resist the power of the dwarven lord's eyes. Tringad had taken his hand, and the lord had kissed him and welcomed him, and right there a sword was brought to him. Tringad had knelt before him, and the lord laid his hands on his head and spoke a prayer to the dark gods, and that was when the visions came upon him.

They were like dreams, the visions, only they were with him every time he closed his eyes, in the dark hours of the night, and in the stillness between every thought. The true magic of the visions was that they were different for every knight, his own path to glory or death.

The strange thing was, Tringad could no longer remember what the visions had been to him.

When his lord died, the visions went with him, for they had come through him, and was of him. Now Tringad was left with a gaping hole in his mind, a gap he could not stop worrying over, like a dwarf who has been to the barber and searches with his tongue his empty lip where his mustache used to be. He knew that the visions had filled him with both terror and wonder. But even the memory of them was gone now, and he knew he would never regain them.

"I'm sorry," Elaninir said at last.

His words infuriated Tringad. Was he sorry for what he had said? Or sorry for him? Even when he spoke humble words such as those it seemed to be with the implication that he was the better of them. Yet there had been genuine remorse in his voice, and Tringad knew he was being unfair.

"There is nothing to be sorry for," he said. "I don't need the visions. I know my key to glory. I'll have it soon enough, once the dragon and I are in league together. With its strength and my brains, nothing will stand between us."

Elaninir shook his head. "Enemies we are in another place, and enemies we still may be, but here and now you are my companion, and so it is not my wish to offend. Yet I still say you are misguided in your intentions. What do you have to offer a dragon? What makes you think you can convince it to form an alliance with you?"

"And what makes you think that if you perform some bone-headed heroic deed that the gods will restore your sight?"

Elaninir winced at his words, and Tringad knew they had struck some sore spot deep within him. *Good. We do not have time for this.* Tringad glanced up at the sky. The sun had passed its zenith and was already starting its descent.

"Let's get going," Tringad said, "if you really want to kill a dragon."

The elf helped him to his feet, and they started up the mountain once more.

After his fall the day before, Tringad should have been more wary of the treacherous slope. But as they climbed on, exhaustion dulled their caution. It was only a matter of time before one of them made a mistake.

It was Elaninir who did so first.

They stood on a slim ledge, a drop of five hundred feet below them. Perhaps he got too tired to think, or perhaps he had grown overconfident. Either way, Elaninir started to pull himself up the rocky shelf in front of them before Tringad had sufficiently guided the elf's hands to the best holds. The crack he had gripped was too shallow. His blind fingers could not dig in deep enough to support his weight. He dropped back roughly to the narrow ledge. His heels skidded on the edge of the precipice, his hands flew out in search of balance. They found nothing. He toppled over backward.

No!

Tringad didn't know if he screamed the word aloud or silently. It didn't matter. Much as he hated to admit it, he needed Elaninir. Tringad lunged for him. Pain surged up his broken leg, but he ignored it. He stretched farther than he thought possible, so far that his joints popped. His fingers just brushed the hot metal of the elf's breastplate—then caught the top edge of the beaten steel. He threw all his weight backward.

The Shanmour Knight sprawled forward, onto the ledge where they had stood. Tringad in turn stumbled forward, felt his leg twist sickeningly, and fell to the side. Before he could stop himself, he rolled off the edge of the precipice.

Tringad scrambled for something, anything, to stop himself. His hands found nothing but smooth stone. He fell. Then one hand slid into a crack in the rock, caught, and held. Fire exploded in his shoulder as his body jerked to a halt. He twisted in midair, suspended from the overhang by one hand. Beneath his dangling boots was five hundred feet of emptiness and, beneath that, sharp stone.

Pain sliced at his hand, blood slicked his palm. He could not hang on for long.

A shadow loomed over him.

"Elaninir!"

Tringad screamed the word. So much for pride.

The elven knight groped along the edge of the precipice in search of him. The elf had cut his forehead in the fall, and blood streamed down to soak the already crusted bandage over his eyes.

"To your left," Tringad shouted. "Farther!"

Hot agony melted his muscles. His blood-wet fingers loosened. Another few seconds, no more. The elf's hand came within in an inch of

Tringad's, moved away, then, as if guided by impossible instinct, slid back.

Contact.

Just as Tringad's hand slid through the crack, the elf grabbed his wrist, then heaved back with all his weight and dragged Tringad onto the ledge.

For a minute they both lay there, panting. As last Elaninir spoke.

"Are you all right?"

Tringad cradled his battered hand. "I'll live."

The relief on the blind elf's face was clear. Somehow, that eased Tringad's pain.

Still shaken by the near fall, Tringad sipped some water, and Elaninir tightened his splint. After that they were ready to move on.

They started back up the peak. Soon it became like a game, albeit a deadly one, and each time they avoided a tilting rock, or survived a tumble down a short slope or scree, or dodged a falling boulder, it was like a personal triumph, a victory that affirmed they were smarter and better than the blasted heap of stone. Before long they were laughing as, battered but not beaten, they fought their way up the mountain.

All at once Elaninir's laughter fell short. The curvature of the peak in either direction was apparent now. They were almost there.

"I thought you were gone, you know," the elf said. "Back down there, after you saved me from falling."

For a moment Tringad was silent. Then, to his own surprise, he grinned. "You'll not be rid of me so easily, Knight of Shanmour," he said.

He didn't know why, perhaps he was growing used to the pain in his leg, but at that moment Tringad slipped his arm off the elf's waist, reached down, and gripped his hand, and they walked those last agonizing steps together.

They reached the summit just as the sun was dying in a sea of bloody clouds.

At first they could see nothing. Grit swirled around them. Then the wind shifted, tore a rent through the veil of dust, and at that moment Tringad caught his first glimpse of the dragon of Blackstone.

It was enormous. Tringad had read accounts of large dragons before, and they had filled him with awe and fear. But this creature was five times larger than the greatest of them. It sprawled across the entire top of the mountain, as black as the stones for which it was named. A serrated ridge ran along its spine like a row of knives. The wings were folded tight against the lean, angular body. Its massive head rested on a heap of rubble, and its maw was cocked open, large enough to swallow a man whole.

They came to a halt behind the cover of a boulder. The dragon was no more than thirty paces away. Tringad's hand slipped from the elf's.

"What is it?" Elaninir asked.

Tringad said nothing.

The elf drew in a deep breath and gripped the hilt of his sword. "You see it, don't you?"

"Yes," Tringad whispered.

Fear slithered up his throat. He gagged and tried to swallow it back down. A part of him had not believed he would really find it. But this was what he had come for. He had not gone through hell and back to get here just to turn around now. Besides, any moment the thing would turn its great, wedge-shaped head—any moment it would detect them standing there. Then it would be all over, one way or the other. Tringad took a step forward.

Elaninir's hand shot out, groped in the air, then found his shoulder, halting him. "What are you doing, Tringad?" he asked in a hoarse voice.

"Let me go."

"No, you can't really mean to do this."

"I said let me go, Elaninir. I have to talk to it."

"And what are you going to say?" The elf's grip on Tringad's shoulder tightened. "What words are you going to use to convince it not to strip your flesh from your bones the moment it sees you? Tell me that before you go, dwarf."

Tringad opened his mouth, but nothing came out. For a long moment they stood frozen, silent. Wind hissed over stone. Then, slowly, Tringad shook his head.

"You don't want to make a deal with it, do you?" the elf whispered. "That's not why you came here at all. You're hoping that it will kill you. Aren't you?"

What could Tringad say to that? Strange, he couldn't remember the visions, but he could remember the face of every person he had slain in the name of one cause or another, each one of them frozen in the moment of terror, or agony, or disbelief when he pulled his dripping sword from their gut. The visions were no more, but that—that Tringad would always have.

"My clan lord told me he would save me, Elaninir. But I think he damned me instead."

Tringad laughed. It was a bitter sound.

For a moment the elf said nothing. If he had had eyes, he would have wept. Then all at once his expression changed. It was anger now. Righteous anger.

"No!" Elaninir said. His voice rose to a shout that rang off the hard stones around them. "No, I will not let you do this!"

Elaninir pushed Tringad aside. Then, before the dwarf could stop him, the elf drew his sword and scrambled blindly up the last remaining slope. Tringad screamed at him, but he did not stop. The elf stumbled, fell, got up, and fell again. Hands bleeding, he gained his feet and lurched on. Tringad thought for certain the dragon would see him coming, would turn and pounce on him like a cat on a mouse. But perhaps it was sleeping, for it did not stir. Tringad started after him, but his broken leg dragged uselessly behind him. Then Elaninir collided with the dragon's shoulder.

He cried out, a wordless sound of rage, of hate, of sorrow—and swung his sword at the beast.

With a metallic ring, the blade bounced off the dragon's skin.

Elaninir gaped in blind confusion. Then he swung again, and again, and again. Each time his sword bounced back with a loud chime. Through it all, the dragon did not move. They both realized the truth at the same time.

Elaninir sank to his knees. Head bowed, he leaned on the hilt of his sword, its blade now notched in a dozen places. At last Tringad limped to his side. He reached out and laid a hand against the beast's neck.

Rock: hard, warm, solid.

The dragon of Blackstone. Of black stone.

There is always a kernel of truth in the stories people tell. But only a kernel. Tringad should have known. There was no dragon here. Only a heap of rocks that, in silhouette, happened to look a bit like one, enough to frighten wayward travelers, enough to make them tell tales to knights foolish enough and eager enough to listen.

Tringad eased himself down beside the elf. "I guess neither of us got what we wanted," he said. "Did we?"

Elaninir did not answer. Bent over his word as he was, it looked almost as though he were praying.

Suddenly the dwarf was angry. "So our dragon turned out to be just a pile of rocks. So what? Find someone else to restore your sight. Find another heroic deed to accomplish."

The elf gasped the word like he was drowning. "No, you don't understand. It has to be this."

Tringad looked into his blind face. "Why? Why does it have to be this?"

The elf shook his head, but Tringad did not find that good enough. The dwarf balled his hands into fists and pounded on the hard armor that encased the elf's shoulders, and shouted the words.

"Why this, Elaninir?"

For a long moment the elf was silent, and Tringad thought he would not answer at all. He let his hands fall. At last the elf spoke in a low voice, his face distant beneath the bloody rag, the expression of righteousness he had worn since the dwarf had met him now gone.

"We were in the midst of a battle when it struck," Elaninir said. "In the east. My brethren and I—mostly Knights of Shanmour—we espied a troop of dwarves. They outnumbered us four to one. We knew that if we engaged them we would almost certainly die. They had not seen us, and the terrain was rugged. It was possible we could have slipped away without them seeing us. But that would have been a cowardly act. Maybe glory is enough when victory is impossible."

No, Tringad thought, *it isn't*. But he said nothing and let the elf continue.

Elaninir's expression became one of remembered fear. "It was the screams that got to me. I guess I never imagined them. I knew there would be shouting, and the clanging of swords. But the cries of the dying were everywhere. I've never heard grown men scream like that."

"It was your first battle, wasn't it?" Tringad asked. The elf did not answer the question, but he did not need to.

"It was almost like a sea," Elaninir said. "The way the battle surged back and forth. Suddenly everything swirled around me, and I was by my commander. He was fighting two dwarves, and though he was bleeding from a wound in his side, he was holding them back, but only just barely. He saw me then, and called to me to help him. But I just stood there. I couldn't move. It was like I was a statue, made all of stone. Except for my eyes. My eyes still worked, blast them. They could see everything. My commander let out a roar and charged one of the dwarves, killing him. But he stumbled and fell to his knees. The other dwarf stood above him and raised his sword."

Tringad could not tear his gaze from the elf. Elaninir's shoulders were shaking now.

"It would have been so easy," he whispered. "The dwarf's side was exposed. All I had to do was thrust with my sword. But I couldn't … the fear … all of me, stone, except for my eyes, my blasted eyes. The dwarf grinned at me. I think he knew I would do nothing. He swung his sword, and cut off the head of my commander. Then, in that moment, I could move again. I turned and ran. The dwarf ran after me. I knew any second I would feel his axe drive between my shoulders."

Elaninir drew in a rasping breath. "Only then it struck me. The sky went dark. The land shook. And in that moment, all of us, all of the Shanmour Knights felt the power of the dwarven magic. The battle turned into chaos. People were running in every direction, and I ran too. It was the last time I saw any of my fellow knights."

Tringad shook his head, sickened by the story. He knew all too well the horrors of battle, had seen how they could shatter the spirits of the young, of the innocent who witnessed them for the first time. People like Elaninir. Yet there was something about his tale that bothered Tringad. Something that didn't seem quite right. Then, all at once, he had it.

"But your eyes, Elaninir," he said. "The Plucking happened before the dwarf reached you. The battle was over, so you ran. So how were you wounded?"

Elaninir hung his head. For a moment Tringad stared at him. Then his mind reeled.

It was like I was a statue, made all of stone. Except for my eyes. My eyes still worked, blast them. They could see everything.

Tringad stared at him in horror. "You did it yourself, didn't you? Your eyes. By all the gods, you did it yourself!"

When the elf spoke again, his voice was barely above a whisper. "Don't you see, Tringad? It was my fault. It was my act of cowardice that caused the death of my commander. That's why I came here, to prove myself with a deed of glory. I knew that if I could slay the dragon, the gods would be pleased and restore my sight and take away the things I have seen." A sob racked his body. "Only there is no dragon, and there will be no glorious deed. I have failed."

The elf bowed his head once more over his sword. Somehow, Tringad gained his feet and stood over him where he knelt. A wave of disgust rolled through him. He wiped the tears from his cheeks and spit out a laugh like a man who has been kicked in the face spits out his teeth.

"Poor Elaninir. You wanted a dragon to save you, and all you got was me."

For a moment the elf was silent, frozen. Tringad started to turn away. Then the elf snapped his head up, and a quiet word escaped him.

"Yes …." He heaved himself to his feet, gripped his sword, and turned toward the dwarf.

Tringad's eyes narrowed. "What are you doing?"

The elf stumbled toward the sound of his voice. "Don't you see? The gods have given me a second chance to prove myself. I was a coward, I fled from the dwarf I should have fought. But here you are, another dwarf of Rachdale. Why didn't I see it before? It's not a dragon I need to fight." The elf raised his sword and took another step. "It's you."

Tringad swore and drew his sword. It was broken, but it would be more than enough. "Don't be an idiot, Elaninir," the dwarf spat. "You're blind. If you come at me, I'll slit your throat in a second."

The elf took another step forward. Beneath the bloody bandage he wore a rapt expression. It was a look of madness. "Do what you have to do," he said.

In that moment, Tringad knew what he wanted. There was only one way he could save himself, one way he could atone for what he believed he had done.

"No," Tringad said in disgust. "I won't help you." He threw his sword and it clattered down the slopes. "Strike me down if you want to, I don't care. But I won't be part of your sick little game."

For a moment Elaninir stood before him like a statue. Then the elf whispered in a reverent tone.

"Forgive him."

Too late, Tringad saw what he meant to do. The elf reversed his sword, grabbed the blade, and thrust the hilt toward Tringad. On instinct, the dwarf closed his hands around the hilt as it struck his breastplate. In that moment Elaninir threw his body forward. The elf gripped Tringad's shoulders, clenched his teeth, and pulled himself toward the dwarf until their bodies pressed together in an embrace. For a moment they stood that way, as one. At last Elaninir smiled.

"Thank you," he whispered.

Then blood poured from his mouth.

The stars faded in the slate gray sky. Tringad gazed at the distant horizon. Dawn was coming.

He placed one last stone atop the cairn he had built for Elaninir. The elf has gotten what he wanted after all. Tringad only hoped there was some peace in it for him, that maybe in death he was finally whole again. Tringad himself was alone now. His lord had died, and so had the visions.

Yet somehow this no longer troubled him as it had. He did not need his clan lord to save him, nor the visions, nor Elaninir.

It was up to him to save himself.

Dawn came then and cast its light on the broken landscape below. It would be a long time before each of their people was healed of the wounds wrought by the folly of the Plucking. But the king was gone now, and those who were left still had the power to choose what they would be. It was not the first time peace had ended. Maybe, just maybe, it would be the last.

Tringad tightened the splint around his leg and started down the mountain.

A Taste of Blood

Richard Fierce

Kirin stepped out of the shadows as the carriage approached, his eyes narrowed against the glare of the rising sun. The transport stopped and he boarded silently. With limited seating, he was forced to sit beside a large female dwarf. She wore a pendant around her neck; the symbol for one of her gods. Kirin shifted as a spring in the cushion probed him obscenely. He rested his hand over the new bag of gold at his hip, half of the payment for the job he'd just taken.

The carriage jolted as it began moving. Kirin stared out the dirty window. The buildings they passed were old and abandoned. He hated the village of Thanalian, wanted to be out of it before the dwarves woke and rose from the gutters and the ruins to begin their work day. At least in Vaelkesh the nasty little creatures kept themselves hidden. Thanalian was a small village twenty miles west of the Verge in elvish lands. It was one of the only places Kirin knew of where dwarves and elves lived around each other without burying daggers in one another's backs. More often than not.

The dwarf leaned toward Kirin, staring out the same window as they passed a small group of elves standing in front of a burnt-out market. One of the elves held a magical ball of fire, a bright tongue of blue flame curling up, searching for a target. Kirin fought a wave of nausea and ducked his head, wondering if they were the ones responsible for the dwarf killings, or the fire that almost killed him. Like it was his fault that the dwarves had been in the same tavern as him.

The dwarf beside him held her pendant tighter, fingering the outline of the symbol. Kirin shook his head, hiding his disdain behind an impassive mask.

"Elves," the woman spat, her face contorting as if tasting her own disgust. "I hope they all die. The city's better off without them."

"Have you ever met an elf?" Kirin asked, taking the middle road.

The dwarf touched her pendant and moved back into her own space. "No. And I hope I never do. Only a fool would want anything to do with one of them."

Kirin knew all too well what someone would do to an elf, which was why Kirin kept his ears covered. In Thanalian, most elves and dwarves remained in a drugged or drunken stupor, selling body and soul for the chance to forget. Kirin knew she would not be sympathetic. This dwarf would condemn him as she condemned the hundreds of others who had not been involved in the Plucking. In this dwarf's world, the words "elf" and "love" could not exist in the same sentence, the same thought, the same breath. Kirin knew it must be a sad existence.

"Fools and worthless trash, they all are," the dwarf continued, rocking in her seat until it creaked. Kirin considered telling her the pendant was useless. He didn't think the dwarf would appreciate a history lesson, so he said nothing, and she let the subject drop. "You're holding onto that bag tightly," she stated almost coyly, as if hoping for a handout without having to beg.

"Yes, I am."

The dwarf seemed to realize she wouldn't get anything without pleading and sat back in her seat to sulk. They fell into silence as the carriage moved on past the void of light that during the day was a large garden, full of dead flowers. At night, it was a black hole, sucking light and energy from the world around it until even the stars above seemed pale. No one went into the garden at night, unless they were looking for something most people didn't want to find. The dwarves in the rest of the city were civilized for the most part, but in the garden, that chunk of wilderness in the middle of town, they were nothing more than predators, without honor, without humanity.

The carriage continued along the nearly deserted street, past taverns patronized by shady types. The carriage slowed as it neared a sparsely populated part of the village. Kirin stood, preparing to leave the ignorant dwarf. She grabbed his arm, obviously preparing to give him some dire warning about this part of the town. Before she could, the pressure of her hand caused Kirin's sleeve to ride down, pulling his cowl loose, exposing his pointed ears. The dwarf pulled her hand away as if scalded, and stared at Kirin, her expressive face registering horror and disgust.

Rage uncoiled within Kirin, overshadowing his mild contempt. This dwarf was his enemy now. That prejudice, once broad and laughable, was now aimed directly at Kirin's soul. As if she could know him, as if she could understand the decisions he'd made. As if she were somehow better because her ears weren't pointed.

Kirin leaned down in her face, sneering. "What's the matter? Never seen an elf before?"

The dwarf sputtered, finally dumbstruck. The carriage lurched to a halt and Kirin turned, holding his anger in his fist and walking stiffly out into the village. The wind beat against him like the wings of a bird trying desperately to escape the beast that has it pinned. The dark morning sky seemed far away now, like a cloak had been lain across the tops of sharp, angry dwellings that closed in on him from above. He shrugged his shoulders, adjusting to the burden, and as the carriage pulled away he turned into the darkness.

A great fire had ravaged this part of the village. The old stone building that had housed his family for generations was still there, a ghost of its former glory. He stared at it for a long, aching moment, slowly walking past the place. One of the doors hung drunkenly askew, and the odor of smoke still lingered in the air. Where light shone through the broken windows and missing roof, he could see black fingers reaching up the walls, their destructive touch caressing the remaining inside, teasing, promising.

He hadn't seen the fire, didn't know who, if anyone, had survived. All he knew was that the fire that had killed so many of the elves milling around outside hadn't killed him. If he had survived, maybe someone else had, too. He could hope.

Hope. The concept seemed so foreign, a foul taste on his lips that knew the pleasures of the present, not thoughts of the future. Hope reeked of the belief that there was something beyond this day, these precious hours. He had given that belief up long ago. Or perhaps not so long. It seemed an eternity, but nothing was forever. If elves could die, then he could remember.

He left the boundary of the village and stepped into the woods. He had a job to do. Reminiscing would have to wait.

The elves named the valley *Tal'Elul*—the Land of Death. Most now called it the Verge, and no living being walked there willingly unless they were desperate or insane. Kirin was neither. He was on a mission.

He had been hunting the creature for days.

Kirin wasn't sure what it was, and neither were his employers. He'd yet to glimpse the thing. It hunted during the night and it was quick, leaving few clues behind. Something was terrorizing the outlying villages, leaving mauled bodies and terrified people in its wake. Kirin had read several reports and there was little consistency among them. Some described a demon, while others talked about a humanoid figure mounted on a horse. He believed he was closing in on it, whatever *it* really was.

Kneeling beside a slow-moving stream, Kirin cupped his hands and placed them in the water. The cool liquid pooled into his hands and felt good against his skin. He brought his hands to his lips and drank some of the water before splashing the rest onto his face, wiping the sweat and grime away. Although it was autumn, summer clung to the land like a child clung to its mother. It was nearing dusk and the sun was descending faster than he anticipated. The temperature was beginning to drop. It wouldn't be long now.

A panicked squeal resonated from the east. His sensitive ears twitched at the sound. It wasn't an elvish squeal. It was an animal. He stood up and dried his hands on his pant legs. He scanned the area in the direction of the noise. His vision was hampered by tall, thick marsh reeds. The setting sun was casting long shadows on everything and he could only see a few feet ahead.

He was a fair distance from the safety of the woods, and he had no time for distractions. Hunting down the creature was his sole task. Besides, he was in the Verge—the narrow strip of land between the elvish and dwarvish kingdoms. It was a dangerous place. Aside from possibly running into one of the short folk, there were dire creatures afoot. It was likely the squeal he had heard was an unlucky animal being attacked by something sinister.

Again, the squeal rang out. Against his better judgement, he drew his sword—a straight, single-edged blade roughly two feet in length—and walked toward the sound. Kirin leaned forward and ducked beneath long strands of foul moss that hung from the lifeless branches of dead trees nearby. In the marsh around him, all sounds of birds and other things suddenly stopped. Only the unending swarms of mosquitoes and gnats continued to make their presence known. The annoying bugs horded around him seeking exposed flesh to bite. These he managed to ignore as his full attention was locked ahead.

As he pushed his way forward, the reeds began to thin. A terrified squeal sounded. He could hear the animal splashing, and he could hear too the sound of a deep, gravelly voice cursing. The reeds parted and he found himself standing at the edge of a quagmire, roughly twenty feet in diameter. Near the center, a pony floundered, giving an occasional terror-stricken cry. Kirin noticed the form beside the fraught pony. Chest deep, struggling and cursing, Kirin's eyes narrowed in a sudden rush of hatred.

A *dwarf!*

Kirin stepped fully out of the reeds and the pony stopped its thrashing. The dwarf looked up and locked eyes with Kirin, his eyes narrowing—just as Kirin's own had—at the sight of his hated enemy.

Silence ensued. Long, tense moments passed as the two glared at each other, neither willing to speak first. Kirin's emotions churned, his mind in turmoil. Seeing a dwarf in Thanalian was one thing. Seeing a dwarf out here … that was another. He stepped toward a log and the dwarf spoke.

"Don't try to help me, *elf.* I'm capable of getting out of this myself." The word elf was spat as a curse from his mouth. The dwarf continued to glare hostilely from his shadowed eyes. Sheathing his blade, Kirin turned to go. Just as he turned, the pony began to thrash again, snorting and rolling its eyes in terror.

Clenching his jaw, Kirin turned back around and grabbed a long tree branch. "I refuse to have this animal's blood on my hands, *dwarf,*" Kirin fumed. He leveraged the branch over the bog and dropped the end of it near the dwarf, leaving the other end resting on dry ground.

Snorting with disgust, the dwarf grabbed hold of the branch and pulled himself out of the muck and onto the branch, wrapping his legs around it for balance. Finally free, he reached with his short arms to grab the pony's reins. He almost fell back in, but he managed to grab them. Clutching the reins firmly, he used his brute strength to pull the pony toward him. Then the dwarf scooted backwards, reset his legs firmly around the branch, and heaved the pony again.

It was a tediously slow process, but finally the dwarf reached dry ground. The pony thrashed free as well. The dwarf stood there, gasping in deep breaths. Kirin couldn't tell what the dwarf looked like beneath the muck and slime. A cloud of insects immediately swarmed both the animal and the dwarf. They smelled terrible. The foul odor of rotten eggs assailed Kirin and it was all he could do not to vomit.

Like all dwarves, this one too was short—standing somewhere between four and five feet. He was thick and looked like he weighed a few hundred pounds. Other than that, Kirin could see no other distinguishable traits. Dusk had fallen into night and the dwarf was nothing more than a vague silhouette.

Kirin stood with his hand on the pommel of his short sword. He stared in loathing at the dwarf. Likewise, the dwarf had retrieved a double-bitted ax and stared contemptuously at the elf. Neither spoke.

Suddenly, the pony reared up and squealed. The dwarf managed to keep the animal from bolting away by holding onto its reigns. Dwarves were known for their strength, and when they plant themselves firmly, it is almost impossible to budge them.

Sss, thwak! Sss, thwak!

Their stalemate was broken by the sound of arrows hissing through the air, striking the ground and dead trees around them. A chorus of wild howls broke the silence. Kirin ducked down and unslung his bow from his shoulder. In a swift, smooth motion, he knocked an arrow to the string and pulled it back. His eyes darted back and forth among the rustling reeds, but he could see nothing definite in the dark.

The dwarf leaped onto the pony's saddle and spoke a word Kirin didn't know. The pony sprinted off. Giving one last look around, Kirin took aim in the direction of the crashing reeds and let his arrow fly. He was rewarded with a wet thud and a cry of alarm and pain. Slinging his bow back onto his shoulder, he sprinted after the dwarf, his feet moving lightly and easily over the slimy terrain.

They headed east, going deeper into the swamp. Dark shapes rose before him. He drew his blade and swung at the shadows. His strikes scored clean hits and black blood splattered him. Ahead, he heard the dwarf's battle cry and heard too the sound of his ax crushing through bone. Behind them, Kirin could hear the howls of pursuit.

He plunged headlong through the thick rushes, passing the cursing dwarf and his pony. Suddenly he was floundering stomach deep in water. He pressed his way toward the shore. The dwarf galloped up, stopping his mount.

"Blast it, *elf!*" the dwarf growled. "They are closing in and you run as though you are blind!"

Kirin pulled himself onto dry ground. "I didn't have to save your l—"

Sss, sss! Black shafted arrows hissed through the darkness.

"Follow me, *elf.* My eyes see better than yours." The dwarf spurred his pony forward, straight into a mob of dark shadows. The dwarf swung his ax mightily, bashing through armor to crush heads. Twisting and turning, the pony zigzagged through the swamp, continuing east.

Kirin raced after the pony, unseen arrows whizzing by him. He could not tell what obstacles the pony was dodging, nor did he know why he was following the dwarf in the first place. Here and there he caught glimpses of the dwarf's dark outline atop the pony.

To his right, he could hear the howling of enemy voices and the splash of pursuit. Out here Kirin was at a disadvantage. He had no idea where he was or where he was headed. He couldn't tell the shadows apart from one another. Finally, the moon broke through the clouds. Kirin welcomed the sight of the soft glowing orb. He began to recognize some of the shapes around him. Gnarled trees, clumps of marsh reeds among other things.

He also began to see the obstacles the dwarf's pony avoided. The increasing light of the moon glistened off surfaces on either side of him. The sounds of the night denizens fell silent as they plodded past, taking up their songs again once they were gone.

The howls of their pursuers grew louder and closer. Kirin could make out the splash of running feet, drawing nearer. He prepared himself to veer left or right, guessing the pony would begin to panic. The dwarf remained in control of the animal and they continued straight.

Suddenly black shapes crashed out of the reeds on either side and intercepted them, swinging wicked blades. For the first time, Kirin saw his enemy: Scourges. There were roughly as tall as dwarves, gray skinned, yellow eyed, batwing eared and their leering mouths displayed pointed and broken teeth. The dwarf spurred his pony onward. There was nowhere else to go but through.

Kirin bore down on a group of Scourges, slashing wildly with his short sword. He felt something strike his back and penetrate his leather tunic. Something warm and wet ran down his flesh, though whether it was blood or sweat he didn't know. His blade sheared through the elbow of a Scourge grasping at him. The creature howled and clutched at his gushing stump. Two more of them jumped in his way, but he cut them down and broke through the mob of creatures threatening to surround him. Ahead, the dwarf and his pony smashed through another group of Scourges, the dwarf's ax awash with dark blood. They continued racing into the night.

Twice more in their flight did the Scourges threaten to overtake them. Each time the pair charged through, smashing and slashing—scattering the Scourges before them. They took several minor wounds themselves, but managed to cross out of the Verge and into the dwarven realm of Rachdale.

They travelled easterly until well past midnight. Neither one spoke to the other. They stopped at an abandoned keep, an old dwarven fortress that had been long forgotten and disused. They staunched the worst of their wounds, each one standing guard while the other bound his injuries. When they each had finished, they glared at each other.

"I am exhausted," the dwarf said, "yet I shall take first watch. You sleep now, and I will wake you when it is your turn."

Kirin considered the offer, wondering if the dwarf planned to kill him in his sleep. "And you suppose I shall just trust you, a *dwarf*, to watch over me while I sleep? You must be more foolish than you look."

The dwarf grunted in agreement, likely thinking the same about the elf. He scratched at his beard in silence before finally muttering, "A truce, then?"

Kirin narrowed his eyebrows. *Was this some sort of trick?* He couldn't know. He was tired and his muscles were aching. Even if he took first watch himself, he knew he would be fast asleep before long. Daylight was still several hours off. "A truce," he consented.

Kirin settled himself in a corner with his back pressed against a wall. He laid his weapons next to him within easy reach. Watching the dwarf take a position at the edge of a crumbling wall, he felt the heaviness of sleep overtaking him. Within a few short moments, he was asleep.

He woke a few hours later to the dwarf nudging him with the butt of his ax. “What’s wrong?” Kirin asked.

“Nothing,” the dwarf replied. “It’s your turn to take watch.”

Kirin nodded and rose to his feet. His entire body was sore. Grabbing his bow, he slung it over his shoulder and then belted on his sword. He exchanged places with the dwarf. As he stared out across the land, he could see why the dwarf stood watch from this place. Although it was dark, the moon was shining bright enough to see a fair distance in any direction. He begrudgingly gave the dwarf credit.

Within a few minutes the dwarf was snoring soundly behind him. They were such loud creatures. Kirin turned his thoughts to the creature he was hunting. Having to run east and cross into Rachdale was going to delay him most of a day just backtracking. He was confident he would be back on the trail by the end of the day, but the creature could attack more of his people by then. Kirin looked back at the sleeping dwarf. The hatred boiling within him told him to leave the dwarf.

What do I owe him, anyway? He’s a filthy dwarf.

His sense of honor was the only thing that kept him from fleeing into the night.

After an hour of watching nothing happen, Kirin decided to explore the ruined fortress. It was standard dwarven architecture. Thick walls encircled the main keep, providing a defense against enemies and the elements. A large portion of the wall where the main gate should have been was now nothing more than rubble.

A noise outside the wall caught his attention. Unsheathing his sword, he crept swiftly to the crumbled section of wall. He listened intently and heard the noise again. Something was shuffling around. Gripping the hilt of his blade in a tight grip, he jumped over the wall and came face to face with the dwarf’s pony. He sighed in relief. He’d almost forgotten about the animal. The pony stared at him as if to say, “What?”

Kirin spotted a wild blackberry bush growing not far from where the pony was tied up. He stripped a few of the branches of their berries, plucking a few into his mouth. They were a little overripe, but still soft and mostly sweet. He fed a few to the pony and then headed back to his position to continue standing guard.

A few hours later, the sun began to peak on the horizon. Kirin was surprised at how quickly the time had passed. He walked over to the dwarf and nudged him with his foot. The dwarf’s snoring stopped, but he didn’t open his eyes.

“Dwarf,” Kirin said, “wake up.” He nudged him again. This time the dwarf opened his eyes. He looked confused for a moment and then his face took on a look of anger. “The sun is rising. I also found some breakfast.”

The dwarf rubbed his eyes and got up. The nasty mud from the bog had dried and pieces fell off as he moved. Kirin scrunched his face in disgust. Holding out his hand, he offered the dwarf some of the blackberries he’d found.

The dwarf snorted in contempt. “You expect me to eat that? I’m not an *elf*.”

Kirin shrugged and dropped them into a pouch on his belt. He watched the dwarf stomp away, muttering into his beard. He was ready to be gone from this place and even further away from the dwarf. Kirin walked to the crumbled wall. The dwarf had retrieved something from the saddle of his pony. As he drew near, Kirin saw it was some sort of meat.

“This is breakfast,” the dwarf said. He held some out to the elf, but Kirin turned away.

“I don’t eat meat,” he said. “I’m not a barbaric *dwarf*.”

“I have a name, *elf*. It’s Drokin.”

“And I have a name, *dwarf*. It’s Kirin.”

They stood there in silence, both fuming with hatred at the other. The dwarf finished his meal and ran his hands through his beard, shaking crumbs and dry mud free. “Which direction are you headed?” Drokin asked.

“West,” Kirin answered. “Back to my woods.”

“That’s where *I’m* going. Don’t think you’re traveling with me, *elf*.”

“What business does a *dwarf* have in my woods?”

“That’s none of your concern.”

Kirin rested his hand on the hilt of his sword. “Don’t think you can enter the elvish kingdom without taking an arrow to the chest. If I see your ugly face in my woods, I’ll—”

Sss, thwak!

A black feathered arrow struck the dwarf’s pony in the neck. A pained gurgling noise escaped the animal’s mouth before it crumpled to the ground. Drokin’s anguished cry broke the spell over Kirin. He looked out past the wall and saw a group of familiar figures approaching quickly. Kirin removed his bow from his shoulder and nocked an arrow, taking aim at the front of the group. He released the bowstring.

One of the figures dropped to the ground. Angry howls filled the air and Kirin recognized them as the same sounds from the night before. He found it odd the Scourges had tracked them all the way to the fortress. They weren’t smart creatures.

Several more arrows skittered against the stone around them. Kirin noticed that Drokin was standing in the open, mourning his fallen mount. He sprinted to the dwarf and tackled him to the ground. Drokin growled in anger.

"I will not be indebted to you twice!" the dwarf shouted. Drokin pushed Kirin off him. Grabbing his ax and a small round shield from the saddle of the dead pony, the dwarf charged toward the approaching Scourges.

Kirin watched as arrows flitted through the air around the dwarf. He fired several more of his own into the group of Scourges, though none of the hits were mortal. He was running low on arrows. Slinging the bow back on his shoulder, he drew his blade and rushed after Drokin. They met the Scourges in a clash of steel. The ugly creatures wielded rusted and chipped swords, likely scavenged from those too poor to afford quality weapons.

Drokin killed most of them himself. The dwarf had turned his grief into rage, and it fueled his strength. When the Scourges were dead, Drokin was covered in blood and entrails. Kirin tried to hide his disgust. They stood in silence, both breathing heavily from exertion.

"We part ways here," Kirin finally said.

Drokin nodded, but didn't say anything.

Wiping his blade clean on one of the dead creatures, Kirin sheathed it and headed back towards the Verge.

Kirin's fears of another attack were justified. He'd crossed back through the Verge and stopped at one of the villages on the border. A small place, housing only sixty people. Elves and dwarves mingled here like they did in Thanalian, but there was a line that divided the village. The two races respected the imaginary border and remained somewhat friendly with each other. The creature had attacked the night before, leaving three dead. One of them a child. Those who claimed to have seen the beast all had varying stories, just like the others. It was surprising that the elves didn't point fingers at their dwarven neighbors.

Kirin stared at some tracks in the mud, his arms folded across his chest. He ground his teeth in frustration. He should have been here. If it wasn't for that blasted dwarf, he would have been. As if thinking him into existence, Drokin appeared on the path, heading Kirin's direction.

Kirin's hand went to the pommel of his blade. When the dwarf noticed him, he stopped. They stared at one another for a moment, then Drokin continued walking. He passed Kirin and kept going, headed for the village.

Kirin relaxed, but kept his hand near his blade. *Forget him,* he thought. Taking a deep breath, he began following the tracks. They led northward away from the village. A short distance from the town, the tracks cut to the left, off the trail. The foliage was particularly dense, but by the way the light was growing ahead, Kirin could tell the trees were thinning. Then he heard a sound other than his own muted footsteps.

A baritone voice carried on the wind. Kirin stepped even lighter, and hunched down among some shrubbery when he reached the edge of the clearing. Peering through the undergrowth, he saw … nothing. The glade was empty. Puzzled, he slowly stood and looked around the woods. He heard the voice pause. Kirin stepped into the clearing and felt magic, ancient and powerful, brush his senses.

The arcane energy disoriented him for a moment. And then he realized the truth. The clearing had been hidden with magic. As soon as his senses cleared, he saw a massive man sitting astride a horse.

"Get him!" the man said.

Then he noticed the Scourges. Roughly a dozen of them stood throughout the clearing and they all rushed him. He drew his sword just as something struck him in the back of the head. He went down hard, his vision swimming. And then several fists pummeled him into oblivion.

When Kirin regained consciousness, the sky was dark. His head was pounding and his right eye felt swollen. A small fire burned in the center of the glade and he could make out the dark forms of Scourges hunched around it. He didn't see the man.

Bound hand and foot, he struggled briefly against his bonds before he quickly realized escaping his bonds was futile. There was a rustling in the bushes behind him. Someone was approaching. His heart started drumming in his chest. *This is it,* he thought, *this is how I die. Finally, peace.*

"Fool *elf,*" a gravelly voice whispered. "What are you doing here?"

Kirin turned his head and was surprised to see Drokin bathed in shadows. "Drokin? What are *you* doing here?"

"Hunting," the dwarf said huskily. Drokin displayed his battle ax and ran a finger down the blade. "How many are there? I've only seen eight."

"At least a dozen, plus the man."

"What man?"

"There was a human. Bare chested, muscular. I think he's their leader. He might be a wizard, too. A spell was keeping this dell invisible."

“A human wizard this far east?” Drokin’s eyes hardened. “Why?”

“Cut me loose,” Kirin said.

Drokin snorted. “I don’t think so. I kind of enjoy seeing you tied up like a filthy rat. I think I’ll just leave you like that for a while.”

One of the Scourges whooped loudly. Kirin looked to the fire. They had spotted the dwarf. The creatures rushed towards them. Drokin shouted a battle cry and met their charge with fury.

Kirin tried escaping his bindings again. The ropes cut into the flesh of his wrists and he could feel warm blood running down his fingers. Drokin made short work of the Scourges. Kirin knew the source of his rage, but wondered what had brought the dwarf into elvish territory.

A blur of motion swept through the clearing and slammed into Drokin, sending him flying. His arms flailed wildly and he crashed to the ground in a crumpled heap. Kirin eyed the dwarf’s ax. It had fallen a few feet away.

His attention was quickly drawn to the figure that stood before the fire. It was no man.

“An orc,” Kirin breathed in shock.

The orc towered at least six feet in height. Judging by his muscular girth, Kirin guessed he weighed a few hundred pounds. Every inch of the beast seemed to be made of corded muscle. It had a low forehead and a pig-like face. Large prominent canines jutted up from its lower jaw. They looked like boar’s tusks. Kirin had never seen an orc before, but he had heard stories. They were raiders, satisfying their bloodlust by plundering villages and slaying anyone that stood against them. Orcs gathered in tribes. The fact that he was so close to an elven village, and keeping Scourges as company, meant that this orc was far from typical.

The beast approached slowly, eyeing Drokin’s lifeless form. As he drew closer, Kirin saw blood on the orc’s face and chest. At first he thought it was injured, then he saw something disturbing. A chunk of flesh hung from its mouth.

Kirin gagged as the realization hit him. The orc wasn’t just attacking elves, he was *eating* them. Drokin groaned. The orc snorted and sprinted to the dwarf’s body. Kirin rolled himself over to the ax and rubbed the ropes binding his hands on the blade. He worked furiously, trying to keep from cutting himself.

The ropes severed and he sat up, quickly cutting his feet free. He looked around for his sword but didn’t see it. Not as skilled with an ax, he was hesitant to use it, but he didn’t have any other options. Hefting the ax with both arms, he charged the orc.

The beast turned to face him. It was shaking Drokin like a ragdoll. An insane rage was in its eyes. Kirin’s resolve wavered momentarily, but then he remembered the bodies. His people slain viciously. A child. *Eaten.*

Kirin swung the ax as he leapt forward. The weight of the foreign weapon threw off his balance and he stumbled, almost driving the ax into Drokin. The orc tossed the dwarf aside and punched Kirin in the face. He reeled backwards and fell on his back. A stick jabbed him painfully.

As the beast closed in, Kirin saw Drokin stagger to his feet. The dwarf retrieved his ax, tilted his head until his neck cracked, and then drew back and threw his ax. It spun end over end and struck the orc in its unprotected back. It howled in pain and blood gushed from the wound. When the orc jerked and spun to face Drokin, the ax dropped to the ground.

Kirin got back to his feet and saw something glint in the firelight. His sword. He quickly retrieved it.

"Beast!" he yelled.

The orc ignored him.

"Beast!" he called again. "Come, fight a foe more worthy than a dwarf!"

The speed of the orc shocked Kirin. It turned and charged him, a look of utter hatred engraved on its visage.

Kirin barely got out of the way as the beast thundered past. It turned and came back at him. Kirin was more prepared this time, and he waited until the last moment before thrusting his blade into the gut of the orc. The charging orc barreled into the elf. The larger creature's momentum forced Kirin to the ground and wrenched the sword from his grasp. The orcs legs faltered; it collapsed.

Wrist burning, Kirin pressed it to his body protectively and watched the orc for movement. He could see the beast was breathing, but it was shallow. Rising, he walked over to where Drokin stood. They both stared at the orc in silence. Finally, the beast stopped breathing.

"You saved my life," Kirin said quietly.

The dwarf grunted. "You saved mine as well."

"Truce?" Kirin asked.

"Aye," Drokin said. "Truce."

Kirin slipped through the dilapidated doors of his old family home. He stepped into the great room, full of echoes and ghosts still dancing to music he could hear in his mind, a haunting harmony of strange and different songs from across the decades. Long even before his time people had danced in this room. He had never danced here but had spent many nights on the balcony above, watching his fellows drunk on life and lust. This room had been the heart of the house.

He picked his way across the ruined hardwood floor to the massive marble fireplace beside the bar. Not even embers—of course not. He'd been gone so long, nothing would be left of that night. He leaned against the marble and closed his eyes. *What was left for him now?*

He walked through the public areas of the house to the kitchen. The fire hadn't reached there, and though nothing had been moved or ruined, it was different from how Kirin remembered it, no longer lively and inviting but instead strangely static, old, unused.

Kirin stared out a soot covered window, watching the populace of Thanalian going about their lives as if nothing had ever happened. He stepped away from the window and removed his shirt. Scar tissue from his own burns twisted and undulated across his back like waves on the ocean. He felt tears and closed his eyes, trying to stop them before he lost control. But he couldn't. Something tore open deep within him, pouring out a pain he couldn't bear. Sobs tore from his throat and he knelt, resting his forehead on the cold floor.

Sometimes it is worse to be left behind.

After he had cried all the tears he had left, he rose from the floor and cleaned his face. Taking one last look around the desolate place, he stepped outside to where Drokin waited. They had claimed the bounty for the orc and split it evenly.

"Do you think that the past will ever be forgotten?" Kirin asked.

Drokin stroked his beard. "No. But that doesn't mean it can't be forgiven."

Kirin liked that answer. He nodded once, then turned to the road that led out of the village. "Where will you go now?" he asked.

"There's a few Scourges out in those woods," Drokin said. "Might need to deal with them."

Kirin adjusted his sword belt. "Well then … let's get to it."

Oilcohol Part I: An Elf's Message

Trevor H. Cooley

"Stupid rock eater!" Stephan swore as he stubbed his toes for what seemed the hundredth time on this dangerous little side trip. That was one problem with an invisibility spell. It hid you from enemies, but it hid you from yourself too. "This is the last message I deliver for her."

Stephan Thistlebaum was an elf and elves didn't belong up in the mountains. This was dwarf territory and in this part of the country enmity between the races ran deep. The war may have cooled but hatred was still high, especially in this region where the elves and dwarves lived so close to each other.

The squat mountain Stephan climbed that morning was called Blackfoot's Nub and was the westernmost mountain in the dwarves' dominion. Its slopes just touched the edge of the Verge and had been the site of many bloody battles over the past centuries. Even now elves stepping into this part of dwarf territory were known to go missing. Of course, the same was also said for dwarves who stuck their blunt faces into the forests at the foot of the mountain.

Fortunately, he wouldn't have to reveal himself at any point. The particular dwarf he was leaving a message for didn't actually need to see him. Stephan's plan was to deliver the letter and leave as quickly as possible. Then he would have done his duty to his cousin and he could return home in peace.

The climb wasn't all that arduous. The trail was steep but well-worn even if, as Stephan's toes kept reminding him, studded with protruding rocks. He was fortunate that this particular route wasn't heavily used. He only had to avoid one group of dwarves along the way.

There were four of them. Squat, smelly, brutish dwarves with bulbous noses and wearing mismatched suits of armor. They were likely low class miners. They were escorting a low wagon weighted down with a huge iron bucket full of thick black oil. There was a heavy lid on top but every sudden movement caused some of the oil to spill over the edge of the bucket. Each dwarf was stationed at one of the wagon's wheels paying close attention, reaching out to steady the wagon with each bump in the trail.

Stephan climbed to the side of the trail, banging his invisible shin on a boulder in the process, but he needn't have bothered. The dwarves were so intent on making sure their oil trolley wasn't upset that he very well could have been standing there completely visible and they wouldn't have noticed him.

Grumbling to himself and cursing his foolish cousin's name, the elf continued up the mountainside. The trail branched several times, but Stephan had been this way before and kept on course. Soon morning passed into afternoon and after a final set of winding switchbacks, he reached his goal.

The trail ended at a wide shelf of flat rock at the base of a sheer cliff. At first glance it looked like a dead end. The only sign that the area was in use was the black tracks left by wagon wheels that had passed through the puddle of oil sludge that glistened at the foot of the cliff wall. A thick and dripping metal pipe that protruded from the cliffside was the source of the puddle.

Stephan wrinkled his nose at the smell of the oil. To his elven senses, this seemed an unnatural or even unholy substance. Only dwarves would see fit to dredge up such filth from the bowels of the earth.

He fumbled at his invisible robes with invisible hands until he found the pocket that the letter was hidden in. Letter in hand, he looked around for the message rock. Where was it? The dwarf always left it not far from the puddle.

The dwarf who owned this oil mine was a recluse. He never met his clients in person. They knew how to place their order. They simply wrote it down and placed it under the message rock. After that, they were to turn around and wait ten seconds and the rock would disappear with the message. Shortly after that, their oil would start to pump out of the pipe.

Stephan turned around a couple times, scratching his head. Then he took a stride forward and his sore big toe smacked right into the rock he had quested for. There was a soft pop as the digit dislocated.

Stephan bit his lip, repressing the curse-filled shout of pain that threatened to leap from his throat as he jumped up and down on his good foot. He would need to pop the joint back into place and use a healing spell to keep it from swelling, but he couldn't do that while invisible. He would either have to end the spell and leave himself vulnerable for the time it took to fix the problem or simply limp all the way down the mountain in pain.

How had he missed the rock? It was square and shin-high! Snarling, he bent down and lifted the edge of the heavy square rock and shoved the message under it. "I hope you choke on it, Daeve Palebeard!"

"If I'm choking on anything, it's gonna be a laugh after seeing you bust your foot on Rocky like that, Stephan," said a familiar rough voice from behind him.

Stephan spun around in surprise. "You can see me?" The elf blinked. He didn't see the dwarf anywhere. "Where are you?"

"What?" scoffed the dwarfish voice. "You're invisible, ain't you? Why can't you see me?"

Stephan frowned at the teasing note in the dwarf's words. So he was hiding somewhere, probably wearing some device allowing him to see magical weaves. The elf let out a sigh at the dwarf's ignorance. "An invisibility spell affects whether people can see me. It doesn't make me see others."

"Then your invisibility spell's stupid, cousin," said Daeve and he appeared out of thin air. The dwarf was leaning up against the cliff face, his arms folded. "You gotta make a qualifier that changes your eyesight when you cast it. That way you see other invisible folk." He barked out a short laugh. "Otherwise you're bound to not even be able to see your own self! Don't tell me you've been tripping all the way up this mountainside."

Stephan's invisible cheeks reddened. He put on an arrogant air. "I am an elf. We don't trip up anything."

"But you do limp," Daeve pointed out. "I think you hurt that toe pretty good. You elves should wear stiffer boots."

Daeve Palebeard looked as scruffy and filthy as Stephan had ever seen him. The dwarf's dirty blond hair was sticking up in all directions and the bottom half of his beard, which was plaited into two braids, was blackened with oil. His pants and shirt were tattered and holed and spattered with more black. His feet were bare and blacker than the rest of him.

All that said, he was still an imposing figure. Though only four-foot-five, his shoulders were broad and his body thick with muscle. Daeve didn't wear any weapons. The only things sheathed at his side were a half dozen flasks, yet Stephan knew he didn't drink liquor.

"My toe will be fine," Stephan declared. To make his point he put his foot up onto the rock and leaned forward, placing his elbow on his knee. "Now, I've left my intended message and will be on my way. Please do not try and follow-."

Before he could lift his foot off of the rock it disappeared out from under him. Stephan's wounded foot stomped onto the ground and a spark of pain shot up his leg. Grimacing, he hissed in a breath.

Daeve was suddenly holding a much smaller version of the square rock in one hand, his other hand clutching the letter. "You'll want to get that foot healed. Now go ahead and disperse your spell, cousin. Ain't no more dwarves anywhere near here or Rocky would've told me."

Stephan's grimace turned into a glare. How dare Daeve know so much about how his magic worked? "It can wait until I get home."

Daeve snorted. "Ain't no reason to act so proud around me. Come on inside and get yourself healed up. Some miners left me some of your favorite grog and you know I ain't drinking it."

As Daeve spoke, a cave opened up into the mountain behind him. It didn't make a sound, just started as a small black hole in the cliff face and broadened into a wide circle large enough for Stephan to walk into without ducking.

"Go inside?" Stephan said. "The mountain? I'm an elf. Not a-."

"Stephan, you're the least elf-like elf I ever met," Daeve said. "It's why I like you. Now get your narrow butt inside."

The elf frowned at the insult and folded his invisible arms. "Whatever you think of me, I'm not stupid enough to follow any dwarf into their mountain hole!"

Daeve blinked at him as if wounded by the remark. "Listen, cousin. How long have we known each other?"

"Maybe twenty years," Stephan admitted. Though it had been three since he had last been to this place.

"And in all that time have you ever known me to hurt any elf, much less a friend?" the dwarf said with a scowl.

Stephan tried to scowl back at him, but he had to admit to himself that his concern about going into the cave had nothing to do with the dwarf in front of him. Daeve had stayed out of the war. It was the reason he lived out here on the border all alone, eking out a living selling low grade oil. The dwarf had proved himself a friend to Stephan and his cousin many times over.

"This isn't about whether or not I trust you," Stephan said.

"Then stop your pussy-footing and get inside!"

The dwarf turned and walked into the cave and Stephan, sublimating every swear he could think of, limped in after him. The elf didn't make it two steps inside the cave before the entrance closed behind him and the two of them were immersed in total darkness. Stephan, his nerves already frayed, felt as if the weight of the mountain was about to crush him. He frantically began the motions of a light spell, but the rock in Daeve's hands began to glow, illuminating the area around them.

The corridor they were in was mercifully short, opening into a large cavern. As Daeve stepped out into the cavern the light from his rock spread throughout the cavern as the stalactites hanging from the ceiling took up a bright luminescence of their own.

This was obviously the dwarf's living area. There was a black-smudged bed in the corner of the cavern and a large cook stove in the center. Dressers and chests lined the walls of the place and dirty fur rugs covered the floor. Stephan wondered what could possibly be in those dressers considering what the dwarf wore, but he didn't ask Daeve about it. Something else was pressing on his mind.

The elf eyed the glowing stalactites that hung from the ceiling like spears of light. “Daeve, how are you doing all this magic?” he wondered, the pain in his foot forgotten as he thought of the rock wall that had moved earlier. “I thought your . . . ‘magic’ only affected your own body.”

“Huh? Oh. This’s all Rocky’s doing,” Daeve said.

“Your pet rock?” Stephan said incredulously.

Daeve’s eyes went wide and he covered the square rock with both hands as if protecting it from hearing the elf’s words. “Rocky ain’t no pet! He’s an earth elemental. He attached himself to me when I moved in here. For years he was content just bringing me messages, but a few months back he became sentient. I think he’s decided he’s my familiar now.”

“You have an elemental for a familiar?” Stephan said. That was quite a powerful being to be a dwarf wizard’s servant. Usually dwarven familiars were semi-intelligent critters or minor demons.

Daeve rolled his eyes. “I know. I know, cousin. I ain’t a Stormguard like my daddy was or my granddaddy before him. But I can’t help it that Rocky likes me.”

“It’s just . . . I’m impressed,” Stephan admitted. “I mean, I heard that Grand Wizard Winterglass had a wind elemental for a familiar centuries ago, but it left him when his powers began to fade.”

The dwarf snorted at the unexpected compliment. “Just stop hiding yourself and fix your foot while I read your letter.”

Stephan’s foot throbbed as if in response to the dwarf’s words. The elf reached out with his magic and cut the threads of invisibility that hid him. It felt good to be able to see himself again.

The elf was a scrawny six feet tall and wore fine green robes embroidered with a multicolored autumn leaf pattern. The colors clashed, but Stephan had never been concerned with appearances. His flowing auburn hair was cut unfashionably short and a pair of silver-framed spectacles sat on his nose.

“It’s not my letter,” Stephan told the dwarf. “It’s from Fleurette.”

“Really?” said Daeve. “Wonder why she went through the trouble of sending you?”

While Stephan searched his pockets for the items he needed for his healing spell, Daeve leaned against a stalagmite and opened the letter. It was four pages long and densely covered in Fleurette’s tight handwriting. The dwarf squinted his eyes, his lips moving soundlessly as he read.

Stephan found what he needed and pulled a pouch of herbs out of one of his pockets. He sat on a bench near the stove and removed the doeskin moccasin from his injured foot. His big toe was bent at an odd angle and his flesh was swollen around it. He opened the pouch of herbs.

"Still using implements, I see," said Daeve, glancing briefly away from the letter at the elf.

"I do what works for me," Stephan replied with a glower. Implements were small items that were used as tools for apprentices to help them learn the ways of magic. True master wizards didn't need such tools to cast spells. Stephan, adept as he had become over the years, had never felt comfortable without them.

The dwarf shrugged and went back to reading. "Bet it makes you tired, all that extra spell movement. You're better than that, I say."

Stephan ignored the dwarf. He began to chant his spell, crumbling flakes of herbs over his dislocated toe as he used soothing energies to reduce the swelling and coax the joint back into its socket.

The elf felt a soft pop as the toe straightened. Then the pain quickly faded. Sighing and feeling drained, Stephan slid his foot back into the moccasin. It would be a while before he could enact his invisibility spell again and head back down the mountain. He frowned and decided to make the most of the situation. "You mentioned my 'favorite' grog?"

Daeve gestured absently, engrossed in the letter. "In the chest next to the stove. It ain't locked."

The elf wizard moved to the chest and lifted the lid. He licked his lips. "There's a dozen bottles here."

"You can take them with you when you leave," Daeve said, a smile bending his lips as he turned a page.

Stephan eagerly pulled out a bottle of the amber colored liquid. He removed the stopper and inhaled the aroma of the liquor. It was a mix of rum and Dwarven spicewater just like he preferred. He lifted the bottle and let the fiery liquid roll over his tongue and hit the back of his throat.

Daeve hadn't been wrong when he'd called Stephan un-elflike. Being a solitary sort of wizard he had developed many eccentricities, one of them being his taste for dwarven rum. Elves were more of a wine-loving people and sippers only. In their culture drinking to a state of intoxication was more than frowned upon.

Stephan took a big gulp, justifying to himself that this particular grog was watered down enough that he'd have to drink half the bottle to get tipsy. The spicewater that the liquor was watered down with was full of flavor notes that enhanced the taste of the rum and left a pleasant heat behind.

"I've never understood you, Daeve," the elf said, smiling at the warm sensation that moved down his throat into his belly. "You're the only dwarf I've ever heard of that doesn't drink. Why is that?"

"The only dwarf?" Daeve lowered the letter and looked back at him with disbelieving eyes. "Ain't you ever heard of Darquethorn Boggs?"

Stephan scratched his head, pretending to know little of the infamous dwarf. "He was one of the Stormguard, right? Wasn't he there when the whole war was started?"

"One of the most powerful wizards of his time," Daeve said. "He powered his magic with booze. Became legendary. But he was also a damn drunk. Drank until the stuff ate out his guts. The stuff nearly killed him before he finally gave it up. I hear tale he's still alive somewhere in Venzor. Taking it easy and sipping tea. Outlived all his famous companions, even my granddaddy. But his magic's gone. Can't do a spell without liquor, but drinking again will kill him so he just lays low."

Stephan raised his eyebrow. So that was the fate of the dwarf who had killed so many elves in the war. He wanted to say the evil monster deserved it, but since he was under Daeve's roof he went with a more polite response. "A sad story for a wizard to lose his power that way. But that's just one dwarf among thousands."

Daeve poked a thumb at his chest. "Well, I'm the same way. My own magic's nothing but a trickle and I found out early on that only liquor would fuel it stronger." He shook his head. "A slippery slope. I liked the brew too much. Then one day my daddy sat me down and told me about Boggs and I knew I'd have to give it up."

"If that's the case, how do you do what you do?" Stephan asked in confusion. In all the time he'd known Daeve he'd never gotten an explanation for the dwarf's magical ability. "The spells I've seen you do take much more than a 'trickle' of power."

Daeve grinned. "Why that's my little secret, isn't it?" He laughed at the look of disappointment of the elf's face. "Alright. Since you're family, I guess I can tell you."

Stephan wasn't sure why the dwarf would consider him family, but he was so interested he let it slide. His study of magic had told him nothing about the type of power the dwarf claimed to have. He had always thought Darquethorn Boggs' liquor-fueled magic to be a yarn the dwarf had told to boast of his drinking prowess. Even if true, the powers had to be a fluke. What were the odds that Daeve Palebeard of all people would have a similar ability?

Daeve didn't read the last two pages of the letter, but folded the message back up and put it in the breast pocket of his ragged shirt. "Come on, cousin, I'll show you."

He tossed the still-glowing Rocky to the elf and walked toward the rear of the cavern. Stephan, who was still holding his bottle of grog in one hand, caught the square elemental clumsily in the crook of his other arm. To the elf's relief, Rocky wasn't heavy at all.

Daeve led him into a downward sloping passageway that branched off of the cavern. The pipe that fed oil to the buyers at the cliff face outside was anchored to the wall of the passage. As they followed the pipe down into the bowels of the mountain, Stephan started to feel claustrophobic again.

He took another big swallow of grog and pushed back at the feeling, reminding himself that he was a wizard; a ranking member of the Maumer house. This was magical research and exploring outside his realm of comfort was an important side of such research . . . He gritted his teeth. Maybe he should have become a hermit like his cousin.

"So after I quit drinking I started to think," said Daeve as he led the Stephan deeper into the mountain. "Why was liquor able to power my magic when other stuff didn't? Why not a roast hog or a sweet cake?" He glanced back at the elf. "Well? Why do you think it was, Stephan?"

"Uh, some sort of mental block I would guess? Belief can be a powerful thing and we wizards are an eccentric people." Stephan knew that his own dependence on using implements to cast his magic was something like that. He kept talking, trying to keep himself distracted from the fact that the tons of rock above him could collapse at any time, grinding him to jelly. "Why, I heard it told that Grand Wizard Routhenstar couldn't cast a healing spell unless he held an eagle feather in his mouth and-."

"Nope! It ain't my head," said the dwarf, waving off the sensible explanation. "It worked because alcohol is fuel. My belly was burning it to stoke the flames of my magic."

"Sounds a bit overly simplistic," Stephan observed.

"Oh, I experimented to make sure," Daeve assured him. "I tried different things. Swallowed sawdust, coal, even cow chips."

The elf wrinkled his nose. "That couldn't have worked."

Daeve shrugged. "Got varying results from each one . . . and a bellyache," he admitted. "But nothing stoked my magic like regular old liquor. That's when I decided I wasn't thinking big enough."

They stepped out of the passageway into another wide cavern and the elemental did its work again, causing the stalactites to glow brightly. The illuminated scene caused Stephan's eyes to widen. Huge cylindrical tanks filled the cavern. Some of them were made of copper and others made of iron, but all were linked by pipes similar to the one that led outside. A few of them leaked black sludge.

The acrid stench of oil filled the cavern. The elf coughed and held the sleeve of his robe over his nose. "Don't tell me you've been drinking crude oil!"

"Nah. That worked better than cow chips, but it still wasn't good enough." Daeve rubbed his hands together and approached a thick pipe that rose from the ground and entered the furthermost iron tank. He slapped the pipe, then ran his hand along the tank. "Problem with crude is that it's full of tar and other junk. Really clogged me up on the back end if you know what I mean. So I figured out how to separate all that stuff out, leaving only the best fuel behind. I sell the sludge that's left over to the other dwarves."

The dwarf pulled one of the flasks out of his belt and held it out to the elf. "Take a gander, cousin."

Reluctantly, the elf set down his bottle of grog and the elemental and took the flask from the dwarf. He opened it up and peered at the clear liquid inside. He sniffed at it and was hit by a wave of dizziness. He wheezed, his sinuses on fire.

"I call it oilcohol!" said Daeve proudly, taking the flask back from the weak-kneed elf. "It's why I started this mining operation in the first place. It burns hotter and faster and more explosively than any liquor. It ain't addictive and best of all, it don't get me drunk!"

"Are you crazy?" said Stephan once he had caught his breath. "That stuff could kill you! It'd definitely do more damage than drinking rum!"

Daeve raised a calming hand. "Now I can see why you'd be worried, cousin. If I was a normal dwarf, it could very well burn right through my guts. But like I said, my magic works different than other dwarves."

"How much of this have you been drinking?" the elf asked, his concern increasing.

"Let me tell you how it works," said Daeve. He held the flask up to his lips and closed his eyes. "First I use that little trickle of magic I already got in me. I cast a spell on my throat and belly, getting ready for what's coming."

He tipped back the flask and took a swallow of the dangerous brew. His fingers started to tremble and he placed the flask back at his belt. He opened his eyes and grinned at the elf. "There it goes. I can feel that power blooming inside me. Now you were right earlier when you said my magic only affects my own body. Can't cast a lightning bolt or fireball. But you've seen what I can do. When I layer spells over myself nothing can stop me."

Stephan lifted his bottle of grog from the ground and took another swig. "It's just . . . I'm worried about what this stuff is doing to you."

Daeve patted his shoulder. "I've been doing this since before you ever met me. The only side effect is that I have to live down in this stink hole. Don't get me wrong. I barely notice the fumes or the filth anymore. But I have to make the stuff myself. If the Trollgrogs or Silvercoats ever got wind of it, they'd just make bombs out of the stuff. Don't need nobody killed because of my discovery."

"You barely notice the filth anymore? How is that possible?" wondered the elf. "You're covered in it!"

Daeve looked down at his blackened beard and feet. "Oh. That's just from this morning. Hold on."

The dwarf held out his arms in a wide stretch, then raised his fists over his head. A brief shimmer rolled across his skin and the oil simply fell away from him, hitting the ground around his feet and leaving his beard and body completely clean. Even his ratty clothes were free of the black stuff.

"I should do that more often but I forget." He saw the look of disbelief on the elf's face and added, "Hey, I don't get visitors down here. Hell, if it weren't for the one time a month I go and visit Fleurette I'd probably forget how to talk."

"You see Fleurette once a month?" Stephan said.

"Of course!" Daeve gave him a pained look. "I hate staying away as much as I do, but it's hard enough keeping it secret as it is. If folks found out about us you know all hell would break loose."

"Found out about you?" said Stephan, a chilly suspicion overcoming him. "What are you talking about?"

Daeve cocked his head. "Don't you know? She was supposed to tell you. She promised she was gonna tell you."

"I'm learning today that there's way too much I don't know!" Stephan exclaimed. He forced himself to calm down. There was no way it was what it sounded like. "So . . . are you two in business together?"

Daeve took the letter out of his pocket and shook it at the elf. "Then you didn't read this?"

"Of course not!" Stephan sputtered. "I don't read my cousin's private letters. Fleurette told me to bring it, she said it was urgent, and that you needed to see it today. That's all I know. Now tell me what this mysterious thing is that she was supposed to tell me."

The dwarf's face was suddenly lined with worry. He opened the letter back up. "Urgent? This message? It's just regular stuff. What was it she needed you up here so quickly for?" He turned back to the opening page and began to talk to himself as he scanned it again. "Pleasant weather . . . her new apple pie recipe . . . her moonlight wards keep going off, but there's nothing there when she checks . . ."

Stephan watched Daeve read the letter, saw the emotion on the dwarf's face, and suddenly the possibility that he had dismissed out of hand no longer seemed so impossible. "Don't tell me you and Fleurette-. You two are . . . together?"

"Married these last fifteen years," the dwarf said absently as he skimmed past the pages he had already read. He came to the third page and slowed down. "She says happy birthday to Rocky . . ."

"What??" exclaimed Stephan. He knew that Fleurette and Daeve were old friends but an elf and a dwarf married? That hadn't happened in centuries. Not since the Plucking and it was rare even back then. Was this why the dwarf kept calling him cousin? "Married? How? When?"

Daeve raised a dismissive hand as he kept reading. ". . . magpies cawing all hours of the night . . ." He flipped to the final page. ". . . Taurine started a turtle farm . . . Wait. This has to be it. Her handwriting changes . . ." His lips continued to move as he read silently to himself this time. His eyebrows, already bushy blond things, were now knit so close together with worry that they were like one long caterpillar squirming across his forehead.

The dwarf let out a pained cry. "No-no-no! The stupid kid!"

Stephan swallowed, shaken by the dwarf's response. "Now you have me worried. What is it?"

"It's Taurine!" Daeve yelled as he rushed over to the furthermost brass tank. Quickly, he began taking the flasks from his belt.

The elf followed him. "Who's Taurine?"

Daeve began using a valve at the base of the tank to start topping off his flasks with more oilcohol. "My daughter! I can't believe Fleurette didn't tell you any of this. She promised!"

"A daughter . . ." Now that part was an impossibility. Wasn't it? If there had ever been a successful conception between dwarf and elf he certainly hadn't heard of it. "When did this happen?"

"She's twelve. We've had to keep her secret, but I think that's about to end," said Daeve as he filled the last flask. "If people find out about her before the time is right you know what they'll do." He placed a hand on the flustered elf's shoulder. "You've gotta help me save her, cousin. Help me save my girl!"

Stephan's mind was a jumble of thoughts and emotions but as he saw the pleading look in Daeve's eyes, the elf shoved everything aside. Family was family, dwarf or not. "What do you need me to do?"

"Follow me," Daeve said and he hurried down another side passageway.

Stephan picked up Rocky and followed him. The elemental continued to glow and light various sections of rock inside the passageway as he went. He yelled after the dwarf, "So what kind of danger is she in?"

"Like I said, the danger is people finding out about her. We've kept her hidden so far by having her hide in the cave under Fleurette's house whenever anyone comes around," Daeve said.

Stephan nodded. The idea seemed ridiculous, but Fleurette was a master of wards. An intricate layer of warning spells covered every inch of her land and if anyone came within a mile of her house she knew right away. She might not have been a powerful wizardess in any other way, but no one was ever going to sneak up on her.

"But early on we found out Taurine was a natural tunneller," Daeve continued as they passed through another cavern, this one empty except for one large iron pipe that crossed through the center and a few clusters of giant mushrooms that grew from the ground beneath it. "She's like her daddy that way. Taurine was always digging at the walls of the caves and when she was ten I gave her her first pickaxe. Any time I could get away to see her, I taught her about mining. How to know where you could dig or couldn't, or when a tunnel needed a brace . . ."

Daeve rambled on as he went through another passage at the back of the cavern. This one was narrower than the others and Stephan began to sweat again. He kept focused on the dwarf's words to distract himself.

Daeve shook his head. "Actually, when I said Taurine was a natural tunneller I understated it. Every time I try to teach her something, she picks it up right away as if she already knows. I tell you the girl was born to it. It's like the gods took the dwarf understanding of the earth and the elf understanding of the rest of nature and mashed it together in one cute little package.

"I think there's magic involved in her talent and Fleurette does too, though it's hard to pin down what it is. Taurine just gets through the rock so fast. She does most of her digging when I'm not around so I'm not sure how she does it, but that daughter of mine would put any six dwarf miners to shame."

The elf let out a low whistle. A twelve-year-old halfbreed and she was able to accomplish so much. It was both impressive and frightening. "How has that put her in danger?"

"Fleurette says she's been digging north!" said the dwarf as if that explained it. "I've told the girl time and again there's nothing but dwarf mines and goblin dens that way, but does she listen to her daddy? No! Little Taurine thinks she knows best!"

"Alright," said Stephan, relieved. The dwarf had been acting like an axe was hanging over her head. "So we go to Fleurette's house and reprimand the child before she gets in trouble-."

"She's missing!" Daeve barked, his voice echoing down the passage as they moved. "Fleurette says she ain't seen her in a day and when she went into the tunnels, she found a place where Taurine had broken into a new side passage."

Stephan blinked. "But say she does stumble into someone . . . Is it that obvious that she's a halfbreed?" Stephan saw Daeve's eyes narrow at the term, "I mean, what does she look like?"

"Cute as a button," Daeve replied. "She's got the build of a dwarf. Not any taller than me. But she has the pointed ears and fair skin of an elf. There was no hiding who she is or we wouldn't have been keeping her secret all these years. If she runs into dwarves, they might kill her."

"They would kill a defenseless child?" Stephan snarled.

Daeve raised an eyebrow. "And what do you think elves would do?"

"Depends on the elves," Stephan said, but he couldn't really disagree. "Still, why didn't Fleurette just tell me all this when she gave me the letter? I would have travelled to you quicker if I had known it was that urgent, invisibility be damned!"

"I don't know! She was supposed to tell you about us years ago. I love the woman, but I could never make sense of her priorities." He shook the pages of the letter. "Like this letter! I understand that she'd wrote most of the letter before Taurine went missing, but why bother sending the first three pages after what happened? Just send the important bits! Am I right?"

Stephan sighed. "That actually might be more of an elf thing. We always tend to leave the important news until the end of letters," he admitted. "But what are we wasting our time down here for? We should be traveling back to Fleurette's. Let's head back to the surface. I have a spell that would help us get there quickly."

"This way's faster," Daeve declared just as they entered another large cavern.

Stephan's breath caught in his throat and he pressed himself back against the wall. There was no cavern floor in front of them. Just a huge empty pit that stretched down as far as he could see. "This is faster?"

"There's a passage at the bottom of this chamber that leads directly to the caves beneath Fleurette's house. I go this way every time I visit. Keeps other nosey dwarves from asking about my business." Daeve laughed at the paleness of the elf's face. "It's not as deep as it seems. Rocky, show him."

A dim light glowed from below and Stephan built up enough courage to look over the edge. There, hundreds of feet down and surrounded by sheer rock walls, was the chamber floor. He pressed himself back against the wall again. "I'm not climbing down that. I can't."

"Come on, cousin! Didn't you see the stairs?" the dwarf asked. He pulled a flask from his belt and took a big swallow of oilcohol. To Stephan's discomfort, the dwarf's skin began to darken.

The elf looked out into the pit again and saw that there was indeed a narrow stairway that wound its way around the outside edge of the pit in a long gradual descent. He nodded, breathing a little easier. The thought of taking those stairs without any sort of railing was daunting, but he reminded himself that it was no worse than the stairs that wrapped around some of the mammoth trees in the elven villages at the center of the forest.

"We ain't taking the stairs though," Daeve said, his skin now almost completely black. "We can shave off an hour's time taking the direct route."

He grabbed the glowing elemental from the elf's hands and it shrank until it was small enough for the dwarf to shove it into the pocket of his pants.

"Direct route?" Stephan said.

The dwarf grabbed the front of the elf's robes. His hands were hard as iron. "You got a spell that'll make you light?"

"Yeah." The elf reached into his pocket, grasping a feather. There was a spell that would allow him to float gently down from high places, but it would take a lot of energy and he wasn't confident that it would last the entire duration of such a long descent. "But I don't like where you're going with thi-!"

"Just hold onto my back," the dwarf said and ran towards the edge, pulling the elf along with him.

Stephan yelped and dropped his half-empty bottle of grog as he tried to pull away. But the dwarf was an unstoppable force. Frantically, the elf started to chant his spell as Daeve reached the edge of the pit and jumped.

Daeve laughed as they fell, a sound full of maniacal joy. The dwarf let go of Stephan's robe and opened his arms and legs, plummeting spread-eagled towards the glowing bottom of the pit below. Stephan gripped the back of the dwarf's shirt and screamed, the chant of his spell continuing in his mind only as he saw death rising up to meet him.

The elf's feather spell enacted twenty feet before they hit the floor of the pit. He let go of the dwarf and floated gently to the ground.

Daeve hit belly first with a thunderous thud. A cloud of luminous dirt and rock obscured his body.

When Stephan's feet touched the earth and he waved the dirt away, he wasn't surprised to see that the dwarf had made an impression in the ground. For a moment, he thought Daeve might actually be dead. Then the dwarf jumped to his feet.

Daeve coughed a couple times and Stephan saw that his skin was lightening back to its normal color. The dwarf checked to make sure his flasks hadn't ruptured and for some miraculous reason they hadn't. He let out another laugh. "Whooee! What a fall!"

"You're crazy!" the elf screeched. "You could have killed us! Or just me, but . . . You could have killed me! You nearly did." He gripped his chest. "I almost died just then!"

The dwarf smacked his arm. "Bah, I knew you'd do fine! You've always been so caught up in your implements and chanting, but I knew that if the situation really demanded it you'd be able to cast a spell without them."

The elf stood rigid. His lips pursed, his hands clenched into fists. "This was a lesson? You, the dwarf who can't cast a spell without drinking poison, was teaching me a lesson?"

"It wasn't something I planned ahead of time, but yeah. You don't have the same problems with your magic that I do with mine. You just needed a little push." He noted the look of fury on the elf's face and smiled. "Come on. It worked. I'll bet you don't even feel tired."

The dwarf was right about that. Right now, Stephan's rage alone could have powered an earthquake. "You may have married my cousin. May have. I still haven't seen proof of that-."

"Your auntie performed the ceremony," Daeve pointed out. "It was sweet, but private. Just the three of us."

Stephan refused to be distracted. "-But if you ever try anything like this again, I will burn you to slag!"

"Deal," the dwarf said and pulled the elemental out of his pocket. He tossed it to the elf and turned to head down another passage. "Now let's keep moving. There's one little trouble spot and then it'll be a smooth journey the rest of the way."

Rocky warmed in his hand as if to comfort him and Stephan let out a slow breath. He was an idiot for doing this, but he had already gone this far. He reminded himself that this was about family and hurried after the dwarf.

They journeyed down the passage for a full hour before another cavern opening came into view. Daeve stopped him again.

"Now be quiet," the dwarf said, raising his forefinger to his lips. "In this next chamber is a big old crab-scorpion. The goblins I bought this mine from called him 'Mister Stabby.' Best we don't wake him."

Stephan swallowed. He had never seen a crab-scorpion, but he had heard of them. They were huge subterranean crustaceans with a crab-like shell and a tail with a spear-like stinger that was more likely to kill you by piercing through you than by its venom.

The elf looked more closely at the opening of the chamber ahead and grabbed the dwarf's shoulder. "I think he's already awake."

There, on either side of the cave opening, Stephan could just make out the serrated edges of one giant pincer. The creature was obviously waiting just inside the chamber, ready to grab them as they entered.

"That's what you get for making such a ruckus," the dwarf accused. "He heard your screaming!"

"He heard me?" Stephan scoffed. "You're the loud one, laughing all the way down the pit."

"Okay, that was both of us," Daeve admitted. "And we don't have time to wait for him to go back to sleep." The dwarf looked back at the waiting pincer and his shoulders slumped. "Damn it! Now I'm gonna have to kill old Mister Stabby. I've always liked the fact that he was down here eating up anything that tried to enter my mine. Thought of him as my guard beast."

"You're going to kill that thing? Without so much as a weapon?" Stephan scoffed.

The elf realized that this was going to be up to him. He wasn't sure how to manage it. Even if he was able to cast a spell without implements again, an unlikely possibility, a spell strong enough to kill or disable a creature of this size would drain him completely. What if he was needed again at the end of the trail?

"You're forgetting my powers," Daeve said with a snort. The dwarf pulled a flask from his belt and drank deeply again. His skin began to blacken once more. "Oh yeah. The oilcohol's burning hot now. It shouldn't be too tough. The key is layers of spells. A little iron skin for toughness. A little boost of strength . . ."

"Right. You're tough. I'll give you that. But you can't just punch the thing dead. You're only four and a half feet tall and that thing's gotta be . . ." Stephan pointed to the cavern entrance. "Hey, the claw's gone."

Daeve shoved the elf against the wall of the passage just in time. The crab-scorpion's spear-like tail shot into the passageway, missing them by mere inches. The dwarf reached out and grasped the segmented tail with both arms.

"This'll be over quick. You'll see. Layers of spells," Daeve promised and then he was gone as the beast yanked its tail and the dwarf out of sight.

Cursing, the elf moved to the entrance and watched as the huge beast skittered backwards to the middle of the chamber floor, dragging Daeve behind it. Obediently, Rocky lit the stalactites in the cavern, bringing the scene fully into view.

The cavern floor was littered with pieces of armor and broken weapons of goblin make. The beast was even bigger than Stephan had imagined, twice Daeve's height, and it must have weighed several tons. It was covered in a rocky shell and had two large pincer arms and that wicked tail. Three sets of pointed legs propelled it across the floor.

Daeve looked tiny in comparison to the beast, but he enacted another spell that increased his weight to the point that it became unable to pull him further. It strained, trying to move him, but he wouldn't let go of its tail. Then it reached out with a pincer and snatched him.

Daeve grunted as it gripped him around the waist, but his iron skin spell kept it from cutting him in two. "Sorry, Mister Stabby! I've got to save my girl!"

The dwarf reached into his still burning magic and enacted a spell on top of the other two, this one enhancing his strength. With a grunt, he squeezed his arms together around the tail. There was a crunch and a gout of ichor as he crushed the pointed end of the appendage and wrenched it free.

The crab-scorpion made no noise. Nor did it visibly react to the pain. It pulled its stump of a tail away and grasped the dwarf with its other pincer, intending to tear him apart. It struggled to lift him off of the ground.

Stephan prepared a spell in his mind. A freezing ray could stop the thing long enough for them to get away. "Should I help?" he yelled.

"Naw! Save your magic," Daeve replied. He brought his elbow down on the surface of one of the claws, causing a spiderweb of cracks to form. He slammed the pincers with his fists. Each blow impacted with the strength of a war hammer. One of the claws broke in two, sending more ichor to the cavern floor.

Perhaps sensing defeat, the creature became desperate. It began striking repeatedly at the dwarf, smacking the top of his head with the dripping stubby end of its tail.

Daeve spat crab juices from his mouth. "Stop! Just stop it! Your stabby part's gone. Can't you see this fight's over?"

If it had been smart, it would have let go of its dangerous prey and retreated to the rear of the chamber so that the dwarf and elf could leave. However, the crabby part of its heritage refused to let a meal go. Instead, it moved its enormous shell-covered body over the dwarf and tried to chew him with its short but powerful jaws.

"That's what I was waiting for," the dwarf said and thrust his hand deep into the beast's maw as he enacted one last layer of spells.

A torrent of electricity rippled from his body, lancing through the creature's soft inner flesh. The thing jittered. Steam escaped from within its shell, filling the chamber with a hissing sound. It stopped moving. Its carapace had turned a deep red.

Sighing, Daeve pulled himself free of its once powerful grip. His shirt now hung in ruins, but his body was undamaged. The blackness faded from his skin as he pulled a piece of white meat free from the creature's claw.

"What a waste," he said, shaking his head as he took a bite. "My guard beast's dead and I can't even take the time to eat the whole thing. All this meat's gonna sit and rot."

Stephan stepped slowly into the room, a look of awe on his narrow face. "That was truly an impressive display. I must say that you have improved even from when I first met you."

"Well, even an old dog learns." Daeve said, glumly taking another bite of the white meat. "Isn't that how the old saying goes?"

"No. No it isn't," Stephan replied.

The dwarf threw the rest of the meat on the ground and pulled out one of his flasks, frowning when he saw that it was horribly dented, clear liquid dribbling down the side of it. He lifted it to his lips and emptied it before tossing it to the ground.

"Ah well. I've seen a couple smaller crab-scorpions in the caves. Maybe the smell of rotting Mister Stabby will bring out a replacement." He shrugged. "Right. Let's keep moving. You got a speed spell in that head of yours? The caves beneath Fleurette's place are pretty much a straight shot from here. Faster if we run."

"I do," said Stephan, pushing away the impulse to reach for the bag of powdered stag horn in his inner pocket. "Do you need me to cast it on you too? You used a lot of magic just now."

Daeve snorted and patted the flasks at his belt. There were four full ones left and they were only slightly dented. "As long as I've got fuel, I've got power. Ready?"

The elf nodded. They enacted their spells and ran down the passageways with Daeve in the lead, their legs a blur. Rocky lit the way as they went.

The dwarf hadn't exactly been truthful when he called it a straight shot. There were many branches in the path and obstacles that made their speed quite reckless. Stephan careened off of the walls many times and by the time they made it to the caves beneath Fleurette's house, the poor elf felt quite battered.

At least the fast pace and constant danger kept Stephan's mind off of the fact that they were so far underground. Nevertheless, the last hundred yard stretch almost broke him. The passage shrank around them until they were forced to stop their speed spells.

Daeve walked hunched over, but the elf had to go on his hands and knees. Rocky kept a warm glow around them, but Stephan wasn't comforted. The confined space combined with the tiredness from his prolonged magic use took its toll. He inched forward, trembling uncontrollably until the exit came into view.

The dwarf was out first. Then a pair of hands grasped Stephan and pulled him to his feet. The elf took a deep shaking breath. He was still underground, but was now in a large cavern. It was well-lit but not by Daeve's elemental. The ceiling of the cave was covered by light-generating fungi. The whole area had a golden glow.

It took Stephan a few seconds to clear his mind enough to realize who had pulled him to his feet. "Fleurette . . . hello."

He looked into his cousin's eyes. They were orange eyes, an oddity among elves. He had always seen them as the color of autumn leaves, but right now they seemed the orange glow of a dwarven forge.

"Stephan! Never in a million ages would I have thought that you would follow my husband here," said Fleurette warmly, embracing him.

Fleurette was every bit as tall as Stephan, though not as slender. She eschewed the formal robes of elf wizards for standard forest garb. She wore plain pants with a blouse and vest, along with a bandoleer of throwing knives. Her long black hair was pulled back behind her head in a thick braid.

Stephan cleared his throat, patting her back weakly as he tried to steady himself. "First I would have had to know you had a husband."

She grimaced. "Sorry about that. I meant to tell you years ago. Really I did. It's just that you hated dwarves so much. You only just tolerated Daeve."

"Speaking of Daeve," said Daeve, spreading open his arms. "I'm here too."

Fleurette turned to her husband. "Of course you are, darling," she said and bent to kiss him tenderly on the lips, something that Stephan found shocking to see even though he knew it had to have happened before. "What on earth happened to your clothes? Did I not ask you to dress properly when you came to visit us?"

"I came in a hurry when I read your letter," Daeve protested.

"Without even wearing boots?" she said, folding her arms.

The dwarf frowned. "You know I don't need them. Now, where's Taurine? Have you found her yet?"

She bit her lip and shook her head. "No, but I think I know where she went."

"Further northward?" Daeve asked.

Fleurette nodded. "She's been digging a new series of tunnels. I've been searching through them ever since Stephan left. One of them intersects with a large chamber. I found boot prints. Dozens of them."

"Goblins?" Stephan asked hopefully. The smelly creatures were mean, but could be reasoned with. Especially if one had coin.

"Worse," she said worriedly. "Dwarves."

Oilcohol Part II: Child of Promise

Trevor H. Cooley

"Where are we?" asked Stephan, staring up at the phosphorescent ceiling of the naturally formed cavern. Stalactites hung down from overhead like teeth waiting to descend, each one set aglow by golden fungi that clung to the damp rock.

"Under the earth just east of my home," Fleurette replied.

Stephan blinked. "But how did you know we would come out here?"

"She keeps all of these caverns warded. Probably felt us coming a long time ago," Daeve told him with pride in his wife's abilities. "Ain't many elves can handle earth wards."

Wards were tricky magical creations, intricate traps that warned a wizard when someone was entering an area. Elves generally used natural sources to power their wards like the light of the sun, moon, or stars. Dwarves were able to anchor their magic to the rock even in the absence of light.

Stephan gave Fleurette a surprised look and she shook her head in response. "They aren't true earth wards. I powered them with the light of the lichen in these chambers. They aren't all that complicated. Truth be told, I didn't know it was you two approaching. The wards just told me that two intruders were entering the caves. If I hadn't recognized Daeve's dirty head coming out of that opening, I might have put a knife in both your eyes."

Daeve grunted out a laugh. "That's my woman. Fiery and deadly as ever. But if your wards were up in the area, how did you lose track of Taurine?"

Fleurette scowled. "I was waylaid. Grand Wizard Winterglass came to visit."

"Winterglass himself?" said Daeve. Winterglass was one of the oldest and most respected elves alive. His powers had faded over the last few centuries but he had been near the top of the dwarves' kill list during the war. His hatred for their people was well known. "What was he doing this close to the border?"

"He is our great grandfather," Stephan reminded the dwarf. Fleurette's mother had been of the Maumer house and a powerful magic user. "So it isn't so odd." He pursed his lips. "Though he hasn't deigned to visit me lately."

"It wasn't just a friendly family visit," Fleurette told her cousin. "He came to urge me to return to my father's estate and take up the mantle of a Moonling lady again."

Her father was of the ruling house; an elf lord, though not of the highest rank. Fleurette could have chosen the life of a noble lady or a pedigreed wizardess. Neither side of her family had liked it when she had chosen to live as a hermit, but Fleurette hated the politics of either house.

"I think he really just wants me to move away from the border," she added with a snort. "For some reason he thinks the war's about to start back up again."

"By the earth's core . . !" Daeve smacked a hand to the side of his head. "Just realized that Winterglass is my great grand-daddy too. By marriage that is. Can you imagine if he found out?"

A brief flash of fear passed through Stephan's eyes. "He'd kill the both of you."

Daeve scowled at the reminder.

"Which is why I could do nothing when my wards told me that Taurine had tunneled outside my reach," Fleurette explained, placing a calming hand on Daeve's shoulder. "I couldn't leave him to poke around the place on his own. Not with his shifty-eyed entourage of hangers on already disrupting my wards. It took me all day to convince him that there was no way I would return to nobility and by the time he finally left she was already long gone."

Daeve pushed thoughts of the vengeful elf wizard out of his mind. "Well, that's enough catching up. Where'd she go?"

Fleurette raised a slender arm and pointed.

Daeve looked towards the northern end of the cavern. There, cut into the rock wall, was one of his daughter's tunnels. He could make out the precise marks left by Taurine's magic pickaxe in the rock. His jaw tightened. He had warned her so many times. "Blast it! I filled that tunnel in last time I was here. Why is that girl so insistent on going north?"

"Because she takes after her mother," Fleurette observed. "And because her father told her not to. All your warnings just made her curious." She sighed. "I don't think it was a coincidence that Taurine chose the occasion of my great grandfather's surprise visit to make her move. She knew that I wouldn't be able to stop her while he was here and that made the adventure something she couldn't resist."

Grunting in frustration, Daeve stomped towards his daughter's tunnel. He understood being stubborn. After all, he too had rebelled from his parents. He hadn't joined the Stormguard like his father, even after learning to use his magic. He hadn't become a Caskpike and worked in his mother's brewery either. Instead, he had taken skills learned from both his parents and used them to forge his own way. The way his story paralleled with Fleurette's had been one of the things that had brought them together.

"Don't give Taurine the right, though," he grumbled. "Ungrateful girl! Don't she understand the sacrifices we make to keep her safe?" All the time he and Fleurette had to spend apart. All the pretenses they had to come up with so that no one would find out that she existed. "I never paddled that girl once in her life, but when we find her I swear her hind end's going to be red for weeks!"

"We both know you wouldn't do that," Fleurette said with an amused shake of her head.

Daeve halted just in front of the tunnel and spun around to face her. "Wouldn't I?" he sputtered though he knew she was probably right.

He found it impossible to stay mad at Taurine. The girl had him twisted around her finger. It wasn't that he couldn't tell her no or lay down rules. He just couldn't hold onto his anger. No matter how frustrated she made him at times, he couldn't get within ten feet of her before all anger faded and he found himself speaking to her in reasoned tones.

It was a maddeningly un-dwarflike way for a father to act. He had learned that if he felt the need to yell at her it was best to do so at a distance, preferably with a door between them so that he couldn't see tears spring up on her cute face. If only she wasn't such a sensitive child.

"Then you'll have to paddle her for me," he conceded.

She barked out a short laugh. "I am just as helpless as you when it comes to her."

Daeve placed his meaty hands on his hips. "What kind of parents does that make us? Do we let our child rule the house?"

Fleurette arched an eyebrow. "It is a good thing she is so humble and kind-hearted. Elsewise we would simply be her slaves."

"Well, we'll see when we get to her. Won't we?" Daeve replied and swung back around to enter his daughter's tunnel. He didn't make it ten steps inside before Stephan called out.

"W-wait!" said the thin elf wizard, still standing in the cavern peering inside after them.

Daeve and Fleurette turned back to glance at him. "What?"

"I don't know if I'll be able to continue," said Stephan. Daeve noticed that the elf wizard was drenched with sweat and he looked haggard, his clothes filthy from climbing through that last stretch of caves to get to this place. Stephan gave Daeve and Fleurette embarrassed glances as he continued. "I've used up all my magic. What use could I be to you down here without it?"

Daeve pursed his lips. The elf had already shown a surprising amount of courage coming all the way here via the underground. Perhaps he had pushed his friend too hard. Stephan wasn't a dwarf, after all. He couldn't be expected to have unending stamina. The elf looked beat down.

Still, Daeve couldn't let him off the hook just yet. He needed all the help he could get. He had been able to urge Stephan onward thus far by ignoring the elf's protests and acting as if his participation was a foregone conclusion. Perhaps it was time to change his motivational technique. He approached his friend.

"You've done good coming this far," Daeve began with an accepting smile and placed a hand on the elf's shoulder, prepared to drop a heavy load of guilt. "I suppose I can't expect-."

"Just a damned minute! He's not stopping now," Fleurette interrupted. The look she gave Stephan was pitiless. "Taurine is my daughter, which means you have a familial responsibility to help."

The elf sighed helplessly. "It's not that I don't want to help. It's just that-."

"You're tired and hate being underground so you want to give up," Fleurette snapped. "That attitude may have served you well when we were younger and you wanted to get out of chores, but you're not a child anymore!" He opened his mouth to say something else, but she didn't let him. "And we both know that your magic will regenerate over time so you can't use that as an excuse. You will stand up and be an adult and help us find our daughter!"

Stephan's jaw clenched and he said through gritted teeth, "I was not going to say any of those things!" The elf no longer looked tired as he stormed past Fleurette and Daeve. He paused at the tunnel entrance and whirled back around to face them. "And I'm older than both of you. So there!"

With that, the elf pulled Rocky out of his pocket and entered the tunnel. The elemental glowed, lighting the way before him.

Fleurette glanced at her husband. "Just guilting him wouldn't have been enough. He has never been afraid to disappoint his family."

"So you went for his pride." Daeve shook his head as he entered the tunnel. "And I always wondered how you managed to get me to do what you want."

She chuckled as she followed behind him. "You're easy. All I need are my feminine wiles."

Daeve laughed in response. She wasn't wrong there. He never could say no to her.

They followed Stephan through their daughter's tunnel. It twisted and turned a bit, but it wasn't all that long. After a hundred feet or so it led into another cavern space lit dimly with green algae. Rocky went to work, spreading his glow into other rocks in the chamber, illuminating the place more clearly. The tunnel came out five feet above the floor of the enormous chamber.

Unlike the previous cavern, this one wasn't icicled by stalactites. The roof high overhead was one enormous pockmarked slab of rock. The floor was littered with towering boulders that had fallen from the ceiling above, causing a mazelike formation that they could barely see over from their position at the tunnel's exit.

"Uhh . . ." said Stephan stupidly, frozen in place as his eyes took the place in.

From the look on Stephan's face, Daeve could see that the elf found this cavern much more terrifying than previous sections of their underground journey. To an aboveground dweller, the place would look like a trap. After all, what if more boulders fell on them as they traversed the floor?

The dwarf hurried to ease his friend's fears and placed a hand on Stephan's shoulder. "Don't worry, cousin. The boulders you're seeing here fell when this thing was first formed. Probably back during the Plucking itself. You can tell from the mushrooms that've grown on them. That stuff takes ages to grow over rock."

His voice was confident and his statement was mostly true. Daeve was certain that no more boulders would fall from above. He'd been in this chamber once before and Rocky had assured him that the solid slab of a ceiling was in no danger of coming down. He had been lying about the mushrooms, though. Those softly glowing things were like the weeds of the underground, sprouting up everywhere as long as the temperature was right. If any of these fallen boulders were new, he had no way of knowing it.

Stephan didn't look all that comforted by Daeve's assurances, true or not. His lips moved as if he was talking to himself and the dwarf worried that he would turn around and flee. Fleurette spoke up before the elf could lose his pride-powered courage.

"I tracked Taurine to the westmost corner of the cavern. That's where she dug another tunnel," she said, pointing the way over the top of the boulders.

"Right," said Stephan, blinking out of his fearful trance. "What are you waiting for, then?"

Swallowing, the elf wizard trotted down the steeply sloped edge of the chamber and came to the floor to stand amongst the boulders. He looked around, frowning. Though he knew the general direction he was supposed to go, there wasn't a clearly defined path across the floor. The rocks he had been able to see over before were now a series of blockish obstacles that he and his friends would have to walk around.

Fleurette joined her cousin and gave him an encouraging nod. "Follow me. I know the way."

Stephan nodded his ahead and Fleurette started across the cavern floor, weaving her way in and out of the boulder field. Stephan followed behind her and Daeve took up the rear.

As they walked, the dwarf thought back to the last time he had been in this place. It had been the day he had discovered his daughter's desire to tunnel northward. He had been so furious at the time and she had done a very good job of hiding from him. Without Rocky's help, he might not have been able to find her. It suddenly occurred to him that she might not be all that far away, but simply hiding again. Then again, why would she do that? No. It was something else.

Daeve pondered the reason for Taurine's decision to leave her home and journey in this dangerous area in the first place. His brow furrowed in concern. What if it wasn't just childish curiosity? What if she was running away?

Daeve remembered how much he had chafed under his father's rule as a child. Daeve's every waking hour had been planned out for him. He had often fantasized about running away and as soon as he had been old enough to get out from his father's shadow he had.

Is that how Taurine felt? The poor child's life was just as restricted as his had been, even more so since her very existence had to be kept secret. No matter how many times he and Fleurette had tried to explain it to her, Taurine had never really understood the reasons why.

The dwarf was so absorbed in his thoughts that when Stephan stopped suddenly in front of him, he walked right into the scrawny elf's back, nearly knocking him over. Daeve scowled. "What are you doing?"

"Uh, Daeve?" said Stephan questioningly and Daeve stepped out from behind him. The elf was staring down at the square shape of the elemental in his hands. Rocky was pulsing with light. "Is it supposed to be doing this? It's vibrating in my hands."

"Uh oh," said Fleurette.

"Rocky's giving us a warning," Daeve explained. Stephan looked worriedly up towards the ceiling but the dwarf shook his head. "Not that. He says someone's coming this way. Several someones."

"What kind of someones?" Stephan asked.

"Not sure. His way of talking ain't precise, okay?" said Daeve. He counted the number of flashes the elemental was giving off. "But there's a whole pile of 'em coming this way. Eight or more."

"Shh! Listen," Fleurette warned. She had drawn her bow and had an arrow nocked.

The three of them held still and Daeve made out what her elf ears had heard. The sound of shuffling feet echoed through the cavern from the direction Taurine had gone. Then came rough voices.

Stephan frowned and whispered, "Goblins! Stupid filthy beasts."

Daeve and Fleurette exchanged concerned glances. Daeve knew from past experience that goblins could be just as smart as any dwarf, though very few of them aspired to be. They were mostly content with being filthy scavengers, surviving by living off the leavings of the higher races, oftentimes stealing or assaulting people to get what they wanted. Dwarves and elves alike considered them to be a nuisance.

The dwarven government had banished the majority of them from the mountains. As a result, the goblins had established several underground villages along the border of dwarf and elf lands. They were fiercely territorial about their tunnels and were known to attack intruders, sometimes capturing them and ransoming them and other times killing them outright.

"Whoa. It be bright in here!" said one gravelly voice. "My eyes!"

There were several awed grunts of agreement and a hesitant goblin replied, "Maybe we don't go this way. The ceiling can fall and crush us to jellies!"

"No!" shouted another voice, this one rough and demanding, probably the boss of this crew. "You squints yer eyes and we goes in. The little half-breed's tracks comed from this way."

"So?" said a fourth goblin. "Why do we care?"

"Cuz of revenge! The chief sended us for it!" replied the demanding voice. "And where there be a child, there be a momma and papa! We grabs them and kills them!"

Daeve bared his teeth in a silent snarl and pulled one of his oilcohol flasks from his belt. He enacted a spell, steeling his throat and stomach, then took several gulps from the flask. The acrid liquid burned on the way down as always, but as soon as it hit his belly he felt a rush of magic flood his body.

"Standard formation," he growled.

Fleurette nodded without complaint and let him walk past her, keeping her arrow nocked at the ready. She knew her husband's capabilities quite well. They had fought side-by-side many times over the years. Or more accurately, they had fought with him barging ahead while she hung back and picked off any creatures smart enough to run away from him.

"Fleurette, my magic hasn't returned yet," Stephan whispered worriedly, coming up behind her.

"They're only goblins," she said with a roll of her eyes. "You just hold on to Rocky."

Daeve headed towards the voices and enacted layers of spells as he went. First he toughened his flesh, his skin darkening to black in stark contrast to his blond beard and hair. Next, he enhanced his muscles until he had the strength of any ten dwarves. Finally, he increased the density of his mass, his weight compounding to the point that his footsteps sent noticeable tremors through the ground.

"You're overdoing it," Fleurette observed in a disapproving whisper.

She was right. Piling up three spells of this intensity pushed his magic to the limit, using up the oilcohol as quickly as his ability could burn it. He probably had ten minutes at the most before he'd need to drink more of the precious liquid.

That didn't worry him, though. Destroying these goblins wouldn't take that long. He let out a low growl to make sure that they knew he was coming.

By the time Daeve came into their view the goblins were nervously wielding blades and hammers. There were ten of them. Squat goblins about the height of dwarves with pig-like ears and skin the color of varying shades of mucus. This particular crew was wearing dented armor of dwarven make.

The nearest goblin stepped forward with a snarl, brandishing a wooden shield that had been reinforced with iron straps. "You stop right there, painted dwarf! You-!"

Daeve didn't break stride. He threw his enhanced strength into a punch that struck the goblin's shield and crashed right through it. The air was filled with splintered wood and twisted shards of metal as his fist continued into the goblin's ribcage, turning its innards to jelly.

"You lowly booger skins looking for the daddy of a half-breed?" he shouted to the rest of them as the goblin collapsed bonelessly to the ground. "Well, here I am!"

The goblins took a step back, frightened by the ferocity of his attack. But their boss was angered by his use of such an insensitive term. "Nobody be calling us snot skins!"

"I said booger skin," Daeve corrected and altered his course to walk towards the leader, the largest of the goblins, who had a torn ear and a thick golden ring through the center of his nose.

"Kill him! Revenge comes to us!" the boss shouted.

Three of the goblins didn't move, but stared trembling at the remains of their dead companion. The other five complied. They came at Daeve, hooting and swinging their weapons.

The dwarf let them strike him, ignoring the hammers that bounced off of his flesh and the blades that sparked off of his hardened skin. He clutched two of the goblins, his fingers tearing through chainmail. He crushed them together, feeling their ribcages crackle as if they were made of wicker.

Next, he grasped one of them by the arm. It was a brutish beast wearing a heavy breastplate and spiked boots. Daeve effortlessly lifted it over his head and began to swing it around.

The three cowardly goblins that had ignored their boss and hung back watched in horror as the black-skinned dwarf used their armored comrade to bash the others to pieces. They turned to run, but were peppered by arrows from overhead.

Fleurette had climbed one of the boulders that towered above them and was firing down at them. One by one, the goblins fell. The boss saw that his cause was lost. He turned to run but was jerked to a stop by an arrow that pinned his hand to the boulder behind him.

When Daeve saw that all of his attackers had stopped moving, he dropped the limp body of his improvised goblin weapon to the ground. The dwarf stepped over the grisly remains around him and strode forward, his eyes focused on the goblin boss.

"You and me have things to talk about," the dwarf promised the boss, who was grimacing as he tried to pull his hand free of the arrow that was pinning it at a downward angle.

Unexpectedly, Fleurette dropped down from above to stand in front of the dwarf. She stretched out her arm and planted her hand stiffly on her husband's hardened face. "No you don't, Daeve. You'll likely kill him outright before he talks. This takes finesse."

Daeve frowned, but realized she was probably right. "Fine."

"We goblins don't be talkin'!" the boss shouted in a surprising display of bravery for a goblin. "Just kills me and be gone."

Fleurette swung around to face him and reached into her quiver. She pulled out another arrow, holding it by the shaft as if it were a knife. She pointed it at the goblin, but he only glared at her until she stepped forward and hooked the arrowhead through the goblin's nose ring.

She twisted the arrow. "You're going to talk to me."

The goblin's bravado faded. "Yah!! What you be doing? We goblins and elves ain't at war!"

Fleurette bared her teeth and growled, twisting again. "I'm the mother of that half-breed you were talking about! Where is my daughter?"

"I don't be knowing! We don't gots her!" the goblin boss squealed, tears of pain streaming from his eyes. "We pick's her up in our tunnels, but loses her in a fight with dwarf scum invaders!"

"She was taken by dwarves?" Fleurette asked, her eyes widening.

She twisted the arrow, causing the goblin to squeal again as the ring tore at its sensitive septum. "Why?"

"'Cause they wants to make her bleed!" it howled. "We tries to sell her to 'em but they just attacks!"

Fleurette's face went white and she eased the tension on the ring as she considered her daughter's possible fate. Daeve stepped up behind her and put his hands on her shoulders, his worries in tune with hers.

Stephan spoke up, his mind in a different direction. "If those dwarves attacked you, then why did you come this way looking to take revenge on the child's parents?"

"They kills too many of us. Kills the chief's wife! And it's that half-breed's fault," the boss snarled, the easing of his pain allowing some of his courage to return. "Goblins don't be sitting in our villages anymore. We be making an army and taking revenge on everybody! The chief sends us here and he goes to kill those dwarves."

Daeve blinked as he pondered the implications of that statement. He reached out and grasped his wife's hand on the arrow. A twist made the goblin cry out again. "Which way did the dwarves go?"

"Ah! East! East! Towards the elf lands!"

Fleurette slapped her husband's hand away, then shoved the arrow through the goblin's nose and into its brain. Its torment ended, she swung around to face him. "We must keep moving."

"I don't know that I've ever seen you be that brutal," he told her, one blond eyebrow raised.

"I don't have the luxury of compassion, Daeve. Taurine's with the dwarves and the dwarves have an army of goblins at their heels!" she said.

"And we'll kill every last one of 'em if we have to," Daeve promised her. "Don't care who those dwarves are. We're finding her and taking her home."

Her eyes burned the color of hot coals as she nodded back at him. The two of them headed towards the tunnel the goblins had used.

Stephan trotted along after them. "I really don't think you need me along on this trip," he observed, frustrated by his inability to match the kind of sheer power that the dwarf and his wife had exerted.

"You're the best healer in the group," Fleurette reminded him without looking back. "We may be taking on an army."

Stephan frowned. "I bet Daeve can heal himself in the doubtful case that he gets hurt."

"Yeah, but I can't heal Fleurette. You know that," the dwarf retorted. "Now come along! We don't got time to waste."

They arrived at the northeastern corner of the cavern and saw the tunnel entrance. Daeve placed his hands on the familiar tool marks his daughter had left behind and stepped inside. He led the way as Rocky extended his magic to illuminate the rock in front of them.

This particular tunnel was longer than the previous one. It curved its way through the structure of the ground for several hundred yards. Taurine's skill was evident in the way she took the tunnel in the safest route, avoiding areas of the earth where a passage might collapse.

"By mud!" Stephan exclaimed after a full hour of twisting turns in the earth, his back aching from walking hunched over for so long. "How long did it take her to dig this?"

"The better part of a year, I'd say," Daeve said, infuriated by his daughter's dogged insistence on defying him and yet admiring the speed and efficiency in which she worked. The girl was only twelve after all! "How did she dig this without you knowing, Fleurette?"

His wife grunted behind him, "I wondered the same thing when I found this tunnel," she replied. "I think she found a way to fool my wards."

Daeve's eyes widened. Perhaps she had inherited her mother's gift as well as his ability to read the rock. "Then when your wards told you she had left the caves-."

"Maybe she made a mistake," Fleurette suggested. "That or she let me know she had gone on purpose."

"Why would she do that?" Stephan wondered.

Neither Fleurette nor Daeve had an answer for that question.

Finally, they arrived at the end of the tunnel and Daeve saw what had frightened his wife. Taurine had dug right into the side of a corridor that was part of an ancient cave system. From the smell of the place it was goblin territory. The fine dirt that covered the floor of the corridor was covered in dwarf and goblin tracks.

Daeve followed the corridor eastward and they soon came upon the large chamber that had been the site of the conflict that the goblin boss had told them about. Signs of the battle were everywhere. The ground was caked with bloody clods of dirt. And the bodies of goblins lined the walls where they had been placed by their brethren until they could be retrieved and given a proper burial.

Fleurette raised a stunned hand to her mouth. "To think that Taurine was caught in the middle of this."

Daeve swallowed. His poor innocent girl. He and Fleurette had done their best to explain the darkness of the world to her, but she was so tender hearted. The only death she had seen was when she and her mother had gone hunting. There was no way she had been prepared to see the carnage that had occurred here.

They followed the tracks of the dwarves, seeing that they had continued in an easterly direction from this point, keeping to the outskirts of the goblin caves. Daeve and Fleurette kept an eye out for any tracks smaller than the others, but saw nothing that specifically gave evidence that the dwarves had kept their daughter alive.

"Perhaps she was being carried," Stephan suggested, but that possibility was no better than the others. The only reason that dwarf soldiers would carry her was if she was a resistant prisoner or if she was somehow injured.

As they neared the outermost edge of the cave complex, they saw evidence that the goblin chieftain had made good on his threat of revenge. Goblin footprints came in from side chambers, covering those of the dwarves. A small army of the smelly beasts had been stalking them.

Finally, at the outermost chamber of the goblin territory they found the results of a second battle.

The chamber was broad and wide and the high roof was pierced here and there by stray roots. This told Daeve that they were no longer under the foothills of the mountains. They had reached the edge of the Verge and were quite close to the surface. If they traveled any further east, they would be under elven land.

The battle that had occurred in this chamber seemed far bloodier than the first, though Fleurette pointed out that it could seem that way just because it was more recent. The chamber floor was muddied with blood. Goblin bodies littered the place in various states of dismemberment. As did a handful of dwarves.

Daeve frowned with concern as he squatted beside one of his fallen people. From the low number of dead dwarves, this was a highly trained group. The dwarf was wearing a full suit of armor in the style of elite soldiers, but without any house insignia or identifying badges or medals. A sword was still gripped in one hand, a fine blade indeed, but plain. There wasn't even a maker's mark.

"That seems odd," said Fleurette, coming to his side and taking the sword from him as he continued to search the corpse. "The other dwarf I checked was clean of house markings as well. Maybe they are part of an independent group. But if so, why not have some way of identifying themselves? Do you think they are mercenaries?"

"Even mercenaries usually keep mementos to remind them of home," Daeve said, the frown on his face deepening as he considered a darker possibility. "No. I think this is a group of government soldiers sent in secret. Whoever sent them doesn't want their deeds to be traced back."

"A secret mission," Stephan mused, standing at the chamber's edge. "To cull the goblins perhaps? Certainly a group of goblins this large will have been causing mischief along the border."

Daeve considered the possibility, but shook his head. "Why keep that a secret?"

"Because an incursion this large under the Verge would be certain to raise the ire of the elves at the border," Stephan said. "Why stir things up? Despite what Grand Wizard Winterglass thinks, I believe that peace could be close at hand. Even if the locals in this area don't want it to be."

Daeve stood. "If peace really is close at hand, there are going to be people on both sides who don't want it. I think these dwarves were sent specifically to stir things up. Notice how they came all the way to the forest."

"They're here to attack elves?" Stephan said with a grimace.

"There is a village not too far from the border above us," Fleurette said.

Daeve nodded grimly. "A quick raid from below under the cover of darkness. All they have to do is make an unprovoked attack on a village and leave via the caves. If any dwarves die and are left behind in the process no one will know who ordered the attack."

"The elf lords won't care who ordered it," Fleurette said, nodding in sad agreement with her husband's suggestion. "The war will go from cold to hot."

"These are the types of dwarves that have our daughter," Daeve said, feeling sick.

"They left the chamber this way," Stephan announced pointing to a passage heading northward, parallel to the forest's edge. "It appears that a few goblins escaped as well."

The three of them left the site of the slaughter and followed the dwarves' trail once again. The dwarves didn't travel very far down this northern tunnel before exiting the goblin territory altogether. Just as Daeve feared, they had turned eastward down a small passage, leading them under the forest.

His chest filling with anxiety, Daeve led his wife and cousin down the cramped tunnel. The two elves had to hunch over to follow him. The air was moist and he could smell the unmistakable scent of fresh soil mixed with something else. Something dank and wild.

The tunnel sloped gently upwards and exited into a damp earthen chamber. Rocky's magic illuminated the veins of rock in the walls. Tree roots dangled from the ceiling like spiders' legs and several side tunnels emptied into the place, some of them coming up from below.

This seemed to be a central hub for some kind of predatory creature.

The floor was covered in bleached bones. The bones were jumbled and mixed together. Daeve saw the skulls of goblins and various other beasts including a few that could have come from dwarves.

"What do you think did this?" Stephan asked, his voice a squeaky whisper.

Fleurette pursed her lips and stepped out amongst the bones, following the signs of the dwarves' passing. "Let's not wait and find out."

Evidently, the dwarves they were following were just as unnerved by the chamber as they were, because they hadn't lingered. Fleurette led Daeve and Stephan across the bone-strewn floor to a tunnel that looked different than the others that came into this chamber. This one was about five feet in diameter and smooth walled. Daeve examined it.

"Dwarves dug this tunnel recently. Probably within the last day," Daeve announced, his eyes examining the tunnel walls. The tunnel had been formed by magic and quickly, something that was possible when tunneling through loose earth. He could see traces of magic like veins of energy hardening the earthen walls and shoring them up. "They have a wizard with them."

"Then let's go in," Stephan said, eager to leave the area and the predator that could return at any moment.

Daeve gestured Fleurette to take the lead and had Stephan follow her, the elemental setting the magically strengthened walls aglow to light the way. The elves forged ahcad, hunched over in the small tunnel and Daeve took up the rear. He was confident that he could handle any creature that tried to come upon them from behind. Nevertheless, he drained a flask of oilcohol just in case.

As the magic burned to life within his belly, he noted that he only had two full flasks left. He would have to make certain that it was enough. They didn't travel much further before Stephan grunted.

"Rocky is giving his warning signal again," the elf wizard declared, and Daeve saw the elemental pulse in the elf's hand bright and hot. "Something's coming!"

The three of them grew silent and listened for some clue as to what it was. A low rumbling noise rose in the tunnel. Daeve could feel a vibration beneath his feet and turned to gaze into the illuminated tunnel behind him. "It's coming from the chamber we just left."

"Feels like something big," Fleurette whispered, and increased her pace.

The rumble increased and Daeve looked back to see something round a bend in the tunnel. Its form filled the passageway completely, its body conforming to the variations in the rough-hewn walls. All Daeve could see was the giant circular maw of inwardly curving teeth that was its head.

"It's a guardian worm!" he shouted. "Run!"

Fleurette and Stephan didn't need any encouragement. They were already bolting down the tunnel as fast as they could while half crouched over.

During the beginning of the war, the elves had been well aware that they were vulnerable to attacks from underground. In order to keep their forests safe from such attacks, the elf wizards had created the guardian worms. The enormous and hungry creatures had patrolled the earth beneath the forest's border, devouring all interlopers.

They were an effective defense. Hard to kill and terrifying to face, the worms had kept all but the most determined of dwarf attackers from attempting an underground approach. Daeve had thought their time had come to an end since the war had gone cold. He hadn't heard tale of the worms in a decade. Evidently, he had been listening to the wrong people.

The worm sensed its potential prey fleeing and increased its speed. Daeve quickly realized that they weren't going to be able to escape it.

"Rocky!" he shouted.

The elemental heard its master's plea. It caused the walls of the tunnel to swell inward behind him in an attempt to block the worm's path. Unfortunately, the walls weren't rock, but magically hardened dirt. The worm plowed through the obstruction and raged on until it was at Daeve's heels.

The dwarf knew it was going to catch him unless he used a spell to increase his speed. The only problem was that Fleurette couldn't do the same. He had a split second to decide what to do about that.

Grimacing, he turned in the tunnel to face the oncoming worm and began to build layers of spells within himself. He only managed to harden his skin before it struck. He took a deep breath and plunged into its toothy maw.

The worm's mouth contracted around him. He could feel its teeth scraping across the hardened skin of his torso, but it couldn't penetrate his flesh. Unfortunately, he was only slowing it down slightly. Daeve enacted the second spell layer, increasing the density of his mass as he slid deeper into the thing.

The guardian worm sensed that something was off about this prey. He was growing heavier and heavier in its belly. It's desire to continue chasing the other two prey ahead of it lessened and it slowed further, contracting it's body in waves to push him further into its body where the intense acids in its stomach could break his flesh down.

Daeve felt the powerful contractions around him and struggled against them. What spell to enact next? His body became surrounded by burning liquid and he knew his time was short. He didn't think it would dissolve his hardened skin, but he would need to breathe soon. He had a spell that allowed him to breath underwater, but that wouldn't work in acid.

Daeve knew he had to kill the thing and get out of it soon or he would pass out and his spell would lapse. He couldn't budge his arms with the worm wedged into the narrow tunnel. Daeve increased his strength until he was able to bring his hands up in front of him. He tried to grasp the stomach wall of the worm but it was too slippery. He couldn't tear his way free.

Realizing that strength wouldn't help him at this point, he abandoned that effort. With only seconds left, spell combinations tumbled quickly through his mind. He chose one almost at random. Daeve's body began to heat up. He poured all the magic he could into it, turning his hardened skin from black to the red of a live coal.

This was something that the worm couldn't ignore. The acid had begun to boil around him and steam built within the beast, causing it severe pain. It surged ahead in the tunnel, panicked, trying to get into open air where it could disgorge this horrible meal. It didn't make it. The intense pressure built within the worm until it's flesh could not contain it. The beast detonated, steam and flesh exploding out both ends of the tunnel.

To Daeve, the sudden release of pressure around him was a relief. He rose to his knees and found that he was still in the tunnel, only now it was half full of gore. The worm's flesh had been liquified by the explosion. He was grateful that the dwarves' enchantment strengthening the walls had held. Otherwise, he would have been buried alive.

He could see the tunnel's exit not far away and hoped that Fleurette and Stephan hadn't been injured in the blast. Grimacing, he half-crawled, half-swam through the muck until he slid out of the tunnel and onto the floor of the chamber beyond.

As Daeve climbed to his feet he found himself standing in a high-ceilinged cave that smelled like fertile soil. The ceiling itself was made of intertwined roots and black earth. There couldn't be more than a few feet between the roof and the forest above.

Standing in the cave all around, staring at him in shock and splattered by worm chunks, were the troop of dwarves he had been following. They were brandishing their weapons, unsure what to do with this slimy intruder. On one side of the chamber Daeve could see Fleurette and Stephan, bound and gagged, their eyes wide.

"By the Holy Earth's Core!" shouted a voice, aghast. "Daeve? Is that you?"

Daeve's jaw dropped at the identity of the speaker. "Father? You're the one leading these dwarves?"

Ritcherd Palebeard looked much the same as he had the last time Daeve had seen him twenty years ago. He wasn't quite as tall as his son, but was wider of belly and his hair was a silvered blond. The fine wizard's robes he wore looked out of place among the dwarf soldiers in their plain armor.

Ritcherd blinked back at Daeve. "Son? What a surprising entrance."

"Got ate by this worm that exploded," Daeve said numbly, though it was an obvious statement. His bare feet squelched in the creature's remains as he approached, his eyes having moved past his father to the child standing next to him.

"Daddy!" shouted Taurine with a gleeful smile that dimpled her cheeks. She rushed towards him, her curly blond hair bouncing above her pointed ears. To Daeve's relief, she looked completely fine, though covered in dirt. Taurine paused before she reached him. "Why are you naked?"

Daeve glanced down and noticed for the first time that his threadbare clothes were gone, along with his belt of flasks. He grimaced and looked back at the remnants of the monster, thinking of the horrible task of retrieving them. "Oh. Uh, worm juice dissolved it, I guess."

"Somebody give my son a pair of britches!" Ritcherd shouted.

A dwarf soldier dragged a pack over to him and pulled out a worn, but serviceable pair for Daeve to put on.

Daeve reached into his reserves and enacted a spell, sluicing the worm blood and bile from his body, then pulled the trousers on and hurried to wrap up his daughter in a tight embrace. "What were you thinking, girl? Coming all this way?"

"I'm sorry, Daddy," Taurine said. She pulled back and looked into his face with eyes every bit as colorful as her mother's. "I know I shouldn't have gone north. I just wanted to see what it was you were so worried about. I knew that other dwarves couldn't be as bad as you made them out to be."

"I'm just glad you're okay," Daeve told her, kissing her cheek.

"You were wrong, by the way," she told him firmly.

Daeve directed his eyes on his father, the dwarf who was leading this vile attack. "Was I?"

Taurine nodded. "They've been really nice. At least once they got to know me. At first they were kind of scary."

Ritcherd gave Daeve a regretful smile. "I'm sad to say that our first reaction upon seeing her wasn't very kind. I didn't want to believe her when she told me who her parents were."

"Yeah, there's a reason I never told you," Daeve said. His father hated elves as much as any dwarf Daeve knew. It had never crossed Daeve's mind that he might accept Taurine.

"But . . . that girl of yours is special," Ritcherd said, walking towards them.

"What do you mean?" Daeve asked suspiciously.

"There is a magic about her. I don't think it's a conscious thing she does, but something inherent within her soul," Ritcherd explained, a look of awe in his eyes. "When you're in Taurine's presence, your judgement isn't clouded by negativity. Emotions like rage or hatred just disappear. I tell you, Son, no matter how any of us felt upon first seeing her, there isn't a one of us that doesn't love her now. All we had to do was get within ten feet of her."

Daeve clutched his daughter tighter to him and thought back to the way he couldn't hold onto anger around her. It hadn't occurred to him that she would affect others the same way. He and Fleurette had never let her be seen by anyone. Even if what his father was saying was true, they would have had no way of knowing.

Ritcherd placed a hand atop his granddaughter's head. "Daeve, I think Taurine may just be the Child of Promise."

Daeve blinked at his father. The Child of Promise was a prophecy so ancient that it predated the war. An oracle had foretold that one day a child would be born that would be a harbinger of peace. The child would come at a key moment in time just as the dwarven people needed it most.

He licked his lips. "I thought the Child of Promise was supposed to be a pure-blood Silvercoat."

"The tale has been embellished over the centuries," Ritcherd told him. "Believe me, I never thought that the Child of Promise would be a half-breed. To tell you the truth, I didn't think it was possible for an elf and a dwarf to be . . . fertile together."

"It was a surprise to us too," Daeve told him. He cocked his head at his father. "If Taurine is . . . who you say she is, what are you planning to do here? The only reason I've been able to think of that a troop of dwarf soldiers this size would come all this way is if they were planning an attack."

Ritcherd sighed. "Well, you'd be right. We were sent here on a mission. See, there has been a strong movement towards peace in our war with the elves lately. There is a certain faction within the government that doesn't want that peace to happen." He winced. "Before I met Taurine here, I've got to admit that I was one of them. But in the time that we've been with her she's convinced us that it's time for old hatreds to end. We were just getting ready to return home."

Daeve gave him a cautious nod. "If that's the case, then why do you have my wife and cousin tied up?"

"They ran into our scouts and were brought to me just moments ago. Taurine was telling me that the elf woman was her mother just as you made your . . . explosive entrance."

"Her name is Fleurette," Daeve said.

"Right. Fleurette," Ritcherd said, swallowing visibly as he realized that he was going to have to recognize her as his daughter-in-law. He may have had a recent change of heart but it wasn't going to be easy to erase decades of hateful thought patterns. He nodded to one of his men. "Let the elves go. It's time we headed home."

Fleurette and Stephan stood and were freed. Taurine rushed over to them and fell into her mother's embrace. "Momma, I am so sorry I disobeyed."

"How did you two escape the worm and get here before I did?" Daeve wondered.

"Stephan managed to cast a speed spell on both of us," she explained.

Stephan shrugged. "My magic returned just in time I guess." He held out his hand to Taurine. "Hello. I am Stephan."

Taurine stepped past his hand and hugged him. "I am so happy to meet you, Cousin! Momma and daddy told me all about you."

Stephan's eyebrows rose and he turned his head to look at Daeve, his eyes welling with tears. He swallowed. "I think your father may be right. What I'm feeling right now about this lovely child . . . there is a magic in this."

Fleurette and Daeve shared concerned glances. If this was true and Taurine was the prophesied harbinger of peace, what did it mean for their family going forward?

No sooner had the question passed through Daeve's mind than the ground around them shook violently. Dirt rained down on everyone from above. Dwarves cried out in surprise as the floor of the chamber began to rise. Daeve was knocked to his feet.

A great crack appeared in the root-filled ceiling above them and yawned wide, peeling open as if pulled by the roots of the plants above. The bright noonday sun streamed down upon them in blinding brilliance and the ground beneath them continued to rise. It didn't stop until they were brought level with the surface. To their surprise, the dwarf troop found themselves in a broad forest clearing not far from the walled elven village they had been sent to attack.

Surrounding them, both in the trees above and on the ground all around them, was an army of elves. The dwarves were outnumbered three to one and Daeve realized that the elves must have been tipped off that they were coming. Elf archers pulled back their bows, ready to fire on command.

"You see! You see!" cried a whiny voice and Daeve saw a rotund goblin chieftain wearing a crude crown made of crooked daggers. His hands were bound before him and he was standing next to three fancily-dressed elves on horseback. Two of them wore robes marking them as wizards. "Dwarves! Treacherous dwarves here to attack you!"

"Indeed," said one of the robed elves, ancient with hair that was silky white. His face was filled with hatred and rage. "You dwarves sought to attack this village! A town of innocents with not a soldier among them!"

Daeve's father stepped forward. "No!" He signaled to his men and the dwarves placed their weapons on the ground. "Grand Wizard Winterglass, I recognize you from past battles and I swear to you that we do not mean your people harm!"

"They lies!" shouted the goblin chieftain. "They be here to slaughter! They be here to-!"

The ancient elf waved his hand and the air around the goblin's jaw solidified and tightened, forcing it shut. Daeve's eyes widened. So this was his great grandfather in law? Power radiated from the elf as strong as any Daeve had seen. To think that the elf was in his declining years.

Winterglass sneered back at Daeve's father. "I too recognize my enemy, Ritcherd Palebeard of the Stormguard. I know of your hatred for my people. I know of the many elves you have slaughtered!"

"That was in the past," Ritcherd said, his face pained. "I have no room in my heart to hate elves anymore. We seek your pardon for being in your lands uninvited and place ourselves upon your mercy."

"My mercy?" Winterglass said with a laugh.

One of the other elves on horseback, a high-ranking Moonling lord by the look of him, spoke up. "An entire dwarven troop taken prisoner behind our lines and in a time when treaties are being discussed," he mused. "Imagine the concessions we will be able to force the dwarves to make with them as capital."

Winterglass snorted, his teeth bared. "Imagine the capital if we bring a troop of corpses taken in attack on a peaceful village and led by an infamous dwarf wizard."

"Great Grandfather!" shouted Fleurette, stepping forward to stand next to Daeve's father. Taurine smartly hung back. "The dwarf wizard tells the truth. They are not here to attack us."

Winterglass frowned, noticing her for the first time. "Fleurette? What are you doing here amongst these foul dwarves?"

"I am here to stand as witness," she told him.

Daeve understood what she was up to. If Fleurette could convince her grandfather not to kill the dwarves, he might use them as leverage at the treaty talks, but it was possible that renewed war could still be avoided.

Fleurette stood tall and proud. "If you were to-"

"And I, Great Grandfather!" Stephan interrupted loudly, stepping forward to join his cousin. "I too stand as witness that these dwarves mean no harm. The goblin chieftain lies. He is merely angry because his people tried to attack these dwarves underground and lost."

The goblin chieftain's eyes bulged and he jumped up and down irately but he couldn't speak past the elf wizard's spell.

The elf lord spoke again, his voice curious. "Then what, pray tell, were these dwarves doing in caves beneath our forest?"

"They are here on a mission of peace," said Stephan to everyone's surprise. Daeve wondered what on earth he was thinking. What Stephan said next sent a stab of fear through the dwarf. "They have brought with them the long prophesied Child of Promise!"

There were several gasps within the elf army at this claim. Stephan reached an arm out to Taurine. Daeve's fists clenched as she stepped forward to take the elf's hand. "This is Taurine. She is here to herald a new age of peace."

"A dwarf child?" scoffed the elf lord. "Nonsense. The Child of Promise will be an elf of pureblood Moonling descent!"

"The original prophecy claimed nothing of the sort, as a reading of the original document can prove," Stephan told him. "But I understand your bewilderment. I was skeptical myself at first. But all doubt will fall away. All you need to do is come down and meet Taurine. You will understand."

"Me? Meet a dwarf child?" said the elf lord.

"That is no dwarf!" cried Winterglass suddenly, his voice shrill with outrage as he saw her pointed ears. "That child is a half-breed!"

This brought another gasp of shock from the elf army. Some of them grimaced in disgust. Daeve, his heart pounding, pulled up his reserves of magic. He had very little left and he had no way to get at his oilcohol. He would be able to manage but one spell and he readied himself to cast it if necessary.

"Impossible!" shouted the second elf wizard.

"It is true!" Fleurette yelled back. "This child is my daughter, Taurine! Her father is a dwarf, Daeve Palebeard! Through me, she carries the royal blood of Moonling and Maumer. Through him she carries the blood Stormguard and Caskpike! She is proof embodied that our people can coexist together!"

There was stunned silence at this revelation.

Finally the elf lord spoke again, his eyes staring at the child. "Is this truly possible?"

"All you need do is meet her and you will see," Stephan promised.

"Enough of this!" shouted Grand Wizard Winterglass. He spread his arms wide and cast a spell of immense power.

A wave of energy flowed across the clearing and the air around every elf and dwarf solidified, holding them in place. Daeve couldn't move. He enacted the spell he had saved up, increasing his strength in an attempt to shove past the magical bonds, but he couldn't budge. The elf wizard was too strong.

Winterglass climbed down from his horse and turned towards Taurine, his gaze fearsome and full of hatred. He pulled a long knife from within his robes. "Such an abomination cannot be suffered to exist."

Taurine took a single step forward. For some reason she was untouched by his magic. Daeve willed her to turn and flee, but she merely stood there. Her gaze was unblinking as she watched the ancient wizard approach.

"Hello, Great-Great Grandfather Winterglass," Taurine said.

"Silence, foul thing!" he said, walking closer.

She cocked her head at him. "Why do you call me a foul thing?"

"Because you are the disgusting result of a vulgar act between elf and dwarf," he said, though as he came closer and fell within the range of the love she exuded the venom in his voice lessened. "I am sorry, but this is an offense against nature. I cannot allow you to exist."

Taurine blinked, but she did not seem afraid. "You would kill me, Great-Great Grandfather? Even though I have done nothing to harm you?"

"It must be done," he said, now mere steps away. He tightened his grip around the knife in his hand, and his lips trembled. There was no repulsion in his voice now. He sounded almost apologetic. "I will make it quick, child. The sins of your parents are not your fault."

He stood in front of Taurine, towering a full foot taller than her, and raised the knife. His arms trembled as he battled with the unexpected emotions swelling within him.

Daeve would be held back no longer. The last of his oilcohol-fueled magic was gone, but he pulled deep within himself, dredging up reserves he didn't even know he had. His muscles bulged and he surged forward, tearing past the grand wizard's spell.

Daeve ran as fast as he could towards his daughter. He would jump in front of her. He would obliterate the wizard with a single punch.

Taurine heard his approach. She glanced back at her father and held out an arm. “No, Daddy. Don’t hurt him.”

Daeve felt all of his fear and anger sucked away by her presence. He stumbled to a stop next to her. Logically, he knew that he should strike out and destroy the threat, but instead he found himself saying, “Please, Great-Grandfather. Don’t hurt my daughter.”

“I must,” whispered the old man, but his face was now a mask of confusion.

Taurine reached out and grasped the front of the wizard’s robes. Gently, she pulled and Grand Wizard Winterglass sank down on his knees before her. Then she wrapped her arms around him and pulled him into a tight embrace. “It’s okay, Great-Great Grandfather. You can let it go now. I forgive you for hating me.”

The knife fell from Winterglass’ fingers. The ancient wizard sobbed.

Fathers and Sons: Part I

pdmac

Thorgil was small for his age, even for a dwarf. His parents attributed it to an elven curse. After all, that was the only rational explanation. They had five other strapping sons who were amongst the tallest in the clan, powerful young dwarves probably better suited to be border guards or miners than ale brewers. But Thorgil, the youngest? An elven curse was the only answer.

How the curse was invoked was another matter, but his father was sure it occurred at the battle before Thorgil as born. The elves had overrun a defense embankment only to be pushed back. Thorgil's father remembered a retreating elf hurling some sort of curse in elvish at him as the elves fell back to the forest.

"We should've wiped them out when we had the chance," his father often complained. "Now it's too late. Their black magic has gotten stronger." Then he'd cast a side glance at Thorgil.

It's not that he didn't love his youngest son. He loved him as much as any father could whose son was such a disappointment.

"The boy can't wield a hammer," his father groused. "Every dwarf can wield a hammer. In it's our blood."

"Your hammers are too big for him," his mother replied. "Every dwarf starts off with small hammers and grows into the bigger ones."

"But he can't wield the bigger ones. He's still using a boy's hammer." His father crossed his arms and stared at her. "How can he be a cooper when he can't even bend the hoops for the barrels enough to hammer in the rivets? So I think to myself, maybe he's a better brewer. But the boy's attention wanders."

Reaching into his apron pocket, he pulled out a small stone carving of a unicorn. "Here, look at this," he said, handing her the carving.

Holding it up to study it, she marveled at the intricate detail. "It's beautiful."

"It's got a horn sticking out of its head," he grumpily pointed out. "What sort of horse goes around with a horn stuck out of its head?"

"Look at how lifelike it is," she said, slowly twirling the unicorn in her hand. "It's as though this horse could come alive at any moment."

"Dang it woman," he snapped. "That's not the point. He's too distracted. He spends his time making things like these instead of learning a trade."

"He's got the talent to be an artist," she countered.

"Don't be a fool, woman. We're brewers and coopers, not artists."

"Maybe he should enter some of his work in the carving contest," she said, ignoring him.

"Carving contest?" he fumed. "We got no time for that. He needs to learn his trade, just like the rest of the family."

"The carving contest is just two weeks away," she said, still admiring the statue. "Why I bet he'd win first place."

"Are you listening to me, woman?" he scowled.

Lowering the carving to gaze at him, she sweetly smiled. "I always listen to you. You go back to your ale and barrel making and let me figure out how to get Thorgil entered in the carving contest." Turning around she called out, "Thorgil."

With a sigh of exasperation, his father rolled his eyes, shook his head and headed to the workshop behind the house. He knew better than to argue anymore. Her mind was made up and when her mind was made up, she was harder to move than any stone known to dwarves.

In a corner of his father's barrel-house, amidst the noise of hammers, saws and bellows, Thorgil slowly walked around a small work table, studying the chunk of blue alabaster nestled in the middle. He had been saving this piece for a special occasion, but when his mother told him about the carving contest, he knew this was the stone to use. The question was, what to carve?

The second question was; did he even have a chance of winning? He would be competing against the very best, dwarves who had decades of experience and talent. Thorgil was barely past his thirteenth summer.

Reaction had been mixed when word leaked out that he was to enter the carving contest. His brothers teased him mercilessly, while his friends gave him encouragement. The grown-ups? Most commiserated with his father, saying it was probably for the best, as Thorgil would never make a good ale master. However, there were a few who were pleased with the prospect, especially the burgomaster who was excited that one of his villagers was entered in the contest, even if he was a mere youth.

As Thorgil studied the stone, he heard a "Pssst," at the window behind him. Turning, he saw Brice, a curly brown-haired lad five summers younger than he, peering over the ledge.

"C'mere," Brice said, curling a hand at him.

"What is it? I'm busy," Thorgil said.

"I wanna show you something," Brice said, looking furtively side to side.

"What is it?"

"You gotta c'mere."

With a sigh of frustration, Thorgil walked over to see that was so important. Leaning out the window, he looked down as Brice pulled back a bit of cloth to reveal a small beautifully carved knife.

"That's an elven blade," Thorgil blurted.

"Shhh," Brice admonished. "Not so loud."

"Where did you get it?"

"In the forest."

"You found it in the forest?" Thorgil's eyes widened in surprise.

"Naw. I traded for it," Brice grinned.

"You traded for it? What did you trade for it?"

"Remember that carving of a bird you gave me?"

"Yes," Thorgil replied, not liking that his creations were viewed as barter.

"I traded that bird for this," Brice triumphantly said.

Thorgil gazed down at the blade and knew immediately it was an expensive piece. Brice had traded well. "Who would trade you that for the bird?"

Brice glanced around again then said, "An elf."

Thorgil's eyes bolted wide. "You traded with an elf?"

"Not so loud," Brice scolded him. "You wanna get me in trouble?"

"How'd you get an elf to trade with you?"

"You gotta come out here. It ain't safe to talk like this."

Without casting a second glance at the waiting slab of alabaster, Thorgil hurried out and soon he and Brice were well away from prying adult ears as they made their way to the back streets then down the paths towards the forest that separated them from the elven domains.

"There's a secret place in the Forbidden Zone," Brice explained when they were finally beyond eavesdropping, "that me and Gunnar go. One time we was there and saw some elf kids, so we ran away as fast as we could, but when we ran I forgot and left a small hammer I was usin' to bang away at a stump. So the next day, me an Gunnar go back and I can't find the hammer, but there's a couple of elf toys on the stump."

"Elf toys?" Thorgil said.

"Yeah," Brice replied. "Stuff like a yo-yo and pinwheels. So me and Gunnar figure they was tradin' us for the hammer. We go back home and I get one of my Ma's small pewter plates, an Gunnar, he brings a couple of his toys he don't use no more. So we take 'em to the secret place and put 'em on the stump. We wait around a bit to see what happens, but no one comes. We go home, but the next day the stuff's gone and there's elven stuff in its place, like an elven shirt my size. An how did they know it would fit me?"

"You have an elven shirt?" Thorgil asked with some envy.

"Yeah," Brice grinned. "We been tradin' ever since. That's how I got this knife. I hope you don't mind I traded your bird for it."

"No," Thorgil said with a shake of his head. "Looks like you got the better deal." Realizing they were getting close to the forest that edged the Forbidden Zone, he said, "I better get back."

"You don't wanna see our secret place?" Brice said, disappointed.

"I can't," Thorgil replied, torn between responsibility and curiosity. "I don't have a lot of time to get my carving done before the contest." He turned to go and a weird feeling of satisfaction filled him. It was the satisfaction of making the right decision. His father always said, 'Do what you have to do now. No dwarf succeeds by wishing he had another opportunity."

"It won't take long," Brice urged. "We're almost there."

"Not today," Thorgil said, feeling like a grownup. "I got work to do. But I'll give you another of my small carvings and let you trade it for me."

"Honest?" Brice said, pleased with the trust.

"Honest," he answered.

The following day, Thorgil had done nothing but stare at the alabaster stone on his work bench, studying the blue coloration, the cloud like patterns and the seeming transparency of the stone.

By late afternoon, his father had come by and fussed at him. "The stone isn't going to cut itself. Get to work. Remember. Do what you have to do now."

"No dwarf succeeds by wishing he had another opportunity," Thorgil finished the proverb for him.

His father frowned and blinked at him, not sure whether he should be pleased or irritated that his son had been listening all this time.

"I know, Papa," Thorgil said. "It's just that I want to make sure I do it right. I've watched the stone cutters and some of them take over two days before they begin carving."

"Well you don't have two days," he father answered, but not quite as gruffly. "The contest is less than two weeks away." He ticked his head at the stone. "Think of something and get going, otherwise you'll rush and rushing never gets the job done right."

"I know, Papa. I think I know what I'm going to make."

"What?"

"A flower."

"It took you an entire day to figure that out?" His father cocked an eyebrow at him then saw Thorgil's look of defeat. "Never mind. Now that you know what it is, you can get to work."

Several days later, Thorgil was focused on the alabaster stone, carefully tapping the mallet against the chisel as he cut away bits of stone. Pausing to study his progress, he heard Brice at the window.

"Yer goin' deaf, Thorgil," Brice said. "I been callin' at ya for the past ten minutes. C'mere. I gotta show you what I got."

With hammer and chisel in hand, Thorgil walked over to lean out the window and look at Brice's latest trade.

"What is it?" he asked when he saw the strange contraption in the youngster's hands.

In the shape of a box, it was small enough to fit in both his hands. Made of thin strips of wood held together by tightly woven string, it had a wooden spring in the center that was attached to a two-sided blade on the top.

"It's some sort o' toy," he explained. "Ya wind this knob here," he said, turning it on its side to show a recessed handle, "an it winds the spring inside tight. Once the spring is tight, ya push this lever here on top and look it."

He released the lever and box lifted out of his hands, hovering a hand's width above his palms then slowly descended as the spring wound down.

"Ain't that somethin'?" Brice triumphantly said.

"I've never seen anything like it," Thorgil replied, amazed at the toy. "Do it again."

Only too happy to comply, Brice twisted the knob to wind the spring then released the lever. The box repeated the same demonstration.

"I bet if I had a bigger spring, I could make it stay up longer," Brice said.

"I suppose," Thorgil said. "What did you trade for it?"

"I traded that one stone you made of the hog."

Thorgil thought of the amount of time it took to carve the sculpture then looked at the toy in Brice's hands, knowing the toy would probably not last the week. Though it was well crafted, it was too delicate a toy to survive the hands of Brice.

"I got to get back to work," he said, reminding himself at the same time to think twice about giving his carvings away.

"Ya still gonna give me a carvin' to trade for ya?"

"Sure," he unconvincingly replied.

"When ya gonna come with me and Gunnar to the secret place?"

"After the contest," Thorgil answered. "I'll come then."

By the end of the week, the petals of the flower were taking shape. Thorgil's father now made it a point to check on his son's progress several times a day, each time offering words of encouragement tempered with realistic expectations.

"Remember who your competing against and don't be disappointed with the results. These carvers have been at it for years. You have talent, but they have experience."

"I know, Papa."

His father then said, "Tell that youngster Brice to leave you alone. You don't have time to waste with him. And while I'm thinking about it, where is he getting all these things he's bringing here to show you?"

Thorgil's palms began to sweat and his mouth went dry. "I don't know, Papa." It was almost the truth, for he'd never been to the secret place in the forest.

His father narrowed his gaze at him then sternly spoke. "Some of those things don't look dwarf made."

"I don't know, Papa. I haven't really been paying attention to him. He comes here to show me stuff, but my mind's on my carving. I can't even tell you all the stuff he's shown me."

Mollified, though doubtful, his father scratched his face through his thick beard. "Well, you tell him to leave you alone."

"I will, Papa."

The following day, Thorgil warned Brice that the adults were on to him and that he needed to be more careful about showing all the things he had.

"I talked to 'em," Brice said.

"Talked to who?"

"The elves," he replied with a confident grin.

Thorgil's jaw dropped. "You actually talked to them?"

"Yup. They're really nice. There was three of 'em 'bout your age. They was tall as I've ever seen."

"What did they say?"

"They asked if there was any more of the carvings 'cause they like them the best. Said there weren't a elf known who could carve like that."

Thorgil's pride grew and he was about to say he would make more when his father came up behind him.

"Get along with you, Brice. Thorgil's got no time to play. He's got work to do. I don't want you hanging around here. Go find some children your own age. Thorgil has to start earning his keep."

"Yes, Sir," Brice said, stung at the inference that he was just a child. Hadn't he talked with elves? What grownup could say the same thing? The only time the grownups had anything to do with elves was by fighting.

As Brice walked away, Thorgil's father said, "You're thirteen summers old now. You don't have time to play anymore. You keep working on your carving. Your mother and I talked and we think we can make some money with your carvings."

"Really?" he brightened.

"Yes," he smiled in reply. "I didn't want to admit it at first, but you've got a gift. Our family has always been brewers and coopers. This will be a first. Who knows, if it's done right, you might be able to make a living do it."

"Honest?"

"Honest," his father chuckled. "Now let's see what you have so far."

Thorgil held out the stone for his father who studied it silently for a bit then nodded. "You're coming along real good. What more are you going to do?"

"I've got to work the flower petals smooth and cut away so show veins on the leaves. I need to find a small enough rasp to smooth the petals."

"Well here," his father said, reaching into the apron pocket and pulling out three small rasps of varying sizes. "I made these for you. Hope they'll help."

Thorgil took the rasps and gazed down at them, hefting each one. They fit perfectly into his hands. "Thanks, Papa," he said and hugged his father.

"Now, now," his father admonished, pulling him away, though Thorgil saw the pride in his father's eyes. "Back to work."

"Yes, sir."

The day before their departure, Thorgil had risen early and wrapped his sculpture in soft cloth then in a more secure box for the journey to

Anghor. His father had yoked an ox to a small wagon used for short hauls of ale. Standing in the doorway, box securely in his arms, Thorgil kissed his mother goodbye and climbed up to sit next to his father. With a crack of the whip, the ox lurched forward, heading towards the great city of Anghor.

They had spent the night in a small tavern where his father pronounced the ale good, but not as good as theirs, carefully instructing his son in the finer points of why their ale was better.

Thorgil did his best to pay attention but his mind was on the contest. His father noted the disinterest and interpreted it as nerves.

The following morning, though Thorgil's stomach was too much in knots to want food, he forced himself to eat as he knew the day would be a long one. It was when they crested a small hill that he sucked in his breath, for in the distance Anghor rose like an impenetrable fortress with towering battlements and thick crenelated walls, all of which emerged out of the mountain as though it was part of the ancient peak.

A single wide road snaked its way to the main gate, which was wide enough for two wagons to pass. By the time they approached the massive portcullis, they were enmeshed in the throngs headed into the city. The gate was guarded by a single soldier on each side whose only function appeared to be to keep traffic moving.

Once past the gate, the road turned sharply left.

"That's to slow down an invading army," his father explained. "The road twists and turns until you get to the main part of the city, most of which is inside the mountain."

"Have you been here a lot?" Thorgil asked.

"Before you were born," he replied, "when I was a soldier fighting elves."

"Was there ever a time when we didn't hate elves?" he asked.

"Not in my lifetime," his father replied. Looking over to a shopkeeper in front of his produce, he pulled to a halt and called out, "Ho friend. Where can we find Carvers Walk?"

The shopkeeper was a plump dwarf with a curly beard that went down to the middle of his ample stomach.

"Ah," the shopkeeper's eyes brightened. "You're a carver then?"

"No, my son is."

"Your son?" he replied with a raised eyebrow. "The tad seems a bit young to be a carver."

"He may be young, but he has talent."

"No doubt, I'm sure," he politely replied the pointed up the road. "Keep to the main road until you get past the main barracks."

"I know it," his father nodded.

"Once past the barracks, take the road to the Guardian Hall. Carvers Walk is on the way."

"My thanks, friend." He flicked the reins and the cart moved forward, blending in to the crowd.

Thorgil's eyes were wide with wonder as he looked side to side at dwarves and wagons and soldiers all mixed going in all directions. Everyone seemed in a hurry.

"Where is everyone going, Papa?"

His father smiled in understanding. "Life here is not like at home where we take our time to do things. Here in the city, it seems that everyone needs everything right now."

As they approached the barracks, his father said, "This is where I lived for a while."

Thorgil looked up at his father. While his father often talked about his time in the army, it was always stories of life living in the barracks. To hear him tell it, life in the army was one of monotonous drills and exercises followed by drinking with friends.

"Papa," Thorgil ventured. "Did you ever have to go to war?"

"Yes," he replied, looking straight ahead.

"Did you have to kill elves?"

"Yes."

"Brice's father says it's an honor to be in the Dwarf Army. He said that to be in battle was glorious."

"War is only glorious to the living," his father quietly stated.

Thorgil gazed at the long barracks building that rose in layers like a pyramid. Soldiers stood guard outside the main doors, saluting officers as they entered or departed. Thorgil was disappointed as he imagined the barracks would be teeming with energy and activity. Instead, it was a solid drab grey stone edifice with little to recommend it.

Just past the barracks, the road split, one way leading straight towards thc main part of the city, the other slowly rising then disappearing into the mountain. His father steered the wagon to the road on the right.

No sooner had they passed the gaping gateway into the mountain that they entered a cavernous junction where at least a dozen roads went off in different directions. His father slowed the wagon to ask again for directions of an artisan dwarf for he wore the apron and collar of the guild.

"Pardon, friend. Might you direct us to Carvers Walk?"

"You're almost there," he smiled and pointed to the far left road. "Take that road. It's not more than 400 paces farther."

"Many thanks."

"Are you a carver?" the dwarf asked, his curiosity obvious. He scratched his cheek through his thick beard.

"My son is."

"Ah," he nodded. "Here to look over the pieces in the competition?"

"Looking to enter," his father answered.

"The lad's work?"

"Yes."

"Forgive my doubt, but might I see what he has?"

Bristling at the condescension, he turned to his son. "Show him."

Thorgil reached behind him and lifted the small box to his lap. Opening it, he unwrapped the carving and held it out to the dwarf, pleased at the change in expression.

The dwarf accepted the sculpture, scrutinizing it as he turned it over in his hands then looked up at Thorgil. "This is your work?"

"Yes, sir."

"You have talent, lad. This is exceptional work." He handed the carving back. "But there are masters with decades of experience who are competing. My advice to you is to enter the novice level where your work will be noticed."

"Thank you," he replied.

With an affable nod, the Dwarf walked off to one of the food vendor stalls that lined the edges of the great hall.

It was then that Thorgil noticed the aromas of baked meat pies and sweet desserts causing his stomach to growl.

"We'll get you entered first," his father counseled, "then we can find something to eat."

The dwarf who sat behind the wide registration desk was a no nonsense dwarf who gruffly said, "Step lively now. Are you here to gaze or compete?"

"Compete, sir," Thorgil answered.

"How old are you, lad?"

"Thirteen."

Frowning, he sighed. "Let's see what you have."

When Thorgil peeled back the layers of cloth surrounding the carving, the dwarf's attitude changed.

"This is your work?" he asked with some doubt.

"Yes it is," Thorgil's father answered for him.

"Hmmmm," the dwarf mused, studying the carving then Thorgil then back to the carving. "You're age should put you in the novice division, but your work far exceeds the level of talent found there. I'm going to put you in the intermediate division."

He pushed a piece of parchment towards Thorgil then twisted it around. "Fill out your name and the title of your piece."

Thorgil accepted the feathered pen and wrote his name, his father's name, town and title of the carving, which he simply called 'Flower.'

Accepting the registration, the dwarf quickly scanned it and placed it on a stack of other registrations. He then penned a small card with Thorgil's name and the title of the carving. Blowing on it to dry the ink, he handed card and carving to a young dwarf standing ready by the wall.

"Intermediate division," he announced then turned his attention to Thorgil.. "Good luck, lad. Next."

"When does the competition start," Thorgil's father asked.

"Tomorrow morning. Winners will be announced in the afternoon."

Nodding his thanks, his father led the way back to the wagon.

"You've got skills better than I imagined," he said, stepping up into the driver's seat. "Looks like your Ma was right."

"Can we look at the other carvings?" Thorgil asked.

"You sure you want to?"

"Why not?"

"Don't want you to get discouraged. They put you in an advanced division and you haven't had any schooling. There's bound to be a lot of talent there."

"I know," he replied. "I still want to see what's there.

"You don't want to eat first?"

Despite his stomach growling, Thorgil was too nervous to think about food. "We can eat after we see what's there."

Reluctantly agreeing, his father stepped back down and they made their way to the Judging Hall. The doors to the Hall were open and as they stepped in, Thorgil's eyes wandered in fascination over the hundreds of creations ranging from tall statures of horses to small pieces of finely crafted marble.

"Where's the intermediate section," his father asked one of the docents, an elder dwarf with thick grey beard.

"The competition Hall is divided into three parts," he explained. "Up front here is the expert division. Behind them is the intermediate then the novice."

Instead of going to the intermediate section, Thorgil led the way to the front section, stopping at the first sculpture, a female dwarf leaning forward on a small chair, arms on her thighs, head tilted as though staring intently at something. The work was incredibly lifelike and Thorgil lingered, studying the way the artist shaped the stone.

By the time they moved on to the next piece, his father was decidedly bored. "You take your time. I'm going to get something to eat. Meet me at the wagon when you're finished."

"OK, Papa," he replied, staring at a sculpture of a swan, wings spread wide as it landed on water.

While is father strolled off to find something to eat and a fine mug of ale, Thorgil marveled at the exquisite detail and movement of the creations. Instead of being intimidated by the talent, he was invigorated to see what could be accomplished and carved. Studying each piece caused him to envision his own work and how he could improve and become a master sculptor.

When he came to the intermediate section, he could see the difference in skill levels in the little things like details of the feathers on a swan's wing. An expert would spend the time distinguishing the downy barbs at the base from the rest of the feather, delicately carving each part. Intermediate carvers, though skilled, spent less time on detail.

Wandering up and down the aisles, he closely examined the intermediate pieces, nodding at selected carvings that got his attention. He paused before one exquisitely carved piece of a flower sculpted from alabaster. The detail was excellent, down to the veins on the leaves. It was a minute before he realized the piece he so liked was his own.

Packed amongst the crowd sitting on stone benches, Thorgil and his father waited for the three officious looking dwarves to finish their tabulations. Thorgil recognized the one dwarf from yesterday as the one who looked at his carving. Remembering the dwarf's praise, Thorgil hoped that would add to his chances of winning.

Clearing his throat, the older dwarf in the center tapped the result pages on the table, aligning the edges.

"We have the results of this year's competition. The entries were many and excellent. We'll begin with the novice class. In third place…"

Thorgil's nervous anticipation increased as the third place winner, a middle aged dwarf, made his way to the front, beaming with pride to receive his trophy and prize money. The same occurred for second and first place.

"Now on to the intermediate division," the head dwarf announced. "I must point out that the entries for this division were the most we've ever had, and the entries were all of outstanding skill, making our decisions quite difficult."

Thorgil frowned as the dwarf droned on. "Come on," he muttered.

The lead dwarf announced the third place winner and Thorgil's hopes rose as his name was not called. His hopes rose further when second place was called. He crossed his legs and his fingers waiting for his name to be called.

The lead dwarf cleared his throat and read loudly, "In first place in the intermediate division is Freydis Hammersmith."

Thorgil's heart sank and his shoulders slumped. His father patted his leg, whispering, "The competition was tough. You'll just have to try harder next year."

Thorgil's disappointment was so great that he contemplated asking his father if they could leave now. He looked up to see his father's attention focused on the dwarves up front behind the table. The dwarf they had met yesterday was speaking.

"Before we move on to the expert division, there is one more prize to be awarded in the intermediate division. Normally we award only three prizes, but we all agreed that this young carver's talent was so exceptional that he deserved recognition. This was his first competition and his talent was so strong that he was placed in the intermediate division instead of the novice division where all first time entries are placed. So, the honorable mention in the intermediate division goes to Thorgil Coopersmith."

Hearing his name, Thorgil's sour demeanor immediately sluffed away and he bounced up to receive his award.

"You have skill, lad," the lead dwarf told him. "You need some training to go with that skill. Have your father talk to us after the program."

"Yes, Sir," Thorgil said, grinning so much that his ears began to ache.

The program ended, Thorgil and his father waited for the crowd to disperse. One of the judges noticed them and waved them over.

"You are his father?"

"Aslauf Coopersmith," Thorgil's father replied.

"I see where he gets some of his talent," the dwarf said kindly. "I've seen the craftsmanship of your barrels. Some are works of art in themselves."

"You are most kind," Aslauf replied, pleased to know his barrels commanded the attention of those here in the capital.

"Is your ale as good?"

"I'll send you a barrel and you can decide for yourself," Aslauf grinned.

"Ha! Well said, my friend. Walk with me as we determine the future of your gifted son. Stay here," he said to Thorgil, "or study the sculptures of the experts. See what they have that you might be missing."

His spirits soaring, Thorgil watched them meander away, chatting and friendly. He wondered what it all meant and how he would learn to be a better artist. Would he become an apprentice to a master? The thought excited and worried him for it meant leaving the security and warmth of his home.

It was as he was closely examining the foot of a sculpture of a stag that he heard his father and the master carver approach.

"It's been decided, lad," the dwarf said. "You'll come here to apprentice under me."

Thorgil's mouth slacked open in joy then quickly closed when he saw his father's pride edged with sadness.

"We'll go home first," his father explained, "to get your things. Then we'll come back here."

"There's no rush," the Master Carver said. "Take a week or two if you need."

"Thank you," Aslauf replied, "but when we Coopersmiths make a decision we see it through. It's like they say, any decision no matter good or bad, is always better than no decision."

"Well said, Master Coopersmith. You can rest assured that your young prodigy will have the best tutors and masters available. He will be like my own son."

On the drive home, his father was unusually quiet. Not wanting to intrude, Thorgil kept to his own thoughts. They were halfway home before his father spoke.

"I'm very proud of you, Thorgil," he said, looking straight ahead, the reins slack in his hands. "There's never been a member of our family or clan who has been recognized like you have. It is quite an honor and well deserved."

"Thank you, Papa."

His father paused and licked his lips. "I know I doubted you at first, but when I saw what you could do, I was more surprised than anything else. We've always been coopers, barrel makers. Never had an artist in the family."

"But, Papa," Thorgil pointed out. "He knew all about your barrels.

He said they were works of art themselves."

His father smiled with pride. "That's because we make our barrels like an artist carves a sculpture." He laughed at the thought then looked affectionately at his son. "I suppose you being an artist isn't all that odd, now that I think about it."

Flicking the reins, he said, "We best get you home and let everyone know my son won an award in the nation's stone carving contest."

When their wagon approached the town, few paid attention other than to wave in friendly recognition. The burgomaster, who was weeding the garden in front of his bungalow, looked up as they passed. Seeing their friendly yet nondescript expressions, he assumed the worst and went back to weeding.

"It's best this way," his father whispered, leaning over to him. "When you become famous, they'll treat you differently."

Back home, his father related the success then warned everyone to keep it to themselves.

"Why, Papa," and older brother asked.

"Because success breeds jealousy," he replied. "Let Thorgil go to Anghor and make a reputation for himself. Nothing overcomes jealousy better than quiet success."

The next morning, Thorgil was at his workbench collecting and cleaning his tools when he heard his name whispered at the window. Looking up, he saw Brice.

"How'd ya do?" Brice asked.

"I did OK," he evasively answered.

"Ya wanna go to the tradin' spot this mornin'?"

"Can't," he answered. "I have to clean my tools and equipment."

"That can wait until later," Brice complained. "You gotta come now. I left some stuff yesterday and I'm hopin' to get another elf shirt. If its' too big fer me, you can have it."

The thought of an elven shirt caught Thorgil's attention. Casting a quick glance around the shop, he figured he'd be gone for less than an hour, barely enough time for them to notice he was missing.

Taking special care not to be seen, the two young dwarves skirted the town and headed to the forest and Brice's secret trading spot. Once in the forest, Brice led the way, snaking his way around trees and clumps of bushes, backtracking and sidetracking to ensure they hadn't been followed.

"Is it much farther?" Thorgil asked, beginning to get anxious about being away too long.

"Naw," Brice confidently replied. "We're almost there."

His space slowed to a creep and Thorgil could see a break in the forest, as the Forbidden Zone opened up in a long strip that separated the elven domain from the dwarves. Trees had been hurriedly cut down and only the splintered stumps remained.

Brice hunkered down and pointed to a low flattened stump with several items on it. One looked to be a piece of clothing.

"There," he quietly exclaimed, pointing. "Looks like they left us some stuff. C'mon."

Thorgil hesitated. "How do you know it's safe?"

"Don't be a scared chicken," Brice sniffed. "I been comin' here all the time. Ain't seen anybody ever."

While Brice stood up and nonchalantly strolled to the middle of the barren strip of land and bent down to examine his prize. Thorgil hesitated then eased out into the open, finally ending up beside Brice.

"Look at this," Brice said, his eyes bright as he held up an elven shirt.

"It's beautiful," Thorgil said when he had a sudden feeling that they were being watched. "I think we need to go, now."

"Just a minute," Brice said, ignoring him. "What's this?"

He held up a wooden carving of a horse then handed it to Thorgil.

Seeing the carving, Thorgil forgot his nervousness and held up the carving, studying it. "It's not bad," he commented. "The artist didn't use the grain very well and you can see where his tool is not sharp for there are tiny cuts burrs that can't be sanded smooth."

They both jumped when a deep voice called out, "And you can do better."

Panicked, the two dwarves snapped their heads to see a troop of elves emerge from both sides of the forest. They were armed with swords and bows and arrows.

Brice began wailing in fear, streams of tears pouring down his face.

A tall elf approached, towering over them. He wore thin and supple green armor that blended with the forest colors. His long blond hair was secured behind his head by a simple leather headband.

"Do not cry little one," he said. "Unlike dwarves, we do not kill children."

"We don't kill children either," Thorgil stubbornly stated.

"You are not old enough to remember," the elf sternly replied. Looking back at the edge of the forest bordering the elven domains, he said, "Bring him out."

Two elves physically escorted a young elf who did not look pleased to be there. He was scruffily dressed, his hair a tangled mess and dirt smudges on his face. He looked to be Thorgil's age.

"Do you recognize this dwarf?" the older elf demanded, pointing to Thorgil.

"No," he said, giving Thorgil a quick once over. "I recognize him." He ticked his head at the sniffling Brice.

The older elf held out his hand. In it was a delicate carving of a small bird.

"Hey, that's mine," Thorgil blurted.

The older elf frowned and looked at Thorgil. "Are you saying your friend here stole this from you?"

"No, I gave it to him."

"Then it is *not* yours," he pointed out.

"I didn't mean it like that. I meant I made it. I carved it," Thorgil explained.

The frown deepened and the elf turned his attention to Thorgil. "You carved this?"

"Yes," he defiantly answered, irritated that grownups, not matter elf or dwarf, always doubted him.

'He really did," Brice said, his sniffling slowed. "I watched him do it."

The elf held the carving up, twisting it slowly in his hands. He then gazed directly at Thorgil. "We shall see. Bring them along."

Brice erupted again in tears while Thorgil's apprehension morphed to anxiety.

"But I'm supposed to go apprentice to a carving master," he exclaimed.

"You should have thought about that when you entered our domain," the elf replied over his shoulder.

"But this is the Forbidden Zone," Thorgil objected. "It doesn't belong to anyone."

"It did once," the elf tartly replied.

The trip through the forest was tedious. While Brice's wailing had diminished to a constant whimper, Thorgil tried to remember the direction of their travel, but soon gave up as he could see no recognizable reason for their sudden turns and shifts. One thing he did notice was the size of the trees increased in both height and thickness. Some trees were so thick that twenty dwarves with their arms outstretched couldn't encircle them.

Abruptly they stopped in the middle of a small clearing surrounded by the grandest trees Thorgil had ever seen. Above them, the branches intertwined so thickly that shafts of sunlight looked like brilliant swords slicing through to the earth.

Thorgil watched as an elf pressed what looked like a large coin against a part of a tree and the outline of a door appeared, widening as the door opened. The older elf led the way inside and soon Thorgil found himself climbing steps in a circular stairwell, wonderfully carved out of the interior of the tree.

By the time they reached the next door, Thorgil's legs burned from the climb.

As he passed through the doorway, his eyes widened in wonder for spread out before him was a town teeming with elves. Paths between trees were suspended wooden bridges that did not sway or move despite the amount of foot traffic. There were carts pulled by oxen, elves on horses, flocks of goats and sheep all moving and flowing in this world about the ground.

Brice took one look and grabbed Thorgil's arm.

"Take them to the Great Hall," the older elf commanded. "Lord Rimuel will decide their fate."

At that command, burlap grain sacks were roughly jammed over their heads and their hands tied behind them. Brice began wailing again.

"Do all dwarves bellow so much?" an elven voice complained.

Guided by firm hands gripping their arms, Thorgil tried counting steps and turns, but gave up when he realized he had no clue where they were to begin with, and the resonance of the city overlapped despite his best efforts to identify sounds. At one point, the noise of the city faded, followed by being led up a long set of hard stairs.

After more twists and turns, they stopped and their covers removed. They found themselves in a room cleverly crafted of intertwined branches, the only light coming through the small gaps in the ceiling. The door closed behind them.

Brice huddled in the corner and shivered with fear, his arms wrapped around his knees.

Thorgil knew he should be terrified, especially after all the stories his father had told him. Elves were their hated enemies. Nothing an elf did was ever good. An elf's sole reason for existence was to destroy everything the dwarves held dear. The only good elf was a dead elf. Thorgil could recite the litany of diatribes against elves.

Yet this place was magical. There was nothing in all Rachdale like this. He touched a branch in the wall and jumped back when it moved, tightening against the neighboring branches, filling in gaps.

The door opened and an elf blocked the light. "You," he said pointing to Thorgil, "come with me. You, little one," he addressed Brice, "will stay here."

This caused Brice to wail until the elf commanded in a loud voice, "Silence. I heard dwarves were brave, so act like one." He spun around and led the way.

Thorgil followed the elf through the hallways, whose walls and ceilings were intertwined branches worn smooth from centuries of touch. Midway down one hallway, the elf stopped before a thick door and knocked then opened the door, ushering the young dwarf inside.

Thorgil found himself standing before an older elf with long hair that had once been blond but was now reveling streaks of grey. He sat behind a wide table. Before him were several small sculptures that Thorgil recognized as his.

"You claim these are yours," the elf said, though not unkindly.

"Yes. I carved them."

The elf stroked his smooth chin. "You will understand when I say that I have reservations as to your truthfulness."

"Why should I lie?" Thorgil defiantly replied. "Who are you?"

An elf guard gave him a not so gentle tap on the head. "Watch your tone, young elf. This is Lord Rimuel, the ruler of this part of Elvenhome."

"My apologies, Sir," Thorgil said, rubbing his head. "You said you didn't believe that I carved those. Give me the right tools and stone and I'll prove it to you."

"That is my intent," Rimuel said, leaning forward.

Before he realized what had happened, Thorgil found himself standing before a workbench not unlike the one at home, except the bench was at eye level.

"How am I supposed to do anything? I can't even see the top of the bench. Don't you have a smaller bench?"

"We're elves, not dwarves," came the reply. A step stool was brought in and Thorgil ascended so that the table was waist high. On the table were tools and rasps and a piece of white alabaster.

Examining the tools, he was surprised at their quality. Unfortunately, they were large and unwieldly. "I need smaller tools," he groused. "I'm a dwarf, not an elf."

While they sent off to find appropriate tools, Thorgil studied the stone. It was cut in a truncated pyramid. Tilting his head, an image emerged from the stone and he knew what he had to carve.

Looking back at the older elf, he said, "What happens when I finish this?"

"It depends on what you craft," Rimuel replied. "You and your friend's lives depend on it." Folding his arms, he stared down at the diminutive dwarf, leaving Thorgil dumbstruck and flustered.

When an elf returned with dwarf sized tools, Thorgil swallowed hard. Then he blinked and tightened his lips, taking a deep breath. If his life depended on this carving, then he would show them just who he was. He would carve them a sculpture they would never forget.

"I need to be alone," he ordered. "If I am to carve this piece, I don't want to be interrupted or disturbed. No one is to see this until it is finished. Is that agreed?"

"That is reasonable," the Rimuel nodded. "But be warned. You only have so much time to complete this. Any longer than necessary and your lives are forfeit. And do not think of trying to escape. You are high above the forest floor and the entrances are guarded. Besides," he grimly smiled, "if you slip, it is a long way to the bottom."

"How long do I have?"

The elder elf gazed at the stone. "You will have fifteen days. At the end of fifteen days, your creation will determine your fate."

"What about my friend?"

"Your friend will be well cared for while you work." Standing to full height, he towered over Thorgil like a colossus. "It is time you began."

It took fourteen days for Thorgil to carve his sculpture, each time refusing to allow anyone to see his progress. He slept and ate in the workshop and quickly covered the artwork any time the door creaked open.

Lord Rimuel came by on two occasions, each time peering in to see Thorgil hunched over his creation like someone possessed.

It was late when Thorgil was finally satisfied. Covering the art work, he let out a sigh of relief that he had completed the work in time. Leaping down from the stool, he walked to the door and banged on it.

"I'm finished," he announced when the door opened.

The tall guard gazed down at him then up to the table where the carving lay beneath the covering. Giving Thorgil a silent nod, he closed the door.

Thorgil heard him say something in elvish to another elf followed by silence.

Pacing the floor, he fretted about his fate. He knew he was a good carver, but suppose they didn't like what he had created? Maybe they didn't know real art. They were elves after all, sworn enemies of Dwarves. His father's words came back to him: "The only good elf is a dead elf."

Thorgil's jaw slacked at the thought that maybe this was a trick. Maybe they kept him captive here to carve this making him think that he would be freed, but they would kill him in the end. This was all just a game for them, a game to torture him because he was a dwarf.

Then he thought of his carving and began berating himself for being so stupid as to think that his creation would make any difference. His mind reeling, he decided to destroy his work. He would not give them the satisfaction of his creation.

His foot was on the stool when the door opened and Lord Rimuel walked in.

Rimuel glanced briefly at Thorgil then at the covered artwork on the table. "Let us see what this dwarf has created." His tone dripped disdain and superiority.

Stepping briskly to the table, he lifted the covering and startled at the craftsmanship of the piece. Yet he was more surprised at the subject, for Thorgil had carved an intricate stone bridge. Beneath the bridge, flanked on both sides by bushes and trees, water flowed in a calm current. A hare gamboled by the stream. On the other side of the stream, a wolf sat on its haunches, watching in curiosity.

Yet the elder's attention was drawn to the two figures on the bridge. One was a dwarf, his hand pointing at some unseen thing in the distance. He seemed to be smiling, extraordinarily pleased about something.

Next to him was an elf, bent over so that one arm rested on the bridge railing. With his other arm, he rested a hand on the dwarf's shoulder, his head tilted back as he laughed.

Rimuel stared at the work, sucked in his breath, turned and, without a word, walked out, the door closing ominously behind him.

Swallowing the lump in his throat, Thorgil stood blinking and bewildered. He had yet to close his mouth when the door opened and two elves entered.

"Follow me," the one elf said while the other picked up the carving.

"Be careful with that," Thorgil cautioned. "It's not a toy."

"Relax, little one," the elf said. "No harm will come to your creation."

Thorgil relaxed and then replayed what the elf said. "No harm will come to *your* creation." He didn't say no harm would come to him.

He suppressed his fear as he followed them down the hallways, but his apprehension grew when he realized they were leading him back to the lock-in place.

Pausing outside the gaol, the elf not holding the carving opened the door and pushed Thorgil in.

Brice leaped up as his friend entered. "Thorgil," he exclaimed. "What are they going to do to us?"

"I don't know," he nervously replied as the door shut behind them.

"Are they going to kill us?" Brice sobbed and began to cry.

"Stop it," Thorgil said with a worried frown. "You can't start crying every time you get scared."

"But they're going to kill us," he moaned.

"We don't know that," Thorgil said though doubting his own words. Pacing the floor, he accidently touched a branch which quickly twisted to tighten against other branches in the wall. He looked at Brice and asked, "Have you tried escaping?"

"I tried," he sniffled. "Every time I touch a part of the wall, it closes in and gets tighter. The only way out is the door and it's always guarded." He sat back in the corner and wrapped his hands around his knees.

Thorgil continued pacing until he tired and sat next to Brice.

They were awoken when the door opened and an elf placed a meal tray on the floor. Behind him, daylight spread outside and shafts of light pierced the gaps of the gaol. The meal deposited, he closed the door.

Thorgil stood, yawned and stretched then went over to see what was for breakfast. Steam curled from plates filled with eggs and sausage. There was also a small loaf of warm bread. Sitting down, he hungrily devoured his meal.

"You better eat," Thorgil told Brice. "As long as they're feeding us, we're OK."

"I'm not hungry," Brice said though Thorgil could hear his stomach growl.

Lifting the tray, he carried it over to Brice, placing it in front of him.

"If we're going to try and escape, we have to be strong. You can't be strong if you don't eat." He held out the plate to him.

Brice took the plate and half-heartedly picked at the sausage. Yet once he had a mouthful, his hunger overcame his moroseness and he stuffed his mouth full.

His meal finished, Thorgil resumed his pacing. He continued until his restricted journeying was interrupted by the midday meal. This time Brice needed no urging and gobbled down the meat and potatoes. There were even mugs of cold cider.

It was not long after the meal that Brice sat and leaned against the wall. For the first time, the branches did not tighten and he found it curious. Twisting to look, he found the gap wide enough to slip a few fingers through. Leaning back, he quickly realized that this part of the wall had the dull flatness of dead branches. Picking up his dinner knife, he jabbed it into the branch.

"This is dead," he softly exclaimed, pointing to the chisel marks on the branch. "We can escape from here."

His spirit soaring, he focused his attention on stabbing, scrapping and cutting away at the branch, but the wood was harder than he realized and though dead, it would yield little to his efforts. By mid-afternoon, he had barely widened the original gap.

He was mid-thrust when the door opened and an elf stepped in.

Casting a stern gaze at Brice, frozen in place, he said, "That wood is elvish oak. You will be old and gray before you cut through that with a kitchen knife. It takes a special saw with razor teeth to make use of the wood. But that is the least of your concerns." He stepped aside. "Come little ones. Your fate has been decided."

Debating whether to hold on to the knife in case he needed a weapon, Brice knew it was useless and flipped the knife to the floor, and then followed Thorgil who had boldly stepped outside where another elf waited.

"Follow me," the elf commanded and turned to lead the way.

They traveled out the Great Hall and through the gates then on the road for some distance as it went into the town, turning onto so many different side roads that Thorgil lost sense of direction. Yet his fascination held as they passed homes and businesses filled with more elves than he would ever see in a lifetime. As they passed, the cacophony of daily life would slip to a silent standstill as elven heads would turn to follow them, their eyes suspicious that two young dwarves were here among the elven clan. Once past, the noise would resume in sibilant whispers that trailed behind them.

After more than two hours of winding and twisting and, Thorgil was sure had been a tortuous circle, they came to a door in a large oak. Two dwarves were waiting for them, two small packs in their hands. Hoisting the packs to their shoulders, they led the way through the door that led to a narrow set of circular stairs that descended from the platform.

"Where are we going?" Thorgil asked.

"You will discover that when we get there," one elf replied.

As they began their descent, Thorgil startled when he realized that he didn't have his sculpture.

"What about my carving?" he pleaded.

"It remains here," an elf firmly replied.

Pausing to cast one last look back, Thorgil found himself not so gently nudged down the steps.

To the two young dwarves, the trip down was as tiring as their trip up, yet soon enough, they found themselves at ground level, standing outside.

"Come," the elf said, leading the way.

This time, Thorgil was certain they were traveling in a circle, for he swore that they passed the same tree at least four times, yet each time they passed it, the ground looked unfamiliar.

It was as they approached the Forbidden Zone, that he recognized the splintered stumps of those by his homeland. His heart soaring, his pace quickened.

"Slow down little one," an elf chuckled. "We are almost there, but we must negotiate first."

"Negotiate? What does that mean?" Brice asked.

"You will see."

They edged up to the end of the forest and Thorgil felt firm hands grasp him at the shoulders.

"Do not do anything stupid, little one," a voice warned.

Across the gap, Thorgil saw several dwarves, among them, his father. His relief flooded within and he chaffed under the steel grip of the elf. He gave a quick wave, hoping his father would see.

"Are you prepared to trade?" a deep dwarven voice called out.

"Yes," an elf called back.

"Let us see them."

Thorgil felt himself rising as the elf effortlessly lifted him in the air, stepping slightly forward to display his prisoner. He then stepped back and called out, "Let us see him."

A young elf calmly stepped out into the Zone. He stood erect, with bright eyes that spoke humor. He then stepped back

"Are you ready to exchange?" an elf said.

"Yes."

There was but a moment's hesitation as the elf held captive by the dwarves bent down and retrieved a small chest. He gave the dwarves a cheery wave then nonchalantly strode out into the Zone.

While the elf made his way across the Forbidden Zone, Thorgil and Brice were handed a pack each. The elf gave Thorgil a sealed letter.

"Give this to your king. Do not let anyone else give it to him. It must be you." he said then returned to the protection of the forest.

Thorgil and Brice hurried to cross the forbidden zone, passing by the grinning elf as he languidly made his way to the safety of the elven forest.

Once across, Thorgil's father swept him up into his arms, tears spilling forth. "I feared you were dead."

"I'm sorry, Papa," Thorgil replied, full of remorse.

"It's alright now," his father said, wiping his tears away with the heels of his palms. "You're home, safe. That's what matters."

Thorgil hugged him then noticed the many dwarves hiding in the bushes close by. Frowning, he turned to gaze across the forbidden zone to see countless elves emerging form hiding spots then disappear into the forest.

"I've got a message for the king," Thorgil said, holding up the envelope.

The dwarf commander reached for the envelope, but Thorgil clutched it to his chest. "They told me I had to do it."

Nodding acceptance, the commander led them away from the Forbidden Zone.

Thorgil and his father stood in the doorway of the great throne room. Perched on the marble throne, gilded in gold and silver, the king looked over towards the doorway and motioned them forward.

"You are Aslauf Coopersmith?" he said to Thorgil's father.

"Yes, Sire," Aslauf answered, placing his hands on Thorgil's shoulders, "and this is my son, Thorgil."

Thorgil felt the strength of his father's hands and the pride in his voice.

Thorgil gazed up at the monarch. He was a stout dwarf with strong arms and a russet colored beard that went to the middle of his stomach. His long hair was thick and fell to his shoulders. His eyes had the sparkle of one constantly amused with life

Noticing the young dwarf staring at his head, the king said, "You're probably wondering why I'm not wearing a crown." He leaned forward and cocked an eyebrow. "Truth is, the blasted thing's uncomfortable. I only wear it when I need to impress someone. I don't need to impress you, do I?"

"No, Sir," Thorgil blinked in reply.

Aslauf leaned down and whispered in his son's ear. "Sire. Address him as 'Sire.' He's the king."

"No, Sire," Thorgil said, feeling his father's reassuring squeeze on his shoulder

The king flashed a smile then eyed Thorgil curiously. "I hear you have been among the elves."

"Yes, Sire," Thorgil politely answered.

"I've been told me that you have a message for me?"

"Yes, Sire."

"May I see it?" he smiled.

"Of course, Sire."

Thorgil started forward when his father held him back. A steward came and took the envelope then climbed the steps and handed the envelope to the king.

Breaking the seal, he pulled out the note.

To His Majesty, Vestar Silvercoat
King of the Dwarves,

This young dwarf is of unequaled talent and possesses the heart of innocence. It would be a pity to the future of both dwarves and elves should he fall in some foolish battle devised by those whose hatred surpasses their wisdom.

Protect him and keep him safe. Perhaps one day his kind will prevail.

The king reread the note then folded it and placed it back in the envelope. Standing, he handed the envelope to his steward.

"Keep this safe for me. I'll want to study this later."

Stepping down from the dais, he walked to stand in front of Thorgil and his father. "Well Coopersmith," he said to Aslauf though looking at Thorgil, "you've an interesting son."

"I know," Aslauf smiled.

Shifting his glance from one to the other, the King finally rested his gaze upon Thorgil.

"Walk with me," he said, his voice kind and fatherly. "Tell me all you know about elves."

Fathers and Sons: Part II

pdmac

Sordyr ambled among the market stalls, pausing as he heard an elf and his wife bickering about the husband's lack of barter skills.

"I'm a warrior, not a merchant," the elf sternly spoke. "You knew that when we married."

"We still have to eat," she protested.

"Then you handle it, like you always have and let me do what I am destined to do."

"There you go again,' she sighed, "you and your destiny. Destiny doesn't put food on the table."

"I am paid just like every other warrior," he huffed.

"Good morning, Master Jandir," Sordyr smiled, interrupting the husband and wife spat.

The elf's irritation vanished when he saw his customer. "Good morning, Prince Sordyr," he said with respect.

"*Prince* Sordyr? A bit formal aren't we?" he grinned. Before Jandir could reply, Sordyr held up a handful of silverware. "I've four settings here, looking to trade. Take a look. They're solid silver."

"The last time we traded," Jandir warily regarded him, "we discovered the Moonling crest on the back of the serving plate."

"Now, now," he said, holding up his hands in defense. "You can't blame me. I'm merely the middle man. Besides," he leaned in confidentially, "these have no markings at all." He handed a spoon to the wife who eyed the settings with more than idle curiosity.

"What do you want for them?" she asked.

"Now wait a minute," Jandir blurted.

His wife gave him a firm stare. "You're a warrior, remember? I'll handle this, like I always do."

"You have the best grain I can find," Sordyr complimented. "Don't know who your miller is, but he does a superb job."

"We mill it ourselves," she said with pride.

"Why am I not surprised," Sordyr said with overt admiration.

"I'll give you half a peck for them," she said.

"Half a peck?" Sordyr repeated in mock horror. "These are worth a kenning at least."

The wife studied him for a moment then said, "A peck. That's the best I can do."

Sordyr frowned as though calculating the exchange then relaxed and smiled. "Done. You drive a hard bargain, Eolin."

Smiling with self-satisfaction, Eolin lifted two half-peck sacks and placed them on the counter while Sordyr deposited the silverware next to them.

"You two have a wonderful day," Sordyr smiled as he cradled a grain sack in each arm.

"Shouldn't you be sword training or something back at the Hall?" Jandir said.

Sordyr smirked and leaned closer. "I should be, but this is far more fun. Besides, I'd rather be with the good and honest down-to-earth folks like you and Eolin than back there with all those stuffed shirts who think they're better than everyone else because they have a job where they can sit on their butts all day. Good day to you both."

Nonchalantly merging into the ebb and flow of pedestrians and merchants, he grinned when he heard Eolin exclaim, "Pity there aren't more elves like him back at the Hall."

Halfway down Merchants Alley, he stopped by a dealer in pewter and copper to admire some of the ale steins and cookware.

"You've some fine pieces here," he complimented.

The merchant looked up, saw the sacks of grain in his arms and gave him an indulgent smile. "Good day to you Sordyr. Out bartering I see."

"I've a peck of fine ground grain here. I'm willing to part with half a peck." He placed the sacks on the table, untied the leather strip to one of the sacks and opened the mouth.

The merchant peered in nodding in approval. "And where did we come by this quantity of such high quality grain?"

Sordyr grinned and shrugged. "Always working in trades. What will you give me for this excellent grain? I'm sure the missus can make any number of mouth-watering pies or desserts with this. You might even trade or sell some of her meat pies. I know she's quite good for I've had her starling pie."

"You're a clever one," the merchant smiled. Appraising the grain in the bag, he reached behind him and selected four pewter steins. "That's the best I can do."

Sordyr lifted and inspected each stein then nodded in agreement. "Done."

The merchant retied the sack and set it below the counter. "I'm surprised your father lets you spend so much time away from the Hall."

Sordyr leaned in and whispered, "He doesn't know I'm here. I'm supposed to be studying battle campaigns and such. You've never been bored in your life until you sit in a mind-numbing lecture as one of the tutors drones on about ancient battles. By the gods, all the motivation for battle can be summed up in three words: we hate dwarves."

The merchant chuckled, knowing better than to get into a discussion of why elves hated dwarves. He had tried that once with Sordyr and the young elf just couldn't get it through his thick skull. To Sordyr, dwarves were nothing more than additional trading possibilities… as if a dwarf could ever have something an elf would want, the merchant sniffed.

"What will you do with the ale steins?" the merchant asked, changing the subject.

"Trade," he grinned back. He turned and jittered to a halt. Standing sternly in front of him was an older elf a half-head taller than Sordyr, with long strait blond hair, secured with a simple leather band.

"You're not where you're supposed to be," the elf said with irritated formality.

"Hullo Fingol," Sordyr lamely greeted the elf. "What brings you here?"

"Your father will not be happy when he finds you gone again." He motioned with his hand to lead the way back to the woodland Great Hall.

"He doesn't need to know, does he?" Sordyr asked, hoping Fingol would again keep his secret.

"He already knows," came the stiff reply.

"Oh," he winced, realizing Fingol had probably received a tongue lashing before hurrying here to find him. "Sorry."

In too short a time, Sordyr, the four pewter steins and the half peck of grain still in his hands, stood before his father who stood behind his desk, an unfurled scroll spread across the top, the two ends anchored by small exquisite carvings. Fingol stood by the doorway.

His face the mask of subdued and cold anger, his father stood to full height and folded his arms. "You continue to flaunt your place in this kingdom. Instead of training to assume your rightful position and role, you purposely neglect your studies, avoid all responsibilities and cause good elves like Fingol to receive punishment that belongs to you. When you're not wasting your time playing chess, you're sneaking out to spend time among the merchants. You are doing everything except be the son of an elven chief."

"I'm good at trading and making deals, father," he said before his father raised a hand to silence him.

"I didn't raise you to be a merchant," he said, leaning forward and scowling. "You are no longer a child, but an elf who has come of age. If a merchant is what you want to be, then I will not stop you.. But know this, there are no merchants in my house." Standing straight again, he called out, "Guards."

Two warrior elves stepped past Fingol to stand on either side of Sordyr.

"Escort him to the gate and see that he does not come back. He is a merchant and not a son of mine."

"But father," Sordyr blurted, stunned. "What am I to do? Where am I to go?"

Locking his eyes on his son, he said, "You should have thought about that when you decided to become a merchant." Turning his back on Sordyr, he slowly walked to stand before the open window and gaze out upon the vista of the courtyard and spreading tees beyond the living walls.

"But father," Sordyr pleaded to no avail as his father's silence stirred the guards into action and they physically dragged Sordyr out of the room.

The last words to echo from the hallway were Sordyr's as his voice rose in anger. "What kind of father are you?"

A thick silence settled in the room before Fingol cleared his throat. "M'Lord?"

"Follow him," he said without turning from the window. "Keep him safe, but do not let him know you are there. Find out where he got these carvings." He ticked his head at the two alabaster statues holding the scroll down. "Those are not elven carvings. I want to know where he got them and who gave them to him."

"Yes, m'Lord."

Fingol hurried down the hall then out the doors to stride across the wide path to his rooms in the walls of the Great Hall. Bursting into the room, he unlocked his safety chest and withdrew a small bag of coins then gave chase to Sordyr. He found him stalking along the road not far from the gates, heading towards the merchants quarter.

Sordyr sensed someone was following him and turned to see Fingol catching up. Thinking his father had changed his mind, he relaxed. "Father send you to apologize?"

Fingol gave him a quizzical look then shook his head. "You are his son, yet you know nothing of your father."

Sordyr's mouth slacked open and his eyes widened. "He really means to go through with this?"

It was Fingol's turn to be flummoxed. "So it's his fault you disobey him?"

"He smothers me," he retorted. "And he doesn't understand me."

"What's to understand?" Fingol snapped.

"That I'm not a warrior like him," he said, his voice rising. "I have other skills."

"Like trading?"

"I prefer to see it more like negotiating," he loftily replied.

The epiphany hit Fingol and he let out an exasperated sigh. "Damn you, boy. You think your father doesn't know your skills?"

"What are you talking about?"

"Bah," Fingol exclaimed and spun around to march back to the Hall.

Sordyr stuck a hand on his arm to stop him but Fingol shook it off.

"What?"

Fingol stopped and glared at him. "You only see trading as a means of making money."

"What else is there?"

Fingol shook his head at him with pity. "There's more to this world than money."

"Oh, that's right," he scornfully said. "We hate dwarves. Dwarves are the cause of our misery. Death to dwarves. Have I got them all?"

"And what would you propose?"

"How about we talk to them? Negotiate."

Fingol fixed him with an intense stare. "It takes someone with skills to do that."

"I could do that," he scoffed.

"All you know about is trading grain for pewter steins," he shot back.

"There's skill in that and what I don't know, I can learn."

"What do you think your father was trying to do?" he said, giving him a look that said Sordyr was an idiot.

"What are you talking about? All he wanted me to do was sit in boring lectures about ancient battles."

"If you don't know our past, how can you be a part of our future?" Fingol lectured. "You were supposed to learn all those battles so that if or when the time came for negotiations you would understand your enemy."

"There's your and *his* problem," Sordyr bristled. "Knowing the past is one thing. Living there is quite another. You spend so much time going over old hatred that it clouds everything you see today."

"You just don't get it, do you," Fingol snapped. "You're an elven prince. You need to act like one."

"Not anymore, remember?" Sordyr shot back. Suddenly the overt reality that he had no home, no place to go and no resources to even pay for a meal hit hard and his shoulders slumped in defeat. "What am I going to do?"

"You should have thought about that before you decided to go your own way," Fingol replied.

"You've said that already," he tartly replied. "I get it. I'm a jerk, a lousy son. OK? Satisfied? Now what do I do?"

Fingol was about to answer when his attention was diverted by two small dwarves with sacks over their heads being led by two tall elves towards the gate. Sordyr turned to see what he was looking at.

"Dwarves?" he gasped. "What are they doing here?"

"They're young," Fingol remarked. "Probably lost their way in the forest." Dismissing them form his mind, he turned to Sordyr. "Where did you get those carvings on your father's desk?"

"I traded for them," he answered, still watching the dwarves as their little legs tried to keep pace with the elves.

"With whom?"

"Someone in the forest," he evasively answered.

"Dwarves?"

"Might be," he shrugged.

"Did you see them?"

"No."

"Then how do you know they were dwarves?"

"Because I set things to trade in the Forbidden Zone."

"You were in the forbidden zone?" Fingol said, aghast.

Sordyr looked down at the four steins and decided he could get more for them in another way. "Not for long," he nonchalantly replied before heading away from the great hall.

"Where are you going?"

"What's it to you?" he sneered. "I'm a merchant, remember?"

Fingol followed in the distance as Sordyr made his way to one of the stairwell-trees not far from the great hall, watching him disappear into the opening. Once he disappeared, Fingol quickened his pace and entered the tree, stopping at the landing and listening to footsteps echoing below him.

Descending the tree tower to the ground, Sordyr stealthily made his way east to the Forbidden Zone to where the trading stump always yielded good trades for him.

Approaching the cleared out area between the two kingdoms, he hunkered down to watch for movement on the other side. After a while, his boredom got the better of him and he did one last scan before standing and sauntering over to the stump.

He was disappointed when there was nothing there. Deciding he could part with one stein, he placed it in the middle of the stump. It was then the hairs of his neck rose and he looked up to see dwarves emerge from hidden places and surround him, each one threatening him with a sword or battle axe.

"You need to come with us," one dwarf said.

"I could go back home and we could all pretend you never saw me," Sordyr said, attempting a show of flippant bravery.

"That won't work today," the dwarf said.

They closed in around him and, enmass, warily pushed him into the dwarf kingdom. Sordyr quickly retrieved the stein before they dragged him away.

Fingol gasped when he saw the dwarves emerge and lead Sordyr away. His first urge was to leap in the middle in a vain attempt to rescue the willful elf, but he knew it would result in at least one death, most likely his, and Sordyr would still be held captive.

Instead, Fingol turned and raced back to the great hall to inform Rimuel that his son had been captured.

Expecting to be thrown into a dank prison cell, Sordyr was surprised to find that he was put into a large high-ceiling, windowless room, apportioned with a fireplace. A thick cushioned chair was positioned by the hearth. Against the wall to the right was a beautifully carved oak chest of drawers and two wide bookshelves filled with thick tomes, while a bed with a thick mattress nestled against the wall to the left.

"Are all your prison cells like this?" he grinned.

"Of course n– " the dwarf began but then smiled. "Why yes. We treat all our prisoners like guests."

Chuckling, Sordyr continued his gaze about the room. Near the fireplace was a small table with two hardback chairs. On top of the table was a board game. Walking over, he picked up a chess piece, a bishop, exquisitely carved from dark amethyst. "This is a chess game, right?"

"That's right," the dwarf answered.

Sordyr picked up a knight from the other side of the board. It was carved from scintillating opal, the workmanship delicate and exceptional. "This artist who made these is indeed a master. I've never seen anything like it."

"Of course not," the dwarf said with a superior sniff. "Elves can't carve like dwarves do."

"I'll grant you that," he readily agreed.

"Do you play the game?"

"I was taught the game when I was young, but it's been some time since I've even seen a board. The game is too slow for my tastes."

Grinning slyly at the elf, the dwarf said, "How about a game?"

"If you wish," Sordyr amiably shrugged, sliding a chair out. "If I remember correctly, white goes first?"

"Yes."

"If I might impose, could you give me a refresher as to how the pieces move?"

The dwarf cocked an eyebrow at him. "You sure you know how to play?"

"Yes, yes," he amiably replied. "It's just that it's been a while. By the way, is it permitted to know the name of my worthy opponent?"

The dwarf warily eyed him then said, "My name's Olaf."

"Olaf," Sordyr repeated. "A fine name, a strong name. It sounds like the name of a chess master. Am I right?"

Olaf subtly preened at the compliment. "I have been known to win a few tournaments."

"Come now," Sordyr encouraged. "Don't be modest. It sounds like you might be a champion?"

Olaf's preen turned into a stiff frown. "No, no. I'm not that good yet."

"Why not?"

"Do you want to talk or play," Olaf gruffly demanded.

"Ah," Sordyr nodded in commiseration. "I understand."

"You don't understand anything," Olaf retorted.

"I understand that you were about to give me a quick refresher," Sordyr kindly replied.

Selecting each piece, Olaf did a quick review then took a white pawn in one hand and an amethyst pawn in the other and thrust them behind his back, exchanging the game pieces back and forth between hands.

"Choose."

Sordyr pointed to the dwarf's right hand.

"You have white," Olaf said, twisting the board around so that the white pieces were in front of the elf.

Sordyr moved the white King's pawn to King four.

Olaf responded with black King pawn to King five.

Eighteen moves later, Sordyr sighed in defeat and leaned back in his chair as Olaf moved his knight and said, "I believe the term is 'Checkmate.'"

Smiling at Olaf, Sordyr said, "I probably didn't give you much of a challenge. Of course this was my first game in a quite a while. I'm sure I could give you a better challenge with another game.

"Why not," Olaf smirked, setting up the pieces.

Sordyr lost again, rather badly this time.

"I can't believe I'm playing so badly," Sordyr frowned. "I know what it is. The last time I played we had a friendly wager on the outcome. I play better when there's money on the line. How about I'll wager one of my steins here." He held one up. "While not of the quality a dwarf would make, they are rather nice."

Olaf suppressed a gloating grin, giving the stein a passing glance. It was well made, solid and functional. This was truly taking candy from a baby. "Fine, fine. It's an adequate piece, but, like you said, not up to the dwarven standards. I'll match it with five coppers."

"Five coppers," Sordyr complained. "It's worth at least one silver. What have you got to lose?"

Olaf barely reconsidered before snorting a laugh. "Fine. One silver it is. Set up the board."

Twenty two moves later, Sordyr flopped back in his chair and uttered an exasperated, "Damn."

Chortling, Olaf, moved the stein to his side of the table.

"One more," Sordyr announced. "I've another stein. I'll stand this one against the stein I just lost."

"If you wish," Olaf cavalierly replied, already mentally replaying how he would expound the story of how a foolish elf wagered all his possessions on a game of chess and was soundly thrashed. As he was white, Olaf made the first move, pawn to queen four, intending to use a queen's gambit. Sordyr answered with pawn to queen five, and the game was on.

It took longer this time, but in the end, it was Sordyr who announced, "Checkmate."

Olaf sat back, stunned.

Looking up at the mystified dwarf, Sordyr soothed, "I'm sure it was just a bit of luck. You weren't playing your best."

"I suppose," Olaf grumbled.

"How about another game?" Sordyr said. "I'd like to try and win that other stein back."

"Of course," Olaf snapped, snatching the pieces and placing them on the board. Sordyr was white this time and Olaf decided he was going to teach this elf a lesson he would never forget. He would crush this cocky elf and rub the victory in his face after winning the other stein.

Sordyr opened with pawn to king four. Olaf countered with pawn to queen's bishop five, intending to use the Jorund defense.

Thirty-eight moves later, Olaf glared down at the board. It was three moves to checkmate and there was nothing he could do about it. He glanced up at Sordyr who, hand at his chin, continued to intently study the positions, revealing no emotion.

Hoping the elf didn't see the mate in three, Olaf moved his rook and waited. He had barely taken his fingers off the piece, when Sordyr slid his bishop forward for the final attack. His shoulders slumping, Olaf tipped over his king.

Sordyr reached over and retrieved the other stein. "A good game. I was beginning to worry."

A snarl curled the lips of the dwarf. "Another." Without waiting for a response, he began setting up the pieces.

"Are you sure?"

"Of course I'm sure, elf." The pieces in position, he moved his pawn to queen four.

"What's the bet?"

"No bet," he growled, "just play."

"I don't play well unless there's money involved," Sordyr answered. "Tell you what. I'll wager both steins against three silvers."

"Three silvers," Olaf sputtered. "They're not worth that much."

"Take it or leave it," Sordyr coolly replied, folding his arms and sitting back.

His face scrunched into a cold glare, Olaf jammed back and reached in to his pockets, pulling out a handful of coins. He then counted out two silvers and ten coppers and placed them on the table next to the board.

Sordyr scooped them up and dumped them into one of the steins. Leaning forward, he grinned, "Winner take all."

Twenty-seven moves later, Olaf's jaw dropped as he saw the forced mate in five moves. He looked up to see the elf watching him, an arrogant smile curling the corners of his lips.

"Damn you," he snapped, flicking his king over with an angry flip of his fingers.

As he slid the steins over to his side, Sordyr said, "You play a good game of chess."

"And you said you hadn't played in a while," the dwarf replied with an accusatory stare.

"I haven't," he shrugged. "But playing for money brings out the best in me.

Olaf fidgeted as he struggled to control his frustration. How was it possible this elf was beating him, in a game where he was known to be just about the best in the kingdom? Purposely settling himself, he knew he had to bring his emotions under control if he was going to teach this elf a lesson. That's what the problem was, he silently chastised himself. He had let his emotions get the better of him. This time he would control himself, play like he did in tournaments.

Locking his gaze on the elf, he said, "Again."

"What's the wager this time?" Sordyr asked, arranging the pieces.

"You have two silver and ten copper of *my* coins," Olaf calmly pointed out. "I'll wager another three to get them back."

"What's the sport in that?" Sordyr chided. "If you win, you simply get the same coins back and we're where we started. How about six silvers against my coins and two steins?"

Olaf furrowed his brows, his lips pursed. He then hunched over to the side and reached into his pocket, counting out the coins on the palm of his hand. Selecting a gold coin and one silver, he slapped them on the table.

"Alright, elf," he sniffed in challenge. "You're on."

Eighteen moves later, Sordyr announced, "Checkmate." Scooping up the coins before Olaf had a chance to complain, he said, "Another game?"

Olaf pushed away from the table and stormed off.

"I take that as a 'No'?" Sordyr called out. Smirking at the largess, he wondered how long it would be before they came in and simply took the winnings from him, as well as his two steins.

He was languidly studying each chess piece as he placed them on the board when the door opened and Olaf returned with an older dwarf with a salt and pepper beard that ended just above his ample belly. What he had in beard made up for what he lacked on his head as he was nearly bald, except for the tufts around his ears and the back of his head.

"Him?" the older dwarf questioned with a doubtful stare and pointed to Sordyr.

'Yes, him," Olaf nodded.

"He seems too young." He cocked his head and studied the elf.

"You do know I can hear you," Sordyr said with a polite smile. "That's the way it is with elven ears. It's a blessing and a curse for we can hear even the softest sounds at great distances. Makes it hard for parents to have private conversations."

Ignoring the banter, the older elf addressed him. "Olaf here tells me you are a fair chess player."

"He's being far too kind. Feeling sorry for me, he's let me win a number of games. I must say," he said, glancing around the room, "you have treated me most royally. Not only are these lodgings fit for a prince, you sent in one of your chess masters and let me defeat him, rather soundly I might point out." Sordyr suppressed a laugh as he saw Olaf bristle at the oblique gibe.

The older dwarf was not amused by the elf's carefree attitude. "Perhaps you would like to try your hand at a game with me?"

"Are you going to let me win like Olaf did, or are you going to actually play?" Sordyr asked with feigned innocence.

The older dwarf moved towards the chair opposite Sordyr, slowly pulling it out and sitting down while letting out an indulgent sigh. "I believe I can give you a game that you will remember."

"And what are we waging?" Sordyr asked.

"Why wage anything?" the dwarf replied. "Why not just a friendly game?"

"I play better when money's on the line. Now I've two wonderfully made elven steins plus the equivalent of two golds and two silvers. How about we make it four gold coins against my newly won treasure?" He piled the coins in neatly descending stacks.

The older dwarf cocked an eyebrow at him. "Is gambling really necessary?"

"Come now," Sordyr lightly replied. "I've heard that dwarves are inveterate gamblers. Besides, you didn't come here unless you thought you could whup my young ass."

"Not so crude, if you please," the dwarf huffed. "Chess is a game of refinement. Leave the gutter talk for the taverns."

"You're right of course," Sordyr apologized then stared intently at him. "Do we have a bet or not?"

The older dwarf studied him for a moment then looked at the two steins and stacks of coins. "Three golds."

"Four."

"Three and two silver."

"Five."

"What?" the dwarf sputtered. "You can't go up when I raise my offer."

"Four is my minimum," Sordyr patiently explained. "The way negotiations were going, I was afraid we'd be here all day until you finally got up to four. Now, do you want to play or not?"

The older dwarf frowned in irritation at him then let out a sigh. "Four it is." He started to reach for a pawn of each color when Sordyr interrupted him.

"Tut, tut. I'd like to see those coins if you don't mind."

"Don't you trust me?" the dwarf replied with some indignation.

Sordyr cocked his head to the side and stared at him. "I'm an elf and you're a dwarf. Need I say more?"

The dwarf grumbled as he reached into his pockets and pulled out a handful of coins. Slowly tallying the coins, he said, "I only have the equivalent of three golds and three silvers." Expecting Sordyr to relent, he was surprised at the elf's reply.

"I'll wait." Sordyr folded his arms and sat back.

"By all the gods," Olaf burst. "Here," he huffed as he slammed down a gold coin. "Take mine. Just play, will you?"

The older dwarf added up the coins totaling four golds and placed them on the table then held out his hands with the remaining coins to Olaf who flipped a hand telling him to keep them.

"I think we're finally ready," Sordyr cheerily announced. "May I ask the name of my noble opponent?

The older dwarf hesitated then said, "I am called Amundi."

"I am Sordyr," the elf replied. "Let the game begin."

Amundi placed the pawns behind him and Sordyr ended up choosing black. Amundi's first move was pawn to king four.

Nearly an hour later, Sordyr announced, "Mate in eight moves."

Startled, Amundi hunkered over the board, his attention focused on the pieces. After an uncomfortably long time during which Sordyr got up from the table, stretched, walked around the room, pulled books from the shelves, Amundi finally made his move, placing a knight in a threatening attack on Sordyr's queen.

Sordyr stood at his side of the table and studied the position for mere seconds before smiling. "Make that mate in six." He repositioned a bishop, exposing his queen.

Amundi's head snapped up at the bold sacrifice. His head then bent forward, the thick eyebrows furrowed, as he focused on the positions only to discover that he would lose the game in six moves, just as this annoying elf predicted. With a lip curled in defeat, he tipped over his king.

"Thank you for the game," Sordyr grinned, scooping up the coins and spilling them into a stein, the rattling noise of gold and silver an arrogant reminder of who won.

"Again," Amundi grunted.

"Your wager?"

"Not that again," Amundi grumped.

"Here's my wager." He slid the two steins containing the coins to the middle of the side of the table. "Let's call it eight gold coins."

"I don't have eight gold coins," Amundi snapped.

"I'll wait." Sordyr walked over to the bookshelves to read the titles etched in gold letters on the spines.

Scooting his chair back, Amundi pushed himself to standing and wordlessly shuffled to the door, returning twenty minutes later with a small chest that he carried with both hands. Placing the chest on the table, he opened the lid to reveal it full of glimmering gold coins.

Sordyr chuckled upon seeing the contents. "You plan on losing a lot?"

"Not so brash, young elf," Amundi retorted. "This will simply make it easier to add your coins to my own."

"Then make it more interesting," Sordyr taunted. "Why not make it two to one, if you're so confident. Sixteen of your gold against eight of mine."

"I will match your eight," the dwarf scowled.

"That's a wise move," Sordyr nodded sympathetically. "That way you only lose eight coins."

"Are we going to play?" he grumbled.

"Certainly," Sordyr grinned, scooting the chair back and plopping down. "You were white last time. I'll be white this time."

By the end of the evening, there were dirty dinner plates piled on the floor at their feet, half empty ale mugs on the oak chest, and three dwarves standing behind Amundi as he pushed the small chest with the remaining coins towards Sordyr.

Without a word, Amundi stood and left the room, humiliated at the crushing defeat. He had won two games, and those were because the elf had made a mistake… or at least that was what it seemed. Yet he knew in his heart that he could beat the over-confident elf.

Sordyr yawned as he watched Amundi leave, the other dwarves following behind. Waiting until the door closed and he heard the bolt slide home locking him in, he gazed down at the chest filled with gold coins. Digging his fingers into the thick coins, he reveled in the touch of hard metal. He didn't know how many were there, but he knew he was very rich. The question was; how could he keep his new found wealth? And then, how could he take it home with him?

For the next week, numerous dwarves came to challenge Sordyr, Amundi and Olaf among them. By the end of the week, Sordyr's winnings were contained in three small chests lined next to the oak chest of drawers. Yet, while Sordyr thrilled with his growing wealth, he chaffed at his confinement. Though he had been treated well, the thought that he was condemned for the rest of his life to playing chess in a windowless prison worried him. The elf in him longed to be outside and the incarceration was beginning to take its toll and he found himself becoming irritable.

It was after one long day of endless chess and challengers that he realized they were trying to break him, that they were purposely wearing him down. By then, the number of chests had grown to five and he decided he had had enough.

Amundi arrived in the morning and moved towards the chess board. Another five dwarves piled in after him. Setting up the board, he looked up to see that the elf still seated, reading a book.

"It's time to play, elf," Amundi announced.

"I'm not playing today," Sordyr said, flipping a page.

Holding a rook, Amundi's hand hovered over the board. "What?"

"I said I'm not playing today," he replied, standing up and folding his arms, "nor tomorrow nor the day after that. None of you is a challenge. I'll play again when you find someone who can at least provide a bit of a challenge."

Amundi glared at him. "You *will* play, elf."

"What are you going to do if I don't? You going to throw me in prison? Starve me? Beat me? I half expect you to do that because wearing me down is the only way you have half a chance of beating me and saving some of your pitiful pride."

Amundi's hand slowly deposited the rook on the board and he stood up. "I'd watch your tongue if I were you, young elf."

"Why?" Sordyr sneered. "Like I said, what are you going to do? Kill me? What else should I expect from dwarves?"

Amundi stiffened while the others behind him began voicing their indignation. "We are not elves," he coldly replied. "We have treated you with respect and provided you with lodgings far better than even our common people have."

"But I am still a prisoner," Sordyr answered.

"You were on our land."

"I was in the Forbidden Zone," he pointedly stated, "and if you remember, at one time that was our land before you dwarves destroyed it."

"That was 200 years ago," a dwarf standing behind Amundi said. "We had nothing to do with that."

"But you've done nothing to change it," the elf replied.

"This gets us nowhere," Amundi said.

At that moment, a young dwarf thrust open the door and announced, "The elf called Sordyr has been summoned to the presence of King Vestar Silvercoat.

Moments later, Sordyr stood before the dwarf king.

"I hear you're a pretty fair chess player," the king said, eyeing him with an air of indifference.

"Better than any dwarf," Sordyr calmly replied.

The king smirked at the answer. "We shall see." Leaning forward, he rested a forearm on his thigh and peered intently at the elf. "Why were you on our land?"

"It was ours before you destroyed it."

"Posh," the king retorted with a flip of his hand. "It's been like that for hundreds of years."

"You mean it's been the Forbidden Zone for 200 years because you pushed your mountains into elven domain."

"It is what it is," the king replied with finality.

"If that is so, and the Forbidden Zone is a no man's land between our two kingdoms, then how can you claim it and by what right do you have to hold me captive?" Sordyr boldly asked.

"By the right that you are here now," the king retorted, "Sordyr, son of Rimuel."

Sordyr startled. "You know my father?"

"How could I not?" he said, shaking his head. "I receive a constant flood of envoys requesting formal negotiations concerning the Forbidden Zone and the never ending appeals for peace. Frankly, he's beginning to become a real pain in the -" He stopped when his chamberlain purposely cleared his throat. Frowning at the interruption, he continued, "All your father wants to talk about is the Forbidden Zone and making it a safe zone, a place where we can conduct the affairs of state between elves and dwarves."

"What's wrong with that?" Sordyr asked.

"What's in it for us? What do elves have that we dwarves could possibly want?"

"For one thing," Sordyr replied with an impish smile, "we could teach you to play chess."

That brought an uproar of indignation in the court, all except the king who grinned at the elf's sauciness. He raised his hands for silence, and the hall slowly settled.

"Besides chess, what else do elves possess that we might want?"

"Markets, Sire," he replied without hesitation. "For example, it's common knowledge that dwarves produce the best ale." His assertion was met with more than a few grunts of approval. "Elves know that and they know the only way they can get the delicious brew is by the black market." Here, silence suddenly filled the hall as a few of those in attendance suddenly found their feet to be of fascinating interest. "I assume you tax the production of ale. If so, you are losing out on lots of income by neglecting a huge market right across the Zone."

The king slapped his knee and exclaimed, "By the gods, this lad speaks my language. All your father talked about was the safety of the citizens of our two kingdoms, and rapprochement and living in harmony. Lofty ideals certainly, but nothing solid like what you're suggesting. Pity he didn't send you in the first place. We could have been trading partners long ago. But…"

"But?" Sordyr asked, his rising hope abruptly checked.

"This last envoy he sent demanded that we release all elves held prisoner or there would be consequences."

"Consequences?"

"Yes, consequences," the king sniffed in disdain. "Of course he gave no names of any elves we had prisoner and the only elvish *guest* we have is you, so I can only assume he means you."

Sordyr was momentarily stung by the thought that his father treated him like some anonymous elf who had managed to get himself captured.

"Obviously the tone of his threat is more than insulting. If he wants a war on his hands, he will get a war." He settled back into his throne chair. "The question I have is what to do with you?"

"Just send me back and all this ugly talk can be avoided," Sordyr cheerfully suggested.

"Too late for that," the king sourly stated. "But I do have an idea." Templing his fingers, he studied the young elf. "I understand that you like to gamble, particularly on your skills as a chess player."

"I've been known to wager a game or two."

"A game or two?" the king guffawed scanning the room. "You've five chests full of gold lost by dwarves too foolish to quit while they were ahead."

Sordyr sheepishly grinned and shrugged.

"I have a wager for you, my young elf," the king said. "You will play one more game of chess. If you win, you can take your chests of gold and go home. If you lose, you lose everything, maybe even your life, for you will spend the rest of it digging in the mountains. But I will grant you a boon if you lose. I will commit to a truce, to peace between us in the Forbidden Zone, so that you might know all was not in vain."

"No truce if I win?"

"Correct."

Sordyr pondered the wager and it seemed too good to be true.

"When I win, I get to take all my winnings with me?"

"*If* you win, yes."

Sordyr thought about the five chests full of gold. He was more than wealthy. Besides, what did it matter to him if the Forbidden Zone remained like it had been for 200 years? His father had disowned him and he now had more than enough wealth to live like he wanted.

"Just to make sure –I win, I get all my winnings so far and I go home."

"That is correct," the king replied. "But if you lose, you lose everything except peace in the Zone. You will never see your home again."

A sly smile curled the corners of Sordyr's lips. He liked these odds. "I accept."

The king flicked his hands at the guards by the far door. "Bring him in."

Heads turned as the doors opened and a dwarf not yet into middle age sauntered in. His thick auburn beard reached his belly and his eyes were bright with confidence. His name, a whisper at first, gained in sound until it became a chant.

"Hakon. Hakon. Hakon."

The dwarf stopped several paces before the throne and did a sweeping bow. "Greetings, King Vestar Silvercoat."

"Well met Hakon Helgason. We have patiently waited your arrival." The king's eyes glimmered with expectant triumph.

The newcomer turned to look up at Sordyr. "Is this the elf pretending to be a chess master?"

Sordyr smirked at the insult. "Are you saying that all my opponents so far have been bungling amateurs?"

"That's not what I meant," Hakon said, eyes blinking wide at the insinuation and his gaffe making it appear so.

"What did you mean then?"

"What I meant is that you haven't played the best yet," he said, puffing himself up.

"So by the best," Sordyr said, feigning understanding, "you mean the others I've played so far are so beneath your talents that there is no comparison?"

"Yes, I mean, no," he sputtered. "Quit putting words in my mouth.

Initially annoyed at Sordyr's verbal sparring, the king began laughing. "Quit while you're still behind, Master Hakon. Save your gloating for after the game. For now, let's get this match started."

Two dwarves carried in a table with the chess board inlaid into the surface. Another dwarf carried a box with the chess pieces and a small box with two timing clocks.

Sordyr glanced up at the king. "Sire. Win or lose, I should like my elven brothers to see the craftsmanship of your chess pieces, for none carve like the dwarves do. There is one carver whose work I've seen deposited in the Forbidden Zone for trading. He is exceptional."

The king's excitement momentarily diminished. "We'll see," was all he said. "For now, let's just give our attention here."

Bowing respectfully, Sordyr waited for his opponent to take a seat before taking the chair opposite him.

Amundi stood to the side, a pawn of each color behind his back. "Choose," he said to Sordyr.

"Right hand," he replied, pointing."

"You are black," Amundi announced, "or in this case ruby red," as he placed the delicately carved pawn on the table.

As the two players arranged their pieces, Sordyr gazed up at Hakon and said, "Pick a number greater than twenty. That will be the number of moves before I checkmate you."

"In your dreams, elf," Hakon retorted.

"Then I'll choose for you," Sordyr smiled at him. "Let's make it thirty one."

Ignoring him, Hakon finished arranging his pieces and looked up at Amundi.

"Each player will have one hour to make at least forty moves," Amundi began.

"It won't take that long," Sordyr interrupted.

"After which," Amundi continued, shooting a glare at the elf, "another hour and another forty moves will be allotted. Agreed?"

"Suits me," Sordyr said with a bob of his head then directed his attention to Hakon. "Your move, O great wizard of the chessboard."

Amundi pressed Hakon's timing clock and the second hand began its sweeping motion.

Hakon serenely smiled and moved pawn to king four. "Your lesson is about to begin." He then moved his king pawn to king four then pressed the button starting Sordyr's clock.

Sordyr placed a hand over his mouth, stifling a pretend yawn. Crossing one arm across his stomach to prop the elbow of the other arm, he rested his chin on the palm of his right hand and intently studied the chessboard. As the seconds ticked away, Sordyr ignored everything around him and focused, never taking his eyes off the board. Occasionally he would sigh and change arms, but his attention never wavered. Every now and then he would utter, "Wow... that's a really good move."

Those in the audience silently fidgeted as did his opponent whose frown deepened as the seconds ticked away. Yet Hakon's frown soon morphed to confidence for he knew that the elf was losing valuable time.

Finally, after almost twenty minutes, Sordyr nodded and said, "Great move," then moved his king pawn to king five.

Hakon quickly responded with knight to king's bishop three.

Sordyr stared at the move as though puzzled with the choice.

Another ten minutes elapsed and Hakon's leaned back to cast a preening grin at the audience. The fool elf had wasted so much time that this was going to be an easy victory.

Sordyr then responded with knight to queen's bishop three and pressed the button for Hakon's clock to begin.

Suddenly, the tempo of the game changed as Sordyr took no time to study the board as he made his move and pressed the clock button. Hakon would make a move and less than two seconds later it was his move again.

Sordyr's speed began to rattle him and he found himself taking longer to study the board. All too soon, the minutes vanished from his clock and he found himself losing time. With twelve minutes left on his clock he heard Sordyr clear his throat and speak.

"Mate in seven."

Hakon's eyes bolted wide and he focused on the positions, the seconds of his clock ticking away much too quickly. Frantically studying the pieces, he played out future moves, unable to see Sordyr's supposed checkmate. Deciding to take the attack to his opponent, he moved his queen's bishop.

"Check."

Sordyr took no time to look at his response and positioned a knight to block the check then said, “Mate in six.”

Hakon’s heart pounded he and leaned over the board, his head twitching as he desperately searched for Sordyr’s checkmate. Four minutes had disappeared from his time and he now had less time remaining than his opponent. It was then he saw it, and the more he struggled to counter it the more he realized there was nothing he could do.

With a deep sigh of resignation, he tipped over his king.

A stunned silence swallowed the hall as the dwarves absorbed the shock that the kingdom’s best chess player had been soundly defeated by an elf, a young elf at that.

Finally, the king spoke.

“You have won, elf. You have defeated our very best. We had an agreement and I will honor that agreement. You are free to take your gold and return to your home. We will provide you safe passage to the Forbidden Zone.”

Standing, Sordyr grinned and bowed with a sweeping gesture. “I have a proposition for you, great king. It is obvious, to me at least, that our two peoples mistrust each other far too much. We are always ready to believe the worst in each other. Great king, I would like to present to you personally, four of my chests filled with gold in exchange for peace in the Forbidden Zone along with establishing trade between us. Not only do you come out four chests of gold richer, you will increase your treasury with the profits in trade.”

A slow smile curled the corners of the king’s lips that burst into a wide grin. “By the gods you are a piece of work. Pity you aren’t a dwarf. I could use someone like you.”

“You already can, Sire. If you agree, I would be happy to act on your behalf.”

Despite the general outcry and objections, the king said, “And how do I know I can trust you?”

“Sire,” Sordyr pointedly replied. “I will act on your behalf to ensure you reap excellent profits while at the same time ensuring elves are not taken advantage of. Good business ensures the customer always comes back. Give me a year. If you are not satisfied, you are free to choose someone else.”

The king slapped his leg, laughed and pointed at him. "See?" he chortled as the twisted his head back and forth, gazing at the crowd. "This elf understands business." Turning his attention back to Sordyr he nodded. "I agree, elf. One year. If I like what you've done, I'll grant you exclusive rights to trade on my behalf."

"Thank you, Sire," Sordyr replied with a grand and sweeping bow.

Sordyr stood at the edge of the Forbidden Zone, talking pleasantly with his escorts and wondering why he wasn't allowed to cross. "What are we waiting for?"

"We're waiting for the other side to show up," the escort commander said. He was a stout dwarf wearing an iron torque.

"I don't understand," Sordyr said.

"You elves have some of our dwarf children and we want them back. You're the exchange for them."

"Ah," he nodded. "I understand. Those must have been the two dwarves I saw before coming here."

"You saw them?" the commander asked.

"They were being led to my father's Hall, which means they were well taken care of if that's where they stayed."

The dwarf commander relaxed until he saw movement on the other side. He signaled with his hands to alert the rest of the escort when he saw several elves and the two young dwarves at the edge of the forest.

"Are you prepared to trade?" the commander called out.

"Yes," an elf called back.

"Let us see them."

Two elves lifted the two dwarves as evidence.

"Let us see him," an elf called back.

Sordyr took a step into the cleared expanse of the Forbidden Zone and gave a cheerful wave.

"Are you ready to exchange?" the elf said.

"Yes," the dwarf commander replied.

Sordyr turned to his escorts. "It has been a pleasure getting to know you. I pray that we see more of each other." Bending down, he hefted up the small chest filled with gold coins, noticing one dwarf seemingly more than a little interested in the two dwarves making their way across the Zone.

He was halfway across the Zone when he turned to watch one dwarf sweep up one of the lads and hug him tightly. A flitting feeling of envy swept through him as he observed the outpouring of emotion between, most likely, father and son.

With a sigh, he turned and trudged home and was soon standing before his father who leaned heavily on his desk.

"What you did was more than irresponsible," Sordyr's father fumed as he stalked about the throne room. "Your foolishness has set back years of careful negotiations."

"But father –"

"No 'but father,'" Rimuel stormed. "I had the perfect opportunity of exerting pressure on the dwarf king with the two hostages we had. Of course we wouldn't have done anything to them. They were fine lads, even if there were dwarves."

"But father," Sordyr tried again to interrupt.

"Be silent while I'm speaking," Rimuel thundered. "Because of you, I've lost an opportunity. Not only do I discover that instead of having hostages and an upper hand, I find out that an elf has been taken and it's my own son. Can you even imagine the utter embarrassment you have caused? Because of you, any chance of peace in the Forbidden Zone has all but vanished.

"But father," Sordyr interrupted, firmer this time, "if I may be allowed to speak?"

"No," his father tersely replied. "I've had enough of your excuses."

"You haven't even asked me what's in the chest," Sordyr loudly exclaimed.

"I don't give a damn what's in that chest," his father exploded. "You think that chest and whatever is in it can replace the years of negotiations, the years of struggling for peace? All you care about is you. You never think about others. You're selfish and self-centered. Life to you is a game, isn't it? One big game of seeing how much you can take advantage of someone else. Well that game won't play here. You're a merchant, remember? Go be a merchant."

Rimuel folded his arms and turned his back on his son.

His lips tightening, Sordyr picked up the chest, spun around on his heels and marched off. He was through the doors when Fingol caught up with him.

"Give him time to settle down," Fingol comforted. "You know how he can get sometimes. You have to understand it from his perspective. He's spent a lot of time trying to get peace between the dwarves and elves."

Sordyr stopped, adjusted the weight of the chest, opened the curved top just enough to withdraw a sealed envelope. "This is what was in the chest. Give it to him. It's from the dwarf king." Without waiting for a response, he walked on.

Startled, Fingol stood and stared down at the envelope. It was addressed to Rimuel of the Moonling House. The script was strong with flourishes of serifs and extended letters. Walking back into the room, he saw Rimuel, chin on his fist, angrily staring out the windows.

"M'Lord," he began.

"Don't start," Rimuel challenged. "I know how much the boy means to you. But what's done is done. I won't budge on my decision."

"M'Lord," Fingol calmly said. "Your son brought a message from the dwarf King Vestar." He held up the envelope as evidence. "It was in the chest."

"Give it here," he demanded, stretching out is hand. Tearing open the envelope, two letters were folded within. He unfolded the larger letter first.

To Rimuel of the Moonling House,

My Brother, I have reconsidered your proposals and agree that it would serve the interests of dwarves and elves if we should set aside our quarrels and seek a harmony of coexistence, especially in the area called the Forbidden Zone. I, Vestar, King of the dwarves, agree that peace shall reign in the Forbidden Zone. Further, that free trade will occur between our two nations. Such trade will be supervised by selected individuals acceptable to both kingdoms. Thus, I have chosen the elf called Sordyr to act as my representative in all future economic endeavors in the elven kingdoms. I trust this will meet your satisfaction.

Vestar Silvercoat

King of the Dwarves

Though frowning in bewilderment at the dwarf king's choice of Sordyr, Rimuel could barely contain his euphoria. He quickly opened the second message.

To Rimuel, father of Sordyr,

I write this as one father to another. You have done well in raising a son you can be proud of. Too often we forget that our children are our greatest treasures. So preoccupied with ruling a kingdom, we sometimes forget that we are fathers also.

Your son is an exceptional young elf. He has the qualities and talents every father wishes for their children – a caring for others at the expense of his own desires. He could have returned very wealthy – he's quite the chess player, as you know – but instead willingly gave up what he had earned so that others could benefit from peace in the Zone.

You are blessed to have a son like him. For my part, I am pleased to call him friend.

Vestar Silvercoat

Rimuel's shoulders slumped as he heaved a deep sigh, his eyes misting as he turned to stare out the windows again. He stretched out his hand for Fingol to take the letters.

Fingol took the letters and read them in the same sequence that Rimuel did, lingering over the personal note the dwarf king had sent.

"What do I do now?" Rimuel asked, his voice forlorn. "I've chased him away."

"Bring him back. Admit you were wrong. Be a father to him."

Rimuel blinked as he gazed vacantly out the windows. "I don't know how to do that."

"Well it's time you learned," Fingol bluntly said, thrusting the letters onto the desk.

Letting Go Is Hard To Do: Part I

Jeremy Hicks

Argus Gravelheel worked the new claim for three bone-aching, back-breaking months before realizing he had a neighbor, much less an elf for a neighbor. The woman waded between a cart loaded with material and a sluice set atop one of the ancient stacked stone fish weirs—attributed to older races than the two that dominated modern Mirstone. She was shorter and even more petite than normal for her fae species. Like all elves, she proved to be stronger and hardier than she looked.

Though he could not hear her over the rushing water, the elf's lips never stopped moving. Many dwarves sang while they worked. His former crew had. Perhaps elves were no different in that respect.

She stopped in front of the azure ox hitched to her mining cart. Her thin lips moved faster. She danced around excitedly. The beast chewed its cud, unfazed by her frenetic display.

The manic girl's fit passed. She stood swaying in the wind for a moment before depositing two handfuls of shiny crystals into a worn leather haversack. Her mining claim proved to be more productive than his current belly mine, responsible for a few measly ounces of gold and a dram of rubies.

By all rights, Argus knew he could take her claim. These were the Hinterlands, stony hills and ridges with narrow, verdant valleys and hollows cut deep by waterways that had once flowed beneath the surface. Both races disputed the area—even the exact boundaries of the region. Might made right here.

Plus, he had a clear shot on her from his concealed position. He hid along the rocky bank above the cut leading to his side of the broad stream. Argus spotted the ox cart the previous afternoon and staked out the area all morning.

He'd learned patience and crossbows during his enlistment with the Thirteenth Hand Ballista Battalion. As far as range and penetration value, his over-and-under double crossbow did not hold a candle to the larger, bulkier repeaters he'd used in the war. Still, he reckoned a dead center torso shot would be easy enough once he factored in bolt drop and windage. That would put the elf down quickly and mercifully.

Why shouldn't I take the shot?

After all, dwarves had warred with elves since the mountains had risen up, a godlike event blamed on his folk for good reason. Their ego-driven leaders, hungry for glory and power, had claimed responsibility for it, inciting a race war fought hot and cold over two bitter centuries. Argus came to realize it no longer mattered if the Dwarves of Rachdale had possessed the means or motives to move their secure subterranean homes above the primordial forests of Topside, his preferred term for the Overworld.

Regardless, the wars had taken their toll on both races, and countless more caught among the chaos and carnage. Now, elf hated dwarf, and dwarf had come to hate elf. Neither population had had time to recover, which meant the conflicts had grown smaller, sparser, and provincial—or in some cases, more personal.

In his experience as a prospector and fortune hunter in the rocky mineral-rich valleys of the intrusive mountains, anyone—dwarf or elf—could be a potential friend or foe. Best friends often became the worst enemies. In the vested interests of his bottom line, and his life, he tended to avoid everyone, especially his neighbors.

If faced with an actual conflict, Argus weighed the odds. He would either end it quickly and move or avoid it and move. He moved regardless. There was too much shiny in the world to deal with unnecessary conflict and drama.

If forced into a social situation, the dwarf remembered the manners beaten into him by his grandmother, a revered Clan Matron among the Whitmasters. Conversation had been the first form of self-defense he'd learned. Her lessons on respect and manners, even in the face of verbal aggression, often took the form of witty caveats and ancient proverbs.

One of her favorite sayings had been: Treat a neighbor like you'd treat a mate; you have to coexist peacefully, unless you plan on sleeping with one eye open. Argus remembered those words well. He had not always applied them, though. Otherwise, he'd still be married and living a lie or wearing a uniform and doing things no dwarf should ever be asked to do for clan and cave home.

Home.

He missed his honeymoon home, but he had sold it and moved. Why? He'd returned home from a tour of duty to find his materialistic wife shaking her bubbly booty for the gemcutter living across the street. Argus divorced her, and she remarried two months later, to the gemcutter's wealthier boss.

Focus.

Argus reconsidered his options regarding the wild, white-haired neighbor. He tabled shooting her, and stealing her shit. He had done desperate, dumb things during the war—and after—but he had moved far from civilization to start over. To turn over a new leaf as the elves say. He reminded himself that he was a changed dwarf, and a better person, if not yet a redeemed one.

Argus glanced back in the direction of his camp. The world was vast, and his current claim was unimpressive. Pulling up stakes and cutting his losses would be the wise move.

Something about the woman kept him watching. She screened material in the sluice, allowing the flowing water to wash away the soil. Her wet clothing clung to her fit form. Tiny nipples, stimulated by the cold creek, protruded through the white fabric.

How low have I sunk to be stimulated by an elf? But how long since I've encountered a woman at all? A year, maybe two.

"Like what you see?" She called across the waterway.

Argus froze in place, arresting his smallest movements. He wondered if she could see him or had simply felt his lingering gaze. Some species of wild game sensed if one dared stare too long. Like those alert animals, elves proved to be elusive game, even if somehow caught unawares.

She reached into the screen and plucked a clear crystal the size of her palm from its contents. She oriented it until a rainbow emerged from the prismatic stone. Sweeping the refracted light across the slope, she honed in on his position with enough precision to blind him.

Argus raised a hand to block the rainbow light, and his crossbow shifted. He caught it. Already off-balance, the burly dwarf wobbled enough for the rocky soil beneath his feet to shift.

The combination of the elf's prismatic beam and the sudden cloud of dirt and dust forced Argus to shut his eyes. He grasped the crossbow tighter, digging its brass-capped stock into the ground. The thin, rocky soil gave way, and he lost his footing. He slid far enough to lose purchase with the steep-sided bank above the confluence of the stream and wagon trail.

Argus landed in shallow water with a rocky bottom. His boot clad feet hit first, but his awkward landing resulted in aching ankles, barked shins, and a sore arse. Despite the pain, he sprang to his feet and shook like a mangy hound after a treated bath. He discovered how cold the water had grown over the past week, which meant winter was closer than the almanac had predicted.

The dazed, doused dwarf raised his right hand, but realized his mistake in enough time to prevent catastrophe. The blunt end of his weapon's upper bow struck his eyebrow, almost poking himself in one waterlogged eye.

"Ah, sh—" His teeth chattered so violently he bit his tongue.

Hysteric laughter penetrated his waterlogged ears. He glanced about, attempting to focus on the source of sudden laughter. By the time he blinked the water from his eyes, the cackling elf stood close enough for him to fall once more, this time into the abyssal pools of her stygian eyes. His breathing slowed, but his heartbeat raced in his barrel chest.

Is this what it feels like to be bewitched? Or is this love on first sight? If so, that's never worked out in the past.

The glint of steel broke the spell. His eyes widened, noticing the knife in her hand for the first time. She raised her weapon hand slowly, until the curved blade was level with her chest. His gaze flitted between danger and delight.

What is my irrational attraction to crazy women with knives?

Argus forced his eyes to focus beyond the blade, beyond her bosom, and focus on her shoulder. If she intended on using the weapon, he'd see movement there first. He'd forgotten his training once before, distracted by his naked ex-wife (though they'd still been married at the time). When caught cheating, she'd reacted in her normal fashion, with harsh words and violent actions. His free hand traced the long scar on his other forearm.

"Don't move! I don't want to kill, but I will if forced. And keep your eyes here." Using her empty hand, she pointed to her face. Shaking her head, she added, "I swear, some things are universal. Be they elf, dwarf, or human, all males are the same. So basic. My Erythmus was little different, but his wandering eye and silver tongue never led his heart astray. Unlike most of you."

"Begging the lady's pardon," Argus ventured a smile, "I was trained to keep my eyes on an opponent's weapon at all times."

"Lady? Opponent? Not enemy? Or worse, elf bitch or pointy-eared whore? Say, Brushtail, this one shows promise. Think we let him live? Or do we feed him to Fudgy? Soggy dwarf is easier to catch than freshwater eel, after all."

Argus risked a glance in each direction, but saw no one else on either bank of the creek. *Unless she's speaking to the ox?* The beast bellowed in response, confirming his suspicions.

"Guess you're right," the elf woman said. "We should give the dwarf a chance to explain himself. But he looks like a claim-jumper to me!"

She jabbed at him with the knife to emphasize her point.

"Whoa! No!" The dwarf raised his hands. He wondered if he should drop the crossbow, but did not want to risk losing such an expensive item. At this point, it was worth more than his life. "I, I'm your neighbor. Name's Argus Gravelheel. I'm a fellow miner. Just not as lucky as you it seems. I have a belly mine on the western slope, but it's provided more blisters and backaches than anything else."

"Why were you spying on me, Argus Gravelheel?"

"I noticed your cart. And your ox. Brushtail, right?" The dwarf smiled, hoping he'd guessed correctly. "Just wanted to make sure its owner wasn't after my claim. Turns out she has a better one already."

The elf lowered her knife, but held it ready at her side.

"To be fair, I inherited it from my late husband." Her big, black eyes wandered as she spoke. Argus wagered he could put a bolt in her neck from this distance, but it didn't feel neighborly. "He was the real miner in the family. Erythmus always did say I had a natural affinity for it, though. He said, 'Lo, I reckon you find stones and gems the way animals find you.' He never was a fan of all the wildlife, but he tolerated them for my sake.

"This one time—"

"I, uh, don't mean to interrupt," Argus said, his teeth chattering again, "buh, but if we're not going to have a, guh, go at each other, mind if we cha, cha, chat in the dry. Lo, is it?"

"Lobianca Willowshroud, but family, friends, and furbabies call me Lo. You're welcome on my side of the creek. As long as you don't cause any trouble. Otherwise." She drew the flat of the knife blade across her slender neck.

The elf backed away from him, neither turning away nor sheathing her knife. The doused dwarf followed, but he remained at a respectable distance. Once they exited the river, each kept an eye on the other, circling like hunting cats.

Lobianca pointed to a flat-topped, moss-covered stone a few paces to Argus's right. "I tire of this dance. I really must insist we invest in a bit of trust. Take a seat."

The dwarf scrambled onto the rock. His legs dangled from the ground. Water dripped from his boots. He set the crossbow beside him, leaving it within easy reach.

She flitted over to the cart, her steps light as a feather and swift as a hummingbird. When the elf spun around, Argus's eyes grew wide. He expected a weapon. Instead, she held a woven basket and a bloated wineskin.

"This is how I prefer to greet a new neighbor," Lo said. "Beats skulking around and sniping people, right?"

"Many of my people might disagree, but I was raised right. By a woman born a century before our people went to war, no less. That's why I didn't shoot. But I had to be sure you weren't a threat first."

"Are you convinced I'm not a threat now?"

"Mostly. I mean, you did offer me food rather than cutting my throat while I thrashed about in the river. Unless I'm missing something, yeah, consider me convinced. As long as the food's good and wine's tasty, anyway."

Argus hazarded a smile to indicate his jest. He hardly needed to, though. Lobianca laughed, chortled really, doubling over. His eyes followed her lean, flexible form, but returned too late to avoid her notice. She averted her gaze.

"Of course, we elves spice our food and drink properly. Consider yourself warned. We like both with as much flavor and verve as our lives. Not like the bland stews and charred hunks of meat your people call cuisine."

"Hah, you're right on that account!" Argus flashed a grin. "My grandma said every war kills people, but that our wars with your people killed the evolution of dwarven cuisine. She liked to cook her own version of elven dishes, even traded precious commodities for contraband herbs and spices."

"She sounds like quite the rebel." Lo set the basket on a smaller stone beside Argus's perch. She lifted the wooden lid and reached inside.

"Not quite." Argus's smile slipped when he recalled his late grandmother. "She just preferred the olden times. The times before the mountains rose up, and all these wars started."

"Smart woman." Lo handed him half a loaf of brown bread and a cheesecloth bag filled with jerked meat. "That's why I'm here now. To find some small measure of peace."

"I can respect that," Argus said. "It's why I'm out here actually. All part of a long, painful journey that would never have happened without the wars."

Lo swallowed a portion of wine before handing him the container. He accepted it with a nod and broader smile. His mouth was full of the jerky, a curious mixture of meat and berries, and he did not wish to be rude. One moment it was salty. Another, it was sweet. Overall, the jerky proved dry. One needed the wine in its wake.

The fluid hit his tongue and exploded with flavor. He tasted honey, flowers, fruit, and something else, something elusive. Argus wondered if the wine was poisoned, but he found the thought to be a ludicrous byproduct of post-war paranoia. After all, the elf drank first and deeper than him. Plus, few poisons and venoms affected dwarves at all. As a result, their food and fermented beverages proved potent enough to be lethal to some races when consumed in large doses.

Seated across from each other, dwarf and elf supped in relative silence. Lobianca's big, dark eyes watched Argus like those of a hunting bird. Her neutral expression defaulted to an ephemeral grin, unless he made a face or emitted a satisfying sound. Then she would smile or laugh or fill him in on the particulars of what he was consuming. After answering a couple of questions, she went on to explain the particulars of the pemmican jerky and pumpkin loaf. He consumed his portion of both, along with her bread, too.

With her blessings, of course. If he wouldn't steal her claim, he wouldn't steal her meal, a meal she'd offered him freely. That would be the height of rudeness.

Lo nibbled at the jerky, but drank deep from the wineskin. Between them, they'd drained it by the time the sun had reached midday. Clouds had gathered above them, mimicking the clouds forming in Argus's brain. He stared at the amorphous blobs of grey and white, wondering if the foreboding weather brought rain or hail. This time of year, one was as likely as the other.

The dwarf stared across the flowing waters. His cart looked so far away. He shivered, envisioning himself trudging across the icy stream. Then the muddy trek back to a leaky shelter.

When he turned back to Lobianca, the elf pointed skyward. "We're going to be wetter and colder sooner rather than later. I don't envy you the trip across the creek."

Argus sucked in his swollen belly and sat straighter, befitting a former soldier. He flashed an overconfident grin. "I'll be fine. We dwarves are built for suffering it seems. Colder, wetter the better, I say." He forced a broader smile.

Lo muttered, "And here I'd have said dwarves were built to make others suffer. At least that's been my experience."

"Excuse me?"

"It's nothing, really. Ignore my ramblings. Look, if you need a place to stay until the storm passes, I have a warm, dry cabin not far from here."

Argus's eyelids grew heavier as he grew colder. The dwarf blinked away nagging fatigue. He grinned once more, slower this time.

Suppressing a yawn, he said, "If it's no trouble. I don't want you to do anything you're not comfortable with. I can understand why you might not want a grubby dwarf darkening your doorway."

"If I minded, I wouldn't have offered. Consider it an olive branch."

"Excuse me?"

"Are you hard of hearing? Or is my accent in the trade tongue that thick?"

"A bit of both, I'd say." Argus smiled again.

Lobianca returned the gesture. "A peace offering. In the past, my people exchanged olive saplings when they made peace."

"Dwarves do something similar, only with statues and monuments to commemorate the war dead. I suspect we owe your people a mountain's worth of them by now."

"You're not incorrect there." Lobianca sighed. "But statues don't replace lives."

"Neither do olives." Argus chuckled.

"Guess that's why the tradition fell by the wayside."

The first drops of rain spattered on the dwarf's helmet. He'd forgotten to remove it in the presence of the lady. His grandmother would have disapproved. No point now, though.

Argus tilted his head, blinking away raindrops, not surprised the storm clouds were overhead. They'd talked longer than he'd intended. Now, he had to ford the creek again. Or trust a virtual stranger. An elf at that.

While feisty, Lobianca appeared harmless enough. Too bad looks were often deceiving. Voluptuous with big eyes and full pouty lips, Argus's ex-wife had seemed the most beautiful woman in the world. In the end, she had turned out to be as ugly and vicious as any goblin. The same could be said for men, too.

Zarkus Pipebender, one of the sons of his former boss, had been the most handsome, distinguished looking dwarf in their military unit. He had been a devil, though, barely kept in check by strict martial law. But as the underboss of a freelance fortune hunting outfit, he had become dangerous, unstable, and murderous. His father and many brothers had secured his position in the gang, or what remained of it after a series of desertions.

Argus had been one of the last to go. After all, he needed the money to fund the search for any family who'd survived the attack on his childhood home. Following a botched and bloody job, he deserted in the dead of night, but was captured a few days later by the Pipebender Gang.

His boss, Papa Pipebender, had used him as an example to the rest of the crew. Beaten, broken, and left for dead, Argus awoke two days later in a shallow grave dug into rocky clay on a piney ridge. They had picked a picturesque location for his grave, but had been in too much of a hurry fill it with enough soil to cover his nostrils.

"Turkeys do the same thing, you know?"

"Huh?" Argus said, pulled from his grim reverie by Lo.

"Turkeys stare at the sky when it rains, beaked mouths agape. Some of them do it until they drown. They think they're drinking their fill, when they're really sowing their destruction."

"I'm not the swiftest dwarf in the mine, but I'm not that dumb."

"That's not what I meant," Lo said. "Don't stare at the sky until the weather makes the decision for you."

Lo pointed toward the creek. It had risen while they'd conversed, which meant the storm front tracked northwest to southeast. Rain falling miles away had flowed into the basin, racing along beneath the clouds. The stream swelled as Argus watched, surging with the rain runoff.

"Seems I'm a turkey, after all."

"Turkey or dwarf, my offer for shelter still stands. But I must away, before Brushtail catches his death of cold out here."

The blue ox dipped its long, curled horns, stamped one massive hoof, and snorted in apparent agreement. The cart's contents rattled. Thunder rumbled overhead, and lightning flashed. The cart shook as the ox lurched ahead a few paces.

"If I've learned anything in life," Argus said with a grin, "it's to never argue with women or livestock."

"Why?" The elf's face twisted into a sinister scowl. "Because we're both stubborn and spirited?"

"No, because you're stronger than you look and capable of killing any man who crosses you."

"You're wiser than you are nimble, Argus Gravelheel."

"Wisdom comes from many mistakes."

Let's hope I'm not making another.

"It'd be a mistake to wade into that creek right now."

"Agreed. Let's get out of rain."

Brushtail snorted and slogged forward toward a makeshift trail through the dense foliage growing in the creek basin. Lo followed, gathering her equipment and tossing the tools into the cart. Argus aided her and then fetched his crossbow.

He doubted anyone would abscond with the weapon. The narrow valley was isolated and sparsely populated, but if the creek flooded, he would likely never see it again. Turning back toward the waterway once again, he wondered about his cart.

Would it be there when he returned? Nothing to do about it now, he feared. The creek had risen two feet or more according to the bank on the far side, which would put it well over his head.

Argus trudged along behind the elf's cart. His boots sank deeper into the mud with each step. At least, he hoped it was mud. The ox had traversed this path before, so its droppings likely lined the rut-filled trail.

Lo stepped lightly along the trail, skipping and bouncing from stone to stone. Her madcap dance in the rain matched her toothy grin. Her smile faltered when she noticed Argus trailing behind.

The elf slipped two slender fingers into her mouth and blew. She whistled over the storm. Brushtail halted.

The woman waited until Argus drew within a few paces and shouted, "It'll be easier riding on the buckboard."

Lobianca flitted to the front of the wagon and scampered onto its plank seat. Turning, she extended one hand downward. The other grabbed onto the seat's edge.

Shifting the crossbow to his right hand, Argus grasped hers with his left. He raised one muddy boot. He strained to reach the lowest rung of narrow steps, little more than iron stirrups welded one atop another and bolted to the cart. With Lo's help, he clambered onto the seat.

Argus found himself intimately close to the elf. The whiskers of his moustache brushed her cheek. She flinched, but she did not move away immediately.

Their eyes bored into each other. Wonder filled his for the moment, but fear, and something sorrowful, lurked behind hers. She stared intently, as if searching his eyes for something. Finally, displaying a flicker of a smile, she edged away from him. Her gaze lingered on him, until she settled on the opposite side of the wagon seat.

Argus averted his eyes and lowered his backside onto the plank seat. His feet dangled over the edge. Once they were moving, he tried to focus on the trail rather than the erratic elf. He wanted to know the lay of the land in case the situation turned awkward. If relations soured, he would walk back in a flood rather than remain where he wasn't wanted.

Judging by her recent reaction and the sadness and fear in her eyes, something haunted the elven woman. Had she lost someone close to her, perhaps everyone close to her? Argus had seen that particular expression on the faces of too many vets, refugees, and war widows. Nearly a decade had passed since the Treaty of Bentfork ended the last total war, but he still saw that look in the mirror most days.

Some who'd experienced loss found ways to deal with it, ways to let it go. Others found ways to hide it. Booze, drugs, and even work became ways to cope with lingering heartache, frequent nightmares, and even full-blown flashbacks. A few, like him, tried to outrun their bitter past and seek a better future.

Whatever her particular damage, he respected her pain and suffering. After all, he'd lost most of his family during the war. When he had returned home, he found it decimated, and everyone gone. Many had died when elves raided the mining town. The bulk of the survivors packed up and left. Some resettled closer to fortified towns and mountain citadels. Others scattered across the Hinterlands.

Argus had spent as much time as he could afford wandering and following leads about various family members, usually based on gossip passed along by survivors who encountered each other at various times and places. The messages often became twisted and embellished as they passed from the lips of one to the ears of another. That process repeated itself across the frontier, producing mostly dead ends and false leads.

After a few years, Argus had located part of his eldest uncle's family. They'd resettled in another mining town, but only Aunt Narn remained in the land of the living. Uncle Yarlt had died with his three sons when a shaft had collapsed, burying nineteen miners with a vein of silver.

By the time Argus found her, Aunt Narn had remarried. She managed the business owned by her new husband, the sole cobbler providing boots for the steady stream of mining recruits. Only a relative by marriage, newly wealthy Narn knew little about the other Gravelheels' whereabouts and cared even less.

Lobianca leaned in close, entering his peripheral vision. She muttered something, but the rain had increased. The deluge drowned out all but the loudest sounds. Plus, her words had fallen on dampened ears and a distracted mind. Argus drifted back to the present.

Moving closer, Lo shouted, "I said, we're almost there, just around the bend!"

"The bend?" Argus stared around, but the trail behind them was barely visible in the downpour. He could not see where water ended and land started in most places. The blinding sheet of rain obfuscated everything beyond the closest foliage lining both sides of the trail.

His attention had wandered with his thoughts. Once again, dwelling on the past intruded into the present. Now, he was lost.

Argus peered through the downpour, stretching his dark vision to its greatest limits. Sooner rather than later, as the ox cart slogged through the mud, details formed of Lobianca's mining camp. A vine-covered cabin stood in the center of a grove of sturdy ancient oaks. The massive trees' canopies provided some respite from the rain, allowing the dwarf to survey the area better.

Rock-lined walkways extended in four directions from the small cabin, the center of her little woodland home. Each winding path was lined with carved poles and covered by an arched roof constructed of woven vines. They were a mix of wild roses, moonflowers, and muscadines, the same vines on the cabin.

One walkway led to a partially enclosed kitchen, complete with an iron woodstove. Another led to an A-frame structure with a set of double doors. Judging by its appearance, it could be a small barn or smokehouse. The third path ended at a workshop, complete with a forge and smelter for processing ore and gems.

The fourth walkway was twice as long as the others. It ended at what appeared to be an enclosed latrine or bathhouse. The boxy structure featured a ventilation pipe and a door engraved with three wavy parallel lines. He recognized it as the sign for the elven goddess of purity and flowing water. Did that make her the patron saint of shitters, too?

His gut gurgled at the realization of a secure dry place to relieve himself. Then it cramped. The dwarf glanced at the elven woman, but she seemed content to wait until the cart closed the remaining distance to the cabin. Perhaps he could wait.

As the pressure in his gassy gut increased, Argus watched the ox veer away from the main structure. The beast circled around a stacked stone well stand—complete with a pump-handle and spigot—and headed for the barnlike building instead. The dwarf looked over at Lobianca again, but her glowing eyes peered into the distance.

"If you'll excuse me," Argus cried, "I need your latrine! I've been surviving on dried nuts and bland hard tack so long that the spiced wine and jerky are warring it out inside me."

Without waiting for a reply, he slid from the seat. He landed in the mud, expecting to sink, but his boots were stopped by the mossy root-riddled soil. He turned back to Lo and his crossbow, but he could not hear the words her lips formed.

"Huh?!"

"Be careful! If Fudgy is in there, don't provoke him. He has an irritable bowel and refuses to eat right, so he spends a lot of time on the pot."

"Uh, okay." The confused dwarf trudged toward the toilet.

His gut growled again. Now that he was away from the comely elven woman, he let a bit of gas escape. But only a little. He couldn't risk filling his trousers on a night he was a houseguest. That would be the height of rudeness.

Argus paused at the edge of the walkway to the outhouse. He pushed through the hanging array of vines, which were meticulously manicured. Cursing, he stopped after a few paces. Thorns dug into his neck, arms, and hands.

"Too late now." When he forged ahead, his skin ripped as the thorns tore free from their fleshy prisons, and his blood dribbled onto the stone-lined walkway. The rain carried it between the cracks. To his wine-sodden senses, the ground appeared to drink his vitae.

Shuddering at the sanguine thought, Argus forced it from his preoccupied mind. He focused on the door, trying to ignore the quivering in his belly and the shaking of his cold, wet limbs. When he arrived at the short set of sturdy steps leading to the latrine's door, he sighed with relief.

The dwarf fumbled with his belt buckle while his other hand reached for the door. He opened the door and raised his head. His bulging eyes met the big orbs of the wet wall of fur filling the outhouse. The bear's eyes disappeared, blocked by its open mouth full of pointed pearly white teeth.

Argus was not sure what happened first, if he screamed at the sight of a grizzly bear wedged into a space the size of a closet or if the beast with the irritable bowel and murderous maw had roared. He did know what happened next, though. The dwarf stumbled, slipped on wet stones, and landed on his backside, right before shitting his pants.

The grizzly loomed over him like a fuzzy shadow. It bellowed again, but stopped abruptly. Sniffing with a nose the size of the dwarf's face, the bear blanched, whined, and backed away.

"C'mon now!" Argus cried. "It can't be that bad!"

Apparently, the odor of his offal had offended the bear's acute sense of smell. The beast retreated toward the latrine, preferring the shithouse's odor to that of the shitty dwarf.

Argus was a veteran of two wars and participant in countless ambushes. He had lain in wait for the perfect shot for up to three days, so he was no stranger to soiling himself. But this was the first time he recalled it saving his life.

"I see Fudgy found you unappetizing." The laughing elf stood paces away on the path. She covered her nose with one delicate hand. The helpful elf walked forward, extending the other hand to help him.

Argus blushed, aware of his situation and its offensiveness to his host and even her pets. On this occasion, he had not just stepped in it. He had fallen back into it.

"No, don't! Just wait there."

Argus struggled to his feet. He tried to smile, but failed. He avoided her gaze. He glanced from the elf to the bear and then the barn. He latched onto a solution.

"By your leave, I will sleep in the barn tonight. Seems I am not fit company to sleep in a house with a lady."

"Nonsense!" Lo said. "Even the best pets just need to be housebroken. Now, take advantage of Mother Nature's bounty. Strip and shower while I bring you something clean to wear."

"What about him?" Argus gestured to the bear.

"Fudgy doesn't need a shower. I keep his arse hairs shaved, so he can stay hygienic. Plus, he sleeps in the barn with Brushtail. Not sure he'd treat you as a bunkmate or a midnight snack."

Argus parted the vines and stepped into the cold beating rain. His hands shook by the time he'd removed his garb. He hung his pants on one of the hooks driven into the wood posts to support the extensive network of vines. With luck, the rain would wash them clean, too.

The shivering dwarf stood in the downpour until everything, but his muddy feet, was clean. He might catch his death from the cold, but he would not die with shit in his trousers. Trudging to the path once more, Argus gasped when the thorny vines pricked his icy skin. More of his blood mixed with the water and earth.

Lobianca waited for him at the end of the path. Her rough silhouette framed by the light shining through the open doorway of her cabin. Drawing near her, Argus's hands kept his helmet over his manhood, preserving some mystery. After all, the dwarf had no desire for her to see his anatomy in its current state. Between his frightful encounter with the bear and his shower in the freezing rain, his cock had crawled back into the rooster house until winter was over.

Lobianca held a furry robe out to him, a mirror of the one wrapped around her. Her pale limbs and bare feet led him to believe she'd relieved herself of her wet garments as well. Blushing at the thought, Argus accepted the heavy garment and swirled it about him, careful to keep his manhood concealed. He didn't mind flashing her a bit of freshly clean cheek, though. It was one of his better features.

Clad in the warm skins of mammoths or buffalos, they sat by the fireplace, sipping a hot spiced cider from mugs made from the acorns of redwood trees. Neither had said a word for a spell. Argus was not sure if they were enjoying a comfortable silence or suffering an awkward one. Either way, he was exhausted.

Lobianca proved a hospitable enough host, even if she was not as entertaining now. Perhaps she was tired, too. Either way, he had no right to criticize her for remaining mum for a spell.

The dwarven drifter was warmer and drier than he'd been since his last stay in a real inn, which had been so long ago he failed to recall its name. His belly was full as was his cup. Between dinner and now, they had chatted in a friendly, if shallow, fashion. They stuck to mining and prospecting, or the weather and local geography, not the wars, not the hardships, and definitely not the losses.

Lo's head poked out of her hooded robe. She peered into the fire, nibbling her nails. The fire hissed. A log popped, echoing in the stone hearth, and its fiery contents shifted. Shadows flickered across her face, but she didn't flinch this time.

Argus sipped at his spiced cider without spilling a drop. Between the war and mining operations, he had a steely resolve when it came to fire, explosions, and the other chaos encountered on the battlefield or that resulted from mining accidents.

Seems my host has a resolve forged by fire and loss, too. I admire a hardy widow surviving in the Hinterlands. There are so many ways one can be robbed of everything and everyone here. How had Lo lost her husband? Was it a mining mishap? Or something more tragic, more violent?

No sooner had he thought it when she said, "My dear Erythmus loved his cider. Prospecting was really just a way of paying for something we both loved. Some might say it was his love of his brew and our cherished orchard that got him killed, not a mining mishap as one would expect from a better brewmaster than miner."

"Orchards, you say." A distant horrific memory flashed across Argus's brain. The flood of colorful images, dominated by red apples and even redder blood, rattled his brain with the intensity of the sudden thunderclap that shook the cabin.

For a long awkward moment, the rain pelting the roof and the crackle of the fire filled the silence between them. Lobianca's head turned slowly and deliberately until her eyes bored into his. The elf's high cheekbones and sharp features cast long shadows on her face. Fire danced in her wild eyes, like the one raging in his head. Memories of his past misdeeds replayed a particularly regrettable scene, one that had led to him being left for dead.

Argus's association with the notorious Pipebender Gang had been doomed from the start. First, there had been a stint of bushwhacking and armed robberies to steal enough capital and equipment for mining operations. Then they had moved from one productive but vulnerable claim to another. They ran off most of the legitimate claim holders, but some proved stubborn and required convincing.

Arson usually did the trick. Failing that assault worked nine times out of ten. Killing over a claim was uncommon, but it had happened, usually because someone on one side or the other lost their cool.

Ultimately, it had been the unprovoked killing of a hospitable elf farmer and the burning of his prized orchard that had caused Argus to sever his ties with the Pipebenders. Yawning, he recalled being on the verge of a dire choice when fate had snatched away his chance for redemption. His hand moved reflexively to his bearded face. He could feel the deep grooves in his flesh beneath the wooly mass. Argus had preferred a cleaner, more manicured beard before the golden eagle. The mad creature had attacked him before he shot Papa Pipebender in the back.

Turning to Lobianca, Argus's eyes met the piercing black eyes of the same eagle. Screeching, the bird-of-prey flew from the chair toward him. Argus flinched and shuddered, closing his eyes. The screech died away, replaced by his screams.

He dropped the mug and covered his face. Fresh pain bit his skin, this time from spilled cider. When no attack came, he felt foolish.

Another flashback, I guess.

Finally, he peeked from behind his hands. This time he saw a freakier sight, the elven woman perched on an arm of the chair. Her eyes fixed him with the malevolence of a predator.

“What’s going on?” Argus asked. “I don’t understand.”

Lobianca screeched, “Sleep!” She waved one open palm.

The word hit him with the force of a flash flood. His arms were leaden. His eyelids closed no matter how much he fought.

“Why?” Argus asked as the world faded to black. “I don’t…”

The treacherous elf’s words reached his doped brain faintly.

“You’ll understand everything once you’re ‘Awake’!”

The dwarf’s eyes snapped open, only to be pelted with heavy raindrops. He shook his head, but it was the only part of his body to respond. His limbs had been restrained, and the more he attempted to move the more needlelike pain pierced his vulnerable flesh. Craning his neck and opening his eyes, Argus realized his body was constricted by the same thorny vines that had covered the pathways connecting Lobianca’s homestead.

What homestead? Argus wondered. *What happened to it?*

The oak grove remained, but the cabin and its outlying structures were gone. A lone flat-topped stone adorned the moss-covered clearing inside the ring of trees. Since he was lashed to it with living rooted vines, the dwarf did not think it too much of a leap of logic to call his resting place an altar.

An altar! The mere word terrified him. It conjured images of elven blood druids dancing naked among the oaks, sacrificing dwarves unlucky enough to wander into their sacred grove. Leave it to him to blunder into one of the silly but grisly legends he’d laughed at in his youth, all while secretly losing sleep over them.

The elf bitch must have doped me? But how? With what?

A flash of lightning revealed another lingering presence from the earlier hallucination, or illusion, whatever he had been seeing. The grizzly bear with the neatly groomed backside emerged from underneath the largest oak. Fudgy huffed and bared his prominent teeth, circling the altar counter-clockwise. A familiar screech drew Argus’s attention from the beast.

Twisting his head to the right, he saw a large feathery blur. The eagle swooped from a tree, provoking the same flashback as before. As the raptor banked and soared around the edge of the clearing, Argus slipped from the present to the past.

The dwarf recalled the confusion caused by the bird when it had launched a surprise attack on the dwarves aiming crossbows at the orchard's owner, an elf rumored to horde a treasure excavated from the mine on his property. Despite their crossbows, three dwarves, including the youngest Pipebender brother, had died fighting the formidable farmer.

Argus had considered the eagle a casualty, too. After all, a bolt, fired by one of the Pipebenders, had missed his face by inches and skewered the bird. He figured it couldn't have flown far, but he'd been wrong. He'd been wrong about so many things.

Now, here in the dark, he'd pay for his sins. There would be no redemption, no turning over a new leaf as the elves would say. Hope flew the coop as the eagle flew low over the bear's back.

The great bird transformed into the elf woman, Lobianca Willowshroud. She landed atop the grizzly, and they circled the altar once. Twice. From what he could observe of her painfully slow victory laps, her eyes never left him.

Argus attempted to return the stare. Not to match the venom he saw there, but to show her he was unafraid. The elven shapeshifter screeched, and he roared at her, a pathetic imitation of her pet bear. The vines tightened, their thorns cutting deeper into his skin. The cold failed to numb him to the piercing pain.

Lobianca slid from the grizzly's slick back and sprinted toward the altar. She drew her shiny dagger on the run. The elven steel rang loudly enough to be heard over the falling rain.

The mad woman leaped onto the stone, straddling the dwarf. Her eyes glowed red in the darkness, and her bone white skin shined with each lightning flash. Instead of raging, cursing, or even praying, Argus cried over the thunder, "I'm sorry!"

"Sorry!" She screamed. The tip of the knife bit into his chest. "You think sorry is going to cut it? Oh no, I think I prefer steel."

"If you were reading my mind earlier, or even just my emotions," Argus said, breathing as shallowly as possible, "you know it's the truth. We did go to your farm to rob it, but murdering your husband wasn't part of the plan. I didn't sign up for that shit! Neither did the others. But Papa Pipebender and his sons forced us to kill more and more people along the way, including your husband."

"Don't talk about my husband!" Lobianca's warm spittle mingled with the cold rain on his face. On the other hand, she hadn't driven the knife into his heart. *Yet.* "Don't use him as part of your lies. That's what your people do, isn't it? Lie, steal, and kill!"

"It's not a lie! Look inside my mind again, if you dare!"

"What if I carve your heart out instead?"

Argus grimaced when the dagger's tip hit his dense sternum, but he remained deathly still. Any movement at this point could be fatal. The same could be said of any further provocation.

Whispering his confessional, he said, "That wouldn't help you, help us, get justice for your husband. And for the others. Sure, I'd be dead. There'd be one less piece-of-shit dwarf stinking up elf lands. But the Pipebenders would still be alive. You would have to find them on your own, fight them on your own, and kill them on your own. Can you avoid every trap leading into their hideout? Can you handle the whole clan? Just you and a bear with bad bowels?"

The elf stared at him for what felt like an eternity. Despite the knife in his chest, Argus was thankful to be shielded from the rain, if only for the last few moments of his life. He made peace with the situation, with failing to find redemption. Perhaps the Underworld would not be as torturous as Overworld.

We should never have come Topside. We should have stayed allies with the elves. Then life would have turned out differently.

No! Hot tears streamed from the dwarf's eyes. *You have no one to blame but yourself. You should have shot Papa Pipebender after the first bloodbath he created. You were in charge then. You had a following then. After appeasing that madman, you became his dog. You were loyal and obedient, until you were beat one time too many. Your decisions damn near killed you then. And they're responsible for killing you now, Argus Gravelheel.*

"What if I told you they didn't have to?" Lobianca tilted her head at an angle. Pity colored her face, replacing her rage. She removed the knife from his sternum, though she kept its bloody tip close to his vulnerable throat. "It's true that I see what is in your heart and head. For now. The combination of drugs I used to paralyze and entrance you makes it easier for me to peer into them, but the effects are temporary. But if you lie to me now, they'll last longer than your life."

"Nothing but the truth, I swear!" Argus meant every word.

I'm your dog now. Just don't kill me.

"Do you truly seek redemption in the eyes of Creator, Mother Nature, and Judges of the Underworld? If so, do you know where these Pipebenders can be found? And will you help me exterminate these vermin?"

Breathing deeply, the dwarf focused his jumbled thoughts before speaking in self-defense. The art had saved him before, and he hoped it saved him now. Argus spoke from the heart.

"I left the night after your husband was killed. When they caught me, I was beaten, stabbed, left for dead, and buried alive. After I awoke in that shallow grave, I adopted a new mission in life, to find and reunite with my family, those who weren't killed by elves in the war, anyway.

"So I understand loss. I understand overwhelming guilt and regret. I also understand the desire for revenge."

Argus was careful to maintain eye contact with Lobianca. No matter how much this confessional hurt him or how many tears he shed while telling it. The elf's face remained impassive like she was looking through him rather than at him.

"Don't think I didn't think about it while sitting on the ridge this morning. I could have sent one elf down to the Underworld to start settling the tab for my dead family. But I didn't. I wouldn't have. It's not neighborly."

"Not neighborly?" Lobianca laughed, spewing more spittle. "You're ridiculous, Argus Gravelheel. And pathetic, I think. But you're not beyond redemption.

"After all, in your heart of hearts, you realize if we keep fighting these wars, even on a personal scale, there won't be any dwarves or elves left one day. Mark my words. Myriad species, and countless cultures, have lived and died because of petty competition over resources easily shared. How many others have died because of a miscommunication during a crisis? How many more must die before the conflicts and miscommunications end?"

The elf stroked Argus's brow with her free hand. "Perhaps you have the potential to learn a better path to walk in this life. But first, we have to take a chance on trust at some point, for the sake of our mutually aligned goals. Do you agree?"

"Yes, of course." His body shuddered once he realized he might make it out of this situation alive. The vines constricted, and thorns ripped at his flesh. "Please just make it stop. I'll help!"

"Do you swear it, Argus Gravelheel?" Lobianca stuck the knife so close to his left eye he could no longer focus on its tip. A moment later, she waved the weapon about her head in a frenetic series of loops, whirls, and circles. "Here in this sacred grove, a holy conduit, you swear an oath in your own blood?"

"Before all the gods old and new, elf and dwarf, I do!"

"Excellent!" Lobianca lowered the knife. "I think we'll get along fine. As long as you remain as loyal to me, and to your oath, as your favorite animal, a dwarf man's best friend."

"So you want me to be your dog, is that it?"

"As a matter of fact, I do. Quite literally."

"I think you mean—"

Argus screamed when new hells racked his body. His muscles spasmed and burned. His bones snapped and shifted inside him. His nose swelled, along with his jaws, and the world exploded with newly discovered odors. Even the rain contained a palpable odor over the strong scent of his blood, sweat, and fear. His tongue stretched and lolled across his pointy canines. When he opened his mouth to scream once more, he howled instead.

Letting Go Is Hard To Do: Part II

Jeremy Hicks

Lobianca Willowshroud perched on the uppermost limb of a great oak, one of the few hardwoods left standing on the rocky ridge overlooking two parallel valleys. Pines had become as invasive as dwarves in this region, replacing much of the old growth burned away when the mountains rose up, a pyroclastic and earth-shattering event that had come to define modern Mirstone. Greedy dwarves, fast-growing conifers, and bitter wars had followed.

Lobianca and her late husband, Erythmus, had survived the wars. For a time, they had lived at peace, farming and mining their sanctuary nestled amongst the rocky hills of the Hinterlands. In a cruel twist—common enough in tales like these—he had been taken from her while she had been forced to watch.

No, not taken. Stolen by thieves and murderers.

The same gang of bloodthirsty bandits she watched from her treetop perch. The same gang that planned to rob a stage coach they believed to be carrying a payroll bound for a garrison of soldiers. The same gang she planned to exterminate.

Or die in the attempt.

The Pipebenders had been military men once, proud patriots who'd volunteered to expand the whole of dwarfdom. Now, they sought to steal from the army who'd cheated them out of occupied land and promised pensions and sent them packing after the war. Rumors of a lightly guarded payroll proved too tempting for Papa Pipebender and his surviving sons to resist.

Baiting this trap would not have been possible without the assistance of the dwarf-turned-dog named Argus Gravelheel. She did not have to glance down to know the dwarf-dog waited below. The hound's odor wafted upward, recognized by the enhanced senses of the elven druid.

Lo turned toward the other valley instead, shifting her gaze from the Pipebenders and their crew. The bird's eye view allowed her eagle eyes to spot the stage coach from leagues away. The thunder of the horses' hooves prevented her from hearing the chatter of the dwarves seated on the wagon.

She would have to work quickly if she intended on keeping her side of the deal with her magically transformed companion. After his transformation, Argus had Lo swear a counter oath because he wanted no more innocent blood on his hands. *Or paws, rather.* To all appearances, the former gang member and soldier had been turning over a new leaf when she found him excavating a worthless mining claim.

Lobianca remained doubtful that the dwarf could be trusted if pressed. That's why she had secured a blood oath from him and transformed him into her trusty sidekick, a Catterand Hound, a breed trained to track dwarves by the elven military. She learned all about them while serving as a scout during the wars.

That was how she'd met Erythmus. He had commanded the company of cavalry to which she was assigned. Tall, lean, and muscular, he had glittered like a silvery angel in his sculpted officer's breastplate and winged helm. His widow had buried his charred remains in that same suit.

Screeching like a banshee haunting a moor, the golden eagle—her preferred animal form—glided from the treetop. She banked, circling the tree and surveying the scene. Gang members moved into position, their stubby legs good for climbing but not well-adapted for the tangled undergrowth between the pines.

If they're cursing the briars now, they'll loathe them for life soon enough. What's left of their pathetic lives, anyway!

Lobianca lighted on the lowest branch of the towering tree, a few centuries younger than the aged elven druid. Her black eyes settled on the big brown eyes of the hound. Despite their fierce natures, Catterands had soulful eyes, another reason she felt it an appropriate form for the guilt-ridden dwarf.

"Stay here! Stay quiet!" Lo cried aloud. "Betray me and die!"

Argus woofed. "You're the one screeching and squawking like a chicken with a snake in the coop."

"Just remember your oath."

"Remember yours. The fleas biting my arse are a constant reminder of my side of this deal, which is raw as my…" Argus chewed at his backside to emphasize his point.

Lobianca did not know whether to laugh or cry. With a beak instead of lips and tear ducts designed to lubricate her eagle eyes' protective membranes, she couldn't do either in her present form. The druid made a mental note to flea dip the dwarf before she changed him back. If she lived to change him back.

Only one way to be sure. Kill them before they kill me.

Lo spread her wings and soared toward the crux of the ambush, the blind bend in the road through the pass that connected the two valleys. While the wagon and its team traversed what amounted to a logging trail through the woods, they would be vulnerable to attack. Focused on their quarry, she hoped the Pipebender Gang would be vulnerable, too.

The lady eagle caught a thermal and rode it, adjusting her wings for maximum lift. Turning tight circles, she surveyed the positions selected by the bushwackers. This part of the plan required improvisation and imagination, for neither she nor Argus could predict the particulars of the Pipebenders' plan.

The gang wore masks, hooded cloaks, scarves, or handkerchiefs to conceal their bearded faces. This prevented easy facial recognition, but then again, she had seen them only once before, the day the orchards burned along with her beloved. In her zeal for revenge, she had forgotten to have Argus point out Papa Pipebender, his sons, and any of their flunkies who had been present that day.

Squawking in frustration, Lo circled again. She looked and listened for clues to their identity. She did not have to wait long before careless words on the wind called her to her first victim. When the speaker glanced at the sky, the disguised elf could see the fear in the dwarf's turquoise eyes.

"I sure wish that bird would shut it!"

"Guess we're too close to its nest," his partner-in-crime said.

"Wish it would bugger off before I put a bolt in it." The robust dwarf lifted the wide brim of his hat and mopped sweat from his forehead with the back of his sleeve. "I hate eagles. Give me the heebie-jeebies."

"'Scary Lerry' Pipebender afeared of a flyin' fowl!" The smaller dwarf laughed. "What'll the others say when—"

Scary Lerry lived up to his name as soon as the jest escaped the other man's lips. He dropped his crossbow and wrapped both meaty hands around the joker's neck. Lerry shook him like a sapling in a storm.

Lobianca made her move the moment both men were distracted. Swooping below the tree line, she shifted forms and landed in a crouch. Beneath her animal guise, she wore leather garments dyed the color of the local clay. The druid could only transform so much excess material at a time, so she traveled light. Her kit included a haversack, a waterskin, a war club with a carved bird's head, and several blades, one of them a khopesh.

Lo drew the short, curved sword and touched its silvered blade to her forehead. She whispered a prayer to Mother Nature, asking her forgiveness for the blood she was about to spill. A sudden breeze brushed across her exposed skin, a warm caress despite the lateness of the year.

Reassured by the omen, she padded across the pine needles and other leaf litter. Her moccasin-covered feet created less sound than a feather drawn across a lover's skin. Briars, privet, and vines parted ways for the creeping druid. The thorny briars and thick vines followed her closely, snaking toward her quarry.

"Don't you ever, ever..." Lerry's voice trailed to a wet gurgle. A crimson line blossomed across his fat neck in her curved blade's wake. The dying dwarf staggered. His grip loosened on the choking man.

The other dwarf fought to raise the alarm, but thorn-covered vines replaced Lerry's hands. The fibrous material tightened, even as the gingery dwarf thrashed and clawed at them. His dark eyes bulged from their sockets, standing out from the eyeholes cut into his canvas mask.

Lobianca placed one slender finger to her full lips. "Shhh."

While the vines lashed the choking dwarf to the closest tree, Lo hefted the dead man's weighty repeating crossbow from the forest floor. When it hadn't discharged earlier, she realized it had a safety catch. She thumbed it into the "Ready" position and leveled the weapon.

With a smile on her face, she squeezed the curved brass trigger. The steel bolt passed between the dwarf's hands, pierced his windpipe, and stapled him to the bluebark pine. The air escaping his garish neck wound sounded like a sad, wet imitation of her shush.

Heavy footfalls on the forest floor wrested her attention from the gory scene. Lobianca did not see the dwarf yet, but knew she had little time before he arrived in the small clearing. Shifting forms again, her whole perspective changed as the forest seemed to grow taller around her. The hare's legs kicked hard, propelling her fuzzy tail toward the dense undergrowth.

Lo exited the opposite side of the clearing ahead of the dwarf's arrival. Darting and dodging through the foliage, the gray streak circled around until she reached fresh tracks. She paused to sniff at the boot prints. Her tiny but sensitive nostrils smelled strong booze, sour sweat, and goat dung.

Low curses reached her ears, the sound coming from the clearing. With no time to spare, she dashed from the foliage into the open. The dwarf had a tan handkerchief tied around his neck and stretched over his nose. Black braids from his beard spilled out from under his poor disguise.

The bandit turned toward her, but stopped short of loosing a bolt. Chuckling, he lowered his crossbow.

"It's your lucky day, rabbit."

If you only knew.

Lobianca's nose twitched. Her furry feet thumped against the ground. She bared her long, flat teeth and charged. Amused by the raging hare, the dwarf cocked his head and chuckled.

The rabbit leaped into the air, but it landed as a mist cat. The dwarf had no time to scream, for his head was caught in the toothy maw of a hunting cat the size of a dire wolf. Lo shook her head until she heard a satisfying snap. The bandit's body went limp, and she dropped him like the dead weight he'd become.

The dwarf's blood tasted like a copper coin on her tongue. Sadly, it was not an unpleasant taste. She licked at her gory snout, cleaning as much of the sticky fluid from it as possible. The mist cat snuck away from the scene of its crime, disappearing into the forest and living up to its name.

Lobianca padded through the forest, staying in the undergrowth despite her form's natural camouflage. The scent of mountain rams grew stronger as she stalked along the woody slope above a narrow hollow, a natural drain for rain water or snowmelt flowing from the ridgetop. The rams' musk mingled with oiled steel, the sour tang of dwarf sweat soaked into leather, and something floral, almost feminine.

Leaping onto a formation of mossy rocks, Lo sought a better viewpoint. Her efforts were rewarded, for she found the location where the Pipebenders had stashed their mounts. The wooly battle rams had curved horns, steel bits and bridles, and tooled saddles. The beasts looked fierce, but proved temperamental if provoked. With the right approach, the rams could be driven into a panic. Unfortunately, three gang members guarded them.

The oldest of the dwarven trio, his beard white as a dove's wing, watched the terminus of the hollow where it emptied onto the road. His repeating crossbow rested in the crook of a butchered rhododendron, mangled for his nefarious purposes. The stout bush's flowery limbs littered the ground at his feet, which were covered by spurred boots favored by their cavalry.

The senseless destruction of the colorful rhododendron typified dwarf behavior. They had to destroy in order to create, unlike her people who had largely found ways to modify their environment without obliterating it. Sounds of more destruction drew Lo's attention from the other two dwarves in the hollow, a well-groomed man in military-style armor and a young woman in garishly-colored clothes, like those of a burlesque or circus performer.

An injured oak's high-pitched scream cut across the dwarves' conversation, for the druid spoke as readily with flora as she did with fauna. Rhythmic thwacks of axes followed the agonizing cry. Neither gruesome sound could be ignored, despite Lobianca's desire to scatter the gang's mounts. The druid retreated from her rocky perch and rushed through the valley toward the scene of the woody crime.

The mist cat cleared the sorry excuse of a road in one bound. She landed in the bushes on the far side and slowed to a crawl. Her nostrils sniffed at the air while twitching ears struggled to hear more than the tree and axe.

The stagecoach's horses sounded much closer now, echoing through the valley. The stage had turned onto the road through the pass. If so, it had been spotted by the Pipebenders' lookouts. Hence the tree slaughter, a distraction to stop the wagon.

Two gang members worked in tandem, each with an axe more suited for felling elves than trees. They alternated blows on the young oak, easy enough to chop down while tall and wide enough to block the whole trail. A third dwarf's attention bounced between the axmen and the trail. The golden-haired guard had enough sense to keep his double crossbow pointed away from his companions. Too bad the pungent cigar he smoked forced him to hold the weapon with one unsteady arm. His carelessness provided Lobianca with all the time she needed.

As she had predicted, the dwarves proved efficient destroyers. The poor oak was beyond saving and in a few blows would shudder and fall into the path of the stage's team of horses. With the blind curve in the road, the animals could break their legs before stopping. While Lo could do nothing for the tree other than provide it with a merciful death and a chance at its own bit of revenge, she could save the horses from harm.

The mist cat circled this particular trio of bandits until she reached the optimum angle of attack. She charged, relying on her natural camouflage and the dwarves' focus on their particular tasks. Lo leaped, extending her claws in midair, and landed on the side of the dying oak.

The sickening snap and sudden shutter as its trunk twisted did nothing to assuage the wailing tree. Its dying screams echoed in the cat's ears. Instead of falling toward the road, the oak fell in the direction dictated by the heavy beast clinging to its trunk. Lobianca rode the falling tree until she was sure it was on target.

By the time the cigar-smoking, crossbow-carrying dwarf turned toward the threat, he had no time to run. The oak struck him squarely, crushing his skull and right shoulder before landing atop his battered body. In full view of the astonished axmen, the mist cat stalked back and forth in front of the gore-covered tree.

The dwarf on her left braced to fight, raising his battle axe and baring his yellow teeth. His partner, however, made a wiser choice and ran for the road as fast as his stubby legs would carry him. The defiant dwarf glanced over at his retreating companion and said, "Get back here, you yellow dog sombitch!"

Lobianca seized the initiative, exploiting the distraction. She jumped, fore claws leading the way, but the distance proved too great to clear in a single bound. She landed in range of his axe.

The dwarf swung, forcing her to retreat several steps to avoid a smashed skull. When he overextended on his swing, she raked a paw across the back of his left arm. The three parallel gashes were enough to disable his unarmored limb.

Hefting the axe with his right arm, the gang member roared louder than any big cat. Even if the dwarf died now, he had raised the alarm. Grinning fiercely, he charged. Her left paw swatted him hard enough to topple him.

He landed in a heap, both arms bleeding from her claws. His mask had been knocked askew, obscuring his vision. The mist cat gave the blinded bleeding dwarf no quarter, sinking her teeth into his exposed back. She shook him until a chuck of flesh ripped free, and he fell to the forest floor.

Lo spat the dwarf meat onto the ground despite her animalistic urge to consume it. The bandit groaned and said something, but the mist cat's pulse pounded in its ears. She did not even hear her own roar when she pounced.

The dwarf flopped onto his back before the beast landed. He raised a D-guard dagger, a sidearm common among dwarf soldiers. The knife bit into her flank, sliding along one of her ribs. She roared in pain and rage and, unable to fit his entire head into her mouth, sank her teeth into the sides of his face.

The dwarf twisted his blade. She squeezed with all the force in her jaws. The dwarf's skull broke before she bled out, and his body went limp. Despite the pain, Lo enjoyed the rush provided by each satisfying step toward achieving justice for her murdered husband.

Voices filled the forest around her, interrupting her appraisal of her sanguine handiwork. The druid wanted to stand and fight, but the mist cat's adrenalin and instincts screamed at her to flee and lick her wounds. This time she did not fight the cat's instincts, bounding into the brush and disappearing from view once more. While she would leave no tracks, there would be a blood trail for the dwarves to follow.

They would find her if they took the time to look, but not before she had planned a new ambush. Curiosity would not kill the cat this time; instead, it should enable the cat to kill anyone curious enough to trail her blood into the foliage.

Finding sanctuary in the shadows of a rock shelter, the big cat circled widdershins before returning to its true form. The elf woman slumped against the cool limestone and slipped to the ground. The wound in Lobiança's side was shallow and bled freely, but turned out to be relatively minor. Her form's sturdy ribcage had protected its innards and, by extension, hers.

She reclined against the low wall of the rock shelter. Closing her eyes, she applied pressure to her wound with one hand and reached into her haversack with the other. The shoulder bag contained most of her remaining possessions, except those she'd stashed in the aftermath of the fire, not that much had survived.

Lo removed a thick green glass jar capped with fine copper mesh and secured with a steel band. She flipped the release on the band and slid the mesh free. Whispering to the lurkers in the dark, she coaxed them from their partial hibernation.

The Chirurgia Spiders climbed from the jar and crossed across her hand, tickling her with their needle-like legs. They scurried toward the smell of fresh blood. Lobianca withdrew her bloody hand from their path, not wanting to confuse the helpful little critters.

The arachnids descended on her wound, aligning over the bloody gash. Their pronounced mandibles opened wide and snapped together, pulling her flesh along with them. Lo gasped and writhed as each of the attached spiders' wove a silk suture, aided by their sharp, skillful appendages. All the while, they drank the remaining blood that seeped from the wound.

Lobianca's eyes fluttered, and her strength flagged. Sighing, she almost fell asleep with the Chirurgia at work on the wound. Suddenly, she sat bolt upright.

"Enough!" When one persisted, Lo plucked it from the suture it had secured minutes ago and dropped it into the jar. "The rest of you, back inside. Meal time's over."

The spiders obeyed, but moved slower this time. Their blood-bloated bodies dropped one by one into the jar. Once the last straggler entered, she capped the container and secured its lid.

Lobianca returned the arachnids to her shoulder bag, and then slumped against the rock wall again. *I'll just rest my eyes.* Her heavy lids closed, drawing a veil of blackness across her vision. The coolness of the shelter shuttled her to the Dreamtime.

In Lo's dream, Erythmus was still alive. The druid was still happy, for she had yet to become a widow, a Willowshroud. Husband and wife walked together in their orchard, the pride and joy of their farm. Every trees' limbs hung low, covered in apples. Harvest time was upon them.

Distant thunder signaled a storm on the horizon, but she could see no clouds. She detected no pressure change. Change was coming, though, for them, for their farm, for the rest of their lives. When they parted company to fill their baskets, she had no idea it would be the last time their lips kissed in this life.

This dream haunted Lobianca most every time she rested her eyes.

Her medicated sleep in the wake of the spiders' suture job proved to be no different. Only this time, a dog's persistent bark joined the sound of the approaching thunder, the hooves of the Pipebenders' battle rams.

Lo awoke to the smell of something burning. The dream evaporated as her eyes focused on smoke wafting into the rock shelter. The new element of her recurrent dream persisted, the deep distinctive barking of a Catterand Hound.

"It's a setup!" The dwarf's voice rose above the dog, which seemed to be circling the area around Lobianca's hiding place.

"How can you be sure, Zarkus?"

Zarkus?! That's one of Papa Pipebenders' boys!

"That's a Devil Dog," Zarkus replied, using the dwarven moniker for the hounds. "The elves used them to hunt us during the war. I'd know that sound anywhere."

"You reckon they bounty hunters, son?" Papa Pipebender asked, his voice sounding farther away.

"That stage was a bust," a third dwarf added. "No telling how many of us are dead already. I say, we high-tail it. The brush is on fire, and some of the trees are catching. We're liable to end up boxed in here."

"For a former knight," Zarkus said, "you sure like to sound the retreat, Silverforge."

"One of the reasons why I survived two wars and this gang's growing recklessness."

"Careful with them loose words," Papa shouted, "Someone might think you're disloyal like that dog Argus. We know how that worked out for him and his supporters."

"Nah, Major, just stating my tactical read on the situation."

"Is that so, Dakken?" asked Papa Pipebender, another former officer, albeit a Sergeant Major, not a knight errant with Dakken Silverforge's noble lineage. "You suggest I leave Lerry and my men out here, not knowing their fates."

"Lerry's dead, Papa," Zarkus interjected. "We found him while you tracked this blood trail. That's what I was coming to tell you when that Devil Dog started raising hell."

"What happened to him?" Papa's voice rose to a shrill pitch before hitching in his throat."

"His throat had been cut. Someone killed Xek and the newbie, too. But it looked like someone stabbed him in the head and then broke his neck."

"My Little Lerrer, I'll make them pay. Oh, you sonofabitches! You hear me. I'll end you!" The old dwarf shouted into the forest, before choking on the thickening smoke.

"We can't do it here," Silverforge said, his voice growing calmer as the older dwarf became more irrational, cursing and shouting more threats into the burning forest. "We'll burn, choke, or blunder into an ambush."

"I can't leave," Papa said, "I can't leave until they're dead!"

"If we stay, we'll be the dead ones, Papa. Silverforge's right. If they want us, they can come get us. We'll be ready."

Lobianca knew Zarkus's statement to be an absolute truth. If they slipped the trap now, she would have to pursue them into the heart of their hideout, a mining town nestled along a river beyond a narrow, steep-sided canyon. The Pipebenders were the closest thing to the law in Lickskillet, owning both the shire reeve and territorial guildmeister. She couldn't let them make it there alive.

When Lo attempted to stand, her legs refused to hoist her to her feet. They felt leaden, drained of strength...and blood. She had exerted herself too much, too quickly, and had become reckless in the process. As a result, her strength and powers were fleeting, but they were not yet exhausted.

Using her sore arms, Lobianca pulled her legs underneath her. The elf rose to one knee and braced her elbows against the wall for stability. Her pale skin scrapped along the rough limestone as she forced her limbs to cooperate. The determined druid stood until her head brushed the top of the rock shelter. Blood from her abraded elbows stained the wall, another sacrifice for her justice.

Lobianca staggered from the rock shelter, glancing in every direction. The Pipebenders appeared to be farther away than their voices had indicated. The steep-sided rocky streambed had distorted the sounds, which meant she had no idea where the hound was at the moment or what was going on in his head.

As if he'd read her mind, Argus bayed from behind her. The Catterand's powerful voice dwarfed a savannah lion's roar. She turned to see the calf-sized hound standing on the outcrop above the rock shelter. He bared his teeth and barked.

"They're above us!" Zarkus cried, returning Lo's attention to the bandits.

"50 gold crowns to the man who kills that blasted dog!" Vonder "Papa" Pipebender posted the bounty with a bellow, but fired his crossbow first. Judging from Argus's stories about the gang leader, the miserly dwarf hoped to save himself the gold.

She shifted her attention fast enough that her head spun, causing her to stumble. The druid knelt in the cool waters of the stream and watched as the dwarves wasted precious bolts firing at the Catterand as it bounced to and fro, barking and howling at their futile efforts. The angle of their shots were too steep, and the foliage between them too thick. The smoke settling into the deeper basin on the edge of the shallow valley did not help either.

Making direct contact with the land, Lobianca could no longer ignore the burgeoning wildfire. As trees and bushes burned and small woodland creatures choked and fled, their screams reached her ears. Thanks to the running water, their terror and pain flowed into her heart. Fresh tears fell, joining the stream and blurring her vision.

The dwarf's cigar! In my haste, I didn't make sure it was out.

Her quarry scattered across her field of vision, almost within her reach. All around them, more of the vulnerable forest burned with each wasted moment. Rising to her sodden feet once more, Lo glared at the dwarves who continued to fire at the hound.

What do I do now?

If she retreated to the shelter, she could call upon the stones to shake the slope beneath the dwarves' feet. If she remained in the water, she could use its powers to summon a rainstorm, the sole hope for fighting the fire. Speaking of the fire, combining it with the wind would allow her to create a perfect firestorm to consume the enemy. Lo could burn them to ash.

Poetic after what they did to my Erythmus!

How much acreage would burn in the process? How many trees, bushes, briars, and nests? How many would suffocate inside burrows and woodland homes? How many lives to avenge a single life, even if it was her Erythmus?

There must be another way. I must restore the balance, level the scales of justice, but I cannot become those monsters.

A low shot bolt struck the stony slope on the other side of the streambed. She turned in time to see the dying spark created when the steel tip bounced against a flinty outcrop. Inspiration sparked brighter than steel-struck flint. By the time she returned her attention to the shouting dwarves, a smile crossed her face.

"Look!" The knight Silverforge pointed at her. "It's the bloody elf controlling that Catterand."

"They're bounty hunters for sure!" Zarkus ratcheted his double crossbow and reached for two bolts.

"Kill that one," Papa cautioned, glancing around, "but watch our flanks. Looks like you're gonna get your wish, yella bellies. We're leaving."

With their eyes focused on Lobianca, the dwarves did not notice the fat, gray clouds gathering above their heads. Another shower of sparks rose from the burning forest into the sky, but a torrent of rain fell to earth. The dwarves fired through the sudden downpour, but Lo dodged their bolts, rolling into the streambed.

She expected to hit water, but her shoulder met with rocks and muddy silt instead. The spell had consumed more material than she thought possible, but the results had to be quick or the fire would spread out of control. *Could still spread out of control.*

Clawing her way to her feet, the druid stayed low and allowed the bolts to skip against the bank and ricochet against the rock shelter. Too tired to transform, she crawled along the depleted waterway. She dragged herself into the thickest foliage available and advanced on the dwarves while they reloaded.

All five dwarves moved as they cranked bows and loaded bolts. Zarkus and the two unidentified dwarves stumbled on the rocks and slipped on the wet pine straw littering the slope. The shorter dwarf jostled Papa Pipebender.

Frustrated and cursing aloud, the old dwarf sat, reloaded, and aimed. From her hiding place, Lo stared too long. The wily old dwarf shifted the crossbow until he met her distant gaze.

Papa loosed. Lo rolled. He gripped the secondary trigger on the double crossbow and fired again. The first bolt hit closer than the second, sliding along her back and setting her skin ablaze with fresh pain in its wake.

“Cover me!” Papa slipped end of the crossbow over his boot and pulled on the first bowstring. “Don’t let that elf bitch escape!”

“I thought we were leaving, Papa!” Zarkus had recovered, but his eyes searched the undergrowth for his quarry. “I don’t see anyone down there.”

“See her? Are you blind, Zark?” Vonder affixed the first bolt and reached for another. “She’s in the creek. Somewhere.”

“You don’t see her either?”

“I did!”

“I got’er, Vonder.” The dwarf who’d slid farthest along the slope pointed in Lobianca’s direction with his crossbow, a heavier repeater. He levered its gearing mechanism into the “Ready” position, but never had a chance to fire.

Argus leaped across the narrow streambed and landed atop the dwarf before he loosed. The Devil Dog’s teeth sank deep into the bandit’s exposed shoulder. The hefty hound twisted and tumbled along with the bloody dwarf toward the dry streambed.

Lo sprinted toward them as they fought. The gang member did not give up, pawing and punching at the snarling dog. But his blood fled him rapidly. From paces away, she noticed that Argus had hit an artery in the dwarf's neck. The poor bastard was dead already, but she admired his fight.

Confident the Catterand could handle the dying bandit, she concentrated on the remaining Pipebenders. Dodging fire from the dwarves on the slope, Lobianca retrieved the discarded repeater. Her leaden limbs responded slower than she wanted, but bolt after bolt left the weapon in search of the dwarves.

"Run!" The former dwarf knight led the charge away from the savage scene. The other unidentified bandit followed Silverforge, but Zarkus was busy dragging his father to his feet. Lo concentrated on hitting them, but firing uphill through smoke and rain was difficult on her best day.

Her quarry reached the top of the slope, but not before suffering another casualty. The dwarf tailing Silverforge diverted to aid Zarkus with their stubborn leader. Papa loosed two more bolts, but failed to hit the druid or the hound. In the process, he delayed his people long enough for Lobianca's last shot to connect. The bolt struck the unidentified dwarf in the back; its shaft snapped in half as the bandit tumbled down the slope.

The dwarf's death bought his cohorts time. By the time the elf returned her attention to the Pipebenders, they were nowhere to be seen. They had slipped the noose once more. They might slip the whole trap if they made it to their mounts.

Lobianca flung the crossbow at the hound, but it hit the wet slope and slid. She gasped for air, feeling her muscles burn and her back bleed. She wanted to choke someone, preferably Argus. Without his warning, she would have been able to lure the Pipebenders close enough to finish them once and for all. Now, they were on the run and had one helluva head start.

"Tell me one reason why I should not transform you into a toad and feed you to a timber rattler?"

"Because I saved you, you foolish elf! You would have died cornered in that cave over there if not for me."

"I was luring them into a trap!"

"How? By snoring loud enough for them to shoot you at twenty paces?"

"I don't—" Lobianca was about to say "snore", when she remembered that Erythmus had taken the secret of her terrible snoring habit to the grave with him. The only man to sleep in her proximity since his death had been the transformed dwarf.

"I, uh, apologize." Lo summoned a smile, but faltered. She grimaced instead. "Thank you for warning me, for spilling blood for me, and for saving me. But that doesn't excuse losing our prey. We'll never catch them now. I failed to run off their rams."

If a dog could smile, Argus would be wearing a smug—if bloody—grin. The hound wagged its tail instead.

"Don't worry about them. I've got that angle covered."

"How? When did you manage to do that?"

"When I worked out that series of signals with our reinforcements." Argus shook his wet fur and then loped along the slope, sniffing at the path taken by the dwarves. "I can't be everywhere at once, after all. We couldn't trust you to follow a plan without improvising, so we planned around it and worked out contingencies."

"Reinforcements?" Lobianca's mind reeled as she followed the dwarf-dog in the rough direction of the gang's mounts. "We? What in Holy Oak's name is going on here, Argus?"

"Do you want me to spoil the surprise?"

"Do you want me to turn you into a tapeworm and force feed you to a hungry hog?"

"I would prefer for you to trust me and transform me back to my old self again."

"If wishes were fishes, we'd all eat every night."

"Fine. Then trust me enough to listen."

"Listen? Listen for what? Rain? The sizzle of dying fire?"

"Not quite." The Catterand sniffed and walked. He paused, cocked his head, and then returned to trailing their quarry. Despite the pervasive smoke, the hound course corrected for the dwarves, mimicking their steps by smelling their tracks.

"What then?"

"You'll know it when you hear it—him—whatever."

"Him?" Lobianca stopped, looked, and listened.

Since dogs could see spirits, she convinced herself Argus meant Erythmus. Somehow his spirit was with her still. Now, in her time of need, her late lover had conspired with the dwarf-dog to help spook the mounts, seek justice, and then rest peacefully.

Perhaps this was the right course of action, after all. After this, my beloved, you can sleep in the arms of the Creator until I am there alongside you for eternity.

An inhuman roar spoiled her romantic—if ghastly—fantasy. The beast's cry proved a familiar sound, a heartening sound. Somewhere in the hollow beyond the next ridge spur, a grizzly bear with a spastic colon had answered the call to battle, even after telling her that he was too old and sick to make the trip.

Tears filled her eyes, but she dismissed them as a response to the growing amount of smoke produced by the increasing rain and diminishing wildfires. She blotted them with the back of her sleeves and realized Argus had been studying her reaction. This time she offered him a tired but genuine smile.

Perhaps a new dog can teach an old elf a few tricks, after all.

"Thank you, Argus," Lobianca said. "Seems like there's one dwarf in this world I can trust."

"That you can trust enough to change back?"

"No time. I'm drained, and you're faster in this form. Even Fudgy is no match for all those armed dwarves, so we'll have to help him before he wades in too deep. But I will have to trust you, if you're willing to trust me."

"I've followed you this far, haven't I?"

"Through blood, smoke, filth, and fire," she said, patting the dog on his head, "which is more than I can say for most elves I've known."

"People are just people, Lo. We all make bad choices. Some of us more than others. But few of us are fortunate enough to live long enough to make better ones. I appreciate the chance to rectify this regrettable part of my life."

"We haven't rectified it quite yet."

"What do you suggest?"

"I suggest you run, run to Fudgy's aid as fast as possible."

"What are you doing to do?"

"Don't worry. I'll be close to you the entire time."

"What do you—" Argus stopped talking when Lo disappeared from view, replaced by a fresh itch on his backside. He gnawed at his flank, but received a stern rebuff.

"Run, you fool dwarf-dog!" The tiny, shrill voice sounded bizarre, but reached his sensitive ears with ease.

Flea-sized Lobianca used her new mandibles to draw fresh blood, the closest thing she could to do spurring her mount onward. The canine accelerated to breakneck speeds, its towering hairs swaying like trees in a twister. At this size, the small feast of dog's blood provided the druid with enough energy to fuel restorative magics necessary to fight onward. The grossly distorted terrain moved and bucked around her, but she remained in place until the Catterand crossed the ridge spur and raced into the hollow.

An oversized scene of carnage played out before her transformed eyes, forcing her to enhance them to discern details. The rampaging grizzly towered over the scene, appearing taller than a dragon and fiercer. Two rams with twisted necks were at Fudgy's feet. The bear held two more aloft, using them as meat shields. Bolts from the dwarves left to guard the battle rams stuck from the dangling bodies of their dying mounts. Of the three bandits she'd spied in the hollow earlier, two survived. The third was in pieces, his body strewn along the forest floor.

The rest of Papa's gang circled the hollow, avoiding the bear attack and not bothering to aid their fellow Pipebenders. They skirted toward the last group of rams, lashed to a solitary oak. Argus growled low, assuring Lo that he'd spotted them, too. The hound did not divert, though. He barreled toward the closest dwarf, despite repeated bites from Lobianca.

Argus jumped onto one rock and then another, before using one of Lo's tactics on a bandit with his back to them. Focusing on the bear, he never saw his attacker. The Catterand landed on him, forced him to the ground, and then sank its teeth into the back of his victim's neck.

The other dwarf turned, revealing itself to be the young woman Lo had spotted earlier. The garishly dressed woman did not hesitate; instead, she lobbed a knife at the hound's exposed flank. The druid leaped farther than she had ever leaped; as a flea, she sailed through the air for what seemed like a league.

Shifting forms while still in the air, Lobianca returned to her true self before she reached the hurled dagger. Her hand slipped around its handle, and her momentum carried it and her to the forest floor. Lo tumbled to a painful stop, but still held the knife.

"Grizzlies, Devil Dogs, and now a flying elf?" The woman shook her head in disbelief as the druid rose from the ground. "I'm outta here. I didn't sign on for this shit."

"Don't forget this!" Lo threw the knife at its owner.

"Consider it a gift." The woman tumbled away from the thrown blade. "Really, I have more."

The dwarf gestured over her shoulder, toward the surviving rams. She backed away from the elf and then turned to run. Argus barked and chased after her.

"No, wait!" Lo worried the transformed dwarf would be led right into the line of fire.

"We have them on the run!"

A satisfied roar from Fudgy confirmed their seeming superiority. Until the remaining Pipebenders loosed their bolts to screen their escape, Lobianca almost believed her animal friends. *Friend, huh?* She never thought she'd use that word to describe a dwarf, but perhaps she had been wrong about Argus. After all, he was risking his life alongside hers, even if he had been looped into her plot to avenge her husband.

Bolts filled the space between the contested parties. With a whimper, the hound's rear leg buckled, clipped by a bandit's crossbow. Instead of leaping onto a rock in his path, Argus collided with it, provoking another pain-filled whimper. The impromptu cover kept him alive, though, as other bolts skipped by him or bounced against the small boulder.

With most of the mounts dead or scattered, Fudgy retreated in the face of the onslaught of projectiles. Lo knew the bear well enough to figure that he would maneuver around them to find a better angle of attack. But this was her fight ultimately.

"Run, Yewstys! I don't want you ending up like Axel!"

Papa Pipebender wiped tears from his bloodshot eyes. His red face and scowl deepened when he spied Lobianca beyond the injured hound. He pointed two fingers at his eyes before turning the gesture in the druid's direction.

Judging by a visual count, four Pipebenders remained, unless others had found alternate means of escape already. Papa and Zarkus covered Silverforge, who worked to free two ornery battle rams, and Yewstys, the retreating woman. Lo had no chance of hitting them with a thrown knife from this distance, but there were crossbows visible among the ravaged corpses in the hollow.

One of the newly dead is his youngest son, but which one? If I knew, I might be able to use that to my advantage.

Lobianca searched her thoughts, attempting to recall every detail of the Pipebenders provided by Argus. Axel Pipebender had been a surviving twin; his elder, Papa's favorite, had been killed years ago in a botched raid on an elven garrison. His death had cemented Vonder Pipebender's hatred for all elves.

From Argus's description, Lo recalled the twins having dark curly hair and a shared love of military-style weapons and armor. One other bandit had worn a breastplate like Silverforge, the flighty knight errant; Axel had been killed by the Catterand moments ago. Vonder assumed it had been on Lobianca's orders.

Papa Pipebender is wrong there, but Axel's death was among my fondest wishes. I like that dwarf-dog better by the minute.

Lobianca seized on a gruesome ploy. Giggling under her breath, she sank to the ground behind a thick pine. She dug her fingertips into the ground, so she could exercise maximum control over the vegetation around her.

Briars and vines responded to her commands and snaked through the trouser legs of Papa's dead son. Several tense moments and close calls by crossbow bolts later, Lobianca watched as her meat puppet rose from the forest floor. Convinced the greenery knew the plan now, she withdrew her fingers from the earth and then called upon the wind.

Axel Pipebender stood amid the hail of crossbow bolts, his herky-jerky movements convincing enough to fool his father.

"Stop firing, arseholes! My boy, is that you, my boy?"

Wind flowed through the wound in the back of the twin's neck and exited his vine-controlled mouth.

"Papa." The hoarse sound was not loud, but it cut across the sound of falling rain, pawing rams, and cranking crossbows.

"He's alive!" Papa lowered his weapon and rose from a crouch. "He's okay. C'mon, son, we're going home. We're leaving this nightmare place."

"No, Papa, no!" Zarkus and Yewstys cried, but it was too late. They only aided Lo's distraction, which provided her with adequate time to retrieve the dead twin's loaded crossbow.

"Papa." Axel's corpse called while Lobianca stabilized the weapon. When the dwarven patriarch glanced between his gang and his dead son, he stepped farther away from cover. Lo loosed.

"Papa!" Zarkus jumped in front of the bolt meant for his dad. The missile struck the loyal son in his chest, puncturing his heart.

One of her husband's killers slumped to the forest floor. Smiling, Lobianca glared at the clan patriarch, a man rapidly running out of sons. Something in his watery eyes died at that moment, leaving him vulnerable. She lifted the crossbow again.

Yewstys rushed to Papa Pipebender's side. For a moment, Lo thought the dwarven woman was acting as a shield. Instead, Yewstys embraced and kissed the old dwarf, blocking his view of his dying son and the dead one still mimicking life. She whispered something in his ear and then led him from the hollow.

Though he allowed Yewstys to lead him, Papa's tear-filled eyes never left those of the druid who'd masterminded the destruction of his gang and death of his sons. What could console a viper like him at a time like this? Had the young woman promised him more sons—more baby vipers to be raised to strike at elves, elves responsible for killing his children?

No, not when I will die childless. I will cut the head from this snake and burn its corpse. Not out of hate. Not out of revenge. His capacity to do harm and infect the world with hate will not outlive my capacity to love and heal the damage he's caused. What I can fix, anyway.

Lobianca rubbed the lower abdomen scar underneath her clothing. When the Pipebenders had arrived on the farm that day, they had killed more than her husband and their farm. The dwarves had killed any chance she'd ever have at having a family, for the bolt that had pierced her side had killed her unborn son and damaged her uterus beyond repair.

As she advanced, the Pipebenders retreated, reaching their mounts before she made it to Argus's position. Their quarry mounted two of the three remaining rams and fled along the forest road.

"Are you going to make it?" Lobianca surveyed his wounds.

"I was about to ask you the same question."

"Who's reading minds now?"

Elf and dwarf shared a laugh. In fact, they laughed until they coughed, choking on the thickening smoke. The storm was working, but if they remained here, the smoky byproduct of the dying fires would extinguish what remained of their lives.

"Are you ready to finish this?"

"Finish this?" Argus laughed again. "How're a crippled dog and a worn-out druid supposed to catch up to those battle rams? Even if that last ram would allow you to ride it, I can't keep up."

"No, but if a former cavalryman rides it, we'll catch them."

"Do you mean?"

"It's already done."

A smile spread across the dwarf's face when he laid eyes on his bare hands instead of a pair of fuzzy paws. Smiling, he ran them along his fully clothed body. When his attention returned to her, he scowled. Had she made a mistake by trusting him?

"Not that I'm complaining," Argus asked, "but why was this transformation so easy? I passed out from the pain last time."

"You're right to be mad. Transmutation magic doesn't have to be painful. But it does help with coercion."

"And dramatic effect."

"Speaking of dramatic effect, how about we chase down some dwarves through a smoke-filled valley during a raging storm and kill them all?"

"We'll never catch them with two of us riding on one ram."

"I won't be riding with you. I'll be riding alongside you."

"I thought you were too tired to transform into anything big."

"I am. And I won't have to. I'm not too tired to call for reinforcements."

"Reinforcements, huh?" Argus grinned at her. "Thought you said that was a bad idea. That trusting a mangy dwarf-dog with your life was dangerous enough without involving others."

Lobianca could not deny that he was handsome, especially when he smiled. It had to be his noble spirit and decision to walk a better path, she wagered. It shined through when he smiled from the heart. Lo had always respected men who would stand against imbalance, injustice, and the forces threatening to rip Mirstone apart.

"I might have been wrong." She gazed into her unlikely ally's eyes. "I might have needed help. I might even want help now. But I'll ask for it on my own terms."

"Do you think Fudgy would refuse to assist you?"

"No, I was talking about you, silly dwarf."

"You don't have to ask. I have already sworn an oath."

"You've done enough to win back your true form and your full freedom. What you do now is on your own accord."

Argus held her hand to his heart and said, "Then I choose to ride the same road as you, fight the same villains as you, and work to restore the balance with you."

"How long do you think that will take?" Lo wondered aloud.

"As long as it takes. Or until we die trying, right?"

"Right."

"Then let's ride like there's no tomorrow, my friend."

"Friend." The reclusive elf had not used the word to apply to a person in more years than she cared to recall.

"Is there something wrong with that?"

"No." Lobianca whistled for the grizzly bear. "It's a fine start to a new life, even if there turns out to be no tomorrow."

The Last Quest of the Drunken Wizard

A.R. Cook

"The Brightness! The Brightness have returned!"

I turn my gaze away from the cup of piss-colored tea in front of me, as a young scout rushes into the tavern, almost tripping over himself. His announcement fills me with sudden nausea.

"The Brightness," I growl. "Gods damn it."

It's bad enough that my insides were shot to hell centuries ago, thanks to that damn Boon that the Brightness gave the Stormguard, but now the return of those pretentious bastards makes me think about how miserable my life has been since they appeared.

I take another sip of tea...*what is this horse drool again, chamomile?...*and grind my teeth. Thankfully, no one scoffs at me anymore about not holding my liquor. You can only jeer at an old man for so long, knowing he's too exhausted to put up a fight about it, before you get bored with it. Also, anyone whose opinion of me I cared about is dead.

It dawns on me why this scout announces this news to all the patrons of the Axe Handle Tavern. Most of the men in here don't have any idea what he's talking about – they were all born after the Plucking, and they've been taught how the Venzor Mountains were raised solely by dwarven might and magic. To say the Brightness had any hand in supplying the incredible amount of mystical energies the Stormguard required for the Plucking would be an admission that our wizards weren't strong enough, were too weak for the will of our king. There's only one man in this tavern who remembers who the Brightness are, and why it's a matter of importance. This scrappy, twitchy messenger is searching for me.

I don't look the same as I did 200 years ago. Part of that, I can thank the daily doses of tea. Once, back when I could swig ten steins of ale at every meal, I had a beard the lush hue of Cherrywood that tumbled to my toes, and a bushel of hair as thick as ram's wool. But my hair has faded to little more than hay, as pale and prickly, and I've cropped my beard to a manageable two feet in length. The tea's also given me an unexpected side effect: longevity. Dwarves already live long lives, not as long as those frail elves, but I bet I'll be outliving those scrawny blighters by a few hundred years at the rate I'm going. Most folks have forgotten I'm still alive, assuming I wasted away to join the rest of my generation's

Stormguard brethren. But someone apparently remembers I'm still breathing, and I'm in no mood to humor them.

I toss a coin on the table and shove myself away from the table with a grunt. I turn, and that kid is smack in front of me, snuck up on me like a bad day. He pulls a small scrap of paper from his pocket, and reads from it. "Are you Master....Darquethorn Boggs of the Stormguard, sir?"

"No," I reply.

The scout snaps his head up at me as if I just told him there was a dragon standing behind him. His eyes drift away from my stone glare down to my left hand. Two rings, one with a night-blue sapphire and silver band, and the other with a lightning-yellow topaz and copper band, glimmer on my second and fourth fingers. Each generation of Stormguard has their own unique combination of bands and stones, and these are distinctive of my generation. I make no effort to hide them.

"Are you...sure?" the scout squeaks.

"You accusing me of lying, son?" It's hard for me to keep a straight face as I watch the kid's face pale to stark white.

"Uh...n-n-n-no! Of c-c-c-course not!" the scout stammers. "But...I was told Master Boggs wears those sp-p-pecific rings..."

"Well, then," I say, raising an eyebrow, "maybe I killed him and stole his rings."

The scout pauses a long moment, and I can almost hear the gears turning in his brain. Finally, he rasps, "I...don't think so. I've heard Master Boggs could turn chimeras into kittens. He could stop a whole army with a pint and a flick of the wrist. Seems like a thief would be the last thing to kill the Drunken Wizard."

By now, every head in the room has turned to look at me. Tales of the Drunken Wizard have been passed down from drunkard to storyteller for ages. The stories have become a bit exaggerated over the years, I grant you, but when every inn and tavern in Venzor offers a drink named "Boggs' Brew," or "A Bottle of Boggs," or "The Hair of the Boggs that Bit You," you know you're a local legend.

I chuckle, shaking my head. "Lad, you run back to your lords and tell 'em there be no drunken wizards here. Just the typical lot of swillers and an old man who can barely down a cup of tea." I ruffle the kid's hair, and brush past him and out of the tavern.

I take one step onto the mountainside path leading away from town, and I look up the ascension towards Crooked Crag. A serpentine spiral of smoke wafts up from the direction of where my cliffside house should be.

I sigh, wiping a hand over my brow. "Aruyin, what did you blow up now?"

* * *

"I swear to gods, it wasn't me! It was that stupid pelican!"

Aruyin's fox-red hair stands on end like a pissed-off cat, and her face is smudged in patches of black soot. She stands in the middle of a ring of ash, which also tarnishes on the walls, shelves and windows of my living room. She looks so small, even for a ten-year-old, wearing a green smock that nearly swallows her, and stares at me with big, wolf-pup eyes.

I grimace at her with my arms crossed, and shift my gaze over to the filthy pelican staggering about the room in a stunned stupor. "I'm fairly certain Warf can't mix salamander powder and liquid lightning," I retort. "Lack of hands and all."

"But he said that it could help me…control my *ghosts*…" Aruyin trails off, as if worried to even speak of the apparitions that plague her. She raises her hands, buried within the long sleeves of her smock. "Stupid lying bucket-mouth!"

Warf honks angrily at the insult, and then smacks into the wall and collapses.

"Don't blame the bird," I say. "If you were apprenticing for any other wizard, he'd turn you into a newt for tampering with his materials and nearly frying his familiar!"

Aruyin beams a big smile, one of her front teeth missing from when she got in a fist fight with the tanner's son—and he faired the worse from it, gods bless her. "But, Master Boggs, I'm *not* apprenticing for another wizard. And I know you won't turn me into a newt, because then who would take care of you?"

I grab a broom by the door and toss it to her. "Don't forget the corners," I say before walking off to my study. I hear Aruyin mutter something in her own invented language, one she assumes I can't decipher, although I'm pretty sure "snork-razzin" means "mean old coot."

A sharp rapping of the front door interrupts the shuffling of the broom on the floor. I sit at my writing desk as I listen to Aruyin go to the door and open the sliding eyehole. "We don't need any more griffin toenails, thanks," she says.

"I…beg your pardon?" grumbles a male voice from the other side of the door. "Young lady, is your master home?"

"Hold on," Aruyin says, and then she appears at the door to my study. "Master Boggs, there's a dozen men here in gray coats. Really shiny beards, braided with ribbons and all. Bunch of poofs."

I rub the bridge of my nose, closing my eyes. Damn Silvercoats can't take a hint. I thrust myself up from my chair and trudge over to the front door, opening it just enough to give each of the dwarves standing there a good, hard glare. "I already spoke to your scout. We have no business here."

The dwarf at the lead of the party, whose flat nose, sunken eyes, wide frown could only belong to someone as brooding at Tawn "Frogmouth" Gizzardstone, strokes his beard plaited with silver ribbons. He clears his throat. "Darquethorn, your involvement in this matter is mandatory. You know the Brightness. You were one of the Stormguard who were granted their Boon. You have a rapport with them."

"Rapport? A fine word, Tawn, but a bit assumptive," I grouse. "I barely remember what happened yesterday, let alone before any of you were born. I have no relationship with those devils."

Tawn wrinkles his nose in irritation. "We must send the proper representatives to meet with them. Naturally, we…" He gestures to his preening flock. "…and a small band of guards will go, but your presence would remind the Brightness that we were the favored faction in the past. Word is that they have set up court by the bridge in the Fool's Marsh."

"How fitting," I reply. "They know where they belong."

"We have to win their favor again, before those blithering elves reach them first. Do you know what will happen if the elves win the Boon this time?"

I scratch my chin. "Oh, I'm sure you've already concocted a perfectly scathing campaign against the elves, without needing my input."

Tawn furls his eyebrows, like two nuzzling mice, and curls his lip. "They will undoubtedly request enough magical energy to reduce the Venzor Mountains to rubble. They will flatten this region of the dwarven kingdom, if not the whole bloody thing, and grow their forest over it. They'll claim it justice for the Plucking, and it will destroy towns, homes, mining operations we've set up here. Thousands of citizens, crushed or buried alive. The minor skirmishes in the Verge will explode into full scale war again, and there will be no diplomacy."

"How do you even know the Brightness will grant a Boon? Maybe they're just in the neighborhood for the summer fishing. Supposed to be a good year for salmon."

"By the gods, Darquethorn, take this matter with a granule of gravity," Tawn barks. "Now gather what you need and let's be off. If we leave now, we should be able to reach the bridge by mid-day tomorrow. Hopefully the elves are not yet aware of the Brightness' arrival."

I smile. "Tell you what, Tawn, why don't you all get a head start, and tell those shining squawkers that the only boon I want is for them to kiss the hairiest part of my—"

I get yanked by the belt from behind, away from the door, and Aruyin pokes her head out and smiles at the Silvercoats. "He hasn't had his medicine yet today. Come back tomorrow." And with that, she closes the door on the group of slack-jawed, red-faced Silvercoats, just as Tawn blusters out a curse that I'm fairly certain isn't dignified for a politician.

*

I wake in the middle of the night to a presence standing over me. My eyes adjust to the darkness but I don't dare to make a move. I can feel it, something hovering in the corner of the room, something seething fear. I twist the rings on my fingers, even though they'll do me no good without a swig of the brew to fuel my magic. Slowly I sit up in bed and focus on the spot where I sense the presence, and I spot two small glowing orbs of blue flame, demon eyes staring back at me.

A soft sobbing comes from outside my room. My mind is now awake enough, realizing the situation. "Yin, come in," I say.

The door creaks open, and the flaming eyes blink out of existence. Aruyin shuffles in, the hem of her too-big nightgown dragging the floor, her eyes red and puffy. She halts, turning her head towards the spot where the demon eyes were moments ago. There is a fading wisp of something still there, a fleck of floating ink, but it blends into the night's shadows. Her face scrunches in misery. "Oh, no…was it…was one of them in here? I…I didn't mean to…I'm sorry…"

I hold up a hand to quiet her, and I roll out of bed. The ghosts are nothing new – they came with Aruyin when I took her in after her parents died, although they still take me by surprise when I'm not fully awake. I've heard of cases like hers before - untrained mages, children and adults alike, who have magical energies that manifest their feelings into physical shapes, but it's rare. It's always a sign she's dealing with some confusing emotions, or at this time of night, she just had a particularly intense nightmare.

"What did you dream?" I ask.

Aruyin wipes her nose with her sleeve, and inhales deeply. "I saw…it was so real, Master Boggs. I saw Venzor, the whole mountainside…it just crumbled apart. I heard screaming, crying, all those people…couldn't get away…I was running down the mountain, looking for you…but you were gone. I was…all alone…again…"

I sigh, shaking my head. "Aruyin, you overhead what Lord Tawn said this afternoon, and it got into your head. Look, I don't believe with a single hair on my beard that even if the elves were to ask the Brightness for a Boon, they would use black magic for such a destructive deed. It's against their morals—"

"But that's the thing, sir! I don't remember any elves in my dream. But I remember…I saw that poof with the silver ribbons in his beard, holding something bright and glowing…that was right before the mountain burst apart. I think… I don't know what a Boon looks like, Master Boggs, but I remember him being there, and he was smiling, smiling! He was happy it was all happening! I felt so, so frightened…" She trailed off, furrowing her brow, trying to make sense of her visions.

I stand motionless for a moment. I could dismiss her dream as wild imagination, but I've lived long enough to heed a premonition when I hear one. Sadly, it strikes me as exactly the kind of thing Frogmouth would do. All that blustering about the elves destroying the Venzor Mountains…hell, I had contemplated for years if Tawn would pay the elven wizards to actually do such a thing, if they were capable. No one profits more from a war than a gods-damn politician. Rumors of the Silvercoats pocketing profits from hired privateers, collecting the spoils of anything left behind from skirmishes along the Verge, were commonplace, if not talked about openly. And Tawn had been vying for years to be the king's advisor, whispering poison into his fellow Silvercoats' ears, encouraging a "pre-emptive" strike against those back-stabbing elves. Losing Venzor would be a small price to pay if it would finally promote Tawn to royal advisor, convincing him to dismiss any hopes of treaty between the dwarves and elves and revive the age-old war full scale. Then, oh, how the Silvercoats' pockets would fill to bursting…hell, they'd become Goldcoats!

There isn't much that makes me change my mind about anything nowadays, but a politician willing to massacre his own people for a bloody promotion…that'll do it.

I put my arm around Aruyin, as fresh tears wash her face. "Now now, little one. Such thoughts are a terrible burden to bear. And I hate to think you going back to sleep with such notions on your mind."

She sniffles. "Then…will you make me some of that happy-dreams tea? With honey and cream?"

"I'll do you one better, lass. How about we go get ourselves a Boon, eh?"

Aruyin cocks her head at me. After a long moment, she replies, "Huh?"

I go to my bed, where my trousers are lying on the bedpost at the foot end. I start putting them on, tucking my nightshirt into the waistband. "Well, it seems to me, if you're worried about that Boon falling into some weasel's hands, then there's really only one logical option. *We* get to the Brightness first, and ask for the Boon ourselves."

A light flickers in Aruyin's eyes, and a smile almost splits her face in half. "Then it's…*adventure*???"

I harrumph, as I slip on my boots. "Aye, wee one. Adventure. Just don't—"

She shrieks like an eagle, her fists in the air, and she dashes out of my room. From the hall, I hear her laugh, "Come on, Warf! We're going on an adventure! Huzzah!"

A few minutes later, once I'm fully dressed and stuffed some provisions in my travel pack, Aruyin appears in my bedroom doorway again, this time wearing her boots and cloak, and holding Warf under one arm. His beak-pouch is weighed down with what looks like rolls of spare clothes and some of Aruyin's favorite books.

She grins at me. "I'm all packed. Can we go now?"

*

It's a short walk past the town of Venzor, down the steep path to the small secluded shack near the base of the mountain, a tattered old pile of stones and discarded metal surrounded by a graveyard of the bones of mechanical beasts, although to the untrained eye, it looked little more than a blacksmith's collection of rejected projects.

Aruyin grouses, which she has been doing since before we left the house, when I told her to unload Warf and repack her things in a proper travel bag. "What are we doing here? Those poofs have a head start on us. Why are we going to the old tinker's house, when you could use a spell to transport us to the Fool's Swamp in half a second?"

"One shouldn't use magic willy-nilly," I say, my boot squelching in a puddle of mud. "Besides…you know I don't drink anymore."

Aruyin knows that my magic is tied to my alcohol consumption. A different spell for every liquor – I once spewed fireballs after a shot of whiskey, could uproot trees after a flask of bourbon, or summon storm spirits with a stein of ale. But the Plucking took it all out of me – even with the Boon, I couldn't channel the Brightness' energies into my aura without the brew. I had to chug so much alcohol to help the Stormguard raise the mountains that my liver practically melted and I was laid up in bed, poisoned and clinging to life for a year. So the Drunken Wizard died, leaving behind a slew of tales and a quiet, non-magical, tea-drinking old man.

Yet Aruyin always hopes I'll perform a spell or two, insisting I don't need ale to conjure. Trust me, if I could still do any spell, it would be to dispel those damn ghosts of hers. But that's beyond my abilities, and that fact makes me want to punch myself in disgust.

Aruyin looks up at the sign over the front door of the shack, a batter plank of wood with the name "Geargrinder's" on it. "So what's Mr. Rusty going to do for us? Replace our feet with wheels?"

"I commissioned Rusty to make me something special," I say. "Said he'd have it ready for me in precisely two months, three weeks…and whatever the rest. I figure it should be done. Will be mighty handy for our purposes."

I knock on the door, and immediately a clattering and clanking comes from inside the shack. "I'm coming, I'm coming!" snarls a voice like sandpaper, and a moment later, the door opens to reveal a pair of owl-eye goggles framed by a mucus-green face and two prominent pig ears. Rusty Geargrinder would've been driven out of dwarven territory years ago, as were all the other goblins, but since the Ashmakers charge an arm and both legs for their blacksmithing, he's the only smith in Venzor I can afford, or like. So I set him up here. Not a bad chap at all, really, and one of the only other people around here who doesn't take guff from a Silvercoat. We could've been brothers in another life.

"Ah, Boggs, you old goat!" Rusty grins his yellow teeth. He checks a bizarre contraption on his wrist, a watch of five faces and more do-dads and numbers and letters than I would bother to keep track of. He grunts. "You're sixteen hours, three minutes and forty-nine seconds early. Lucky for you, I worked ahead of schedule. You are here for your commission, yes? It's a beaut, my best work yet!"

He ushers us into his shop, and Aruyin's jaw drops open at a glistening sight in the corner. A nine-foot-tall, sleek, avian mechanical marvel stands there, the fires of Rusty's furnace reflecting off of its chrome scales. It was designed with hints of wyvern in it – long powerful legs, a round sturdy body, a tall curving neck, and a small head with ruby-inlaid eyes on top—but the tail on the end is fan-like, and can fold out or tuck in to adjust the speed.

"Wha…." Aruyin gasps.

"That's one funny-looking chicken, Rusty," I joke.

Rusty doesn't pick up on sarcasm well. "What do you mean? I duplicate exactly as instructed! You gave me illustration of this thing, this…" He yanks a scroll out of his back pocket, the one I gave him at the start of the commission. He lifts up his goggles to read. "…oo-sta-ri-ch, and I make exactly like your sketch, but better! With this design, it can reach speeds of 45 miles per hour, a whole 5 miles per hour faster than those rams you use. Is no chicken!"

Aruyin goes over to the metallic ostrich, tapping her fingernail on its scales. "An ostrich? Master Boggs told me about those…you said they live in lands far, far away, like where Warf came from. Where do you learn about all these weird birds, master?"

"I make it my business to understand 'weird.' That way I'm never surprised." I walk to the ostrich, which has a leather saddle built into its back, and heave myself up onto it. It's a comfortable seat, although after years of riding rams, the height is a bit disconcerting. Still, not as bad as being on a horse, which I'd rather eat sheep dung than ride one of those temperamental long-faced mules.

"This is fastest device I've ever created," Rusty answers for me. "Boggs said he wanted something faster than ram, or wolf, or goat, or horse. He will be faster than anything in the whole realm! And best part, it is machine, so does not need food, water, and can go for days and days without stopping! Well, except for fuel…it runs on serpent oil, I've already filled her up but I've got a quart in the back you can have for 10 gold pieces…"

"Oh, neat!" Aruyin says. "But…why do you want a mount that's so fast, master?"

I pause, scratching my chin. "Well, been thinking of…going places, Yin. Maybe getting away from here…" I chuckle. "But don't you fret about that. We've got an adventure first, you know. Those Silvercoats have a good half-day lead on us, but they're not accustomed to that much travel. They'll need to take rests often. We can easily make up for the lost time on this mount."

Aruyin clambers onto the ostrich to sit behind me. She wobbles, as she hasn't ridden anything except a cart, and she grasps onto my middle to steady herself. "Okay, I'm ready, I think," she says.

Rusty comes over to the back of the ostrich, and under its tail is a hand crank. He cranks up the machine, which jerks to imitation life, scratching the floor with its silver-clawed feet. I take hold of the steering mechanism, like a miniature ship's wheel, right in front of the saddle. As the chrome beast begins to step forwards, I turn the wheel to maneuver it towards the door.

"Hey! Where is my pay?" Rusty asks, his gnarled hands on his hips. "This costs 5,000 gold, Boggs!"

"That's really the sort of thing you should've asked before cranking up the thing!" I respond. The ostrich begins to break into a run, and before I'm done saying, "Put it on my tab!" it shoots out of the shack, breaking the doorframe into splinters, and streaks like a silver comet into the forest.

I'm pretty sure Rusty is face-palming himself and committing to memory, "ask for pay first, *then* hand over commission" as we speed off into the night, while the first hues of dawn peek through the trees.

*

"This is why I didn't want you taking the wheel, Yin!"

"How was I supposed to know the wheel would just come off like that? And we could've crashed a whole lot worse."

"*Worse*??"

"Hey, at least we're not hurt, right?"

"We'll see how long that lasts, given that you have the impeccable talent of crashing into the only damn bear for miles!"

And it's not too happy. For the moment, the grizzly is pinned under the prone, twitching remains of the mechanical ostrich, roaring and flailing to get the metal bird off of it. The contraption had already been rendered broken from the tumble we took downhill, after Aruyin grabbed the wheel and steered us right off of a ledge and down a fifty-foot decline into this ravine. Landing on the bear that had watched us fall the entire way in bewildered fascination was just what we needed to top off this manure stew we were in.

"Then…we should probably run before it gets free, right?" Aruyin says, already backing away.

I grab her by the hood of her cloak, pulling her back. "And go where, missy? You're going to climb all the way back up that muddy slope? Or just go running through this ravine until a pack of wolves finds you? And you're not even going to apologize to this poor bloke for dropping an ostrich on him? Manners, girl, manners!"

She gawks at me, sweat forming on her forehead. "Apologize? To a BEAR?? I'm pretty sure he'll show forgiveness by tearing my head off!"

The bear wriggles and squirms its way along the soft dirt of the ravine floor, regaining its footing so it can heave its body to the side and push off the jittering ostrich. It smashes one of its huge paws on the bird's skull, crushing it into the mud and causing one of its ruby eyes to pop out.

Rusty won't be happy to hear about this, I think.

The bear then turns its massive head in our direction.

Aruyin pulls hard against my grasp, and fumbles to undo the clasp of her cloak. "Uh, Master Boggs…we should *really* go now…"

The bear lumbers slowly towards us.

I stand my ground, switching my hand from her cloak to grasp her arm. "Now, Yin, don't be rude."

The bear is now five yards away, and its lips curl back to show its flesh-ripping teeth. It growls like thunder.

Aruyin's eyes are wide enough to fall out of her head. "What the *hell* are you doing!!"

"Where do you learn language like that?"

"FOR THE LOVE OF GODS!!"

"Shh, bears don't like screaming."

"I'm going to kill you!"

"I guess that'll be after the bear poops you out."

The bear rears up on its hind legs, towering over us and raising its front paws over its head. It bellows, its eyes and breath fierce. I notice a patch of its fur by its armpit is missing, showing an old scar – a brand shaped like a lion's face. I thought I knew this big lump of fur and teeth from somewhere.

"Arth! My, it's been years! You've gotten big!" I say.

The bear lowers his arms, and stops bellowing. He tilts his head at me curiously.

"Arth, you remember me. Darquethorn Boggs. I punched that good-for-nothing beastmaster bastard who chained you up and made you do all those dumb tricks for his traveling show? By gods, you were only a wee cub back then. Glad I got you out of there so you're not juggling melons and jumping through hoops of fire anymore, right?"

Arth snorts, and then he plops down on all fours and sniffs me, deeply. His eyes light up, and he happily licks my face, putting a paw on my shoulder in a half-hug. I can't help but laugh at the enthusiastic greeting. "Look, no hard feelings about us landing on you. My apprentice doesn't know how to steer. Right, Yin?"

Aruyin stares at me darkly, her face's color changing from terror-white to rage-red. "You…jerk…" she wheezes.

"Anyway, Arth, I hate to bother you, but we're on a bit of a hunt. We're looking for some folks who aren't from around here. Shiny, tall, supposedly hanging out around the bridge in this marsh. You've seen anyone like that?"

The bear blinks, and then turns his head and points with his nose down the ravine behind him. He grunts.

"Well, that's a bit of good news. Would you be so kind as to guide us a bit of the way, until I can get my bearings? No pun intended, of course."

Arth turns around, and sits down with his back to us.

"That's downright generous of you, Arth." I climb onto Arth's back, and look back at Aruyin. "He's offering to give us a ride the rest of the way to the bridge. Hop on."

Aruyin crosses her arms and narrows her eyes on me. "You knew who this bear was the whole time, and just wanted to torment me??"

"Consider it an education," I say. "Now would you like to walk the rest of the way by yourself, or get on the bear? It'll be fine this time. There's no wheel for you to rip off."

"IT FELL OFF BY ITSELF!" she snaps, but she stomps over and gets onto the bear behind me, wrinkling her nose at the odor.

Arth stands up and lumbers off down the ravine at a steady pace. Aruyin holds onto me again, grumbling, "You can be such an ass sometimes, master."

I smile. "Oh, but I have a lot more fun that way, kid."

*

The Marsh Bridge was once a mighty stonework known as Bridgefaire—four towers topped by crown-shaped parapets, guarding an arched deck of cobblestone that once upheld a marketplace of colorful tents over the great river—but over the centuries has become a moss and vine-invaded ruin watching over a trickling creek of what the river once was.

One might have looked upon the Marsh Bridge with some reverence of the great structure it once was, but any awe to be had was squelched by the two processions of dwarven and elven aristocracy arguing in front of it. The Silvercoats clearly had not had a tidy journey, as they and their ram mounts were mud-caked, but the elves managed to keep a clean countenance – no surprise, given that the forest is their domain and they probably knew how to avoid every puddle in their realm. They're also swathed in finery fit for royalty, long flowing silks and vine-twisted tiaras on their brows. The Moonling House, most likely. Clean or no, both parties are as polite and calm as a nest of startled vipers.

Even from a distance, I could hear Tawn hollering, "It's only right that we get first audience with the Brightness! Our ancestors built this bridge, and they chose to take respite here. It's a sign they prefer *our* hospitality!"

"They are taking respite in *our* forest!" argues one of the elves. "Besides, we arrived at this bridge first. First come, first served."

"Balderdash! We should be first served, for we heard of their arrival first!"

"How like a dwarf, twisting the truth to his own benefit." The elf inhales deeply. Elves don't like to show their temper, in particular to a dwarf. "But there is a more diplomatic way to settle this. We brought a gift for the Brightness. I trust you did as well?"

Tawn snorts. "Of course! We've brought the finest jewels from the king's personal collection. The most valuable prize in all the land!"

"Jewels, how quaint. We brought the only seed from our eldest sagewood, the most ancient, mystical tree in the forest. Such a seed can cure any ailment, dispel any madness, enlighten the dullest mind…" The elf gives Tawn a pointed look, with a grin. "…and purify the darkest heart. There is no other like it in all the world. Therefore, our gift has more value than yours, and we should go first."

"I've got a bear," I say, riding up to the lot of them, "so I trump all of you."

Arth grunts in agreement.

Both parties are shaken by the sudden grizzly in their midst, and the elven guard ready their longbows and arrows in barely a breath's time. The dwarven guards raise their warhammers in defense, but Tawn gestures for them to be at ease. "Ah, Darquethorn! You've changed your mind, I see. The Brightness will be delighted to welcome an old friend, I'm sure. A dear, old *friend* of theirs," he says, grinning smugly at the elves.

"Get off your high ram, Tawn," I reply, dismounting Arth. "I'm here representing myself, so don't be getting any ideas."

Tawn and the Silvercoats look like they've all swallowed their tongues, while the elves snicker. "Well, a dwarf double-crossing his own kind? I shouldn't be surprised," says the lead Moonling elf. "At least we elves always stand together as brothers and sisters, even in the temptation of individual profit."

"Why don't you choke on it," hisses Tawn, and I'm not entirely sure if he means the elves or me. He then sneers at me. "I'm afraid it wouldn't be good manners, Boggs, to ask the Brightness for an audience without a gift. As we were just discussing—"

"And who said I didn't bring a gift?"

"I doubt the Brightness need a smelly, tick-infested bear."

Arth would have bitten Tawn's head clean off for the insult, but we are all silenced that moment by a sudden warmth that washes over all of us. A being stands at the entrance to the bridge, taller than even the elves, shining with a silver-blue glow. The light makes the figure's features difficult to discern, although the face is like that of a barn owl, a pale heart-shaped mask with two massive black eyes, but no nose or lips to speak of. Wings like a shawl cascades down its shoulders, and any hint of a body underneath looks little more than essence. The figure floats a few inches above the ground, not of this world. A ghost, an angel, a god.

"We shall speak to Master Boggs and his apprentice now," the Brightness says, despite having no visible mouth.

Every jaw drops to the ground as I saunter past everyone. I look back at Aruyin. "Coming, lass?"

Aruyin looks more mortified now than when she thought she was going to be a bear's snack. After a moment of consideration, she scuffles up next to me, and grips my hand so tightly, I think she'll snap my finger bones. We follow the Brightness onto the bridge, our boots scraping the cobblestone. I can't help but feel a twinge of sadness for the marvel this place used to be, and the graveyard of memories it has become.

But the sadness is quickly replaced with surprise as in an instant we are no longer on the bridge, but in a rounded room with no windows or doors. All I can see are eleven shining figures like the one who led us here, who whisked us through the invisible barrier masking this inner sanctum. I experienced the same thing the last time I met with them, but it still catches me off guard. It completely shocks Aruyin.

"Wha...What just...how? How??" she stammers, darting her eyes about. Her gaze quickly lands on the Brightness, and she squeaks in astonishment.

"Put your eyes back in your head, kid. Remember your manners," I say.

Each of the Brightness radiates metallic colors, from silver to gold to bronze to copper to dark steel. They all examine us with those huge eyes, like doors to the cosmos. Finally, the silver one speaks. "What would you ask of us, Darquethorn Boggs of the Stormguard?"

I stick my thumbs in my belt, and give them a small bow. "Good to see you lads and lasses. You haven't aged a day, and here I am, an old, withered goat. You'll have to tell me your secret sometime...special soap? Meditation? Stretching?"

They all stare at me, unblinking, humorless.

"Joke...it's a joke. Sheesh, I would think you all would grow funny bones in two centuries," I say.

Aruyin looks up at me with an exasperated glare.

"What would you have of us, Master Boggs?" The eleven Brightness repeat, in unison.

"Now, why does it always have to be business?" I say. "Can't an old friend just drop in and say hi? As a matter of fact, why do you need to go giving any of those fools out there a Boon? I'll be the first to tell you Frogmouth and his clan are idjits, and the elves, eh, they wouldn't even be able to look you in the eye, what with their heads so far up their—" Aruyin elbows me hard, and I sigh. "—with their noses so high in the air."

"It is our purpose," the Brightness reply. "We are the embodiment of fate and fortune, we guard hopes and wishes. If prayers are not answered, people lose faith in goodness. We must give a Boon, or we have no purpose. If we have no purpose, we are nothing. Now what would you have of us?"

"You really want to know what I want? I want to give you something, for old time's sake." I reach into my pack, and pull out a thick-glass bottle of burgundy liquid. "Recognize this?"

The Brightness reply instantly. "That is the vessel in which we bestowed the energies to give you and your people the magic to raise the mountains, for your king's Boon," they reply.

"Yep. Hung onto it all these years, and you know why?" I unstop the cork and take a whiff of the bottle's contents. "Had a little leftover mystical mojo lacing the inside of the bottle, and when mixed with a Valdian ale and rum, it makes one helluva brew. How about we split a pint, eh?"

"We don't partake in vices," the Brightness say automatically.

"Aw, come on. Once I leave, you're gonna sit through the ramblings of two blabbermouths who are gonna do everything from kissing your backsides to holding a measuring contest between 'em – if you know what I mean - and trust me, it'll try even *your* patience. This will make it at least tolerable. And the way I see it, how can you be truly wise about what goodness is, unless you've tasted a bit of the bad too?"

The Brightness are dead quiet. I can actually feel their amused and bewildered contemplation radiating from them. Finally, one of the figures, glowing magnesium white, says, "I have always been curious what these creatures find so pleasurable about such infusions."

"It would be educational," says another.

"Such concoctions would inhibit our judgement," another counters.

"Only if one overconsumes," replies yet another.

"Right, right. Here," I say, pulling a shot glass from my pack. "Just a small taste, one quick round. Can't do you harm, eh?"

*

"What in the gods' names is taking so long?"

I had no idea how much time has passed, but apparently enough that Tawn and his entourage, as well as the elves, didn't feel like waiting outside anymore. Having watched where we vanished on the bridge, they had followed and stumbled straight through the invisible barrier into the room. It took them a moment to adjust to the sudden change in surroundings, but nothing prepared them for what they saw next.

"Hey, fellas!" I call out, waving to them. "Thought you'd never join the fun!"

And what fun we are having – in all honesty, I hadn't had a rumpus like this since the time the Stormguard got so drunk we turned all the local pigkeeper's sows into maidens and sent them into the tavern, whereupon any bloke who kissed them instantly returned them to pig form. But this, watching the Brightness get stone-cold drunk, giggling and floating around the room like they were possessed, was by far the funniest thing I have ever witnessed.

"Oh my gods-s-s-s, di-we…did we leave you ou-thar waitin'?" says one of the Brightness, whose golden glow has flushed to a ruddy pink. He blinks at the dwarves and elves, as if half-asleep. "I am…I'm s-s-s-so, so s-sorry. Didjou…didjou bring bacon? I really, really want some bacon…"

The Silvercoats and the elves stare, just stare, at the room of drunken immortals, who each has by now downed at least ten shots. It takes a solid minute before Tawn roars, "What the *hell* did you do, Boggs??"

"We're making merry! I'd give you a swig of the nectar, but…" I turn the bottle upside down, and one measly drop falls out. "I fear we ran a bit short."

"They're absolutely inebriated!" The lead elf cries. He goes over to one of the Brightness, who is doing lazy somersaults in the air. "Excuse me, your Brightness, are you well?"

"Well? I'm *ffffantastic*!" The Brightness replies. It reaches over and tugs at the Moonling elf's ears. "So *pointy*…you're like a bunny person…"

The elf forces a smile, despite his obvious discomfort. "Yes, well…we were hoping to gain an audience with you about the Boon—"

"Oooooh, no no no nooooooooooo," the Brightness all moan.

"No business, *no business*!" groans the one tugging the elf's ears. "It's always business. Why can't we…why can't we jus' have fun? No Boons tonight, no Boons …"

"Damn it, Boggs! You got them so drunk, they're incapable of granting a Boon!" Tawn growls at me. His face is as red as a tomato, but he purses his lips. "Fine, you've had your fun. Big laughs all around. We'll just have to wait until they sober up."

"You know what I hear is beautiful this time of year?" I say, loud enough for the whole room to hear. "I hear the moon is gorgeous in the autumn. A nice, golden harvest moon. And the view from there is supposed to be amazing."

"OH MY GODS, YES!" The Brightness all say in unison.

"Let's go visit, right now!" says a pewter-gray one.

"I always wanted to take a holiday on the moon," another one agrees.

"To get thar, that'll take…all the magic we can s-s-spare for…a c-c-century or so," an aged copper Brightness slurs.

"Is that all? Then dash it all, why are we waiting?" asks a bronze one.

Tawn waves his hands frantically. "Wait, no! You can't—"

Too late. The Brightness vanish from the room in a blink, and then we're all back on the bridge in the cool, evening air.

Every vein on Tawn's face pulsates. He roars, shaking his fists at me. "I'M GOING TO KILL YOU, BOGGS!"

I roll my eyes. "Why do people keep saying that today?"

Tawn launches himself at me, hands aimed at my throat, but the lead Moonling elf trips him with his longbow, sending Tawn flat on his face.

"I want to hear the rogue dwarf's reason for this," the elf states, icy hate in his eyes as he turns to me. "You gave up the chance to have a Boon yourself. Why deprive us all of the Brightness' gift? Do you enjoy causing chaos?"

I scratch my chin. "Nah, chaos is a lot of work, and I'm too old for it. If anything, I just prevented a huge helping of chaos. Do you really think a bottle full of wish-granting pixie-dust is really going to solve all your problems? Look what happened last time. I'm not proud of the Plucking, not one bit. It was a fool's wish, and I was a fool for having any part of it. I deserved getting my guts blown to hell for it. And here you all are, trying to repeat history all over. No matter who gets the Boon, it's nothing but trouble. Nothing good comes from that much power. Is this what great leaders do? Rely on magic to get vengeance on old wrongs, and create new ones?"

The elves and dwarves glance back and forth at each other. For a bunch of blowhards, they're all speechless.

"Here's a thought - just a small thought, mind you - but how's about since you're all here, you start a conversation, eh? And don't just talk…bloody *listen*." I turn to the elves. "You're angry. That's fair. I'd be too. But we dwarves can hear you all the way down here, and we're not stupid. Not only do we have brains, we have hearts. And we do use them, from time to time. Give us a chance." I turn to the Silvercoats. "And you, maybe if you listened to more than the coins jingling in your pockets, you might learn something. Gold tarnishes with time, but your deeds, those're what lasts. That's what you take with you through life, and death."

I kneel down to Tawn, who is still prostrate on the ground. I lower my voice, narrowing my eyes on him. "I know what you were planning on doing with that Boon. You'd bring down a mountain just to gain the king's ear and some gold. To hell with you."

"What's he talking about, Tawn?" asks one of the Silvercoats.

Tawn pushes himself up onto his knees. "Nothing, nothing. This senile old man is talking nonsense." He stares daggers at me, whispering, "You can't prove anything. I don't care what you say. No one cares about you. The Drunken Wizard's a forgotten myth, a fairy tale. I'm the most respected man in all Venzor, in all the mountains! You're *nothing*!"

"Tawn, I would consider taking an early retirement from politics, if I were you. Because I don't just listen to visions - I love to collect dirty little secrets. I've been around since before you were born. I've known you a long time. And if there's one thing that kills a political career, it's a dirty little secret."

"You don't have anything on me—"

I smirk. "Kiss kiss, oink oink."

Tawn's mouth slacks, and his eyes bulge. He doesn't say another word.

* * *

On our ride back to Venzor on Arth's back, Aruyin asks, "Master Boggs, do you really think the poofs and the elves will listen to each other? Will they make peace?"

I shrug. "It's not as easy as that, I suspect. But the look in their eyes makes me think they want to give it a shot, at least. At least if Tawn isn't croaking his nonsense in their ears."

"That would be nice." She is quiet a moment. "Didn't the Brightness say they *had* to give a Boon to someone? What will happen to them if they don't?"

"About that." I tug on Arth's fur, and he halts. I dismount and hold out my hand to Aruyin to help her down. Only when her feet touch the ground does a silver-blue light shine on us, and the form of the Brightness who first appeared on the bridge materializes.

Aruyin gasps. "Oh…are you back from the moon already?"

"I chose not to partake in Master Bogg's gift," the silver Brightness replies. "I decided my education was to observe its effects on my brethren. Rather unsettling. But…amusing."

"And I may have discussed acquiring a small Boon from him," I explain.

The Brightness nods. "It will not be as impressive a Boon as when all of my kind can contribute, but there are certain abilities I possess on my own." He stands before Aruyin, his voice soft and tender. "Your mentor has told me of your struggles with controlling your magic, that your fears manifest as spirits. This is something no one can unburden from you – it is part of who you are, and something in time you will learn to control. However…" He holds out his hand, and a thumb-sized, golden music box on a chain swirls into existence. "Wear this close to your heart, and it will give you peace of mind when you need it. May it remind you that you are not your fears. You are full of love, and that love gives you strength."

Aruyin is almost too amazed to reply. "Wow..th-thank you, your Brightness sir." She carefully takes the trinket from his hand. She sees a small windup key in its side, so she winds it up, and a gentle, tinkling melody chimes from it.

"I remember that song," she says. "My mother used to sing it to me." Tears begin to well up in her eyes, and she wipes them away with her sleeve. "I miss her, a lot."

"By remembering those who have passed, do they continue to live on, through us." The Brightness looks at me. "Master Boggs, by nature I grant requests, I do not make them. But I ask of you, do good by this child. Will you do good, Boggs?"

"Hey, when do I not?" I ask with a wry grin.

The Brightness gives me a cock-eyed look, and then in a quick flash of light, is gone.

"Now, see, you can't say old man Boggs doesn't do nice things," I say, as I start walking down the path with Arth on one side, Aruyin on the other. She puts the music box necklace on, and hums along to the melody.

"Would you like to sing with me?" she asks.

I scratch the nape of my neck. "I'm afraid I don't know that song."

"I can teach it to you."

I smile. "Yeah, Yin. I would like that."

I don't know if I'll live another 200 years, but I know that song, that moment, that Boon, will make every last year of my life worth it.

Demons in the Pages

From the journal of Llewellyn Angolneth, Apprentice Scrollkeeper of the Wizards' Archives at the Laewaes Public Library

Translated by A.R. Cook

Third Quarter-Moon, 7th day, Winter Season, Year of the Black Stag

I saw the demons again.

On my usual walkabout, as I checked the wizards' archives one last time before I closed the library for the night, I spotted them in the Botanical Elements section. Burly, bulky shadows that were two-thirds my height, wide eyes of green fire, their ephemeral bodies glowed violet with patches of what I think were tattoos, or perhaps runic markings, but unlike any runes I am familiar with. They held hands, never breaking their grip on one another as they stared at me, scrutinized me, and all I could do was stare back, dumbfounded. These ones were bigger than the fiend I saw a fortnight ago, the rabbit-like shadow I had seen creeping around the Animal Enchantments collection. That small demon, while it had surprised me and endeared me with cautious curiosity, had in no way threatened me, even though its burning crimson eyes were disconcerting. These two larger demons, like wraith guardians of the gates of Hell, filled me with such dread that once I regained my senses, I bolted for the exit without a single glance back.

I know I'm not seeing things. I know this library as well as myself. Even before I started my apprenticeship, I came here as a child every day after my daily lessons and explored every nook and cranny of this library. Sometimes I think this trove of tomes is an embodiment of my own mind, so much knowledge but still so many secrets. And if the library reflects my thoughts, then perhaps these demons are an extension of my unconscious.

Master Plavius would tell me I'm overworking myself, that I don't get enough sleep and that's what is causing these apparitions. For being a headmaster of the House of Maumer, wizards who deal in all matters of the mysterious and fantastical, he doesn't give ghosts or demons much stock. *Even if I did believe in such things,* he'd say, *this library has wards all around it. They keep out those that would abuse or misuse the knowledge of the library. In all my hundred and nine years, I've never seen a demon haunt these archives* and so on and so on until my mind eventually wanders.

Perhaps that's my problem. My mind tends to wander, and often I don't know where it's wandering to until it gets there. ~~Like how it keeps wandering back to Vivaine…~~

I should consult Scrub. He might be of some help, if for no other reason than he might believe me. I'll send Cloudstriker to him tomorrow. He will be happy to have some time out of the aviary, although I always fear what would happen if the dwarves should catch an elf's hawk in their territory.

Third Half-Moon, 14th day, Winter Season, Year of the Black Stag

I think it is important that I write here a possible symptom for these phantoms I have observed. Scrub answered my letter yesterday, and I was too eager to read the scroll delivered in Cloudstriker's talons. If Master Plavius, or anyone, knew about my letters with my pen-pal – how scandalous! It hardly seems so strange to me now, after five months of sharing letters with Scrub. Our correspondence began when those old books that the Shanmour raiders brought back from the Verge. They were clearly written in dwarven script, from the inelegant scratchy penmanship, and Master Plavius would have had them burned if I had not suggested that if we could translate them, the books might hold some secrets that could prove useful. *Preposterous,* he said. *No good can come from such dark records.* But oh, the look on his face when I deciphered that one could counteract a dwarven fire spell not with a component-heavy water spell, but a simple earth-based cantrip! How remarkable, that the dwarven magic is so unlike ours, yet once you unfurl the tapestry, the threads are no different than those of elves, just in a different order. Master Plavius was impressed, I think, so allowed me to continue my studies of the dwarven books in secret. Once I have found all I can, then I must incinerate them – but how can one destroy knowledge, even if it is dwarven?

But my ability to translate dwarven is limited, and as this was a secret project, there was no one to consult. Unless…dare I attempt to consult a scholar from the dwarven realm? Did dwarves even have scholars? And why should any dwarf answer my request, even if I made it sound innocent - masquerade myself as a human, perhaps, with a wish to understand their written language to further diplomatic relations or establish trade, or some such façade? I considered the option, deciding the worst that could happen would be that Master Plavius or my other mentors would discover my letters, and I would promptly be relieved of my position as Assistant Scrollkeeper and Guardian of the Archives. Perhaps this possibility would frighten some, shame others, but I realized it was not my lofty position that I held dear, but the knowledge. And to not have the knowledge I sought would be a slow, miserable death.

So I trusted Cloudstriker with the task. *Seek out a dwarf with a great mind and an open heart,* I asked. *Be quick and cautious. If you find no dwarf who may listen, then bring my letter straight back to me. Let no one else see it.* I secured my letter with a green ribbon, and sent the hawk out into the cover of night. Nearly two weeks passed, and I began to lose hope. Then one morning, I awoke in my chambers to Cloudstriker perched on my windowsill, with a scroll clutched in his talons, a brown parchment tied in a strip of red cloth. *Someone had answered!* My first assumption was the letter was a warning: *Dear Stupid Maiden, don't even write to us again with your clear attempts to trick us, or we will bring an army to smash your house to pieces.*

But it was not a threat. A simple note, one of blocky, yet precise lettering. Naturally I had to burn the letter after reading it, but I remember every word of that letter – being a scrollkeeper, I was trained to remember every word of every text I've ever read.

Dear Miss Featherpen (I had decided to not reveal my true name), *your wish to understand the written language of the dwarves is an odd inquiry for an elf, for I am certain by your style of writing that is what you are. No human has yet to master the delicacies of Wisdom Script, as clearly you have. Yet your curiosity intrigues me, and I am not one to deprive an intelligent mind of learning. Send me your questions, and I will judge which I may answer without risking either of our wellbeings. Your hawk knows how to find me, and I don't travel far from home. Signed, Scrub Bramblebeard*

How exciting! A dwarf with not only a great mind and open heart, but such sophisticated words! And so intelligent as to identify Wisdom Script, which it had not even occurred to me that such penmanship could be identified by a non-elf. He had a rather distasteful name, granted – who names their child Scrub? – but then again, the prickly Skinklefruit belies a sweet, delicious flesh beneath its unbecoming grayish-green skin and ridiculous name. So thus began our correspondence, and what began as a deceitful means to an end has become an enjoyable give-and-take of knowledge. So far there has been no question Scrub has not sent reply, no request he found too impertinent or silly.

Now, as to my latest letter, Scrub says it is important that I be true to myself, that if I and no one else can see these demons, then it must be for a reason. That it is some inner part of my soul taking a malformed shape, a poltergeist of sorts. Or, if these be external demonic beings, then they appear to me because I hold something they want. They may be searching, and I can determine what they seek by looking inside of myself and facing the darkness within. And I must be willing to unburden this dark truth from myself – so I pray writing it in these pages will do.

It seems unfair to say I trust Scrub more than even my own kin, my teachers and the masters of Maumer, but it's the truth. And thus, I must record my truths here, if I am to understand these demons before they might inflict harm upon the knowledge – or worse, the visitors and students - of the library.

I have never written this down before…it fills me with embarrassment, even a bit of self-loathing…

~~It started with Vivaine~~ ~~in the academy~~ ~~when my parents arranged for me to wed~~ ~~with a horrible realization~~ ~~with Vivaine~~

No, I must wait on this. There must be a book I overlooked somewhere in the archives that covers this matter, an article I have not yet studied. To pour my worst secrets out onto these pages is too much for me, and I must explore every option before I can bring myself to do such a thing.

I know Scrub means well, but I must postpone his advice. To face what I have buried may be too much for me to bear. Yes, I fear the devils of my memories even more than the undead of Hell.

Third Waxing Moon, 15th Day, Winter Season, Year of the Black Stag

What have I done?

The fire, oh gods, the fire! The horrid smell of burning leather and paper, the crackling heat from flames licking every bookshelf, the flecks of ash that poured through the archives like gray grains of sand in a flipped hourglass. Such loss, such hell, and all because I was too afraid…too afraid to face myself. Now I know, these demons – *that* demon – is no phantasm of my mind, but it feeds on my fears, my doubts, my sins…even if I did not manifest it, it is no less my fault, for I lent it strength.

The rabbit demon was little more than a messenger of what was to come. The twin demons, horrific scouts that paved the path. But what I saw last night… I smelled the burning all the way from where I was, shelving volumes of the Histories of the Moonling House, and I broke into the fastest sprint my legs have ever mustered. My soul shattered as I saw the flickering lights coming from the Wizards Archives, the purple fire writhing and dancing like dervishes among the stacks of books. My heart will forever ache for those pages that have burned away, and it still makes my stomach churn knowing I had not read all the books that were lost, so I cannot even console myself with the hope to replicate them myself.

But that *thing*...that monster, standing among the flames as if they were no more than a summer rain...it was nearly as tall as the bookshelves, curled horns like a ram, eyes of glistening blood, four hooved feet and two arms as thick as tree trunks – some horned centaur? No, there was no hint of intelligence in those bloodthirsty eyes. It was doused in blackness, with the same glowing purple runes painted across its skin, just like the demons I had seen before. But unlike the others, this one had a mouth – a monstrous maw! – from which the violet flames spewed, dripping embers onto the floor like hot drool.

How could this beast ignite such a blaze, when the entire library is protected by magical wards? The library has always been safeguarded against elemental damage, everything from fire to water to book lice and mold, but I could sense instantly that the wards were disabled – was that the creature's doing? Or someone else's? I had no tools to perform any magic, even if I was capable of any spell that would help, so all I could do was flee from the library and get Master Plavius from his quarters at the academy. He returned with me in quick time, but it was too late; sadly, by the time Master Plavius doused the fire, a fourth of the archives were lost, and the demon gone without a trace. Not even a hoof-print was left behind in the ash.

I can only pray that between me, Master Plavius, and the other scrollkeepers, we can recall and rewrite all the burned tomes, although it will take much time and patience. The knowledge may be saved, but it is like when a warrior loses an arm in battle and has it replaced with a wooden or iron replica. It will do, but the original power, the soul of the lost thing, is gone. Its heart is weakened, its legacy tainted forever.

I wasn't blamed for the fire – it was clear it was the work of arcane black magic, and I am barely capable of basic white magic, let alone black – but I fear Master Plavius no longer trusts me...perhaps he thinks I allowed some malevolent person into the library. I don't recall having seen anyone that aroused suspicion, but my judgment has always leaned too trusting. I am to be accompanied by Shanmour guards now, patrolling the corridors at all hours, which unnerves me some. As I have said, this library is like my mind, so now my own mind has no privacy. To even write these words makes me nervous, as I feel eyes over my shoulders even when I think I'm alone.

But I must. I must face my truths now. I cannot risk such a travesty again. I cannot lend this darkness strength, and perhaps in my purging, I shall weaken the demons enough to find a way to extinguish them once and for all.

Vivaine Morningsong. I met her when I was attending academy, in a course on first-level defensive spellcasting. She is such a natural at magic, and why shouldn't she be? A tenth-generation Morningsong, one of the oldest families of wizards in Laewaes. How could anyone not agree how striking she is – long platinum-blonde hair braided down her back, skin somewhat tanner than most elves I know, for she loves to be out in the sun; lithe as a willow, yet confident as an alpha wolf. And eyes like polished lapis lazulis, eyes you could happily drown in…

And I knew. With a twist in my gut—oh gods, I even feel it now –I knew I was hopelessly entranced by her. The way she curls and flexes her fingers with every spell, the way she moves like every step is a dance, the way she ~~smiles at me~~ No, admit it, Llewellyn! The way she smiles at me. Talks to me. Every word she speaks is a musical note, every sentence a melody, every story a symphony.

And I was, *am*, mortified, for my family had for some time been certain I would be betrothed to Farolynn Graywing before I had completed my schooling. An honor, of course, to be promised to one of the Moonling House, and Farolynn is a perfectly fine gentleman. He is a master with the longbow, and most importantly he has an intellectual mind. A perfectly good man that would provide any woman with ~~love~~ decent companionship. A bit…frosty, perhaps, which could be thawed by the right match. I, however, don't think I am the springtime he needs.

But Vivaine, she loves books as much as I do. She's even read *Master Alcour Winterlight's Complete Studies of Dragon Telepathy*, which almost no one checks out of the library these days and that's a crime, if you ask me. But how is it possible I should feel this way about her? I assumed my feelings were rooted in a desire for friendship, as I don't have too many friends – that aren't made of ink and paper, I mean. But soon I found my words fumbled in her presence, my skin heated to sweating, and I went out of my way to braid my hair or put on the nicest tunics I owned before each class we shared. One didn't do such things merely for friendship, I realized. No. I was…*in love*.

I have heard about couples of the same gender – I recall gossip about two young men, a soldier and a cobbler, who had removed themselves to the forest, or some isolated area where the glares and the heated words of the townsfolk couldn't reach them. I had asked my mother about it, since I was unfamiliar with such coupling at the time. She had given me a withering look, and tightened her lips into a thin pale line. *It's obvious such a…*thing *is fruitless,* she had said. *Elven children are so rare as it is. To pair with someone without regard to legacy or the future of your kind…it's selfish and senseless. The poor families of those two boys…what a disgrace!*

What could I expect from such a love with Vivaine, even if she, as impossible as it is, should reciprocate such feelings? I could never make her leave her life in Laewaes to scrape by in some hovel in the woods. She would resent me, eventually grow to hate me. I would destroy her future, not to mention my own. All of that is irrelevant, however; I have seen the way she gazes upon men, the way she whispers to her friends as a handsome boy walks by. To even fancy she would look upon me or speak of me in the same way is idiocy.

Upon the realization of my attraction, I immediately dismissed myself from any classes in which I shared with Vivaine, trying to find alternative courses. But that didn't change the fact that we would pass each other in the hallways or spot each other in the academy gardens. It became too much to bear; my heart incessantly ached, and my mind was incapable of focusing on anything but the image of those deep ocean eyes. It was so terrible, I quit my schooling altogether, much to the consternation of my parents. Master Plavius was kind enough to give me a position in the library, knowing I was a diligent student and he hoped that being surrounded by knowledge would convince me to return to my education. But I have bound myself to the vow not to do so until Vivaine Morningsong has completed her training and moved on…or until *I* move on.

On the positive side, my change from wizarding student to assistant scrollkeeper deterred Farolynn from pursuing me as a potential wife. He says that I clearly desire seclusion, as those who invest more time in books than people tend to do, and it would be rude of him to force me out of willful isolation before I am ready. A sweet sentiment, I suppose, but I believe he's courting Astra Starcatcher now…or maybe Illiane Foxglove? I can't recall, since he can't seem to keep any courtship going for long. I may have, in fact, dodged an arrow with that one.

So that is the truth. I hope it is enough to purge myself of these demons. I shall find out tonight, I suppose, and if all is clear and the demons gone, I shall thank Scrub for his advice.

But if I am now purged and clean of my darkness, why do I still feel so terrible?

Third Waxing Moon, 18th Day, Winter Season, Year of the Black Stag

I thought they were gone. How relieved I was when, the night after the fire, not a single shadow, not any glowing purple lights or blazing crimson eyes, plagued the library. Then the second night came and went without event. While I felt like a blanket of iron chains had been lifted from me, I also cursed myself; it really was my own darkness that had brought the terror, my secrets that had caused so much trouble. After all, it was after my purging into this journal that peace returned to these halls.

It is, therefore, a mixture of panic, and perhaps some relief that I am not the horrible person I thought I was, that I heard the whispers in the walls, a chill breathing from somewhere down the passage towards the private alcoves where the students from the academy come to study.

No, no, no, they're back! I realized as warning horns blared in my mind. Yet, this was different. The previous demons had all been silent; I had stumbled upon them by accident or because of the fire. These whispers seemed to be beckoning, calling, wanting me to find their source. I thought to run and fetch a guard, as they were patrolling the west and south wings, but I feared the whispers would cease if I left, and if it wasn't my darkness responsible for these demons, then what was? I had to know before another incident, perhaps worse than the fire, could happen.

I removed my keyring from my belt, and unlocked the door to the alcoves, since we must keep them locked for the students often leave personal items in their designated study desks. Nothing appeared out of the ordinary – everything was in their places, no one had left any strange magical items behind that weren't spell-protected and safe. I began to think I was simply paranoid from the events of the past weeks, and I was alone, but then the whispers whimpered, as if pleading for me to stay. The chill whipped at my face again, and it was with dread that I realized where it was coming from – the one alcove I hadn't planned to check, because I had just been in it less than an hour ago.

My alcove. The place where I had been working on my secret transcriptions. The place with the dwarven books.

By the gods, Master Plavius was right! What darkness had I allowed into this library by not burning those dwarven writings? But I had been with those books for months; why would they summon demons only now? And why did I not sense the same malice from these whispers as I had from those rune-branded shadows? With slow, tense caution, I moved toward the door, quietly unlocking it. I pushed open the door, and the whispers got louder, the chill got stronger. I thought I would see some devil apparition in the room, but no one was waiting for me. Instead, I felt a pull towards the wooden chest in the corner, where I kept the stack of dwarven books locked away.

I went to the chest and unlocked it, and looked down at the books, exactly as I had put them away. Wait, not exactly. One book, near the bottom, looked to have had its spine pulled out a bit, so the edge of the book was sticking out. That would be unusual for me to not stack books with the spines in perfect alignment, so I moved the other books aside and pulled out the one on the bottom.

I remembered it, although I had not thought to peruse it much. It was one of little text, but many pictures. Not masterfully drawn, certainly nothing of elven quality – just simple charcoal and ink drawings, and yet there was an eerie, earthly air to them that had intrigued me. I guess it to be a children's book, given the sparse text and the simplicity of the drawings. I had first thought a children's book might be helpful for me to gain a grasp on basic dwarven language, but I hadn't given it as much attention as I had the spell books and the diaries. Flipping through the pages, I found myself grinning at the crude pictures, the images of the mountains and the trees and the little mischievous black rabbit and the twin dwarf children holding hands…

A rabbit…twin dwarfs…something like a hot steel glove tightened around my lungs. As I turned the page, sure enough, there was a picture of a large ram-like creature, huge curled horns, four hooved legs and two great arms, standing on a mountaintop like some ram god. *Thealxethor*, the text read below it, and the dwarven words roughly translated to, I believe, *Keeper of Dreams, Herald of Adventure.* And yet, even in the smudge of charcoal and ink, there was kindness and compassion in Thealxethor's eyes, not the burning raw hatred I had seen in the eyes of its demon doppelganger.

I inspected every page, and all along the cover inside and out, looking for hints as to what this book truly was, or who had once owned it. At the very end of the book, I found a small piece of parchment folded and stuck in a pocket of the back cover. There was dwarven scrawl on it, and I believe it translates to "don't forget my little moonbeam" or close to that. Perhaps I should send it to Scr

Third Waxing Moon, 26th Day, Winter Season, Year of the Black Stag

It has been over a week since my last entry, given that I have been afraid to put pen to paper since my surprise encounter. I have no idea if anyone shall read these entries after my death, so if you are reading these words, you shall have to forgive my delay in documenting recent events. Apparently, some apparition was meaning to be helpful – or, perhaps, forceful – by whispering into my ear while I was writing in my journal, and I'm sure the spirit was not intending to frighten me so badly, but I refused to pick up a quill for a week. Even now I write with trepidation.

The disembodied voice, with the delicacy of flute music but the grating urgency of ravenous rats, had whispered, *Give it back.* That's all I remember before I broke the tip of my quill on the page and ran from my chambers.

I have no misgivings about the supposed "it" the voice referred to. After all, had I not been writing about the picture book just as the voice spoke to me? Did these strange paranormal activities not intensify the moment I found "it"? Naturally, something needed to be done with this book, and the demonic energy attached to it, which is why I'm out here now.

I have just spent the last four days trekking through the forest, and now I sit beneath a tree near my camp, with the dying fire from the cooking pit the only reliable light source I can write by. The night sky is cloudy, and even though the moon is near to fullness, it continues to play games, hiding behind wandering black clouds. All around me is still, save a few chorusing crickets, and my thin cloak protects me from the icy touch of the moaning night wind. I should enjoy this quiet moment, since I am on a rather suicidal quest toward the Verge. There is too much to relate as to what has brought me to this precarious situation, so I will make short summary of it.

Naturally upon telling Master Plavius about the book, he desired to have it burned, but I reminded him of the findings in Kalstorm Greenriver's studies of the dark wizards of Highstone – while demonically possessed items should be destroyed, gateway keystones formed by wizards to summon hellish forces should not be, for it could cause a backlash of dark energy that could be even more damaging. I doubted this book was merely possessed, but was a keystone for a still living wizard – scrollkeeper's intuition, I guess, or perhaps the voice that had whispered to me made me believe so. Besides, if this book did belong to a wizard of malevolent intent, didn't it make more sense to use the book to track down the wizard, to arrest him for his crimes and prevent him from doing further malice? I remembered a tracing spell from my academy days, to use an object to lead one to its original owner. I proposed to use the book to find its keeper and report back about any wizard who meant us harm.

Or maybe, deep down, I want to see if that ghostly voice has an owner, and returning its stolen book seemed to be the most decent thing to do, even if it is for a dark wizard.

Plavius, of course, was reluctant to me undertaking the task of tracking down a rogue sorcerer, but he didn't want to risk any further destruction to the library. He granted me permission to go, as long as I was accompanied by two Shanmour guards and a spellcaster with the capabilities of defending against a dark wizard, should we encounter one.

I should have known, given that she has the highest marks in her class in defensive magics, that my bodyguard would be Vivaine.

Our trek has gone without incident so far, and I have remained quiet for most of the journey, which I supposed perplexes Vivaine. She has tried to engage me in conversation several times, but I find no words to reply with – at least, none that she should know. My feelings for her have not dampened with time, and I find her a terrible distraction. I have mainly busied myself with the care of Cloudstriker, who I brought with me in case we needed to relay messages of our progress back to Plavius. But you can only tend to a hawk for so long, and eventually Cloudstriker had to fly off for a while to find food. I did manage a short talk with Vivaine in regards to her family's wellbeing, her studies and such – she seems to be doing quite well on all accounts, although she persists in wanting to know what I quit the academy. She seems, in fact, to have been hurt by my departure, for what reason I can't imagine, since she barely noticed me back then. Perhaps I am simply imagining that I see melancholy pain in those perfect eyes. What would she think of me, if she knew...

But then again, once my quest is done, will I ever see her again? Or worse, what will I do if this quest puts her in danger? What if I have made a horrible mistake?

Third Full Moon, Winter Season, Year of the Black Stag

I have witnessed what may be both the most incredible and most soul-shattering thing of my life.

I envy those who have never known the desolate, war-torn waste of the Verge. My tracking spell bound the picture book with a homing energy only I could see, and I followed the gossamer thread of magic linking it to its place of origin – or at least its most recent owner. To follow the thread through the forest was the easy part – as the trees thinned out, the grass darkened from a cool green to a brittle brown, the rocks and sun-baked earth claimed domination over the landscape, my will to follow the thread weakened, my resolve wavered.

Vivaine, however, remained steady and resolute – in her physical countenance, at least. What was going through her mind, I can imagine – *why did I agree to follow this academy drop-out to the most horrid place in the realm?* That was most likely her thoughts, and I wouldn't blame her. As we approached the Verge, she cast a cloaking spell on our party, which makes one invisible when holding still, but can't entirely mask our movements. Moving too quickly breaks the spell, so we knew we still needed to proceed stealthily. Silence reigned, which was more worrisome than hearing the echoes of a skirmish or a brigade trampling through. The Verge is littered with privateers, vagabonds, scavengers of elven, dwarven and beast variety, and now with us coming closer to the dwarves' territory, we were at risk of much more than a lone dark wizard.

My hands shook as I clung to the book, the magic thread guiding me deeper into the Verge. Vivaine put a hand on my shoulder, and I don't know whether she transferred some calming magic into me, or if it was just her natural touch, but I felt stronger, more confident. We continued on for what felt like hours, occasionally spotting a murder of crows pecking at the decaying carrion of deer, or the remains of a bloody scuffle, broken shields and abandoned swords, warhammers and arrows. It was not until close to evening, when I considered us returning to the edge of the Verge to make camp, that I saw movement in the fog ahead of me, and I froze.

Wolves, Vivaine whispered to me. *They can smell us.*

Wolves, by nature, don't want much to do with elves – dwarves have far more meat on them, and elves are quite stringy to a carnivore – so hopefully these wolves weren't starving or at least knew there was easier prey they could pursue. We proceeded with extreme caution nonetheless. Yet despite giving them a wide enough berth for us to move around them, soon enough I glanced over my shoulder, and there were those glowing eyes in the fog, closer than before.

I think they're following us, I told Vivaine.

She knitted her eyebrows in either curiosity or concern. *If they're planning to ambush us, they're not doing what wolves typically do. I would sense if there were more wolves hiding in wait ahead, which the wolves behind us would try to drive us into them. But it's just that small pack behind us. It's as if they're just…waiting.*

I looked behind me again, and I realized something. I was sure at that distance, I would be able to make out more distinct features of the wolves, even with the fog. But even as close as they were, they still looked like black silhouettes, just shadows with those glowing eyes…

Not glowing, burning. Burning eyes of hell flame. And beneath all that black fur, the faintest shimmer of purple runes flickered on their skin.

But that wasn't what worried me, or if it did, I quickly disregarded it as I saw something that terrified me so badly that I felt a searing sensation so deeply in my skin that it made my bones ache.

Standing among the demon wolves was a child. Dirt and blood-caked skin, a tattered tunic, bare blistered feet, and green eyes so big with fear that they could have swallowed all the misery in the world. A mop of red hair, tangled and mud-crusted, sat atop a round pale face that was unmistakably that of a dwarf, no more than five or six years old to my best guess, yet it was one of the sweetest faces I had ever seen. And all I could think of, looking into that fearful face, was how I needed to save her from the demon wolves.

My legs moved of their own accord, beyond my sense of self-preservation. I broke into a run towards the wolf pack, which instantly disrupted the cloaking spell around me and brought me back to visibility. The child's eyes grew even wider, and she screamed at the sight of me. Her screams startled the wolves, and one of them latched its obsidian teeth onto the back of her tunic and dragged her away, as the pack carried her off into the mist.

For the gods' sake, they have a child! I screamed to my party, but I couldn't wait for them. Cloudstriker took off from my shoulder and flew on ahead, keeping the wolves in his sights. I kept running, but Vivaine caught up and surpassed me. I kept up with her as best I could, and could hear her call back to me, *I don't understand. These beasts don't leave any pawprints in the mud or any smell behind. I can't track them!*

They're not real! I called to her. *They're like the demons in the library. The dark wizard must have created them to hunt us!*

But if that was the case, why did they run when I revealed myself? Why not attack me? And why did they kidnap that dwarf child instead?

We found Cloudstriker perked on a dead shrub, waiting for us. About fifty feet ahead, a wagon appeared in the fog, or what was left of a wagon, at any rate. It once had a white wool cover, but now only scraps of fabric clung to the skeletal bows, creating the illusion that ghosts fluttered about in the wind. The wagon was missing a back wheel, and one of the front wheels was smashed. Shattered barrels, smashed crates and empty torn sacks were strewn across the earth like slain soldiers. Yet the wagon was not entirely forgotten, as I could see the light of a lantern coming from the back end of the bed. A collection of smaller barrels, most of which looked to have collected rainwater, were placed around the wagon. And the faint sound of sobbing broke my heart in half.

Vivaine, bow and arrow at the ready, advanced slowly toward the wagon. *Could be a trap,* she whispered to me.

I looked at the picture book in my hands. The tracking thread…it led straight into the wagon. Not past it, not around it. The end of the thread was in the wagon. I opened the book, and flipped to a picture I recalled, a pack of white wolves standing among a group of mighty dwarven warriors. The Guardian White Wolves of Warriors Past. The demon wolves hadn't been created to hunt us; they had been created the protect their master, like the wolves in this story.

Vivaine, I whispered back. *I don't think this is a trap. My tracking spell shows the owner of this book is in that wagon. What sort of dark wizard lives in a broken-down wagon? And don't you hear that crying? I think...she's alone.*

Vivaine looked at me, blinking those magnificent eyes. *You're not saying…that child?*

I approached the wagon, pulling aside one of the mangled folds of fabric to peek inside. The dwarf child was scrunched up into a ball in the corner, her head to her knees, her body shivering as she cried. The little demon rabbit was curled up on her feet, as if trying to keep her bare toes warm. As I looked in the wagon, the rabbit sensed me, lifting its head up and perking its ears towards me. It made an alarmed squeak-scream, and the child snapped her face towards me.

Go away! She shrieked, and instantly the demon wolves formed around her, snarling and growling at me.

I'm not going to hurt you, I promised.

Elves are evil! She retorted. *You're evil! Leave me alone!*

I knew there was animosity between elves and dwarves, but it had never occurred to me that a dwarf would regard elves as evil. To hear such a belief come from one so young made me want to weep. I couldn't think of anything to say, except, *I have your book.*

This curbed her anger for a moment. I held up the book so she could see it. She wiped away her tears with the back of her hands, smudging the mud her face, and blinked. She leaned forward, but then shrunk back again. *This is a trick,* she said.

No, little one. We never should have taken this. Here, please, have it. I placed the book down on the bed. One of the demon wolves slunk over, sniffed at the book, then picked it up in its teeth and brought it over to the child. She hugged the book to her chest, and eyed me suspiciously, as did all the wolves and the rabbit. *Who are you?*

My name is Llewellyn. I'm a scrollkeeper. I heard you asking for your book back, so I came to find you. Who are you, small one?

She was hesitant, looking at her feet as she bit her lip. *Yin*, she finally said.

Yin, what a lovely name. May I come in? I only want to talk.

The wolves growled, and Yin stared at me, silently, untrustingly.

That's all right. I can stay right here. I would like to help you, Yin. Are you here, all by yourself?

Not by myself, she said, and she pointed to the wolves.

But where are your parents? I asked.

Yin looked away again, and her face scrunched up, and the tears flowed again.

I'm so sorry, I said.

I just wanted to drive the bad elves away, she choked. *Dad and Mum's crops all died because we didn't get rain, and the sheep ate all the grass and were hungry. We went to the forest to pick berries and hunt deer and cut grass and get water from the river. But then the bad* *elves showed up and tried to take everything. They said it was theirs because the forest is theirs. I was so scared. The bad elves...hurt Mum and Daddy...*She was crying so hard, I could barely understand her. *I knew the White Wolves would save us, so I prayed for them to come. They appeared and scared off the elves, but everything was gone. They looked like you! Bad elves!*

My heart splintered more, and I took a deep breath. It dawned on me – Yin's family had been in the skirmish that our raiders had returned from, bringing those confiscated books. I had had the books for five months. Had Yin been living this way all that time? Alone, with only her demons to provide for her? Scavenging for food and avoiding all the dangers out here? It seemed impossible, but then so had the idea of a six-year-old dwarven summoner before all of this.

Those elves did the wrong thing. They were ignorant to your troubles. But we're not all like that. I want to help you. I give you my word, I said.

Yin looked up at me again, her face almost washed clean from her tears. *Who's that?*

I hadn't even heard Vivaine sneak up behind me. She looked at me, and I think she was caught off guard by my emotion, particularly sympathy for a dwarf. But her hard countenance softened, and she sighed. *Llewellyn, a child with such abilities is dangerous. She could hurt herself as well as others.*

I nodded. *What do you suggest we do?*

Vivaine tightened her lips, and gave me a pointed look. I knew what she was thinking. If this child was allowed to live, she would become a dangerous enemy to elves. Yin thought elves were evil, a threat. And given how strong her powers were now, who knew how much they would strengthen as she grew up? Any elf with common sense would make the logical decision: put this dwarf out of its misery. Protect our own kind.

I stared back at Vivaine, my eyes hardening. Would she do such a thing? To a child? For a moment, those beautiful blue eyes looked gray, lifeless, like two granite stones. I turned my gaze away from her. If she was going to do it, then I'd finally be free of her. I'd never look upon her with love or affection ever again. Perhaps, then, it was best, both for elves and for me. I could return to the academy without distraction, without fear. I'd never think of Vivaine again. I'd ignore here every time we passed one another. I could move on, because my heart would be dead.

I know what I would do, Vivaine said. *But I know you can do better.*

Her words fell on me like sunshine in winter. I looked at her, and there was nothing but compassion and understanding. It took everything I had not to leap at her and kiss her. I knew my love would never bereciprocated, but even unrequited love is better than hate. Vivaine turned and walked away, as the two Shanmour guards had been waiting several yards away.

Llewellyn wants to use a Forget-All spell, she told them. *The dwarf will forget how to use magic. Then we will leave it to Nature to decide her fate. She'll most likely die out here without her demons to help her. Let's given Llewellyn some privacy, she doesn't want us to be within range in case the Forget-All might affect us, too.*

The guards agreed. Vivaine glanced back at me, and in a way I think she might have hoped that I would actually make such a decision, but she led the guards away into the fog, out of sight.

Yin was staring at me with renewed fear. She had heard Vivaine. *Please, please don't make me forget!* She pleaded, wrapping her arms around her demon rabbit. *They're my friends! I need them. I don't want to die out here alone. Please, please...*

Vivaine just told them that so they would leave, I explained. *I want to return you back to your people, Yin. I can take you as far as the border guard of the mountains. Can you find your way back home from there?*

Yin looked hopeful for a moment, but shook her head. *Even if I go back, I have no family. I'll be alone. And I don't think the grown-ups will let me bring my friends.*

For a six-year-old, she is awfully bright. I'm sure the dwarves wouldn't allow any demons roaming around anymore than elves did. And where would she go, an orphanage? A workhouse? I've kept her company for the past hour, thinking of the best course of action to take. I hoped writing in my journal would provide some clarity, but nothing has come to me.

I am half-tempted to bring her back to Laewaes, but there is no way the Moonling House would allow a dwarf to live among us. Even if she were permitted, she would face nothing but ridicule, distrust, hostility – what kind of life would that be for her? If only I could ask—

Fourth Waning Moon, 2nd Day, Winter Season, Year of the Black Stag

Forgive the abrupt end of my last entry, but the answer I needed hit me like lightning in that moment, and swift action had to be taken.

I sent Cloudstriker to carry a hastily scribbled message, and he returned from successful delivery in short time, but it was well into night by the time Scrub arrived. I had done the courtesy of bringing Yin a quarter of a mile from the mountain border guard, so he didn't have to come far to meet us. He rode on the back of a ram, and a medical satchel hung from the ram's side – he said he had fabricated a medical emergency for a "relative" that lived near the Verge in order to get past the border guard. It was odd to finally meet my pen-pal in person. I hadn't thought much about how Scrub would look, but he held true to his name – his bristly beard and scruffy hair reminded me of dried sagebrush scorched by summer. He was much older than I had envisioned; the wrinkles in his time-worn face spoke volumes.

Well, Miss Featherpen, Scrub said as he dismounted his ram. *I would say this is the most daring inquiry you've made of me yet.*

I know, and I thank you for agreeing to meet with me, I said. I looked down at Yin, who was holding my hand – a good start for someone who didn't trust elves. *This one is special. She needs a family. Would you please see that she is cared for?*

Scrub stepped towards Yin, and knelt to look her in the eye. He was searching for something, analyzing her. He held up a hand towards the spot over her heart, and I noticed a pair of rings on his hand flickered with an unearthly glow. Lights glimmered from the sapphire and yellow-topaz stones on his rings, pulsating a message that I believe only Scrub could understand.

My gods, he sighed. *Yes, this one is special indeed. What is your name?*

Yin paused, staring at Scrub with fascination. *Aruyin, but Mum and Dad called me Yin.*

I was captivated by the rings on Scrub's fingers. They reminded me of something I had read about in one of the dwarven books. *Scrub, are you a wizard?*

Scrub chuckled, standing up. *Nothing gets past you, Miss Featherpen. Although, that's not your true name, now is it?*

I chuckled. *Llewellyn Algoneth. I felt it safer to use a pseudonym. I hope you're not offended.*

Scrub laughed. *Miss Algoneth, just about everything is more offensive than you. You can stand to loosen up and not be so formal all the time. If it makes you feel better, I didn't give you my real name, either.*

He did tell me his true name, but I feel he would like to keep himself anonymous, so in the event someone else reads these pages someday, I'm afraid I'll have to keep that information private.

It was nearly dawn when I returned to my party, and I had to invent the excuse that the Forget-All spell temporarily affected me and I wandered around the Verge for hours, forgetting where and who I was until the side effects wore off. Honestly, I don't think the Shanmour guards were all that surprised by the excuse – after how nervous they've seen me the last few weeks, I'm sure they view me as scatter-brained. I don't think Vivaine was fooled one minute, though. She just gave me that all-knowing smile of hers.

As we begin our journey back to Laewaes, I wonder how my actions will have affected the course of Yin's life. Will she still be a threat to elves years from now, or will my one seed of kindness take root in her heart?

Second Waxing Moon, 14th Day, Spring Season, Year of the Silver Fox

It has been quite some time since my last entry, but there hasn't seemed to be anything noteworthy to document by comparison to that unusual encounter. I continue my apprenticeship at the library, although I am quite close to becoming an official scrollkeeper according to Master Plavius. How quiet these halls are now, free of demons and disembodied voices. I find myself thinking back to those strange events of that winter night. I still get the occasional letter from my pen-pal, although I haven't see Scrub or Yin since that night. He sends me updates on Yin, who is gaining better control on her abilities, although she will still every now and then summon a "friend" when she's had a bad dream. And Scrub remains as good a friend and advisor as ever. Amazingly, he's quite knowledgeable of teas, my favorite drink, so I shall send him a packet of chamomile sometime.

I must make note: I found a remarkable gift outside my chambers this morning. It was a rare copy of *Master Alcour Winterlight's Complete Compendium of Cosmic Elementals,* which I have been trying to hunt down for the library for years. Inside was a note: *I knew you could do better.*

I think I shall consider returning to the academy this year.

The Company King

David Alan Jones

Chapter 1: Fastness

It was a fine day. Fine. That's what Moorlamb Woolshanks kept telling himself.

And it would have been fine too, if Moorlamb hadn't sank his considerable life's savings into a mining company that was now forty-seven days dry.

Moorlamb drew in a calming breath of mountain air. Dwarves weren't supposed to like fresh air. Oh, they liked clean air, the kind pumped through a maze of rocky caverns via intricate ventilation shafts. The kind of air with grout in its crevices. But not air scented with the early morning tang of lilac and pine needles and musty forest loam. Moorlamb, being a dwarf's dwarf, didn't like it either on principle. But he breathed it in deep between puffs on his pipe.

"It's a might bright without rock overhead, wouldn't you say, king?" Doolen asked. He fidgeted with his ridiculous purple robe, adjusting the tasseled hood to better shade his eyes.

"A might," Moorlamb allowed. "And, you probably shouldn't call me that."

"King?" Doolen asked. "But you own the company, sir. That makes you the company king all right. And if there's one thing my masters taught me, it's the worth of titles. Why, I—"

Moorlamb tapped his teeth with his pipe stem. He had stopped listening. That tended to happen whenever the young wizard got going. Doolen had claimed he could find precious metals and gems with his divination, which was why Moorlamb had hired him. The other company kings, the ones with actual mining experience, had scoffed at Moorlamb, and they had probably been right. So far, the only gold Doolen had found had come from Moorlamb's pocket.

Not that Moorlamb took Doolen for a human—he wasn't a liar or con artist. He was just inept. He had done nothing supernatural since following a bent oak branch up the side of Mount Venzor to this spot.

Forty-seven days ago.

Moorlamb sighed.

The whole of Crumble Valley, so named for the many loose boulders that studded its forests, stretched out below them. A peel tower rose above the trees to the west, marking the dwarf garrison there—a buttress against supposed elven aggression.

To the east lay pasture land cut from the valley forest like a bald patch on a dwarf's chin. Sheep grazed on its rolling hillsides. Moorlamb could almost hear their incessant bleating—almost smell their ripe stench.

"That was your, uh, farm?" Doolen asked, following Moorlamb's gaze.

"Still is, for what it's worth," Moorlamb said, nodding. "My cousin is running it."

"Hmm," Doolen said by way of assessment, neither approving nor disapproving. It was a very employee'esque sort of "Hmm."

That was the best Moorlamb could expect from fellow dwarves when they learned he was—had been—a shepherd and weaver. Decidedly un-dwarven vocations those two. Every dwarf appreciated wool-lined cloaks and boots, woven rugs and satchels, but they didn't contemplate where such things came from. To any gold-loving, gem-digging, hammer-wielding dwarf the stink of a farm was manifest vileness. The same went for the stink of tanning and dyeing.

Of course, disdaining an occupation and needing it were two gems of a different hue. A mountain full of dwarves needed swineherds and shepherds, tanners and tinkers, cartwrights and even weavers. What dwarf wife would settle in a cozy cave home without rugs and rushes? None Moorlamb had ever met.

According to elves and humans, and even goblins if you had the knack of their guttural talk, dwarves were all miners and smiths. Never mind the fact they had to eat, and sleep somewhere besides a rock, and wear clothing.

"They'll find something today," Doolen was saying. He watched his company king with expectant eyes.

"Something precious?" Moorlamb said, echoing the wizard's oft-repeated words. Was mage what you called a pup wizard? Moorlamb didn't know the way of such things—magic was as mysterious to him as gravity—but that felt right.

Doolen nodded. "Yes, exactly! Today. Something precious."

Overeager. That's what Doolen was. A little mage fresh from his lessons, trying to impress his fist patron. Moorlamb couldn't blame him. He had been the same as a young weaver.

He hadn't the heart to tell Doolen the enterprise was a failure. The weaving money—every copper dragget Moorlamb had inherited from his father—was gone. How was that for a company king? In two hours, he would call the crew together, thank them for their efforts, and send them on their way.

As for Moorlamb, it would be back to the farm—back to the stink of sheep and the click-shudder-rattle of the loom. If he wore his fingers to the wrists for the next four months he might just have enough to eat next winter.

The sound of raised voices made Moorlamb and Doolen turn to the mine entrance. Someone was clomping their way.

Bramlee Grammelstock, the crew's master miner, stumped out of the shaft, his face alight though he was squinting against the noonday sun. He carried in his hand a stone colored green, black, and...

"Gold?" Moorlamb shouted. "Is that gold, master miner?"

Grammelstock rolled his watering eyes at his employer's ignorance. "No! No. That there's copper. And from a thick vein too. We must have ten tons if we've an ounce."

Moorlamb's knees turned to water. He put a hand on Doolen to steady himself.

"I told you, king!" shouted Doolen, whooping like a kid. "Something precious! And there it is!"

"Praise the brothers!" Moorlamb said.

Grammelstock frowned. The master miner handed the copper-laced stone to Moorlamb. "It's hard going down there, but I think we might have found a natural opening on the seam. We'll know by tomorrow. That'll save us moving spoil. Otherwise, we'll need more hands up here, and maybe even an ass or two. And definitely some lumber to shore things up."

"With this in hand that shouldn't be a problem," Moorlamb said. He tossed the stone and caught it on the fly. His mind burned with possibilities.

Ten tons! That should turn some heads in the great clans. Getting an investor, even one belonging to the Whitmaster clan, the very lords of dwarf mining, wasn't out of the question. Those shrewd graybeards knew profit when they saw it. Not even the prospect of working with a former weaver would divert them from that!

Three more dwarves exited the mine carrying pickaxes and shovels.

"Tendaub, you gnome," Grammelstock said, "I told you to start in on that seam. What are you doing up here in the open?"

"Sorry, Gram," Tendaub said, shaking a shovelful of dirt from his tunic, "but there's something you should see down there. You too, if I may be so bold, King Woolshanks."

Grammelstock shook his head. "Ain't nothing to be bothering the company master over. I'll have a look."

He started toward the shaft, and the others followed.

“I’m coming,” Moorlamb said, tugging Doolen along after.

“Have it your way,” Grammelstock called over his shoulder.

Darkness swallowed them. The crew had hung glowworm lanterns at intervals along the way, which were no doubt sufficient for the experienced miners, but Moorlamb’s night vision was poor even when he hadn’t been outside. He ran his fingers along the uneven shaft wall to keep his bearings.

“Can’t you conjure some sort of magic to light our way?” Moorlamb asked, letting some of his embarrassment spill into anger at Doolen.

“Yes!” Doolen cried. “Yes, of course.”

The mage clapped his hands, an altogether intrusive sound in the close confines, and rubbed them together. Nothing happened.

“Is that it?” Grammelstock asked without stopping. He seemed to have no trouble seeing his way in the dark.

“No. That’s, um, well there’s this.” Doolen brought his hands apart in a swift motion. A scant, bluish light flickered between them and died. “That worked better when I was training.”

“Don’t trouble yourself, wizardling,” Grammelstock said, pulling a torch from a sconce as they passed.

Moorlamb hadn’t even seen the thing.

Grammelstock lit it with flint and stone in one hand. Squinting at the sudden brightness, he handed it back to Moorlamb.

“Thank you,” Moorlamb said, glad of the dark to hide his burning cheeks. None of the others, including Doolen, seemed to need the light. Not for the first time, Moorlamb wondered if being raised on a sheep farm had ruined his dwarfishness.

The shaft widened into a room about six dwarves across and two high. Twelve miners, the remainder of Moorlamb’s crew, stood about a crevice in the rock on the south wall, their shovels and pickaxes forgotten in their hands.

“What is it?” Moorlamb asked.

“What have you found, lads?” Grammelstock asked.

The miners parted. Moorlamb lifted his torch, revealing a low niche in the solid stone wall. Inside it, their arms entwined like lovers, lay four small skeletons.

“Elves,” Doolen breathed.

“Elf children,” Moorlamb said, matching the young wizard’s tone.

“What do we do with them, king?” asked one of the miners, his hat rolled in his hands.

Everyone looked to Moorlamb.

Later, he would wish he had said something noble, something worth adding to a dramatic monologue chanted over stout dwarven ale. He didn't.

"I need some air."

Chapter 2: Profits and Prophets

"The thing about elves," Moorlamb's father had once said, "is they don't have many children. Just the one usually. Makes 'em all sad like, I think."

The wind had shifted since that morning. It smelled of honeysuckle. Moorlamb leaned against a Settler Pine that grew up the mountain's arched back, soaking up the scent, and thinking about his father.

The old codger had been right about elves and their children. Elves were anything but fecund. Moorlamb had lived on Mount Venzor all his life, right against the most hotly contested lands between dwarf and elf settlements, and he had never seen more than two elven children at a time. They were rare as two-headed lambs. Finding the bones of four of them huddled up like that meant something.

They had died in the Plucking.

Two-hundred years ago the dwarves of Mount Anghor had found their ancestral home overrun to the point of bursting. To alleviate the problem, the greatest dwarf wizards of their generation had raised Mount Venzor from the crust of Mirstone.

The decision to perform the Plucking had been long in coming. It had involved every great dwarf clan and even the commons like Moorlamb's family. It hadn't, however, involved the elves who had occupied the previously flat Danshur forests where Venzor was raised.

The ensuing war, known as The End of the Long Peace, was immediate. The elves took the Plucking as an attack, not just on their people, but on their very homes.

"King?" Doolen said, drawing Moorlamb back to the present. He stood a few paces off, gripping a pine sapling for balance and looking not at all comfortable.

"They're a long-lived people, the elves," Moorlamb said.

Doolen nodded.

"There are still plenty who remember the Plucking, you know," Moorlamb said. "To them, it might as well have happened last week."

"Master Ramsland says that's part of the reason our people's fight. We dwarves forget our trespasses and the elves never do."

Moorlamb chucked a rock down the side of the mountain. It spun and bounced, bouncing off trees as it went, making a satisfying racket.

"The master miner says we should bury the elf children. He says they're safe where they are—have been for two-hundred years."

"I'm sure he did," Moorlamb said, running his fingers over his expertly woven beard. That was one of the perks of being a weaver. Everyone might look down on you, but none could work a better braid.

"I came to tell you, sir," Doolen said. "The miners, they're listening to Grammelstock. He's been telling them the bones are no concern of dwarves."

"Have you heard the new prophet speak?" Moorlamb asked.

Doolen lifted his eyebrows. "I—yes, king, I have."

"My betrothed, Ruby, she's quite taken with his words."

"Oh," Doolen said, noncommittedly.

"You're not, I take it?"

The wizard's jaw worked as if he had something to say but no outlet for it. Finally, he said, "His ideas are...interesting."

Moorlamb smiled.

Every dwarf believed in the twin gods, Creosote and Bismuth. But Creosote, the older twin, had been the favored of the two since time before time.

Jhorhan Jadespar, a silversmith turned prophet, had lately begun teaching that Bismuth was equal to his brother. They were, after all, twins. According to Jadespar, Bismuth wanted peace between dwarf and elf, while his older sibling cared not.

Prophet Jadespar taught that such peace would never come from the great dwarf clans: the miners, smiths, and wizards. Their livelihoods depended too much on hostility between the two races.

Such an indictment of his own class, for Jadespar was a master smith, went far to convince Moorlamb that the prophet was right. Peace, true peace, not just a downturn in fighting so both sides could rearm, could come only if the common folk willed it. What would the war masters do if regular dwarves refused to fight as a nation? Or if the tinkers and swineherds, and yes even the weavers, shut down their trades until peace could be had?

"King?" Doolen said tentatively.

"It's decided," Moorlamb said, though his heart was racing. "We should—we must—return those children to their people. There's an elf village just across the Drake Valley. We can—"

"Go off on a human's errand?" Grammelstock asked. He and seven of the others clomped down the mountainside, ungainly outside a cave, to face their company king.

"It's not foolish," Moorlamb said. "It's kind."

Grammelstock huffed out a breath. "Those bodies have lain

entombed for two centuries, Woolshanks. Why should we go disturbing them now? It's not our place. We have copper to mine."

"The elves don't entomb their dead. They bury them in their forests. It's their sacred rite. We're the ones who found them, so it's our place to help."

"Creosote's left knee, dwarf. You're squandering precious mine time for a bunch of elves. If you hadn't noticed, we are at war with those knife-eared dogs. Now, I know your wife-to-be is listening to that blasphemer, Jadespar, and I respect that you'd want to please her. But don't put the lads' future in jeopardy just because your lady has your beard by the roots."

Moorlamb stood. He wasn't quite as tall as Grammelstock, but years of lambing, shearing, and weaving had filled out his shoulders and chest to match the miner's. "Who owns full stock in this venture?"

"A shovel's bite is only as good as the boot that kicks it," Grammelstock said, meeting Moorlamb's gaze. "You and I both know you haven't the funds to run this company another day. You should have sent someone to seek investors already. Instead, you've been out here, in the gods cursed open air, dithering about elf spawn."

More miners had joined the others while Grammelstock spoke. Most of the crew stood behind him, nodding at the master miner's words.

Moorlamb thought his face might catch fire from the boiling blood racing to fill it. He took a slow breath—honey suckle again—before he spoke. When he did, he turned his gaze on the gathered dwarves, purposefully ignoring Grammelstock.

"If any dwarf among you wants to quit over my decisions, then go. But you've seen the copper in that mine. You know I have the funds to pay you handsomely, or I shall soon enough. The mine master hasn't got the claim on that metal. It belongs to me, and to you, if you'll stay the course."

"I'll stay," one of the miners said. "I need the work."

Grammelstock glared up the hill at the offending dwarf before turning back to Moorlamb. "How are you even going to reach some elven village? You can't leave the valley without getting inspected at the garrison. It's illegal to transport elf artifacts. And the commander there ain't exactly friendly to elf kind. You go moving their remains and the army will have hard questions for you."

"I have some ideas," Moorlamb said. "Who's with me? I will pay every dwarf among you a day and a half per day worked during the trip. And all you have to do is walk."

"Day and a half pay without swinging a pickaxe?" asked one of the dwarves, a fresh-faced youth with silver rings on each finger and a grin on his face. "You've got a walking dwarf, king."

"Bah!" Grammelstock said, throwing up his hands. "I've heard enough." He stumped back into the mine.

None of the others followed.

Chapter 3: By Four Legs and by Two

The mountain road meandered through what seemed to Moorlamb an endless set of switchbacks. It took the better part of a day for him, Doolen, and seven of the miners to travel its length between the mine and Moorlamb's childhood farm in Crumble Valley.

Doolen yammered every step of the way.

"—and that's how Clan Stormguard got the Bluffsburg telescope to the top of the mountain. It wasn't magic at all!"

They were three quarters of the way back to the mine. The sun was setting, but still tinged the western sky in brilliant yellows, reds, and oranges.

Moorlamb swatted a wayward sheep with his father's crook to keep it from trotting off the path. He had brought eight of the stubborn beasts along with old Kelb, his best herd dog. Kelb faithfully trotted over to take the stupid sheep in paw.

"You know, the true root of magic doesn't lie in spells," Doolen was saying.

"Watch your step there," Moorlamb said, pointing his crook at a fresh pile of sheep leavings.

"Oh, ho-ho," Doolen said, just managing to save his boot from the excrement. "Healthy fellows, aren't they?"

Moorlamb had to admit, despite his annoying habit of filling every silence with his gabble, at least Doolen was more accepting of the sheep than the miners. They refused to walk closer than three feet from any animal, and that included Kelb and the ass Moorlamb had borrowed from his cousin. The miners grimaced like tart-eating babies if the sheep so much as sneezed.

But they had come along, marching with grim determination. Truth told, Moorlamb hadn't needed them. He had forced them to come so they could grow accustomed to the animals. With seven of the company so inured, the rest would fall in line on principle. No dwarf would show weakness with another dwarf standing firm next to him. And the extra hands had been useful when it came time to load the wagon with half-cured sheepskins and bales of unkempt fleece.

The miners made certain to walk upwind of the rank load, which made Moorlamb grin.

Silence had fallen. Moorlamb, surprised, glanced over at Doolen, fearful that to make eye contact might bring on another gout of words. But the young wizard only gave him a faint smile.

"I talk too much," he said in a low voice.

"You do talk."

"It's armor," Doolen said.

Moorlamb raised an eyebrow at the younger dwarf.

"If I'm talking, no one's asking me to perform magic. I'm no good at magic."

Moorlamb kept silent for probably too long. He wasn't certain what to say.

"It's okay, king," Doolen said. "I know."

"It's just I haven't seen you actually perform any magic per se," Moorlamb said. "There is the mine, of course, but—"

"—but that could have been a fluke," Doolen said.

"Was it?"

Doolen shrugged one shoulder, not meeting the company king's eyes.

Moorlamb considered the wizard. It said something about his character that he would admit his lack of magic to the dwarf paying him for said magic. Was that trust or stupidity?

"I passed all the tests," Doolen said, his gaze roaming to the miners, but none of them were listening. They were occupied with avoiding sheep.

"You mean the magic worked or appeared or whatever it does when you were training?" Moorlamb asked.

"Every time. But out here, away from the guild hall...I don't know. I can't seem to find it, or when I do it just fizzles or goes sideways."

They were climbing a particularly steep part of the mountain pass. The mine lay just beyond the next wooded ridge. Moorlamb's breath came heavy. He wasn't in the mood to talk, but Doolen seemed to need a word.

"What's it like?" Moorlamb asked. "The magic, I mean. Is there some difference between the way you called it during your apprenticeship compared to now?"

"Magic doesn't come in one piece," Doolen said slowly. "My words and my thoughts are one part. The easy part for me. But the second is made of ephemeral stuff: life energy, the cold of the underground, the heat of the sun, a thousand wriggling things. A wizard spears those with his thoughts and his words, giving them shape and purpose. Or, he's supposed to anyway."

"So," Moorlamb said, trying to picture what Doolen had said, "the words and the, uh—"

"—the power."

"Right, the power, they work together, and with them you can do what exactly?"

"Anything," Doolen said, though he sounded less than confident.

"Call down fire from the sky?"

"Or raise mountains," Doolen said.

Moorlamb nodded.

They had reached the mine. The remaining dwarves Moorlamb had left behind stood just inside the cave mouth, darkling shadows in the evening dusk.

"Where's Grammelstock?" Moorlamb asked, counting beards.

"Gone, king," said one of the miners.

"He dug heels in the trail not a quarter hour after you left," said another.

Moorlamb grunted. "Good riddance. Did you haul up the bones?"

"Aye," said a miner, making way as several others carried four small forms wrapped in linen from the shaft.

They laid them inside the wagon. Moorlamb watched, taking care that his people were careful not to harm the little things as they covered them in sheep skins and fleece.

"Do we strike out tonight, king?" Doolen asked.

Moorlamb shook his head. "The night may shroud us, but with the wagon we'll be forced to take the garrison road across the pass. It'll look suspicious if we're caught traveling in the dark. We'll set out in the morning."

"What of the beasts, king?" asked a miner.

"You're afraid I'll take them into the mine?" Moorlamb asked.

The miner said nothing in a pointed way.

"The sheep have already grazed and I have a feedbag for the ass. They'll be fine sleeping here. I'll stay with them while the rest of you sleep under stone."

"King," Doolen said, frowning, "you would sleep out in the open? Under the stars?"

"A company king does what he must," Moorlamb said.

The miners looked on him with awe. It was the first time Moorlamb had ever felt their pride in him. He wasn't about to tell them he preferred sleeping under the sky, that he had been doing so all his life.

"Get some rest, lads," Moorlamb said, shooing his crew into the mine.

Chapter 4: Warp and Weft

Moorlamb woke with the dawn. He had expected fitful sleep what with the sheep bleating and moving about all night. Instead, the old familiar sounds had lulled him into deep slumber wherein he dreamed of weaving.

Inside an hour, he and the others had breakfasted, posted three of their number to guard the mine, and set off west along the garrison road. The mountain air was crisp, the morning bright and cloudless.

For once, they traveled in silence.

Doolen walked next to Moorlamb behind the wagon amongst the sheep while the miners did everything possible to stay ahead, and therefore separated from the animals.

Moorlamb eyed Doolen, waiting for him to break into some tale about ancient wizard lore. But he didn't. He walked with his thumbs hitched into his lapels, his face sober.

"Are you feeling well?" Moorlamb asked at length.

"The things I told you yesterday," Doolen said, checking that none of the miners was close enough to hear. "About my magic, I mean. I've never told anyone that."

"You're worried I'll dismiss you?" Moorlamb asked.

Doolen swallowed loud enough for Moorlamb to hear. "A little, king."

"I don't know if it was magic or luck that led us to that copper," Moorlamb said. "But I know it was you."

"But I also led us to these bodies," Doolen said. There was a suggestion of pleading in his voice, though Moorlamb wasn't certain of the aim.

"Yes, and to them."

"You'd be mining copper now, if it wasn't for that," Doolen said. "Why couldn't I have found a nice gold mine with no skeletons hanging about?"

"Maybe that's not how your magic works," Moorlamb said. "Don't your masters teach that it's different for every wizard?"

Doolen grinned. "You were listening to my stories?"

"Sometimes," Moorlamb said. He rifled in his breast pocket and withdrew a length of braided wool. He handed it to Doolen.

"Thank you, king," Doolen said. "What's it for?"

"I was thinking about what you said—how magic works with first your thoughts and then all that energy and life and—" he shook his hands in the air—"the fiddly stuff. It reminded me of a loom."

"A what now?"

"A loom, boy. You've never seen a loom?"

Doolen shook his head. "I don't think so, king. Is it a kind of duck?"

"It's a large wooden contraption. The top pulls wool thread tight in many bands, while the side pieces run still more thread across it to make a weave." Moorlamb pointed at the braid in Doolen's hand. "That isn't loom-woven, I did it by hand, but it's near enough to serve my point. Look close. The up and down part is the warp and the side bits are the weft."

Doolen peered at the wool. "I see it. That's...interesting, king. But, please forgive me, it's just, I don't think you should go comparing something as wondrous as magic to hair off a sheep's back. I mean no offense, of course, sir. It's just there are wizards in the mountain whose ears would raise to their crowns if they heard such talk."

"I'm not trying to offend all of magic," Moorlamb said. "It's just the picture I see in my head."

"A braid?" Doolen asked, one bushy eyebrow lifted.

"Warp and weft," Moorlamb said. "You claim your thoughts come first."

"And my words."

"And your words. With those you tie together all these energies from growing things and storms and what-have-you."

"Yes," Doolen said, a hint of comprehension leaking into his voice.

"That's weft," Moorlamb said. "I might not know magic, but I know weaving. All that energy can't be driven straight, it needs a pointer, something to weave around. Given the two, you get your magic."

Doolen stared at Moorlamb with his mouth open, then turned his gaze to the braid. He ran his fingers over its elaborate twists. "I see."

"It was just a thought I had upon waking this morning," Moorlamb said. "Does it help?"

"It does," Doolen said, nodding. "May I keep this, king?"

Moorlamb nodded.

For a long time, Doolen walked without looking ahead. His eyes were on the braid.

Gradually, the garrison road evened out as it meandered into the valley. The trees grew thick around, hemming in the travelers with greenery. Birds flitted amongst the limbs, chasing one another with spring joy and song. The shade was a welcome respite from the sun, even for Moorlamb, but more so for the miners who had spent so little time under its radiance.

A bend in the road led into an open field where the trees had been cleared. A stone building overgrown with crawler ivy stood off to one side. Four dwarves dressed in chainmail and armed with pikes, hammers, and short swords sat on wooden stools in the shade on its leeward side. They stood when they caught sight of the procession.

"Whoa," said one of them, a red-faced, red-bearded dwarf dressed in a gold cape and sporting a badge in the shape of a rose on his chain shirt.

Moorlamb brought the ass to a stop and the sheep, following the wagon, followed suit.

The soldiers, like the miners, kept their distance from Moorlamb's animals. They all grimaced at the smell, not just of the living beasts, but the rank hides in the wagon. One of them even covered his mouth and looked as though he might be sick.

"What's this then?" asked the gold-caped soldier.

"Trade wares," Moorlamb said, trying to keep his face placid despite the fact his heart was currently using his breast bone for an anvil. It was likely smithing him a nice iron coffin.

"Who ya trading with going this direction?" gold cape asked. "There ain't nothing but rocks west of here for fifty miles."

"Elf village," Moorlamb said. He figured the less he spoke the better.

"Elves?" asked gold cape, his upper lip curling. "You trade with those bastards?"

Doolen's eyes went wide as he glanced back and forth between gold cape and Moorlamb.

"I do when the tanning goes bad," Moorlamb said, hooking a thumb over his shoulder at the wagon. "This batch took on something foul. Stench worse than a goblin latrine."

"Well, you ain't lying about that," gold cape said. "What's in there?"

"Twenty full-length sheepskins, six sacks of raw wool, two drums of tallow I rendered. Every bit of it's got that stench though. No dwarf'll come near the stuff, let alone buy it."

"And you think elves will?"

"Snooty as they may be, they like their fleece. I've heard tell the lambing sickness took most their herds east of Vaelkesh last year. So, I'm thinking they'll buy, stink or not. I'll give'em a good deal and they can figure how to get the smell out themselves."

Gold cape nodded, a slow smile creeping across his lips. He liked the idea of elves wearing fouled fleece.

"Do you need to have a closer look?" Moorlamb asked. "I'll warn ya, getting closer don't improve the odor."

"Hah! I'll take your word for it, master weaver. No, you go ahead—get these smelly beasts away from here."

Moorlamb smiled and bowed and was just getting his ass moving when the sound of thundering hoofbeats from the road ahead reached them.

"What's that?" asked one of the miners.

"Horses," Moorlamb said. "Coming fast."

"For us?" Doolen asked. His hands were shaking.

"Why would you think they were coming for you?" asked gold cape.

"The lad's a nervous sort," Moorlamb said, smiling as if confiding a secret.

Gold cape squinted one eye, his gaze ranging back and forth between Moorlamb and the loaded wagon.

Five ponies galloped into the clearing. Four carried steel-armored dwarves wearing masked helms. The fifth, being led by a rope, carried a very put upon and yet determined looking Bramlee Grammelstock.

Moorlamb groaned.

Chapter 5: What is Hidden

"That's him!" Grammelstock shouted. "That's the dwarf!"

Moorlamb, his face burning, bent to whisper in Doolen's ear. "Is there something you can do with the skeletons? Some magic to make them invisible perhaps?"

Doolen shook his head. "You've seen my magic, king. What makes you think I can disappear a grain of sand much less four skeletons?"

"You're our only hope," Moorlamb whispered.

Doolen cursed.

Gold cloak watched them, but his attention was focused more on the approaching riders. His eyes went wide with recognition as they neared and he thumped his mailed fist against his chest in salute.

"Major Shalegroove," he cried. "What brings you here, sir?"

Major Shalegroove dismounted with the grace of a long-time rider. He returned the salute, though his steel-gray eyes never left Moorlamb.

"My name is Staven Shalegroove. I'm commander of the garrison at Drake Passage. What is your name, sir?"

Behind Shalegroove the other soldiers and Grammelstock dismounted. Grammelstock caught one boot in his pony's stirrup and had to be rescued when the beast threated to kick him free.

"I'm Moorlamb Woolshanks, commander."

Shalegroove glanced back to Grammelstock who was looking embarrassed after his near tumble. The mine master gave him a definitive nod.

"And what's in the wagon, master Woolshanks?"

"Trade wares, sir," Moorlamb said. He was beginning to sweat. "Sheepskins, tallow, fleece blankets, and raw wool. Nothing terribly interesting."

Shalegroove watched him, his face unreadable. He motioned to his escorts to approach the wagon. "Move these sheep so my men can see."

Moorlamb set about shooing the sheep away. As he did, he shared a meaningful look with Doolen, flicking his gaze at the length of woven wool in the young wizard's hand.

"They're inside, under the skins," Grammelstock said, hurrying to keep up with Shalegroove's soldiers. "I'm sure of it."

"Stand back," Shalegroove commanded, bringing Grammelstock up short.

The soldiers began unloading the top layer of bagged fleece, grimacing at the stench. In a moment, they would uncover the tiny skeletons.

"Warp and weft," Moorlamb breathed, standing next to Doolen.

The wizard ran his fingers across the braid in his hands, tracing the tightly packed fibers. He drew a long breath then clenched the material in a fist.

Frigid cold air kissed Moorlamb's bearded cheeks and uncovered nose. If he didn't know better, he would have sworn someone had dumped a bucket of snow over his head. He peered at Doolen. The young wizard's eyes were squeezed shut.

The soldiers, with help from the waypoint guards, unloaded the wagon to its bare floorboards under Shalegroove's penetrating gaze.

"Empty, Major Shalegroove," said gold cloak. He appeared as relieved as Moorlamb felt. No doubt allowing someone to smuggle elven artifacts past his waypoint would have been deleterious to his career.

The major turned to Grammelstock whose jaw worked up and down as he struggled to find words.

"You said these dwarves were smuggling contraband," Major Shalegroove said, his voice mild, his manner cold.

"They are, sir! I swear it. Surely, they've hidden it somewhere. We should search the woods. Some of his hirelings are probably out there now, skirting the waypoint."

Major Shalegroove made a subtle motion and three of his soldiers seized Grammelstock. The shocked mine master looked affronted. He tried to wrest his hands away from his captors, but they were too many and too strong.

"This is an outrage!" he shouted as they led him back to the pony that had nearly kicked him.

"I apologize for this misunderstanding," Major Shalegroove said.

"It's fine, sir." Moorlamb had been holding his breath without realizing. It was nice to breathe again. "The master miner and I had a disagreement. I'm afraid he tried to use you and your men to get back at me."

"Foolish."

"What will happen to him?"

"We'll send him to the clan magistrate in the morning. The mountain can deal with him."

Moorlamb nodded, trying not to show triumph on his face. The other miners weren't so restrained. Several of them made not-so-covert gestures at the struggling Grammelstock. He may have been their mine master only a day ago, but no dwarf could respect a miner who turned against his company king.

"Sergeant Aygorsson," said Major Shalegroove, "help these merchants repack their wagon."

Gold cloak came to stiff attention. "Yes, sir."

Together, the miners and the guards made short work of it. Moorlamb lent a hand mostly so he could see the empty wagon bed for himself. The remains were missing.

"Is something wrong with your man there?" Shalegroove asked, lifting his chin toward Doolen.

The wizard hadn't looked up once for several minutes and stood even now with his head bowed, his eyes squeezed shut. His lips moved though he made no sound.

"A devout dwarf," Moorlamb said. "Doolen. Doolen!"

The wizard let go a sudden breath as if he had been holding it. He looked up, his eyes bloodshot.

"Doolen, the inspection is over," Moorlamb said, grinning. "I don't think your prayers were necessary. Not every soldier is looking to clamp fetters on innocent dwarves, you know."

Doolen looked momentarily confused, then managed to whip up a shy grin. "Yes, sir. I just get nervous."

Shalegroove grunted and pulled himself into his saddle. "Again, my apologies for the delay."

"No trouble at all, Major."

Shalgroove led his retinue back the way they had come, Grammelstock once again astride the pony on a leader line. He threw angry looks over his shoulder at Moorlamb and the others until the ponies disappeared into the trees.

Moorlamb got his people moving again, his heart light, his thoughts free. It felt good to be on a mission of reconciliation. He couldn't know how the elves would react to having dwarves return the remains of their children. He hoped his explanation about peace and prophets might assuage them.

A sudden realization sent hot fear coursing through Moorlamb's chest.

"Doolen," he said. "The elf children's bodies. They're back in the wagon, yes?"

"Oh, yes, king," Doolen said. "They never left. I just made them invisible."

Moorlamb sighed with relief. He put a hand on Doolen's shoulder. "Well done, master wizard."

Doolen beamed. "It was you, king. With your wool and your warp and your weft. I was staring at the braid and it all just came together. Made sense to me. My masters would never have deigned to compare magic to weaving, and yet it makes the most sense to my mind."

Moorlamb thought about his fiancé, Ruby, and the prophet, Jadespar, and how so much of life was bound up in what dwarves were willing to do or willing to accept. The great wizards of Clan Stormguard could pluck mountains from flat forest, and yet Moorlamb would wager not one of them could weave the braid Doolen held in his hand. Yet, it was such a simple thing.

The prophet taught peace borne from the commons. People scoffed at him, saying his ideas were too simple, too lowbrow.

"Maybe the complex things in life exist only because they are built upon the simple," Moorlamb said, talking more to himself now than Doolen.

The young wizard glanced at the braid and grinned, nodding. "Yes. Yes, I think that's exactly right, king."

The Beetle's Wing

David Alan Jones

Chapter 1: A Stiff Spine

They named her Keleran. It meant dragonfly wing in the old tongue. That, or beetle wing. Keleran wasn't certain which she preferred. At twelve, most days were beetle wing days. Days when she'd rather scamper through the ancient forests surrounding the elven city of Laewaes than spend time in a stuffy great hall studying magic.

Oh, magic was interesting, even exciting on occasion, but working it was...well, work. Keleran much preferred splashing through clear streams, breathing in loam-rich air, and climbing trees older than the oldest elf.

That, or swordplay. Swordplay was fun.

"Daydreaming will not help you seize the flame in the ice," said Shandres, Keleran's mother.

By utmost dint of will, Keleran managed to keep her eyes from rolling. It wouldn't be proper. Elves were supposed to be reserved in all things, especially those gifted with magic.

"I'm trying, Mother," Keleran lied.

They stood in the family's great hall, a black dining table before them. Though the table was made of some exotic ebony wood from far off human lands, the hall was hewn from stone. This was a precaution on Shandres's part for, though Keleran might not be adept at pulling flame from ice, she had managed to set her mother's practice cottage ablaze last week. Shandres had quelled the flames easily enough, but the cottage still stank of soot.

A single candle in a silver holder stood near the table's edge, its wick stubbornly flameless. Keleran glared at it, lifting one slanted eyebrow.

"Making faces will not help," Shandres said. "How is it you can summon flame one day and fail the next? How will you ever progress this way?"

"Sorry, Mother."

"What has your mind awhirl? Clearly, it's something besides your lessons. Is it the humans? I told you, they're of no consequence."

"The humans, yes," Keleran said. "But more so the dwarves."

Shandres pursed her lips and folded her hands into the long sleeves of her gray silk casting robes. “Not this again.”

“But Lord Dowling says they’re making their way here along Altrede Road. They’ll pass right by our estates. I’ve heard a hundred elves have joined them.”

“Hinter elves,” Shandres said, her tone flavored with disdain.

“Prominent ones too. They say Lord Marjorg walks next to the wagon from dawn to dusk. He could have sent a valet in his stead, but he wants to be near the bones.”

“Lord Marjorg knows an opportunity to curry favor with the common elves when he sees one,” Shandres said. “It’s a political ploy, dear, not rapture. Our family needs no part of that. For the last time, we will not be observing those remains. They’re a forced icon, one that doesn’t deserve the attention it’s receiving. If enough of us ignore it the rapacious stoats behind all this will lose interest, and those poor children can be interred somewhere fitting.”

Keleran sighed. Her mother didn’t understand. Neither did her father. Perhaps they couldn’t. It was hard relating to your parents when you were twelve and they were twelve-hundred. They refused to see the significance of things that seemed world-shattering to Keleran. Couldn’t they comprehend that this event, which was fast becoming known as *The Token of Peace*, might well change the world forever?

Three months ago a cadre of dwarves had arrived unannounced in some obscure elf village away south. They brought with them the crushed remains of four elven children entombed two centuries ago when dwarven wizards had coaxed a new mountain from the mantle beneath their forest home.

These dwarves were under no compunctions to deliver what they had found. And by all accounts, they gained nothing politically from the act. They were common dwarves, not elitists bent on garnering some type of favor from their elven counterparts. The act, so far as anyone could tell, was borne of pure altruism. That had to mean something.

“The candle, Keleran,” Shandres said.

Keleran ground her teeth, hiding her frustration behind a bland expression—an elven mask knit by years of training—and raised a hand, focusing her mind on the candle’s wick.

To her surprise, her fingers grew instantly cold. The magic was there, where before it had been absent. Encouraged, Keleran summoned her will, plumbing her inner self, the place master mages named the maelstrom. Outside, it was a chaotic ball of thought and feeling, rife with fears and desires and unrequited self-expectations. Within, however, lay a space of stillness and cold fire.

Hoarfrost formed on Keleran’s fingers, nipping at her flesh. It spread across her palm and the back of her hand almost to her wrist—thin white tendrils like spiders' webs stretching and elongating. They gnawed at her flesh, determined to sink their teeth to her bones.

She ignored the pain, and redoubled her effort. Ribbons of steam rose from the ice as it expanded, crawling up her arm.

The candle wick glowed orange, duly at first, a finger of smoke rising from its tip. Then the glow intensified, turning a yellow-gold before it birthed a small, flickering flame.

Exultant, she released the magic, rubbing at her hand. A patina of ice shards pattered on the stone floor like bits of rice. Not for the first time, Keleran wished she could steal someone else's heat to make the fire, but that skill was as of yet beyond her. Still, suffering frostbite to create a lick of flame seemed a poor trade of energies. Of course, as her mother so often reminded Keleran, practice was the surest path to efficiency. True masters of ice and fire grew but a little cool when tossing gouts of flame from their fingertips. Or else they siphoned it from other sources around them: the ground, the life energy within plants and animals, even the very air itself. Keleran had seen her mother do such, and though she abhorred the long hours of practice required, she couldn't deny her desire to do likewise.

"Sufficient," Shandres said with a nod. She made a tiny gesture and Keleran's hard won flame died with a hiss. "Do it again."

A knock at the door interrupted Keleran before she could scowl at her mother.

"Pardon me, Lady Shandres, Lady Keleran," said their butler, Guintad. "Lord Nycrom bids me inform you that Baron Strickland has arrived with his entourage. He asks that you join him in the receiving hall at your first convenience."

"We shall be there momentarily," Shandres said.

Though she tried, Keleran could not hide her giddiness, nor the smile that split her lips. No more practice today! And, even better, she was about to see her first humans.

Some said humans were near-elves, a cousin perhaps, with rounded ears and thick chests. Brackeran, her parents' head stableman, said humans were cunning and sly and good with horses. But others said they were near dull-witted as dwarves, and fit for little more than tilling fields.

Keleran had begged her father to attend today's meeting, only to have him rebuff her time and again. He had relented yesterday, likely more due to Shandres's intervention than Keleran's cajoling. Her mother thought the meeting would broaden Keleran's understanding of diverse cultures.

Guintad had hardly exited the room before Keleran was hurrying after him. She would gladly suffer the ignominy of entering on the butler's heels if it meant getting there faster.

Shandres put a hand on her daughter's arm, staying her. "Decorum, Keleran. No need to be hasty."

"Of course, Mother," Keleran said, bowing her head and mastering her expression, though she was nearly shaking with excitement.

"Better," Shandres said. She stared at Keleran for a long moment, long enough that Keleran felt discomfited.

"Mother?"

"I know you may not believe me, but I remember what it means to be a young girl, to have flights of fancy. I do not condemn you for these feelings."

"I know, Mother," Keleran said, though she wasn't certain that was true. Had Shandres ever in her life felt giddy? The very idea was ludicrous. Her mother was the epitome of cool control and disapproving looks. Keleran wouldn't have been surprised to find the woman's skeleton was made of steel.

"This meeting is important to your father. You know this, yes?"

"I'll behave, Mother."

The ghost of a smile kissed Shandres's lips—a stillborn thing. "That is all I ask."

Though still large, the receiving room was far more intimate than the stone dining hall. Decorated in the colors of an autumnal forest with inviting cushions for sitting, and several shelves of her parents' most interesting books lining one wall, the room was bright with candles and stand lanterns. Keleran always found this space inviting. She had spent many a happy hour here reading fantastical histories about the accomplishments of elves and men.

Nycrom, Keleran's father and the finest blade master for a hundred leagues, stood across the room in a tailored suit of black silk brocaded in swirls of gold, azure, and silver. A bronze coronet encircled his forehead, offsetting the auburn hair that hung to his shoulders.

Next to Nycrom stood a human. Keleran would have recognized his race anywhere from the many woodcuts she had examined in this very room. He was taller than any dwarf, though a hand span shorter than her father. His hair, which was black with spots of silver at the temples and across the crown, was short-cropped as if to accentuate his blunt ears. He wore a well-kempt beard that somewhat hid his features, but did nothing to shroud his ice-blue eyes. They too were round, not the almond shape of an elf. Like Nycrom, the human wore black, but his gambeson surcoat was something more akin to armor than the garments of a high-born lord.

Next to the man stood a female human who, though still more robust than any elven woman, appeared willowy and fragile beside the male. She wore a white dress printed with a thousand different flowers in varying stages of bloom. Her hair was golden like the sun and hung past her shoulders. Her skin the color of clotted cream.

Keleran felt her eyes threaten to go wide at the sight. She had never seen any person so light-skinned as this creature. It called to mind stories she had read of wights and vampires, though this woman exuded no evil Keleran could discern.

Two human boys stood next to the woman, both slim and nearly pale as she, though the taller of the two favored his father.

"Baron Strickland," Nycrom said, "may I present my wife, Lady Shandres, and our daughter, Keleran. Ladies, I would like you to meet Lord Willtrem Strickland, his lady wife, Ursula, and their two sons, Pol and Sachar."

Keleran followed her mother in bowing to their guests. The humans returned the gesture, though Lady Ursula curtsied.

"It is a great honor to make your acquaintance," Shandres said. "Have you been made welcome? Have you taken refreshment?"

"We have been made most welcome," Baron Strickland said. "Thank you."

"Your home is exquisite," Lady Ursula said.

Keleran's mother inclined her head demurely at the compliment.

"Yes. Yes, a fine home," the baron said. "Now, my good elf Nycrom, shall we get down to business? You've had my letters of introduction and you've welcomed my envoys thrice. I think it high time we talk swords you and I!"

Though her father's features remained as immovable as a plug of diorite, Keleran knew Nycrom had taken offense at the human lord's brash overture. She doubted the humans noticed the miniscule tightening of Nycrom's shoulders, or the way his left hand fingers curled slightly as Baron Strickland spoke.

Of course, humans were known for their impetuousness. The scholar, Deschaen Horlum, attributed this to their short lifespans and incessant need to prove themselves the equals of any race, even elves.

"I have had your letters upon my desk, and your men at my table," Nycrom said, his voice even, showing not the slightest hint of pique. "But in all our communication, you never indicated how you discovered me and my art."

"Ah! Twas in the field of battle," Baron Strickland said, relish in his voice. Using his belt knife, he stabbed a pear slice from a table laden with fruit and crammed it into this mouth. He chewed as he spoke, juice moistening his fleshy lips. The sight turned Keleran's stomach. "The third battle of Vaelkesh it was, though why your people insist on calling it such I can't fathom. It took place fifty miles from that city. Anyway, there were the dwarves, all arrayed in their fine plate armor, hammers and axes at the ready. Must have been five-hundred of the buggers if there were two. And out came perhaps a hundred elves, gleaming no less than the dwarves mind you, but far fewer in number. Yet, would you believe, and I think you would my lord, those elves fought the dwarves to a bitter stalemate, such that the dwarf commander ceded the field after four hours. I'd never seen the like, so I inquired after the elven officers where they had learned such mastery of the sword. To an elf they gave me your honored name."

"You watched the third battle of Vaelkesh...for sport?" Nycrom asked, the barest hint of reproach in his voice.

"Of course," Baron Strickland said, unaware of Nycrom's tone. "It's fine entertainment so long as you keep clear of the catapults and arrows. I took the family. We shared a meal on a ridge above the fray. Pol was but a babe on his mother's teat back then, but it's never too early to start shaping a young lad's martial mind, wouldn't you agree?"

Keleran imagined she could feel the disdain pouring from both her parents in equal measure. She felt much the same. Death was no sport. No elf of breeding ever drew a sword in haste, or without a tinge of sadness for the consequences that might follow. None trained by her father at any rate.

Nycrom wanted to dismiss the man immediately. Keleran could see it in her father's eyes. He looked to Shandres for her estimation.

Shandres gave the barest shake of her head, forestalling the dismissal.

Keleran felt her brows rise. What was her mother thinking? This human was a boorish cur with manners to match. How could Shandres consider one such as he worthy of Nycrom's tutelage? It was scandalous. Did she think the humans needed the discipline and humility of mind that went with the mastery of the blade? Or could it be that Shandres was as secretly tantalized by the baron's lack of manners as Keleran? This was better than any play the girl had ever seen! The sheer lewdness of it gave her a thrill unmatched in all her twelve years.

"So, Lord Nycrom," Baron Strickland said, oblivious to the interplay between his elven hosts. "How much?"

This time Keleran's father did react. He flinched at the mention of cost, his dark brows knitting together. "Excuse me, sir?"

"Price! How much to train say, fifteen of my guardsmen in your techniques. And, while we're on the subject, how long will the training take? A few weeks? A month? Two?"

Keleran wasn't privy to her father's negotiations, or hadn't been before today, but she knew talk of price and time were the height of social blunders. Prices were to be haggled over by common folk in the press of crowds for things like meat pies and tinkered cutlery. The blade art of Nycrom, son of Shirsta, daughter of Jordrob the First Sword of the Moon King, had no price! Of course, students paid for the privilege of studying under Nycrom, but the money had nothing to do with the gift of the sword. To suggest otherwise was tantamount to cursing Nycrom's family root, branch, and leaf.

The air had gone out of the room, though Baron Strickland, who still munched on his fruit like a monkey, appeared unaware of it.

Nycrom drew a long breath during which Baron Strickland paused in delivering a cut of apple to his red lips.

"Have I said something wrong?" asked the baron. He glanced at his lady wife who, though Keleran had no practice in reading human expressions, seemed to be giving him a rather severe tongue lashing with nothing but her eyes. At least she had noticed something amiss.

"Fifty-thousand staters," Nycrom said.

"What?" Baron Strickland's eyes went wide.

"You asked the price for training fifteen men," Nycrom said. "That is the price."

The baron made a strangled noise not unlike a gelded hog. "You must be mad! I could hire a pox-cursed mercenary army for that amount of gold, and feed them for a year besides! No training's worth that much."

"Mine is."

"I possess trained swordsmen," Strickland said. "Some of mine are the finest of any house from the Fool's March to the Verge."

"Human houses," Nycrom said.

Baron Strickland's cheeks grew rosy where his beard didn't cover, and his eyes squinted nearly shut. "You pointy eared—"

"Willtrem," Lady Ursula said quietly. "We are guests in this home."

"Leave over, woman, this is no concern of yours."

Keleran pitied Lady Ursula. She had never seen an elf of any gender dismiss their mate in such a manner. She likewise pitied their sons. The youngest, Sachar, looked on the verge of tears, while the oldest, Pol, stood with his jaw tight, his blue eyes narrowed at his father.

Nycrom appeared more affronted by the way Baron Strickland treated his wife than anything the man had said to him. His amber gaze bore into the man like an auger.

"You say your men are trained?" Nycrom asked. "Go, call for your best. I would show you the worth of my art."

The baron was already shaking his head before Nycrom finished speaking. "No one's doubting your skill, master elf. I wouldn't be here if I thought my men could best you in swordplay."

"Not me," Nycrom said as he drew Thaqub, the sword passed to him by his mother upon her death. Its name meant *pierce* in the old tongue. He turned the silver weapon about and offered its hilt to Keleran. "My daughter will best any of your men. You choose which."

Chapter 2: Affront

Nycrom gave Keleran no instructions. He nodded to her once as he pressed the sword into her hands, and then drew her to the center of the room. Keleran would have sworn she saw her mother bite her lip for the barest of an instant, but Shandres's face was placid by the time Keleran got a good look.

Blustering and spitting, Baron Strickland hustled to the receiving room doors. Guintad pulled them open and Strickland stuck his head through.

"Sampren!" he shouted. "I need you, man!"

A large human, who stood a head taller than Nycrom, strode into the room. He wore a stiff surcoat not unlike his master's, but his was reinforced with chain links that covered him navel to neck. A longsword hung at his side paired with a curved dagger.

"What is it, my lord?" Sampren asked.

"A ruddy joke. That's what it is," Baron Strickland said. "But one I can't let pass. See the girl there?"

Sampren's pale eyes—they were the color of garden grass—fell upon Keleran. No sympathy lived in that gaze. No heart. The man might well have been surveying chattel on an auction block for all the warmth Keleran found in their depths.

"Aye," he said.

"Our host says she can defeat my best swordsman. Prove him wrong. Disarm her, but take care. Don't harm her."

Without a word, Sampren started Keleran's way, drawing his longsword as he moved. It hissed as it left his scabbard.

"My lord, no!" cried Lady Ursula. "This is madness. Sampren, stop this!"

"Shut your mouth, woman!" Baron Strickland shouted. "He won't hurt the girl. He's simply teaching these elves manners."

Just as she did when drawing magic from her inner self, Keleran found calm inside the maelstrom of her mind. She was fit for this battle. Her father had taught her the art of the blade from her youngest days. Larger opponents held no fear for her, even one so tall and heavy as the baron's retainer. She had never fought an opponent her own size.

Sampren flicked his longsword her way, the strike tentative—meant only to test her defense. Had she stood still it would not have struck her. The human expected Keleran to knock his blade aside so that he could rebound and repost, perhaps with a parry meant to take her sword.

It was just the sort of measured approach any adult master might take with a novice child, and it was an affront to Keleran's skill. This man had no knowledge of her. He should have treated her as an equal no matter her size or age until she proved otherwise. These humans knew nothing of proper manners!

Keleran side-stepped Sampren's blow, careful to place her feet just as Nycrom had trained her over long hours on the practice field. With a deft flick she slapped Sampren's unprotected hand with the flat of her blade eliciting a hiss of surprise from the big man. It was a master's blow of chiding for an ill-prepared student.

Nycrom almost smiled.

Sampren, eyes wide, shook his injured hand. Need Keleran have pointed out she could have pierced him in any of at least six places while he bemoaned his reddening knuckles? Were the humans even aware?

"What are you doing man?" Baron Strickland shouted. "Have done with her already!"

Teeth bared, Sampren brought his sword down in a long arc, the weight of his massive shoulders behind it. This was no tentative blow, but a slice meant to cleave Keleran in half.

Lady Ursula gasped and hid her face. Keleran's parents looked on without expression.

Were humans naturally this slow, or was it Sampren's ponderous blade that made him move like dry season slurry? Keleran evaded the blade and struck it in the air, adding that much more power to its flight just before it bit into the receiving room floor with a thud.

Having no desire to harm the human, though she wondered if he felt the same considering that last strike, Keleran kicked the back of Sampren's knee, forcing him to kneel. She snatched his dagger before the big man had even hit the floor and pressed it to his throat.

Silence fell upon the hall as a bewildered Sampren strained to look up at Keleran without letting the dagger taste his flesh.

"Blight my fields," breathed Baron Strickland after a moment. "How is this possible? Is it magic?"

Nycrom shook his head. "It is our family art."

At a motion from Nycrom, Keleran withdrew from Sampren. The big man stood. Though he glowered, he made no move to resume the fight.

Keleran reversed her grip on his dagger and he swiped it from her. It took a deft hand to keep the edge from biting her palm.

"All your students move like this?" Baron Strickland asked.

"Some are better than others," Nycrom said, giving Keleran a significant glance.

Keleran's heart sped more than it ever had when facing the human. Her father's compliments were as sparse as August snow.

The baron rubbed a hand over his whiskers, his blue eyes contemplative. "That sort of skill is worth any price. You'll have your staters, my good Lord Nycrom, and willing men to learn your art if you're likewise willing to train them, but only on one condition."

Nycrom inclined his head, wary. "What condition, Baron?"

"That you accept my humblest apology for ever doubting your worth." Strickland bowed and remained so until Nycrom returned the gesture.

Chapter 3: The Adulation of Children

The humans sat at table with Keleran and her parents that evening. The servants supplied a sumptuous meal of fresh vegetables and pheasant with a barleycorn soup and roasted pumpkin seeds as a second course. The scent of good things to eat made Keleran's stomach rumble.

The adults, which included several of Baron Strickland's closest guards, Sampren among them, sat at the head of the table conversing while Keleran and the human boys sat at the far end.

Was this arrangement her father's doing? Perhaps Nycrom was more sensitive to the humans' moods than Keleran had believed. While Baron Strickland appeared unconcerned at having Keleran sup with him, his man Sampren cast baleful looks her way whenever he thought the others weren't paying attention.

"Ignore him," Pol said. The human boy, whom Keleran had learned was also twelve, cut his eyes at Sampren and shook his head. "He's always been a poor loser."

"I didn't mean to embarrass him," Keleran said, picking at her peas.

"You couldn't have avoided it and still won," Pol said. He smiled and his green eyes shone in the candlelight. His were darker than Sampren's—almost jade.

"Can all elf girls fight like you?" Sachar asked, and received an elbow in his side from his older brother. "Ow, Pollll! What was that for?"

"Lady Keleran isn't an *elf girl.* She's the daughter of a noble house in these lands."

"It's fine," Keleran said, her cheeks warming. "I'm both an elf girl, and a titled daughter."

"But can they?" Sachar pressed. "No girl can move like you back home. No woman either."

"Or man," Pol said.

"No. My father's sword style is unique. There aren't many who have mastered it."

"But you have," Pol said. It was not a question, and his voice carried only utter sincerity.

"I'm no master," Keleran said.

"If you're no master then I would hate to see your father in battle."

"Hate?" Keleran asked.

"I'm not one for carnage," Pol said. "I appreciate the sword, but death is...sad."

"Your father and his retainers don't share your opinion."

Pol nodded, looking down the table at his father's men. "We don't share a lot of things."

That seemed a sore subject. Was Pol's mother, Lady Ursula, to blame for his gentle spirit? Having seen the human woman's reaction to that afternoon's swordplay, Keleran didn't find the idea far-fetched. Nonetheless, she thought it better to change the subject than pursue that line of thinking, especially if it would somehow press a wedge between father and son.

"Have you heard about the dwarven caravan headed this way?" Keleran asked.

Pol and Sachar shook their heads.

"Isn't that dangerous for a dwarf? Traveling deep in elven-held lands I mean," Pol asked.

"It would be," Keleran said. "There's no hatred lost between our peoples these past two centuries, but these dwarves are on a march for peace. They've brought the remains of four elven children to be entombed here in Laewaes. And they're doing so without provocation."

"Never heard of such a thing between dwarves and elves," Pol said.

Keleran nodded. "That's why it's important. I think this could be a turning point for our races. It could mean a lasting peace."

A lopsided grin turned up one corner of Pol's mouth. "I gather you want to see them?"

"Yes!" Keleran said, matching his grin before she realized it. She stole a glance at her mother. Thank the stars, Shandres wasn't looking her way and so hadn't seen her daughter's slip.

"When are you going?" Pol asked. "I might like to see them with you."

Keleran's cheeks burned under Pol's green stare. Her grin tried to return, then faltered. "I can't. My parents won't let me."

"Why not? Can't you travel?"

Keleran shook her head. "I've only been off this estate three times in my life. And each of those was to visit cousins across the city."

"Why so few?" Pol asked.

"My parents," Keleran said. "They're—"

"—over protective?" Pol said.

"Elves don't have many children. I'll likely never have a brother like you. Sometimes that makes elven parents feel like they've got to keep us hidden from danger."

"I'm sorry," Pol said as if Keleran had told him her favorite pet had died. "Father allows me to travel our lands all I like. If an interesting caravan came through, he would let me visit it."

"Alone?" Keleran asked, scandalized.

Pol shrugged one shoulder. "I'm twelve."

"I've visited our liegeman villages with Pol," Sachar said, sounding boastful.

Keleran harrumphed. She was twelve. Where was her freedom?

"How far away is this caravan?" Pol asked.

"Two days, last I heard. So, perhaps one day now. Maybe even less."

His grin sharpened into a smile. "Would you like to go meet them on the road?"

Keleran glanced at her parents. Surely they had heard the boy's outrageous suggestion. She half expected to find every adult in the room staring at them. But no, they were deep in their own conversation.

"I can't," Keleran said. "My parents' rules—"

"We're twelve," Pol said. "When else are we supposed to break rules? Haven't you ever broken a rule before?"

Keleran shook her head. She hadn't. Not since she was old enough to reason anyway.

"You want to see the caravan, right?"

Keleran bit her lip. "Once they reach the city they'll be mobbed. I'll never get through the crowds to see them. And they're to be entombed here. After that, all I'll be able to see of them is a stone sepulcher."

"So you might never get the chance to view them at all?" Pol asked.

"Perhaps not," Keleran said, a thrill of excitement brimming inside her despite her efforts to quell it.

"Then we should go."

"My parents would never forgive me," Keleran said, though she could feel that pesky grin tugging at her lips.

"Never? Elves live a long time, thousands of years, right?" Pol said.

"Yes."

"We humans live seventy, maybe eighty years if we're lucky, so I figure I've got to do things now before my life is over. You're gonna live so long what will it matter what you did when you were twelve? Do you think your parents will still be angry over a day trip you took a hundred years from now?"

Keleran shook her head slowly, allowing herself a smile.

"Good. Then we're going."

Chapter 4: The Boy and The Peryton

Stealing horses wasn't the exhilarating adventure Keleran had romanticized it to be in her imagination. Part of that was owed to the fact that her father's stableman posted no guard by night. The estate was secure, and the head stableman trusted his fellow servants. No one had ever stolen anything from her parents so far as Keleran knew, especially not one of Nycrom's precious steeds.

Besides, stealing wasn't the right word for their deed. Keleran rode her own mount, a roan her mother had given her two years before named Talka. Pol's horse was likewise his own, a shaggy black gelding he called Cook. How could they steal their own horses?

Keleran wore her riding leathers, and carried a forearm-long dagger at her hip. She smiled to see Pol had dressed in similar fashion. The human boy looked dashing in his riding gear, his dark hair framing his pale cheeks.

They set off leading their mounts on foot through the forests that bordered the eastern side of the estate so as to avoid the main entrance. This way was longer, and the undergrowth made the going more arduous, but it kept them from happening upon any of her father's guards.

Besides, the forest was pleasant, the night air cool and alive with the sounds of insects and frogs and owls. Pale moonlight slanted through the trees, picking out silvery moss in high branches and the dew-kissed scaffolding of spider webs and vines.

Pol slapped a mosquito on his neck, and Keleran handed him a jar filled with waxy ointment from her saddlebag.

"What's this?" he asked.

"Purified strunk weed," Keleran said.

"Smells...uh—" Pol began.

"It's foul, I know. But it keeps the insects off." Keleran daubed a bit of the smelly stuff on her arms and neck to reassure him.

He did likewise and they strode on in silence for a time.

At length, Keleran led them to a game trail that paralleled Altrede Road, which ran from Laewaes to all points southward. The trail would eventually merge with the road, which was good since Keleran's mental map reached only a few miles past her parents' estate.

"This is a wide path," Pol said. "What made it? Moose? I didn't know you got those here."

"Peryton," Keleran said.

"Never heard of that. What is it, some sort of hog?"

"Winged deer."

"You're stretching my eye teeth," Pol said.

"I'm what?"

"Jesting. Joshing. Trying to trick me, because I don't know your land."

Keleran shook her head. "Perytons are real. We'll likely see one if we keep our voices down. Father says they're overpopulated this year due to the mild winter."

"Deer that fly?" Pol said, sounding doubtful.

"Yes."

"But wait, if they can fly why would they make a game trail?"

"They don't fly all the time," Keleran said. "They're like turkeys. They spend most of their time on the ground."

"I don't believe it. You're just—"

A sound in the trees brought Pol up short. Keleran drew her roan to a stop, obliging Pol to do the same with Cook.

As Keleran had hoped, a peryton stag strode into view, the eight points of its horns limned in silvery moonlight. Behind it came a two does and a fawn.

A silent moment passed before the winged deer caught scent of the horses, the elf, and the human. The stag snorted in alarm. Twisting and spreading his wings, he reversed course, leading his tiny herd away down the trail, the others following in graceful bounds aided by mighty flaps of their wings.

"Hah!" Keleran cried in triumph, giving in to a winsome smile. "See? I told you. I know it appears black at night, but by day you'd see their plumage is a most pleasing emerald green."

"Winged deer, eh?" Pol said, laughing. "You had me for a moment there."

Keleran tilted her head at the human boy. "Yes. You saw them just now."

"Those were deer, Keleran. Just deer."

"You didn't see their wings?"

"Of course not. They didn't have any," Pol said, his voice serious.

"But the way they were moving. Didn't you see how far they leapt? What deer jump that far?"

"I'll admit they were energetic," Pol said. "But I didn't see any wings. They were merely bounding down the trail."

"They were perytons," Keleran said. "I swear it to you."

"Then I believe you," Pol said, nodding. "Maybe I couldn't see their wings in the dark. We humans have poor night vision. I guess I just missed it."

"And you didn't hear the flapping?"

Pol shook his head. "Honestly? No."

"Well, let's go on," Keleran said, disappointed. "Perhaps we'll see more once the sun is up."

They walked another half hour, talking quietly about their homes, their families, and the things they wanted out of life. Pol would one day inherit his father's holdings, a large territory of human land granted to his family by their king. He wished to rule it well, and find ways to help his people prosper.

Keleran told him of her studies—how her mother insisted she devote her every free moment to mastering magic. She hardly had time for swordplay with her father let alone exploring the countryside.

"You make magic sound boring," Pol said.

"It's not really," Keleran said. "Not always. But she never allows me any free time. It's all part of what she terms a cultivated mind. She says every thought, every motive must be examined in order to live the most fulfilling life possible."

"You have no free time?" Pol asked. "When do you have fun?"

"I don't," Keleran said.

They had reached the point where the game trail meandered close to Altrede Road. Keleran led Talka onto it, the nighttime sky opening above them as they left the forest's dark canopy. Pol followed suit and they mounted, walking their horses slowly in the dark.

"I find it odd that elves, who live so long, begrudge their children a childhood," Pol said after a minute. "Seems to me, you're an adult for over a thousand years. You should cherish your youth."

"I think you're right," Keleran said.

"Do you get punished for playing, or shirking your duties?"

"I don't—" Keleran began, but was cut off by the sound of pounding hooves behind them. Her heart caught in her throat.

"Do we hide?" Pol asked. "Back into the trees?"

Keleran shook her head. "We're faster on the road, and I don't know the forest here. We'd get lost."

"Wait," Pol said. "Perhaps we're overreacting. We don't know these riders are after us."

"True, but why take the chance?" Keleran dug her heels into Talka's flanks and the mare launched into a gallop. "Follow me!"

They flew down the lane, their horses' hooves kicking up clods of dirt. This was a dangerous way to travel by dark. Keleran couldn't count the times her lord father and his stable hands had warned her against galloping on a night-blind horse. She was liable to get her neck broken.

And it was exhilarating!

Hair whipping behind her, Keleran let go a laugh that echoed over the hills and into the forest like the peal of a bell. She didn't mean to make such a commotion, for surely her pursuers, if they were such, could hear, but the thrill of the run, the freedom, the giddy excitement at stealing away into the night made her elven heart sing.

Galloping next to her, Pol let loose a whoop of his own, his smile shining in the velvety darkness. He laughed, and the sound of it filled Keleran's heart with song.

Keleran looked his way, her smile so wide it made her cheeks ache. And thus she saw the moment when a hempen net sprang from the darkness behind them to engulf Pol and drag him from his saddle.

Chapter 5: Fetters

Two hulking riders raced after Keleran on either side. They held between them a net like the one that had dragged Pol from his horse.

Panic-stricken, Keleran dug her heels into Talka's flanks, urging the horse to even greater speed. Desperately, she glanced behind in an effort to see what had become of Pol, but a bend in the road had put him out of sight.

Keleran bit her lip. She wanted to go back for him—cut him free from his bonds. These men were likely his father's retainers, but what if they weren't? What if they were brigands or slavers? How could Keleran live if she abandoned Pol to such a fate?

She had to evade her pursuers. Talka was a fine mare and fleet of hoof. Surely, she could out turn the steads behind, forcing their riders to tangle their net. The idea was no more than a sparkle in Keleran's head before she was hauling back on the reins and pulling Talka's head hard left.

But the men must have seen Keleran's design, for no sooner had she slowed than they matched her tight turn stride for stride. Seizing their moment, they flung the net over her head. Talka screamed, bucking and heaving, trying to dance away.

Keleran reached for her dagger with a mind to cut herself free, but the men hauled her off Talka's back before her hand found the hilt.

She fell, and would have hit the road, but the guardsmen secured the net between their horses, allowing Talka to gallop away south.

Heart pounding first with anger and only then with fear, Keleran screamed in rage. She fought against the ever-tightening ropes, but could not free herself, nor draw her weapon.

"Stop yer caterwauling," said one of the men.

The other gestured, and his partner handed over his end of the net. Bundling it, the as yet silent guardsman heaved Keleran over the saddle before him.

"What are you doing?" she demanded. The saddle horn dug painfully at her ribs. She tried to scramble down, but the man cuffed the back of her head.

"Squirm again, and it'll be my fist."

Keleran froze, the immensity of her trouble only now dawning on her. She recognized that voice. It was Baron Strickland's champion, Sampren.

"Go into the woods," Sampren commanded the other guard. "Hide till I come back. If one of the others comes looking, ride out and tell them the girl won free, but that she's hid herself in the forest. Tell them we've been searching for her, and they should join the hunt. Lead them west. You shouldn't have trouble. The others will be some time getting Pol back safe."

"Yes, sir."

"Where are you taking me?" Keleran demanded as Sampren turned his horse to follow Altrede Road south, away from her father's estates.

"Hah!" Sampren called to his mount, a black gelding with the girth and strength of a fine warhorse, sending the beast into a lopping canter that flung Keleran about like a sack of beets.

She tried to protest, but the pummeling stole her breath.

They rode for some time. Keleran struggled in vain to reach her dagger, but the ropes held her fast.

Sampren meant to kill her. She was certain of it. Why separate her from Pol? Why send the other guards into the forest on a fool's errand?

Fear gripped Keleran's mind, threatening to stymie her thoughts. Was life so cheap to these humans? It didn't seem so with Pol, but his father and Sampren were different leaves from the same branch.

It seemed an eternity before Sampren drew rein at a spot where the road narrowed and the surrounding trees grew thick above, forming an irregular roof. Though shafts of moonlight dappled the ground, the shadows here were deep and pervasive. Without warning, Sampren heaved Keleran from the horse. She landed on her back with a jarring thud that knocked the wind from her lungs. She would have cried out, but had no air to manage it.

Sampren dismounted to loom over her. "Stop moving."

Keleran ignored him. Still struggling to draw a full breath, she squirmed and fought against the net, her bound hands inching ever closer to her knife.

Sampren kicked her, almost casually, the way a man might kick a stray bit of garbage in his path. The blow sent a fresh stab of pain through her ribs making her eyes water. She tried to roll away, even managed to get her weight onto her uninjured side, before Sampren seized the net and hauled her back.

He put a knee on her gut, and bent close so that the sour tobacco scent of his warm breath caressed her face. She tried not to breathe, but her body demanded air, and she almost gagged. With deft hands, Sampren relieved her of her dagger and shoved the blade into his own belt.

"What are you going...to do with me?" Keleran asked, every word a struggle.

In lieu of answering, Sampren seized the net and heaved Keleran over one shoulder with no sympathy for her cry of pain. He forged into the trees, pulling his gelding along behind. Ten paces in, he looped its reins about a forked branch, and proceeded with Keleran alone, thrashing through the dense underbrush.

It was clear the human was night blind, for several times he ran into thickets he could not pass, but had to untangle himself from thorny vines.

The stab of thorns was a trifle for Keleran compared to the ache in her ribs made all the more painful by the man's ungainly steps.

Was this human about to murder her because she had bested him with a sword? Was human honor so fragile a thing as that? The utter unfairness of it sent a spark of rage burning through Keleran's mind.

No. She had no time for anger, no time for recriminations. This man, this human soldier, was bent on ending her life. If she had any means of surviving she had better reason them out now or resolve herself to dying here in this trackless wood, her bones likely lost forever.

Perversely, the thought of bones brought to Keleran's mind the dwarves who had come to this land bearing the bones of elven children dead these two centuries. Was that her fate? Was she destined to become the unwitting symbol of enmity between elves and humans that is nevertheless transformed into a loadstone for peace over the march of centuries?

More likely, her bones would rot away, undetected in this primordial forest, fodder for the land. Her parents would never know what had become of her, and Sampren would go free despite his crime.

Keleran set her jaw. That would not happen. She had a life to live. Her one act of rebellion in twelve years of near-perfect daughterhood would not be the end of her!

As if cued by her thoughts, Sampren came to an abrupt stop. With a grunt, he dropped Keleran, adding a fresh set of bruises to her bottom and back.

She ignored the pain, focusing instead on freeing her hands from the entangling nets.

"Don't bother," Sampren said. He dropped to his knees beside her, the rancid stink of him overwhelming her nose. "You'll not be leaving this place."

He slipped a gloved hand through the net and seized Keleran's throat.

Pain flooded her senses, marching along her jaw and into her temples. She struggled for breath, but could find none. This was worse than having the wind knocked out of her. In desperation, Keleran's mind yielded to panic. She screamed inside while her body flailed against the human's grip, which might as well have been the pressure of a mountain for all the give she could find in it. Splotches of purple and red danced in her vision.

Mostly by happenstance, Keleran managed to bend one elbow so that her hand drew near her throat. She grasped Sampren's wrist with all the strength of a butterfly lighting upon a leaf, but she held fast.

She cast about, looking this way and that, ever avoiding the visage of her murderer, her only consolation that lack of air and blood would soon blot out his loathsome face. And there, not ten feet from where she lay, Keleran spotted the cloven hooves of a peryton. The creature gazed upon her with implacable dark eyes, turning its head first this way and then that, its majestic rack of antlers catching the moonlight in subtle displays of streaking silver.

Turning, the buck spread its wings and launched itself deeper into the wood. The sight, though dim in Keleran's waning vision, brought to her strength and courage and, most surprising of all, pity.

Pol had not seen the peryton's true form. It was a creature of magic, and Keleran realized now the human boy was not. No doubt Sampren, had he looked up from his grizzly task, would have seen naught but a deer, same as Pol. Perhaps such was the reason for Sampren's avarice and Pol's lack of wonder. Their race had all but lost its hold on magic; they had become blind to its glamour and sway.

But for an elf, even a non-mage like Keleran's father, magic was the song of life, the breath of reality.

Fear and pain fled Keleran as, with the last spark of life left in her, she reached inside the maelstrom of her mind, seeking the void where lay her magic. And when she found it—a bundle of calm wrapped in fury like an obdurate stone at the center of a cataract—she discovered something more. Something surprising. A thing both frightening and delightful.

The magic was not hers.

Magic lived within Keleran, but was not of her. It dwelled within all things, even Sampren. Because of this, her command of it would be ever fleeting, for she could lay no true claim upon it, save in all too brief moments over a lifespan that, though long compared to some races, was nevertheless as ephemeral as the batting of a gnat's wing. And yet this sudden awareness, as humbling as it may have been, opened Keleran to the magic in ways her mother's instruction never had.

Keleran was not magic. She was borrowing magic. And that realization made all the difference.

Heat ebbed from Sampren's wrist, hand, and forearm to fill Keleran with fire. Steam rose from his exposed skin in rushing tendrils. The man screamed, realizing his sudden pain, and jerked away from her.

Keleran gasped for breath. Her throat felt as narrow as an acorn. But there was no time to worry about that now. She focused on the blue flames engulfing her hands and seized them with her mind. Azure fire poured like water from her fingertips, disintegrating her bonds. The net blackened to ash, and what remained fell slack around her.

Keleran stood to face Sampren. He leaned heavily against a birch, holding his frozen wrist, his face a rictus of pain.

He spit at her feet, hurling curses at her.

Sunrise neared, brightening the eastern sky. Sampren's damaged hand appeared black in the early morning light—not the healthy nut brown of skin, but the inanimate hue of obsidian. His fingers did not move.

"Let me pass," Keleran said, her voice a hoarse croak. She considered dousing her flames. The magic was still leeching heat from Sampren's damaged arm, though so slowly he wasn't aware of it. Despite his actions, Keleran abhorred hurting any living thing without need, even this murderer. But the human's next words decided her against the idea.

"You could have gone to sleep with little pain. I would have given you that. Now I'm going to make it hurt." Awkwardly, Sampren drew his sword left-handed.

"Please, no," Keleran whispered. "Let me pass. I'll tell them you ran away."

"If I can never go home again, then neither can you." Sampren raised his sword and advanced, his frozen arm tucked against his chest, his eyes mad with pain and rage.

Keleran refused to immolate any living thing. It was not in her. But she would protect herself.

Raising both hands above her head, tears sparkling her cheeks for the pain of what she must do, Keleran called forth a dizzying torrent of magic. Blue fire exploded from her fingertips into the misty morning as if it would burn away the curtain of darkness, and paint the sky with its hue. The flames roared, their upper tongues licking at the canopy above, setting leaves and branches ablaze to crackle and hiss under the onslaught.

Sampren screamed, but the sound choked off as ice engulfed him. It raced up his neck, laying claim to his jaw, his lips, even his eyes. The crackling sound of it competed with Keleran's flames in volume, as did the hiss of steam that rose from beneath his surcoat.

Keleran released the magic, her heart pained at what she had done, her spirit satisfied by its necessity. The blue flames died, leaving her hands numb with cold but in nowise damaged.

Sampren, now a monument of ice solid to the core, toppled onto his face, sword still clutched in his left hand. The human's frozen arms caught him, sinking into the forest loam, though something, perhaps a blackened finger, cracked on impact.

Keleran dropped to her knees before her would-be killer, bowed her head, and gave herself over to her tears.

Chapter 6: Reconciliation

The sun had lifted far off the horizon when Keleran stumbled from the forest onto Altrede Road. She wasn't certain how many hours had passed since her altercation with Sampren. She didn't know how far she had traveled in the forest, or in what direction. She knew only one thing.

She had killed a man.

That thought kept rushing to the fore in her mind. With it came the image of Sampren's ice-blackened flesh, his stiff frozen form lying prone in a tangle of thorns, and the steam rising from his corpse.

Keleran shook her head, banishing the image for the thousandth time.

Her mind was cluttered, disoriented. She stared at the roadbed, trying to comprehend its significance. Should she turn left or right? Home was north and the sun rose in the east. Keleran knew these things should tell her the direction to choose, but in her muddled state they became two more incomprehensible facts littering her mind.

At length, she turned onto the path, giving no thought to her direction. What did it matter? She stared at her feet. Her ribs and throat pulsed with her stride. She embraced the pain, focused on it, let it push away her memories, her thoughts. She walked and hurt and tried not to remember, though now and again the memories came unbidden.

The road was dry and dusty. The dust aggravated Keleran's damaged throat. Sunlight clawed at the back of her neck, threatening a burn. She was considering leaving the road to travel under the forest's shade, when the creaking of wagon struts and the clomp of many boots reached her ears.

In the distance, rounding a bend, came a procession of elves. They wore a mix of fashions from the dun colors of hinter families to the eye-watering dyed silks of dynastic scions—hundreds of them: male and female, young and old.

At their center, guarding a low-slung wagon drawn by two stout donkeys, ambled a cadre of dwarves. Most wore hoods to protect their heads from the noonday sun, though one did not.

Keleran stopped in her tracks, unable for a moment to comprehend what she was seeing. Then a voice, familiar and distraught, caught her attention.

"Keleran!" Her mother dashed from the throng, all pretense of sternness forgotten; her face alight with joy and amazement. She gathered Keleran into an embrace, her almond eyes sparkling.

Keleran groaned at the pain in her ribs, though her mother's embrace worked as a balm against her tortured mind.

Shandres pulled back, her gaze drawn to Keleran's throat. "Gods, sweetling, what happened?"

Before Keleran could answer, her father was there. Defying all custom, all understanding Keleran had of the world and elven culture, he too embraced her, including Shandres in the circle of his arms. Like his wife, Nycrom's eyes darted to Keleran's throat. His brows knit downward, forming a ridge like granite.

"Who did this?" he asked, his voice seething. In all the battles Keleran had seen her father fight, no look of anger this hot had ever crossed his face.

To Keleran's utter surprise, Baron Strickland, his wife, and Pol had, like her parents, extricated themselves from the caravan. They stood respectfully nearby, Lady Ursala's arms about Pol's shoulders. Pol watched Keleran intently. He looked distraught by her bruised and bedraggled appearance, but gladdened by her presence.

"Did that human boy hurt you?" Nycrom asked, jabbing a finger at Pol.

Keleran shook her head. With gentle movements, she took her father's hand in both her own and kissed it.

"No," she whispered against the pain in her throat. "It was Sampren."

Baron Strickland's eyes went wide. "That cur!"

Nycrom scanned the road and forest behind Keleran as if he expected to see Sampren loping after her. His free hand strayed to his sword.

"He's dead," Keleran whispered. The admission made her heart ache.

"Oh, my love," Shandres said. She squeezed Keleran's shoulders in lieu of another agonizing hug.

The procession had come to a halt, the gathered elves and dwarves watching the tableau with interest. A tall elf dressed in sky blue silk approached. "This is the missing daughter, I take it, Shandres."

"Yes, Lord Marjorg," Shandres said without sparing the newcomer a glance.

"I'm pleased she found us. Is there anything amiss?" Lord Marjorg's eyes lingered on Keleran for a long moment, concern replacing feigned interest in his expression.

"There is much and more amiss," Nycrom said, turning a baleful scowl upon Baron Strickland. “This human brought a murderer into my home.”

Strickland, though he must have known he would stand a flea’s chance in a lion’s maw should Nycrom draw his sword, nevertheless placed himself between Keleran’s father and his family.

“No, Father,” Keleran said, mustering all the volume her voice would allow.

Nycrom spared her a look, though his usually placid features were strained.

Keleran turned to her mother. “Have you seen them?”

Shandres appeared perplexed before comprehension dawned and she shook her head. “We’ve only just arrived. We were searching for you along the road when we happened upon the caravan. We must have somehow passed you by. You were in the forest?”

Keleran nodded. She took her parents by the hands and drew them toward the dwarves and their wagons.

“I don’t think now is the time for a viewing,” Lord Marjorg said, trailing after them. “We have a schedule to meet.”

Keleran ignored him.

“Come,” she said as she passed Pol and his family. The humans joined them, walking reverently in their wake.

“Master Moorlamb,” Lord Marjorg said, “this child is...” he seemed to remember he hadn’t asked Keleran’s name and stumbled over his words before finishing, “this is the elf child who was missing.”

“Hello, young lady,” said the dwarf who wore no hood. The morning sun picked out flecks of silver in his brown locks and whiskers. “I’m Moorlamb. What’s your name?”

“Keleran.”

Moorlamb beamed at her. “Did you know that means beetle’s wing in old dwarfish?”

“Old elvish too,” Keleran said, matching his smile. It was infectious.

“Come to see my treasure, have you?”

Keleran nodded. Her heart was thumping in her chest as the gathered elves looked on with a mix of expressions from indulgent smiles to impatient frowns. Lord Marjorg was most definitely frowning.

“You know,” Moorlamb said, “I’ve been in your lands for eight weeks now, traveling the countryside from village to village, and I believe you are the first elf child who brought her parents to see. It’s usually the other way around.” He gave her a lopsided grin. “You realize the worth of this treasure, don’t you? You know what it means?”

Keleran nodded. She looked at her father, whose brows were still knotted like an old stump. His expression softened, and she turned to gather in Baron Strickland with her gaze. He gave her a solemn nod. Then she looked upon the crowd—elves, humans, and dwarves—and saw that she had their rapt attention. It was as if they had all secretly wondered at the meaning of this thing, and had been too afraid to ask.

"It means peace."

ABOUT THE AUTHORS

Richard Fierce is a fantasy author best known for his novella *The Last Page*. He's been writing since childhood, but became seriously vested in it in 2007. Since then, he's written 7 novels and a few short stories.

In 2000, Richard won Poet of the Year for his poem *The Darkness*. He's also one of the creative brains behind the Allatoona Book Festival, a literary event in Acworth, Georgia.

A recovering retail worker, he now works in the tech industry when he's not busy writing.
He has three step-daughters, three huskies, two cats, two parakeets and a dwarf hamster.

His love affair with fantasy was born in high school when a friend's mother gave him his first fantasy book.

You can visit Richard's website at www.richardfierce.com

—

Trevor H. Cooley
Since putting out his first book: Eye of the Moonrat in May of 2012, Trevor H. Cooley has sold over 200,000 copies of his books in ebook and audio formats.

He was born in South Carolina and has lived all around the United states, including Utah, New Mexico, Michigan and Tennessee.

His love of reading started in the second grade with Lloyd Alexander's Chronicles of Prydain series. He couldn't get enough and continued with David Eddings, Tolkein, Robert Jordan, Stephen King, and many others. Since then, all he wanted was to become a published writer.

The characters and concepts that eventually became the Bowl of Souls series started in his teens. He wrote short stories, kept notebooks full of ideas, and generally dreamed about the world constantly. There were several attempts at starting a novel over the years.

Not long after he was married, his wife told him to stop talking about the story and write it down. Many years and rewrites and submissions and rejection letters later, he finally put the books on Amazon. In August of 2013 he quit his day job and started writing full time.

He is happy being a self-published writer, but is open to inquiries by agents and publishers.

You can visit Trevor's website here: https://trevorhcooley.com/

—

pdmac is the author of the epic Science Fiction adventure series **Wolf 359**, which garnered 2nd place in Science Fiction in the Bookbzz.com Prize Writer of the year 2015 competition. His most recent publication is a Steampunk Western **Fool's Gold**. A diverse author, writer, and editor, he has also edited a Literature anthology, served as managing editor of an archaeology magazine, ghost-written an autobiography, and has had poems, short stories, articles, and editorials published in various literary journals, magazines and newspapers.

His latest short stories appear in the **Short Story America** anthologies III and IV, **Poets in Hell**, and **The Mulberry Fork Review**. He has a MA in Creative Writing and a Ph.D. in Theology, and is a member of the Steampunk Writers and Artists Guild, and the Georgia Writers Association. He has also sung back-up for Broadway plays, provided voice for radio plays, and acted and directed theater stage productions. In his off time, he and his wife race mountain bikes, kayak, and occasionally backpack sections of the Appalachian Trail.

You can visit pd's website at
http://www.pdmac-author.com/

—

Jeremy Hicks

After an exciting but debilitating career as a field archaeologist, Jeremy Hicks teamed up with longtime friend Barry Hayes to realize a creative dream and turn their nightmares into fiction.

The writing team of Hicks & Hayes created an original fantasy-horror environment (Faltyr), wrote a screenplay (*The Cycle of Ages Saga: Finders Keepers*) to introduce it, and then adapted it into a novelization with the same name. The first novel was published by Dark Oak Press in

2013. Its sequel, *Cycle of Ages Saga: Sands of Sorrow*, was published in 2015. The third installment (*Delve Deep*) was released in 2017, along with new coordinating cover editions of the first two novels.

Jeremy co-founded Broke Guys Productions and expanded the company to include publishing. In addition, he writes poetry and short stories. Some of his stories appear in Dark Oak anthologies (*Capes & Clockwork 1-2*; *Luna's Children: Full Moon Mayhem*). Others are available online through Pro Se Productions, Amazon, and Smashwords.

You can visit Jeremy's website at https://jjeremyhicks.com/

—

A.R. Cook is the author of *The Scholar and the Sphinx* young adult book series published by Knox Robinson Publishing. She also has short stories published in the anthology "The Kress Project" from the Georgia Museum of Art, and the dark fairy-tale collections "Willow Weep No More" and "Shadows of the Oak" from Tenebris Books.

She is also a playwright and aspiring screenwriter- her plays have been staged at the University of Iowa in Iowa City; Western Springs, Illinois; and Atlanta, Georgia. She currently lives in Gainesville, Georgia, with her husband David and their husky Daisy May. A.R. is thrilled to be a part of "The Chronicles of Mirstone" with her fellow fantasy authors.

Learn more about A.R. and her books at
scholarandsphinx.wix.com/arcook

—

David Alan Jones is a veteran of the US Air Force where he served as an Arabic linguist. He is also a martial artist, a husband, and a father of three. David writes novels that draw upon his experiences in intel and martial arts combined with his love of all things literary. An eclectic reader, David counts Anne Tyler, Stephen King, Lois McMaster Bujold, Robert J. Sawyer, J.K. Rowling and many others among his favorite, and most influential, authors.

You can visit David's website at http://davidalanjones.net/about-me/